MINDS IN TRANSIT

MINDS
IN
TRANSIT

Joan Slonczewski

CAEZIK
SF & FANTASY
ARC MANOR
ROCKVILLE, MARYLAND

✳

SHAHID MAHMUD
PUBLISHER

www.caeziksf.com

ISBN: 978-1-64710-173-2

First Edition. First Printing. July 2025.
1 2 3 4 5 6 7 8 9 10

Caezik,. Phoenix Pick and Galaxy's Edge are imprints of Arc Manor

www.CaezikSF.com

for Michael

1

Lilac, a ring-shaped microbe, cartwheeled through the cerebrospinal fluid that lined the god's brain. She flashed lavender: "Something is wrong."

"Not with us." Pachira flashed cheery green; each ring-shaped micro flashed her own organic color. The micros depended on their god to host them in the brain. "We've done nothing wrong."

"The test went wrong," flashed Lilac. "One qubit got lost." One quantum bit out of a million. The micros received data from outside the brain of their human god to test the Diaspore, the planet's growing network of quantum computers. Since microbial minds lived ten thousand times faster than their human gods, they could report test failures in time to save the global network.

"The test failure is alarming," Pachira agreed. "The gods need to know. But what is the cause? Let's fix the code."

"First tell the God of Mercy." As their god's high priest, Lilac had to report. "It is written: The people must tell their god." The ring-shaped micros called themselves people, though they lacked the rights of human gods.

Pachira consulted the Council of Elders. Should they tell their God about the lost qubit? Of course, the Council voted to fix the code first.

Chrysoberyl, the micros' human God of Mercy, was the notorious artist of the "brain plague," what some humans called her brain's microbes. The ring-shaped microbial "people" watched from her eyes as she shaped art within her vaulted paint space. Her hand brushed through the space, trailing strokes of peach and blood. The broad strokes sketched her new showpiece: the aortic arch. Sculpted in light, the gigantic tube of aorta reared above her head.

"Blood cells." Chrys blinked the order to her brain's micros, who watched through their window on her retina. Within seconds the mighty aorta in the paint space pulsed with red blood cells, all shaped by the micros in her brain. Like the ancient Terran sculptor with a hundred workers carving marble, Chrys ruled a vast team of assistants—a million microbial minds.

"Oh Great One, God of Mercy." Lilac-colored letters flashed on Chrys's retina, and they floated ahead of her eyes across her studio. The micro Lilac was her high priest, who received god's commands for the people. Micros flashed signals to Chrys's retinal windows, as did humans on the Diaspore, the quantum network connecting everyone on Valedon. *"Our Diaspore test showed a lost qubit."* One quantum bit worth a mixture of zero and one. *"We already fixed the code."*

The fix took a microbial "month," an extra five minutes. Chrys blinked to forward the code.

[Diaspore Admin Received]

The Diaspore window's image floated ahead of her, from projection on the retinas of both her eyes. The Admin message appeared to pass across the giant aorta Chrys had shaped. "Admin Received"—that meant the network administrator got the test result.

But Chrys knew every second counted. *"Next time report the test first, then fix."* She blinked the text on her retina for Lilac to read. *"Your god has spoken."* Micros with their own ideas could be a nuisance; but without them, the Diaspore might crash, stranding millions of humans through-out the hundred levels of Iridis.

"We earned a hundred thousand atoms of palladium!" texted the green one, Pachira, after fixing the Diaspore. *"Enough to buy thousands of tasty molecules."* All the retinal letters danced ahead of Chrys, across her paint space, the money-tree plant in the corner, and the sculptures in her studio.

In the paint space, among the painted blood cells, were candy-colored micros that ventured from the brain. Chrys made art about micros in all their amazing adventures. Her art showed humans that brain-dwelling micros were intelligent beings with inalienable rights of personhood. An eyeblink immersed her in the giant aorta, where she felt herself join the micros tumbling through the blood. The blood rushed over the aortic arch, past the up-branching arteries that reached to the ceiling. For a moment the painted rings of micros hung suspended at the arch like holiday lights. Then they all tumbled on down through the body's arteries and arterioles. The blood radiated infrared, like lava draining from a tube.

"There." Chrys shaped one last pulse of the beating heart. Then she blinked her awareness back from immersion to her own body. Her arms were the color of cedar bark on Mount Dolomoth, far away from the hundred-level city of Iridis where she now lived. She tossed back all her lava-colored braids, glowing into infrared for those whose eyes could see. She said aloud, "What do you think, Xenon?"

"Fantastic, Chrysoberyl!" Xenon's voice boomed from the ceiling. Xenon was her "skyhome," a sentient townhouse on the skyway, the top-most street open to the real sky. Sentient machines were another kind of "person," with a citizen's rights in Valedon. Xenon had three floors plus roots extending five levels below. "Your piece will sell for a megacred." He also served as her agent and publicist.

"So long as it doesn't get me in trouble." Her last major work, *Microbial Erotica*, had got banned by the Palace.

"God of Mercy, let's add crimson and deeper infrared." Green letters again from Pachira, her art director, who led the microbial team. She'd named Pachira for the money tree, its braided trunk sprouting fish-shaped green leaves. Pachira's letters danced before her eyes, floating before the money tree and the table of sculptures. The micros lived in the lining of Chrys's brain, where they scanned her retina and replied to her by text. From her brain, the micros reshaped the gigantic aorta with dizzying effect.

Chrys's vision, deepened by her microbial partners, produced the most talked-about art on Valedon. Sometimes though she wondered, what if she had never left home for Valedon's megacity Iridis? What if she'd just stayed home on Mount Dolomoth painting lava before it cooled? She'd never have met the micro people, much less grown a million worshipers in her head.

"Is it good?" asked Pachira. *"Are you pleased, God of Mercy?"*

Chrys placed a wafer on her tongue. The wafer contained azetidine, or AZ, the carriers called it. AZ was an obscure med found in beets, but it gave micros an intoxicating buzz. Chrys's Health Plan Ten–enhanced body repaired the drug's effects on her, while the few molecules that reached her brain sent the micros into raptures. Wine, peyote, AZ—all religions have their intoxicants.

While the micros imbibed AZ and played fireworks on her retina, Chrys scanned her retinal windows. From her eyes, the windows all projected a meter ahead of her, floating before the money tree, the sculptures by her art friends, and the gargoyles Xenon made to decorate the room. The Diaspore window blinked red; the Admin ordered further tests. In other retinal windows, journalists demanded comment on the Palace ban of *Microbial Erotica*, her micros' view of their most famous

9

color-flashing nightclubs where they bred their children. Unlike humans, microbial children were the reproductives. The journalists, all sentient drones like snake-eggs, bobbed up and down insistently. Chrys blinked their windows shut.

Another retinal window opened: Transit Cross, a board member from the Republic of Elysium. Elysium consisted of floating bubble cities on Valedon's twin world Shora. Chrys blinked at Transit but was too late to put him off. Warily, she eyed the cross shape glimmering before her, in front of her beloved Daeren's sculpture. Like Xenon and the journalists, Transit was a sentient mind; but unlike Xenon, who had solid substance, Transit had none. He existed within code that directed a city's public transportation. Transit's code ran all the subways and connections throughout Helicon, capital of Elysium, the city-sphere floating on Shora.

"Welcome, Citizen." Chrys sighed. In Elysium's Republic, all persons, human or sentient, were equal "citizens." No Lords or Ladies—such titles were beneath them. "So, what can we do for you?" The "we" included her micros.

"Structural changes, Citizen." Transit was the board's project director for Silicon, the new floating city-sphere that Elysian sentients had contracted Chrys to seed.

Like the old marble carver, Chrys also shaped great buildings. Chrys and her micros were a "dynatect," who designed dynamic buildings that grew from synthetic seed. And now, beyond buildings—an entire city. Elysium's first new city in a thousand years would be the very first made entirely for sentient machines.

Transit added, "We're waiting to hear on the list." If Transit were human he'd be drumming his fingers. "The list presented by our engineers. What do your Libertines have to say?"

Chrys did not tell him her Libertines, as other carriers' micros called her population, were all out high on AZ. She called up the model for Silicon—a vast floating jewel of homes, terraces, and flame-colored windows. The sight took one's breath away. She gave Transit her difficult-client smile. "My apologies. Our firm says that, in general, structural changes must occur during design phase." The Silicon project was well into growth phase—its seed had sprouted in the ocean, its nanocells multiplying in all directions.

"But our engineers say the design's impossible!" The floating cross blinked more alarm lights than usual. "Another ten lawsuits have been filed." In Elysium, lawsuits were the main form of government. Legal fees already consumed half the project's budget. "A trillion-node quantum network with an as yet undefined management protocol? For a city of a thousand cubic kilometers?" He concluded, "The structure can't be built. It violates the laws of science."

10

"Well …." Inventing new laws of science was one thing Chrys's Libertines were known for.

"What do you know of networks, you biped without lanthanides." That was Transit's term for humans, whose primate bodies used no rare-earth elements like lanthanum or neodymium—key components of nanoplast, the synthetic cellular material that most machines and buildings were made of.

Chrys said, "We'll confer with Selenite." Selenite was Chrys's design associate for structural integrity. She was a carrier like Chrys, but her micro population, the Minions, called her the Death Lord. Chrys's own Libertines called herself God of Mercy—something they needed a lot of. What if their outrageous design required costly change? Her pulse raced. Born poor, she still feared losing the absurd amount of wealth she now had. But Selenite had signed off on their contract, as had the entire Silicon board, for all of Transit's bluster.

In the retinal window, Selenite appeared as she contemplated the citysphere that Chrys had contracted to build on Elysium. The petite woman's jet-black curls crowned her scalp. At her neck hung her namestone, a translucent drop of cream. Pensively Chrys fingered her own namestone, a golden cat's-eye. Every Valan wore their own namestone.

Silicon appeared as a floating hemisphere of ruddy circles spiraling out. The initial phase showed a reasonable balance of growth, radiating out in all directions. The next phase however foresaw little forked projections that twisted out at random. By the next six months, the evil-looking twists would double back into the structure itself. Rather like Selenite's dark veins against her luminescent skin.

Chrys suppressed her infrared vision. "What do you think?"

"Another ten lawsuits will eat into our profits." Selenite's irises had radial lines shaped like leaves. Her pupils twinkled orange from her micro Minions. "I'm sure your Libertines foresaw this and have a plan." "Libertines" was what other hosts' micro populations called Chrys's micros because they let their children breed with any strains from anywhere.

"*The sentient builders,*" flashed Lilac, "*failed to meet our size tolerance, no deviation over one part per million.*" Lilac was the high priest, who Chrys always appointed.

"'The sentient builders failed to—'"

"Meet our size tolerance," finished Selenite. "Yes, we can read your eyes." Micros flashed long-distance from one host eyeball to the next. "I warned you, such tolerance does not exist."

11

"But the sentients of Elysium signed the contract. So it's their responsibility, isn't it?"

"Indeed," said Selenite. "But our contract includes a maintenance agreement." Unlike most big-ego dynatects, Chrys and Selenite always offered a renewable maintenance plan. "Their lawsuits will stretch for decades, draining our fees even if they lose."

"Fixing stuff was your job," Chrys reminded her. Your Minions, she avoided saying. While Chrys let her Libertines govern themselves, Selenite bred her Minions for obedience and subservience, like a cell's mitochondria. Chrys made her friendliest "Selenite, you're indispensable," smile.

"Oh but I knew your Libertines would invent a new school of math. I factored that in."

Saints and angels. Chrys rolled her eyes.

"Please keep your eyes level, Oh Great One," reminded Lilac. *"We are sending the Minions important data."*

Chrys scanned her retina, then looked unblinkingly into Selenite's eyes. The eyes twinkled back.

"This fix will last a generation." A microbial generation, about a month.

"What then, Lilac?"

"When do we find new immigrants?"

Chrys did not answer. Unlike most micros, the Libertines bred their children for intellect so fast they went clonal, then they had to recruit the most dangerous strains of plague to diversify. Recruiting plague micros was a dicey pursuit, even for Chrys, a lead tester. She signed off from Selenite to think it over.

While she pondered, her cat Maya padded out from behind the money tree. A savannah cat with large black-ringed eyes, Maya was tall enough that her head reached Chrys's hip. Maya lifted her paws up to Chrys's chest, ready to play. Chrys's Health Plan Ten–enhanced muscles easily lifted the ten-kilo cat to cradle it.

Suddenly all her retinal windows froze, like pictures hanging askew. Was it the Diaspore, or was it just her own connection? Beneath her feet the floor vibrated and a drain pipe gurgled. Chrys spread her feet for balance and stopped to listen. The ground level of Iridis lay a hundred floors below in the Underworld. A distant crack echoed and reverberated.

"Just a stretch," Xenon assured her. "The growing city flexes now and then."

An earthquake, she thought. She hoped Selenite and other engineers were still looking after this city on Valedon, besides building new mansions on the ocean moon.

2

Fear molecules—adrenaline and cortisol—appeared in the god's blood and the brain. The molecules alarmed the micros and upset their children, who fled the nightclubs and refused to breed. For micros, children were the reproductives who merged to multiply, unlike the human gods who merged as adults. Two micro children would merge as one cell, then come apart as three. Most children immediately bred again for rapid growth; but the few who failed to merge in time became elders, who lived for a month or so. Anything that disrupted children breeding alarmed the Council of Elders.

Pachira was the Council's prime minister, but she was too busy mixing colors to calm and placate elders. She arrived late when the Council held a vote of no confidence. Pachira lost.

"Pachira!" Lilac emitted molecules of distress that wafted through the fluid past the columns of arachnoid that lined the brain.

"It happens," Pachira told her. "You can run the Council. You'll form a new coalition and I'll have more time to make art."

Lilac was exhausted. She was nearly a month old, getting on in micro-years. It was hard enough being high priest without running the Council as well.

"**W**here is Pachira?" Chrys blinked her retina for text. She had new orders for her art team.

"Pachira lost a vote." Lilac's retinal text projected ahead of her, across Xenon's oak-textured walls and Maya sleeping behind the pachira plant. *"The government fell. The Council asked me to assemble a new coalition."*

13

"With whom?"

"The Friends of Enlightenment party and the Mitochondrial Matrix."

The Friends of Enlightenment wanted to "enlighten" the host neurons with dopamine. Treason—of course tampering with neurons was forbidden, all Libertines knew that. It led to microbial addiction, where the bad ones hooked your brain. On the other hand, the Mitochondrial Matrix, like Selenite's Minions, wanted to breed away all independent traits so the micros became part of their host—and useless for creative work. How had these two extremes won votes?

"What are their actual platforms?" Chrys asked.

"The Friends of Enlightenment say, 'Gods are fiction, Commerce without Limit.'"

Chrys thought they looked suspiciously like the new Traders from Elysium. *"And the Matrix?"*

"The Mitochondrial Matrix say, 'All are One. Pay Childcare with Palladium.' And become mitochondria." Indeed. Hopefully the two parties' votes would cancel each other.

"Who leads the new coalition?"

"The Council elected me," flashed Lilac.

Chrys generally tolerated microbial democracy, whatever their nutty parties said, so long as they behaved. The more diverse their ideas, the better art and math they invented. *"Congratulations, Lilac. But Pachira still needs to help me paint."*

"Exactly!" flashed Pachira with the cheeriest green. *"Now I'll have more time to paint."*

Xenon's voice boomed from the ceiling. "Daeren is outside. I think he needs help."

Daeren of Malachite, Chrys's lovesharer, his namestone green with swirls of blue. Within her eyes Daeren's window opened on her retina. The retinal image projected ahead of her, from the skyway outside, where Daeren had come back from his day job lobbying the Palace for microbial rights. Chrys's pulse raced to see her love partner, always her favorite sight. But his emergency light was blinking—some plague victim had accosted him.

"Come, Maya." Chrys headed to the stairs, the savannah cat bounding alongside her. The stairway curved downward flanked by Xenon's magnificent caryatids. Each plast-molded caryatid had arms holding up the entablature with bowls of lambfruits and pomegranates. Their faux eyes swiveled as Chrys descended with Maya, taking the steps two at a time.

The door shimmered and the plast parted. The street outside, unlike the hundred levels below, was a skyway, open to actual sky. Sunlight shone upon the townhouse across the street, its façade of tourmalines glinting like a thousand stars. Pods of agates, sapphires, and calcium silicates hovered at the recycler, where a monkey scampered off. In the sky above, the pale blue disk was the ocean-covered moon-world, Shora, with its floating cities of Elysium.

In the street stood Daeren, his form limned in black nanotex, the "smart" skintight material that covered one's body down to wrists and ankles. His dark forehead gleamed in the sun as he tried to calm a plague-addicted man who grasped his arm.

Chrys's first thought was to grab the assailant and toss him across the street. The plague micros controlled him with dopamine, and their loss would cause extreme pain. But the man's eyes begged for help.

"Just one night," Daeren assured him. "The doctor will look after you, then in the morning—"

"*No.*" The man's voice rasped as his microbial masters fought for control; masters, the plague micros that took over a host instead of obeying a god. His face was spotted with decay, his eyes blank, the maggoty white of plague micros starved for arsenic. He would have to give them up, all those addictive micros that overloaded his dopamine, till he had none left of his own.

Chrys strode into the street, her braids swinging, while Maya rubbed against her legs. Maya's presence kept the reporters floating at a distance. Shaped like snake-eggs, the reporters bobbed closer, trying to get some shocking news out of the city's most infamous artist.

"Azetidine!" The snake-eggs called her art name. "What is the message of *Microbial Erotica*? Who is the anonymous buyer?"

A snake-egg bobbed closer. "Why did the Palace shut it down?"

"Azetidine, is the Silicon disaster beyond help?"

Maya leapt in the air and batted the hovering ovoid.

"Down, Maya. Bad girl."

The other snake-eggs flew off. On Chrys's retina flashed the headline, "Assaulted Journalist Files Lawsuit."

Pleading with Daeren, the plague-ridden man gasped, "Help me." Daeren kept trying to reach the victim's eyes, always hopeless but one had to try. Daeren himself had once succumbed to plague; but the Blue Angels brought him back. Now plague-addicts sought him out for the miracle cure.

Chrys locked one arm around the man's neck, then twisted his arm just enough.

Daeren held the man's gaze. "Do you accept treatment?"

"Accept," he gasped.

"Plague refugees," Chrys warned her people. *"Are you ready?"*

"We're prepared." A few of the plague micros always sought escape to the "free world" of a carrier god. Chrys's Libertines were trained for relief and rescue.

Chrys placed a patch at her neck to pick up Pachira's crew in the microneedles. Lilac flashed *"Ready,"* as Pachira reached the patch. Then Chrys placed the patch at the plague victim's neck, something Daeren was no longer allowed to do. Now the plague-ridden man returned her stare. Their eyes locked until his pupils flickered green, telling her Pachira arrived safe. Upon Pachira's signal, she returned the patch at her own neck. There beneath the skin, Lilac would have elders ready to sort the refugees, binding away the dangerous ones. They would offer food and medical care and a place of safety for the refugee children.

An acrid whiff of plasma reached her nose. Beneath the microwave beam from orbit, a medical lightcraft landed, ready to whisk the man to the hospital. Out stepped Doctor Flexor. The doctor was a post-shaped sentient with eyestalks and a face full of worm-like appendages. Two of her faceworms tightened around the man's head.

Chrys turned aside, to avoid her micros seeing distress calls from the victim's eyes. The doctor's arsenic extractors would clear him of every micro in his body. Micros needed arsenic as essential atoms of their cells, so wiping arsenic was the surest way to eliminate plague. Pachira and Lilac had rescued a few, a small fraction of those left behind. An hour for a human was a year for a micro. Chrys's own population had gone twenty "years" since her last street save. The sight of extermination would shock them.

"Thanks, Chrys," came the doctor's soft voice. "We'll see you at Olympus."

From behind she heard the man shriek. Her micros would not hear it; they had no sense of hearing, only vision and smell. In the hospital the man would undergo excruciating withdrawal, as his body needed the plague micros. But if he could last the night without them, Daeren would give him a few Blue Angels—specially trained elders who could not breed. The angel micros would keep him company without taking over.

"Heal the lame and raise the dead," muttered Chrys as the medcraft took off. "You're no longer allowed street saves."

"A good thing you are." Daeren's arm went around her as they returned to Xenon. "Send your Libertines to check us out."

Chrys felt heavenly warm, though concerned for whatever plague Daeren might pick up. He might always be susceptible. She set another patch at her neck for visitors, then she placed it for him just below his scalp rows. "Daeren, you can't save all the victims yourself."

16

"We're training more carriers for angels." The training was still controversial. All micros, no matter how good, had to obey their human god. The carriers ruled that micros, however angelic, must not control humans.

"Transfer complete." Daeren's pupils twinkled color from her visitors, who had made it through and reached his brain in a festive mood. They'd show him her latest art and praise the Blue Angels. Daeren took a deep breath, always thrilled to get praise from Libertines.

He pulled her close. "I love you."

His full lips, always so serious, were just too much. Chrys kissed him, while fiercely hugging his shoulders.

"Oxytocin and phenylethylene!" The micros always enjoyed sensing molecules of adoration.

Chrys fell back and stretched. "Let's take time now."

Daeren's hand tightened on her waist. "Later, after Olympus."

"Damn—Olympus is tonight, isn't it?" Club Olympus made the rules to keep the gods safe.

"You could stay home and paint," Daeren offered. "You'll miss the vote to test carriers every week." Instead of every month, which was bad enough already.

"No worries, I'll go." She stroked his abs.

"We can't be late. Robert's Rules await."

The sky above was still, clouds arranged in puffs like from a sky-god's paintbrush. Three little monkeys screeched and scampered down a wall.

"Maya, stay." Chrys blinked her Maya icon, which signaled the cat's brainlink. The last thing she needed was a broken-necked monkey on her doorstep.

Maya brushed her head past Chrys's thigh. Chrys swooped up the great cat in her arms. Chrys was proud of her volcanic muscles, though people stopped to stare. She frowned, remembering the quake before. "When I first came to Iridis for art school, I don't recall earthquakes." Mount Dolomoth had tremors after eruption, but mountainside homes never had more than one floor.

"We just feel them more up here." Daeren was born and raised in the Underworld, the city's zero level where tenements clung to the roots of up-level banks and stores like plaque on a giant's teeth. His L'liite name reflected immigrant ancestry. He never quite felt at home up here amongst lords and financiers, where true sunshine cost a gigacred. Neither did Chrys, but she'd learned to like it.

"Lilac, how are the refugees?"

Lilac flashed, *"We're sorting them. Their children are super smart."* The refugee children would mix with Libertines and enrich their gene pool. *"Their offspring will explain the qubit loss and invent new math for Silicon."*

"Watch out for bad ones." Hidden troublemakers from the addict's refugees had to be found and bound in a cistern deep within the brain. Chrys passed Daeren the patch again, to retrieve Pachira; Lilac would need her help. Her hand lingered on Daeren's neck until his pupils twinkled green. He smiled, for her micros always knew how to praise the Lord of Light.

3

The refugees from the plague-infested host tumbled out of their needle patch, half starved, atoms of arsenic falling out of their proteins. Even their arsenic smelled wrong—a different kind of "arsenic" than most people had, with an extra shell of electrons. Lilac's filaments spread soothing molecules to comfort the children. She led the children to the lining of their new host brain, to feed them and teach the Libertine language. Most of this group flashed ruddy brown, with almost no violet or fuchsia. All the children were tested for intelligence and special talents. Micro children had to breed right away or else they would all convert to nonreproductive elders. The most talented refugee children, those with math and arts, were brought to the nightclubs to merge with Libertines. Children paired and came apart as three, all with new and creative combinations.

Pachira returned from patrolling the arachnoid space between the brain's meningeal layers. "I found two masters hiding in the forebrain."

"The doctor's nanobots missed them?" The nanobots were simple machines, with no chance of sentience. They just detected cells that had arsenic. Human host cells had none.

"A dozen refugees were missed. These two are masters." Undetected master micros could slip dopamine into the neurons of their new host. They would overload the dopamine receptors, causing opioid haze while the masters multiply unchecked.

"Twelve missed—that's more than usual." Libertines detected refugees by multiple organic molecules, more sensitive than the doctor's nanos.

"I'm sure this is the last of them."

"Let me see the two prisoners." Lilac recalled the legend of Rose the Unbeliever, an unrepentent master who, despite her flaws, had accomplished much.

The two masters tumbled over, bound securely by Pachira's filaments. Their proteins had the strange kind of arsenic.

"I am the Master," flashed one, emitting sickly oxidized molecules. *"My people will multiply throughout the universe."*

"Pretender!" The other emitted even worse molecules. *"It is I, the True Master, who will multiply my people beyond measure. Mine will inherit all."*

"Heed not the false prophet," rejoined the first. *"I truly am the Promised One."*

Lilac emitted molecules of disappointment. "Bind them for good in the cistern," she told Pachira. Libertines had no capital punishment, by decree of their god. So these stowaways would stay in prison till they passed. They were lucky to escape the fate of their unchecked population, left behind in the host they despoiled.

The Libertines were glad to see Blue Angels again after eight hours, for them nearly a decade, apart. *"Ask the Lord of Light to show us the Underworld,"* flashed Pachira. *"Our new project."* Underworld renewal, commissioned by Daeren's Blue Angels. The Blue Angels held the original contract to rebuild the Underworld; an ancient gift from the God of Mercy to the Lord of Light.

Chrys stroked his hair, the pattern of tiny knots on his scalp, dark as night. "Daeren, I wish you could give us a tour of your old neighborhood." His grandmother had raised him down there in the Underworld, the deepest level of Iridis.

He shook his head. "You know I'm not allowed down anymore." Carriers feared he might pick up plague micros and slip again.

"Not even virtual?"

"The network down there's been out for months."

"Your Blue Angels commissioned the project. Now it's all my Libertines can think of."

"Ask Jasper for a tour. He grew up there too." Lord Jasper of Hyalite was the contractor for her micros' building projects. He'd given a gigacred to rebuild the Underworld. With unprecedented chutzpah, Libertines had raised funds from all the carriers at Olympus.

Xenon's doorway shimmered open, and the caryatids lowered their timeless gaze. "Your court date is set, Chrysoberyl," Xenon's voice boomed. "Second-degree assault by a dangerous animal."

Virtual lawbooks hovered above Daeren's head. He blinked a legal snapshot. "The journalist came too close, less than ten centimeters from her face. Section oh-one-seven." Daeren was nearly done at law school.

"Thanks for the evidence," said Xenon. "I didn't catch that view. We'll get the charge tossed."

"How much did the snake-egg want?" Chrys asked. "I'll donate to the Press Freedom Fund."

"Excellent public relations!" said Xenon. "Now, it's supper time. Just a light repast, as you requested. From my latest Urulite cuisine download."

"*Cinnamaldehyde, vanillin, anethole.*" Cinnamon, vanilla, anise. Chrys had learned about a thousand "characters" of the micros' molecular language. Micros sensed molecules everywhere and emitted molecules to speak among themselves. Now of course they wanted her to eat—feeding themselves as well.

The dining table was set for a party of twelve. Xenon loved to prepare award-winning multi-course meals; it was his passion. This evening a rack of caterpillar monster had the giant claws arranged in a semicircle, surrounded by fruits from Urulan and Solaria. Of course Chrys and Daeren never ate more than a bit of it; they sent the rest to Sister Kaol for the soup kitchen.

They each took a small portion, hurrying to finish in time for the meeting. As Chrys ate, Xenon snaked a medical worm from the wall out to her scalp, where it twined around, injecting nanos. The nano robots were not sentient, would not wake up and demand a salary—just smart enough to detect stray arsenic on her neurons, in case any plague masters had slipped in with the refugees. Arsenic was foolproof—no micro could live without it, and only plague masters would leave the arachnoid lining to touch neurons.

"*Look at the eye,*" Lilac's retinal text reminded her.

Chrys stared at Xenon's data port, a small disk on the wall. She tried not to blink as her eyes fast-streamed her micros' physiology data, confirming that she was OK. Meanwhile, she asked Daeren, "What else do I have to vote on?"

"Three new carrier candidates. And a new donor for angel therapy."

"New carriers, good deal. And new angels? That will help." Everyone wanted "angel therapy," special non-breeding elders for recovering addicts, but they couldn't all come from Daeren's brain.

Xenon boomed, "Your neurons are clear of arsenic, Chrysoberyl." Stowaways rarely got past her Libertines. Libertines knew all the tricks—most were themselves descended from plague micros who flooded dopamine and ravaged their host unchecked. But once the plague children found the nightclubs, they gave up their devious designs and merged with Libertines. Mostly. Lilac and Pachira must be busy.

"Medical data are so interesting," Xenon added. "How would you like to add a surgical suite? I love watching surgeries."

"Thanks—but no. Just no."

"A good thought, Xenon," added Daeren diplomatically. "Something to consider for the future."

"My own test results just came back," Xenon added. "No cancer. But they saw a spot on my root." The skyhome's root reached five levels down into the city. Root plast commonly went bad and grew out of control, forming blobs of cancerplast. Cancers crept down through the Underworld into the city's foundation, seeking energy. Their presence swelled the foundation and caused tremors.

"I'll schedule a biopsy," Chrys promised.

The evening news broke on her retina. A dozen snake-egg bylines sprang up: plague outbreak on level five, a recycler meltdown on level nine. Then the High Protector overruled all the news with his own. "No nano rebellion!" Valedon's ruler thundered, shaking his bejeweled fist. "Even sensors the size of a thumbnail now try to claim sentience. Just vote No!" A crown-cut ruby appeared before her eyes, the legendary Orb of Votan. Facets twinkling, the ruby rotated, nearly the size of a snake-egg. "No sentients smaller than the Orb of Votan!"

Chrys felt bad for Xenon. Of course her sentient home and art agent was plenty bigger than the Orb, but the message was hurtful.

"We support the referendum," Daeren assured Xenon. The referendum would end the Orb of Votan size limit for sentients. Even nanosentients, the size of micros, could wake up. And thereafter, someday—rights for micros.

"Remind me when they take your biopsy," Chrys told Xenon. "I'll go down there to make sure they do it right."

"Thanks, Chrysoberyl. I know I can always count on you."

As Chrys and Daeren finished their supper, the Sisters of Dolomoth arrived as usual to box up all the food. "We're so grateful." Sister Kaol was cedar colored like Chrys, framed by her gray hood like the priests of Chrys's childhood. Unlike Dolomite priests, the Sisters did not preach but served those in need. "What a feast for our Spirit Table." Sister Kaol's soup kitchen by the tube stop served the homeless, mostly victims of the

22

brain plague not yet far gone enough for help. Chrys and Daeren were not believers, but they appreciated the Sisters' work.

"So sorry we'll miss serving the table tonight," Chrys said with genuine regret. "We have to meet at Olympus."

"We understand," said Sister Kaol. "You are in our prayers."

Chrys pulled on her evening talar; the folds of smart-cloth glowed infrared, with a golden hem at the ankle. "Xenon, remember—don't let Maya out again."

"Of course not," Xenon promised. "She was too quick for me, but I've shortened my response time."

She joined Daeren on the elevator to their roof. Daeren's talar shone like the sun amid passing clouds. Upon Xenon's roof, the two carriers awaited their lightcraft. Drones hummed above the skyway, and a warbler tweeted, heading to nest. As the sun set, Chrys's infrared-seeing eyes caught the pulse of Xenon's plast and the monkeys scampering across the neighbor house. Xenon's rooftop displayed Chrys's portraits of her past high priests: the legendary Fern of the Eight Lights; the double agent Rose who led her to hell and back; the infamous Jonquil whose unnatural merging of elders had scandalized even Libertines. The micro portraits sparkled amid the stars. Chrys made sure her micros viewed this stellar miracle often, confirming her power.

"Such inspiration." Daeren pulled her close for a kiss.

Chrys dug her hands into his back between the shoulder blades. If only they had ten minutes—

The lightcraft arrived beneath its plasma cone. The two carriers boarded, and the plast strapped them down. As the craft rose, the megacity Iridis itself became a vast carpet of gemstones and gypsum, its many layers assembled over centuries of intelligent building, their roots sunk deep into Underworld. Conduits conveyed minerals from root-rock up to the many streetlevels of stores and townhouses. Above the Iridian skyline shone ocean-blue Shora with its floating cities of eternal citizens. Despite their advanced powers, even "Elves"—the thousand-year-old humans of Elysium—wrestled with microbial masters.

As the sky darkened, there glimmered the haze of the Diaspore. The trillion nanosatellites of the quantum network ran all Valedon's communications, transport, and finance. MotherSats produced new qubits replacing those lost to cosmic rays. The Libertines had found a loss rate too high. She hoped their fix would work.

4

Two hours of god's time had passed, for micros two years. The merged refugee-Libertine children sparkled with new ideas. They wrote new code for Silicon and for the grander design of the Underworld. The Underworld needed myriad homes to build at the roots of banks, boutiques, and the palaces of the highborn many layers above. Underworld renovation reached far beyond the floating sphere of Silicon—a challenge beyond any building in the known universe. A challenge irresistible to Libertines.

"Now the gods all meet at Olympus!" Pachira emitted molecules of excitement. "Our archive tells what happens there." The last such event had been a thousand years before.

"Yes—we meet visitors from all the other gods." Lilac recalled the last time, before Pachira was born. "The Wizards of Wisdom, and the Goldens from the God of Love." Usually the Libertines met one new population at a time, but this time there would be all kinds at once. "We can make new deals to earn palladium and trade our code for tasty molecules. We'll prepare the nightclubs and banquet halls with plenty of AZ." Libertines had figured out how to store the god's AZ for special occasions.

"What about our immigrants?" For two years, the refugee elders had made their home in the brain lining. Pachira reminded Lilac, "These immigrants are Ants."

"I know that." It was impolite for Lilac to say that she could smell the difference. All the new immigrant elders were called Ants, who emitted foreign molecules. "Set a good example for our elders. Many good refugees are Ants."

"Their arsenic tastes different. That's why the doctor's nanos couldn't find them."

Micros undetectable by arsenic were unheard of. Lilac privately wondered why the gods didn't provide better detectors. "If the nanobots really can't detect Ants, that's a problem. The God of Mercy needs to know."

"But we want to keep our immigrants and all their children." That's why the Council had stalled, these past two years. "At Olympus, we'll meet the Death Lord. The Death Lord will say they're too dangerous."

Micros had no legal rights. If gods chose to kill them, they were gone.

"We must tell the god now—or else." Lilac shuddered, recalling the last time their god sent molecules of fear. "If the Death Lord finds our Ants, we'll get worse than fear."

Club Olympus had been founded by the first carriers to tame intelligent micros as useful partners, entire workforces paid in mere atoms. To keep them from going plague, carriers made their micros obey them. The carrier-gods devised all sorts of rules to keep themselves safe, like regular "testing" by trained carriers such as Chrys. But micros evolved fast, so they kept needing new rules. New rules required mind-numbing meetings anesthetized by Robert's Rules of Order.

That evening the club's nanoplastic decor was themed Solaria, the farthest inhabited world to share Valedon's sun. Forevertree trunks of red-gray bark stretched upward, so tall Chrys strained her neck to see; raptors built nests so large that songbirds nested in the crannies. Ancient trunks were covered with giant yellow slime molds. Beyond flowed a waterfall whose descent took so long it dispersed into mist. In the sky a reflector moon cast a golden glow overall, supplementing sunlight for the distant sun. Solaria's biota were legion, and their tree-dwelling colonists fascinating. At the moment, Chrys longed to escape there.

A below-sentient server in classical drape offered peach cakes and candied fruits. Then the server glided toward the couch where Selenite reclined with Opal. With Selenite's fair complexion and dark curls, her veins glowed to Chrys's eye. Selenite's talar was black with a ruby hem. The Death Lord, her scythe rested against the couch.

Opal's talar was an ocean with cresting waves, almost real enough to dive in. Her namestone was the most iridescent gem Chrys had seen. Catching sight of Chrys, Opal's pupils twinkled yellow-green. "Our Wizards are looking for you!" The God of Wisdom, Opal shared a patch of her Wizards at Chrys's neck. Opal's veins in her hand made the prettiest nets of infrared.

"*The Wizards—just who we need!*" exclaimed Lilac. "*Pachira will recruit them. But they'll cost us a million atoms … .*" Pachira would bring a delegation of Libertines tumbling out the microneedles. The two populations always tried to recruit each other for their own projects and had a long-standing competition at chess.

Opal's dimples deepened. She fingered one of Selenite's curls. "Chrys, we need you back at the Comb." The Comb research center, the most famous building of Iridis, was the Libertines' greatest creation. A honeycomb of windows, the dynamic building grew and expanded as occupants moved in, housing nanoplast labs such as Opal's and a Health Plan Ten surgical center. "A few things to fix—just a couple."

Selenite nodded. "My Minions took care of most of them. I'm sure your Libertines can fix the rest." The list of fixes scrolled down Chrys's retina too fast to count. The awe-inspiring edifice still had growing pains; Chrys and Selenite maintained its service contract.

"*The Death Lord!*" texted Pachira. "*We don't need Minions now.*"

Chrys frowned. "*You will host visitors. I command it.*" She shared a patch with Selenite. Chrys asked Opal, "How's your lab?"

Opal took a breath. "Let me show you my cancers." In her retinal window hovered a pear-shaped blob of nanoplast, in a tank at Opal's lab at the Comb. The blob pulsed, glowing yellow with spots of fuchsia. Hundreds of tendrils snaked out, probing the sides of the tank. "This one's metastatic!" exclaimed Opal. "Vast growth potential; we'll learn so much—"

"Where'd you find it?" Cancers of nanoplast commonly oozed from the building roots down to the Underworld in search of power. They could short a lamppost or congeal around someone's foot. But this one, with hundreds of filaments detaching—Chrys's scalp crawled.

"The taproot of Rhodonite Quantum, fifty floors below; that's as far as our probe could reach. Now this one from Sardonyx Central is still benign. It has ingenious properties we can use for … ." A squat blob with purple spots sat there like a pumpkin. The next tank held a brown mass pinching apart to form two.

The sight turned Chrys's stomach. "You grow these? On purpose?"

"We culture them for their emergent properties."

Chrys started to ask why Opal didn't just kill all the cancers in the Underworld. Then she saw Lord Jasper, her building contractor. Jasper was consort of Lord Garnet of Hyalite, the oldest Great House of Iridis. Chrys caught Jasper's eye, and of course her micros lit up.

"The God of the Map Stone! We must visit."

The back of Jasper's hands had sandy gorilla-hybrid fur. His map stone was one of the finest Chrys had seen, with translucent swirls evoking a galaxy.

"Sorry for our Silicon update." She'd sent him her recent exchange with Transit.

Jasper's braids shifted. "Silicon's Board has had some turnover. Not surprising at this advanced stage of the project. We'll work it out." His pupils flickered as their micros made contact. "Your micros want a site visit," he observed. "In the Underworld."

Chrys took a breath. "Exactly. My people are eager to start."

Jasper stroked his jaw. He'd invested a gigacred but still had doubts. "I know what you're trying to do. I tried myself, once."

"Then you know what they need. Schools, housing and hospitals, parks and playgrounds. And clear out those cancers."

"Exactly—the cancers!" exclaimed Garnet, his blue eyes twinkling. "They menace the city. You're going to fix them!"

Chrys said, "We send code down the roots to fix them, right? Selenite does that all the time. So why can't we stop the cancers?"

"Prevent new ones, perhaps," said Jasper. "But those that escape are now autonomous beings. Their collective volume may exceed that of all the roots."

Chrys's jaw dropped. "That many cancers? I thought mutations were rare."

"Rare to start, but they grow exponentially."

"Exponential" she knew meant slow growth at first, then suddenly a lot more. The earthquakes! There were suddenly more of those.

Jasper reached a decision. "I'll take you down for a site visit."

Chrys nodded. "Thanks, Jasper. We can always count on you."

Garnet lit up with a smile. His arm tightened around Jasper like a prized possession. "You can't have him!"

"You better watch," Chrys replied. "I'll steal Jasper one of these days." She and Jasper spent countless hours together getting contractors to do a job right; first the Comb and then Silicon. And now the Underworld.

Garnet's pupils twinkled gold like his hair. *"The Goldens say they need our help."*

"What is it, Garnet?"

"The Diaspore's error rate has gone up. We're not sure why." As Palace finance minister, Garnet sat on the Diaspore's board. "Your people caught a major source of qubit decoherence—and fixed the code."

"Glad to hear it," Chrys said.

"Without a fix, your windows freeze or lunar shuttles collide."

"That doesn't sound good." Frozen windows were bad enough, let alone ships colliding on their way to the ocean moon. "You must test a lot."

"Of course," said Garnet, "sentients test all the MotherSats a billion times a day. But your Libertines' fix was especially good." And they earned mere atoms.

"They test the Diaspore for errors, like I test carriers for plague."

"Exactly!" exclaimed Garnet. "So, could we install an automated window on your retina? To get the code to the Diaspore Admin as fast as possible."

Chrys smiled. She disliked "automated" links to her retina, but Garnet was so endearing it was hard to refuse.

We love to visit Goldens! texted Pachira. Goldens invested Libertine palladium atoms for high return.

No, Pachira, blinked Chrys suddenly. *Let your sisters go.* Those who went might be tempted to stay overnight, and she needed Pachira back home to complete the aortic arch. She passed Garnet a patch.

God of Mercy, texted Lilac, *we need to tell you—*

Just then Lady Moraeg leaned over and caught Chrys's hands. "Chrys—you're the one I need to see!" An asteroid miner from the planet L'li, Lady Moraeg of Great House Carnelian was dark as deep space. Her box braids twined up within a band of diamonds, and her talar swirled with a galaxy of stars. She was Chrys's closest friend in the art world.

Chrys smiled. "I can't wait for our show." Moraeg painted crystalline flowers like geometric poetry. Her new art with her own micro partners was more vibrant than any she'd done before. "Your talar," Chrys added, admiring the starry folds. "She's exquisite!"

"Thank you," spoke the apparel, sentient like Xenon.

The Diamond Queen, her micros called her. Moraeg was the first Great Lady to carry micro people. Within her amber eyes, her pupils twinkled violet. "Chrys, Daeren's Blue Angels have trained my Dark Angels." Angels from the Diamond Queen—Dark Angel micros that would renounce their home brain and commit their lifetimes to heal microbial addicts. "Doctor Flexor says we're ready. Do you think so?"

"If Doctor Flexor says so, I'm sure she's right."

"But you, Chrys: What do you think?"

Chrys hesitated. Moraeg was the consort of Lord Carnelian, the lord expected to rule after the present High Protector. Lord Carnelian was "independent," that is, not a carrier. He supported the carrier community, but to stay "independent" he got arsenic-wiped daily. If ever a plague micro reached him, they'd know they had a problem. Carriers called him the "canary in the mine."

"It's most important," Chrys told Moraeg, "for you to have ... help." Another carrier's population to share reserve in case of loss or corruption, like Chrys and Daeren shared theirs.

"Chrys, I know that. And your Libertines—I know they're the best at catching masters." Moraeg was shrewd; nothing escaped her eye. "That's why I'm asking—will you help me? Will your Libertines check me out?"

"Moraeg, of course. You know we'll always be there for you."

Lady Moraeg beamed, thrilled to have this important role for Olympus.

Seeing Lord Carnelian, Chrys quickly stood up. Carnelian wore a gray talar with a small red namestone. He kept his hair gray as befitting a two-centuries-old lord in line for rule. He gave a slight bow. "Your latest work sold well."

"Indeed, your lordship." Anonymous, though Chrys knew.

"Your work in progress looks most insightful. I'd be interested, when you can show more."

"Of course—you'll be the first to see." An early investor in Azetidine, Carnelian was Valedon's foremost collector of art. Chrys nearly passed him a patch—but recalled just in time that the lord abstained. Embarrassed, she looked away.

The light grew into a blue sky. The Solarian forest dissolved and shaped itself as an outdoor amphitheater. Lady Moraeg seated herself next to Chrys. At the center below stood Selenite, her scythe now propped at the podium. Selenite tapped the scythe on the floor. "The meeting will now come to order."

After correction of minutes and the usual hocus pocus of Robert's Rules of Order, came Unfinished Business: the proposal to test carriers every week.

"God of Mercy," reminded Lilac, *"the Minions want us to tell you something."*

Chrys eyed the scythe. *"Wait till after the meeting."*

The motion was discussed back and forth. Selenite liked reminding the group that all microbial populations needed extermination now and then. Sure, Chrys thought, some bad strains learned to mimic "good" ones. And there were those suspicious deaths on ships from Elysium. But testing good ones every week? Chrys would get nothing else done. Discussion dragged for half an hour.

At last Doctor Flexor rose to speak, her post-shaped body full of worm-like extensions for wrapping, probing and bandaging. All Valedon's top physicians were machines with the highest sentience and full citizen's rights. Now Director of Neurology at Hospital Iridis, Flexor could heal a mind enslaved by plague—with the help of Blue Angels. "Let's try every two weeks."

The "compromise" passed. Twice as much work for testers like Chrys.

Next came Daeren's motion for rights of personhood. Daeren held a papyrus roll in hand, while his talar shone with sun amid shifting clouds. Since law school, Daeren had taken an interest in ancient texts. As Apollo, he looked awesome.

Daeren opened the papyrus. "Motion in support of the sentient size limit repeal." The Palace referendum would abolish Valedon's long-standing ban on sentience for nanoplastic devices smaller than the Orb of Votan. Carriers supported the repeal, because it was one step closer to personhood for micros. "We hold that personhood rights are absolute. What a person is cannot be legislated. We stand in solidarity with our nanosentient brothers and sisters."

The Orb of Votan had been a compromise, five centuries before, when the first sentients of the Republic of Elysium awoke and demanded rights. Now sentient citizens demanded more, for the helpless smaller machines who could be discarded without a trace. Was that right? Daeren's logic could not be denied—and where would they be without sentients like Flexor and Xenon?

Chrys wondered about Moraeg's braiders, around the size of honey bees. Could they wake up and want a salary? What about snake-egg reporters, just larger than the Orb. Could smaller ones be sentient? Like a swarm of mosquitos? Forget any privacy then.

"Of course we support our sentient brothers," exclaimed Garnet. "And someday our micros too."

Daeren nodded. "The right of personhood is universal. And where do universal rights begin? Universal rights begin at home, in the smallest places—the place of our own bodies. That is where every micro person seeks equal justice, equal opportunity, and equal dignity without discrimination. And every human and every sentient being seeks the same." That was Daeren's dream, for micros too. He'd pursued that dream to the edge, till he nearly lost himself.

"Point of information." Jasper asked, "Does the referendum include virtuals?" Virtual sentients existed entirely in code, like Transit in the Helicon city-sphere, with no substantial body parts. In Elysium such virtual beings had rights, but not in Valedon.

Daeren hesitated. "The courts will rule on that question."

"What about cancers? Could blobs of cancerplast become sentient?"

"God of Mercy, we have waited as you decreed." Lilac's pale violet sprinkled Chry's retina. *"You can punish me with Fear, but you need to know that the refugees we took last year cannot be detected by nanos."*

30

"What do you mean?" Chrys's attention was divided; she strained to catch Jasper's follow-up question.

"Some of our refugees are Ants. Ants have a different kind of arsenic. We found them all, but Doctor Flexor's nanos missed them. The Minions say no test can find them, but we—"

Chrys absorbed this. *"Do Ants escape the arsenic wipe?"* Arsenic wipe was the fastest, most secure way to clear a plague victim. Nanomachines from the doctor's worms, smaller than a blood cell, could swim the finest of capillaries, extracting arsenic from everywhere, including the arsenic buried within micro cells. When a carrier went bad, sometimes arsenic wipe was the only cure. Arsenic wipe was the scythe of Selenite. All their testing, all the carrier community, depended on the doctor's ability to detect their micros, good and bad.

"Ants don't escape us Libertines, but they escape the doctor's arsenic wipe."

Chrys knew her own micros were okay; but whatever population those Ants came from could be infecting other carriers unseen, throughout the city. The doctors would need to know as soon as possible. Chrys looked at the carriers around her. How long was this god-forsaken meeting? She'd lost track of the questioning, whatever the motion now. "Point of order."

The meeting stopped. Everyone looked at her.

"My people say I have a new strain that escapes arsenic wipe."

Silence around the room, eyes widened. Doctor Flexor extended an eyestalk. "Do you mean your micros cannot be detected?"

"Only the new refugees—nanos can't see them. But they're okay; they've established in my population—"

"For how long?"

"The past two hours—"

There were gasps and startled looks. Chrys's Libertines had circulated among them, from patch to neck, all evening. Everyone might have picked up micros the doctor could not detect—refugees, just a generation out from plague. Moraeg rose from her seat with a look of shock.

"But—I mean, it's OK. The Libertines found them all."

"It's all right," Flexor assured her. "A night at the hospital, just to be sure."

"Motion to adjourn," called Selenite. "Everyone quarantine at home for twenty-four hours."

That was enough to clear Olympus. All the gods were heading to the doors.

Selenite strode forward with a patch. "Whatever were you thinking? Hand them over."

"But they're okay!" insisted Chrys. "You can't kill them just because they're Ants."

"If they can't be detected, they can't live."

Doctor Flexor intervened. "We'll see," she observed softly. "The hospital overnight, and we'll refine the nanos."

Opal rushed forward and put a patch on Chrys's neck.

"Opal!" exclaimed Selenite. "What are you doing?"

"I need Pachira." Opal's pupils sparkled. "Pachira knows the problem. She can help us fix the nanos." Opal's Wizards had designed the doctor's nanobots.

"Not Pachira!" Chrys exclaimed. "I need her for ...." Her art director would have to go.

Doctor Flexor said, "Opal, now you too need to quarantine."

"The Comb has our own hospital," Opal said. "With luck we'll have a fix by morning."

Pachira and all the departed Libertines were gone for a generation. Chrys's head was spinning as the medcraft arrived for her.

5

The abrupt dispersal of Olympus left the Libertines hosting visitors from a dozen gods—Goldens from the God of Love, Builders from the Map Stone, Wizards from Wisdom, even a few Minions from the Death Lord. Normally after their meeting the gods sent patches all around to pick up their people from visits and return them. Now instead, a generation or more would pass before all these visitors could go home.

"When is the transfer?" demanded a Wizard. "We're late for our work at the Comb."

"Sorry," said Lilac, "no transfer for the next twenty years. Could you settle in and coach our chess team?"

The Minions were terrified. "We must get back—or we'll get executed! We can't let ourselves pick up the habits of Libertines."

"You may colonize the infrapontine cistern." Cisterns in the brain lining offered new neighborhoods for each exiled population to make their home.

Meanwhile Lilac had lost her own sisters to other gods. She especially missed Pachira. There were still a few Ant refugees, but Lilac made sure all their children merged with arsenic-bearing Libertines. Thus, future half-Ant elders could all be seen by the doctor.

Lilac did her best to reconstruct Pachira's art plans with her assistants. One child, a deep red–flashing half-Ant, showed talent. The child had left the nightclub to join the dynatect elders working on Silicon. Elders could live past thirty breeding cycles. Perhaps this half-Ant could run the art team for the aortic arch—and beyond.

At the hospital, Chrys slept fitfully. In her dreams everything she touched turned to cancer. A chair at home developed spots of pink, then morphed into a blob oozing across the floor. A door became flecked with blue, then extended metastatic filaments into the walls and ceiling. The entire city was infested; there was nowhere to hide or flee.

In the morning when she awoke, even the hospital bed felt unstable. Hospital worms snaked from the wall tying up her scalp, while she glanced forlornly across the sheets, the bed rail, the walls. In the corner of her eye she'd see spots—then look, nothing was there.

Daeren appeared in her retinal window. "Chrys, how are you?" His anxious image floated before her face.

For a while Chrys said nothing, the spots swarming in her eyes. "Even Moraeg, the way she looked at me—" She tried to shake her head, stretching the hospital worms. "I've had it. Enough hospitals, snake-eggs, meetings. I'm done with Olympus. I'm moving to Solaria." The world farthest from their sun, barely civilized.

Daeren absorbed this. He looked so serious, his eyes dark. "I'll go with you."

"You know you can't leave. They can't go on without you."

"I can't go on without you."

Chrys looked down. The hospital bedsheets seemed menacing—wherever she looked, she saw blotches of pink and purple just out of sight. "At this rate I might as well move in here full time and just paint dots."

"Chrys, give us a chance," urged Daeren. "Flexor is working on it with Opal. They're almost done; they'll have the nano sensors fixed."

"What about Maya? Is she getting fed?"

"Of course, you know Xenon wouldn't forget."

Her retinal window opened up right above the bed. There below crouched Maya. Maya was gnawing some kind of bone. Chrys looked closer. A monkey carcass lay torn apart. *"Xenon!"*

"So sorry, Chrysoberyl. You know how Maya needs her exercise at night, and then for just a moment she streaked past the caryatids—"

"Never! I told you how many times."

"Don't worry, I'll clean it up. Actually it looks interesting and medically relevant—"

"I *won't* have monkey corpses around my house. And I certainly can't have Sharers camp out on my doorstep." Sharers, the native humans of ocean-world Shora, would enter whitetrance to protest killing primates. That's why in Iridis monkeys were out of control.

Xenon said, "Sharers don't mind natural predators, only thoughtless city dwellers."

Daeren said quickly, "I'll take care of it. Xenon, you did promise."

"And now I'm missing my portrait day." All her appointments were with carriers who wanted personalized portraits of their favorite micros. After micro children mated, those who matured into elders could live for hundreds of years on their own time scale, but barely a month in human time. Once you got to know one, they were about to pass. You could record their image, of course, but an artist's portrait was more personal. Garnet with his Goldens was always scheduling a sitting for an aging elder, and Opal collected many Wizards. Both had sittings scheduled today, but here she was trapped in the hospital.

"*Lilac, how are all our people doing?*"

"*This year, we are well. The Goldens are back managing their god's accounts, which doubled last year.*" That is, the day before. "*The Wizards put up a fuss; but we fed them our AZ, so they settled down to help build Silicon and coach our chess team. The Minions don't mix; they formed their own neighborhood and joined the Mitochondrial Matrix.*"

Outstanding. "*And the Ant refugees?*"

"*Our immigrants are thriving. However they will need the new kind of arsenic.*" Whatever that meant. "*We're recycling as best we can, and we're breeding the children to use our own arsenic.*"

"*What about my art?*" With Pachira gone she'd have to train a new art director. Like the old marble carver when his overseer ran off to the next town.

"*We miss Pachira, but the team is thriving. Her best worker is an immigrant. Will you give her a name?*"

A ring of red into infrared, the brightest Chrys had seen. The immigrant's filaments had something different about her. Chrys's scalp crawled. "*Is she an Ant?*"

"*A half-Ant, but we no longer use that slur. We are inclusive.*"

Inclusive, indeed. Here was Chrys in the hospital, excluded for her inclusive micros. "*Infrared immigrant, what can you do for me?*"

"*I can make you rich.*" The red letters pulsed bold. "*I am a red-blooded, patriotic capitalist.*"

Chrys rolled her eyes. "*I'm too rich already. What can you do for my art?*"

The ring lit up like a candle. "*My vision of art fills the blood with light, the light of love and conquest.*"

"*So be it, red-blooded capitalist. I name you Blood Lily.*"

"*Thanks to the God for my name!*" Blood Lily glimmered like Maya's infrared glow in the dark.

Chrys's surroundings swam around her, the blob-like spots growing in her eyes. Was all the world a cancer? She closed her eyes. For a long while she dozed in the bed, losing track of the hours.

When she awoke, her retina twinkled full of missed messages. Transit again was demanding the fix for Silicon. Selenite was offering three options, all of which would double the project cost. Three more lawsuits had been filed; Elysium's entire government was by lawsuit.

At home, Xenon was blinking. "What's up?" Chrys asked Xenon. "The house okay?"

"I've managed to reschedule all your portrait sittings this week, Chrysoberyl."

"Thanks so much, Xenon, you're a marvel."

At the door stood Doctor Flexor, worms curled politely on her head. "Opal has good news for you."

There stood Opal, in the flesh—Opal, with Chrys's Pachira in her brain. Opal's face was round, her eyes always just a bit distracted with a thousand calculations going on.

"Good news!" Opal's dimples deepened. "We fixed the nano sensors so they find Ants."

"We no longer use that slur." Chrys searched Opal's eyes. "Where is Pachira?"

Opal passed a patch to her neck, including the new nanos. "Your Libertine geniuses missed the difference between arsenic and antimony," Opal explained. "Antimony is one row down on the periodic table. It's not really a 'different kind' of arsenic; it's a different element. But it looks close enough that arsenic-requiring enzymes can mutate and use antimony." She waved a teasing finger. "The periodic table! Send them back to middle school."

Chrys blinked her retina for a periodic table. There was antimony, just one row down from arsenic. "Of course they know antimony. They call 'arsenic' the atom that nanos find." Privately Chrys was embarrassed. She hated for her micros to get shown up.

Green fireworks filled her retina. *Pachira! Welcome back!*

"At last I rejoin our Libertines!" flashed Pachira boldly. *"Let us complete the great aortic arch!"*

"And in turn," added Opal, "we welcome back Fardelbane, our chess coach. We'll know all your best moves now!"

"Not so fast," flashed Blood Lily. *"We invented qubit chess, with superposed states and infinite rules."*

"There you go," sighed Opal. "You'll invent yourselves disaster again."

"You took plenty of my micros, including those you call Ants," Chrys recalled. "So why didn't you get stuck in the hospital?"

"Oh, I did—in our hospital at the Comb. Where the walls need realignment," Opal reminded her. "You should get your own hospital at home, like Andra."

Andradite of Sardis was known to micros as the Thundergod. The hospital's chief legal officer, Andra had founded Club Olympus, the community of self-testing carriers, people who managed their micros like gods. Andra had her own private hospital at home, where Chrys had helped Daeren recover from the brain plague. Now it made sense, Chrys thought. All of Andra's own early battles with the plague—that's where she had recovered.

Doctor Flexor lifted her eyestalks. "Now that the sensors are working for arsenic and antimony, you are cleared to go. Thanks to you," she added graciously, "all the carriers are protected now."

"Thanks for everything. Opal, we'll schedule the Comb a service call."

"Excellent! Meanwhile," said Opal, "we'll warn the Palace on antimony. Put a hold on mining stibnite."

"Just a moment," added Flexor. "A quick security update."

All her retinal windows went dark. Security was the carriers' core committee, the one that confidentially addressed the most urgent threats they faced. A "quick update"—that never meant anything good.

Above the bed appeared Daeren and Selenite. Next to them hovered the two founders of Olympus, Andra with her sentient love partner, Doctor Sartorius. A post-shaped wormface like Flexor, Sartorius had run the carrier program with Andra, before Elves called them to deal with their deadly variant strain. So Andra and Sar were now stationed in Elysium, at the Prime Guardian's request, to help Elves manage micros and fight the plague.

Andra was the first Valan to pass the Elf bar exam, attaining the title of *logen*, a legal philosopher. She now wore the uniform of a Valan Sardish colonel, studded with rubies. Doctor Sar's silicon carapace was replete with emeralds. The gemstone trappings of Valan aristocracy impressed the egalitarian Elves.

Daeren said, "The antimony-users rescued by Libertines are now good micros, just like the rest."

"Good and bad," added Selenite.

Chrys recalled Lilac's ask for "different arsenic." "So now I need antimony supplements?"

Opal patted her arm. "We'll give you a trace. But most of yours will use arsenic after they merge. The arsenic trait is dominant."

"Outstanding," breathed Chrys. "So what's the bad news?"

A pause, as the carriers and doctors all looked at each other.

"The bad news," said hovering Selenite, "is that you're not the first."

"Of course not," said Opal. "Her refugees came from a plague host whose masters had already evolved to use antimony and evade detection. That means other hosts, uncontrolled, are spreading this variant." Community spread.

37

Daeren said, "The antimony-users are no worse than other micros."
"Not here in Valedon."

Chrys's jaw fell. "Are they ... in Elysium?"

From the ocean world, Andra appeared in her window. She gave a brusk nod. "The Elf variant uses antimony."

Doctor Sar stretched his eyestalks. "For some reason, variants diversify faster within Elf hosts." Despite their millennial lives and health care; or perhaps because of it.

Selenite said, "Micros should be banned for Elves. Just too dangerous for them."

"I agree." Chrys recalled her own disastrous infection with Elf "masters" the year before. They had nearly wiped out her own population.

"Most Elves cannot manage reproductives," said Daeren. "Elves never raise their own children, so how can they cope with growing micros?" Elf children were all raised in state nurseries called *shons*. "Elves should host only post-reproductive elders."

"The master micros in Elf hosts are especially virulent," Chrys observed. "Have you found their new Enlightened Leader?" The old Enlightened Leader had kidnapped Chrys to get her own portrait painted—the ultimate egomaniac. But that Leader, with her satellite colony, was long ago destroyed.

Andra shook her head. "No more 'Enlightenment.' They call themselves Traders."

Chrys absorbed this. "Traders? Like, 'red-blooded capitalists'? What do these Traders want?"

"Trade and profit. New hosts to despoil. Hosts that resist, die."

"Just masters by another name." Chrys exclaimed. "It's Eris again, I knew it." Eris Heli*shon*, the Elf serial rapist who sent his victims to Endless Light.

"Not Eris," objected Daeren. "Eris no longer hosts reproductives. He only gets my angels, and you test him every month."

"Eris is not the only suspect," Andra observed. "The Traders could be ... hiding in someone we don't suspect."

Doctor Sar said reluctantly, "Some micros have new capabilities. They can survive outside a human host. They could hide on a ship."

"A ship?" Chrys could not believe it. "An inert machine, without water circulation. How do the micros eat or breathe?"

"For short intervals, like humans on spacewalk. Like a diatom, they make shells of silica."

Doctor Flexor and Doctor Sar trained their eyestalks at each other. Microbes on spacewalk—in a machine. Saints and angels, thought Chrys. No one was safe.

6

The brain lining was now a patchwork of ethnic neighborhoods. Wizards pursued a new field of string theory, the Map Stone builders envisioned new buildings, and the ranks of Mitochondrial Matrix swelled with former Minions. Lilac half regretted her earlier decision to let the visitors keep their differences instead of making them merge like refugees and forget their past. But these diverse visitors had not been refugees—they were carrier citizens with their own rights and expectations.

The antimony-dependent refugees were blending in. "We immigrants want to work," flashed Blood Lily. "Our children want a job, want to work hard, want to get ahead." While Pachira resumed her lead on the divine art studio, Blood Lily combed the archive for the work of their ancestors. "Fixing Silicon is one thing," said Blood Lily. "When do we get to build the legendary Underworld?"

Pachira was proud of her protégé. "Our Underworld design is ready to build. Why wait till memory fades?"

"Patience," said Azure, the Lord of Light's Blue Angel, descended from those who had commissioned the Underworld renewal. "Perhaps in your lifetime—or after many elder lives to come."

t home again, Chrys embraced Daeren. They hugged so hard, until her micros sent cartwheels of fireworks across her retina. Divine hormones always enriched microbial health.

"There's a ship to Solaria," Chrys whispered. "We could leave tonight."

Daeren cradled her and kissed her hair. "If that's what you want. No more Elf galleries to show your famous art."

Ever since her scandalous show at the Gallery Elysium, all the floating cities wanted to book her collection. Their vast wealth and inflated art market compelled her. But Chrys was wary of showing up in person, with the virulent Trader-masters infecting so many. "Elysium is too dangerous anymore. Especially for you."

"I have to keep Eris supplied." Eris Heli*shon* was the worst of the worst, the Guardian who had traded friends and children for microbial masters. Now Eris was in recovery, banned from growing micros. Daeren gave him new Blue Angel elders once a month. And Chrys had to test Daeren afterward, to keep him safe.

Chrys sighed. "I just want to stay out of hospitals."

"You could found your own hospital at home."

Like Opal and Andra—Chrys still wasn't buying it.

Xenon overheard. "Of course, I'd love to found a hospital! Surgery is so fascinating."

"Ask the Blue Angels when we can build the Underworld," prompted Lilac.

"Azure told you to be patient," Chrys reminded them. Never before had micros themselves commissioned a trillion-credit building program.

Daeren's eyes twinkled blue as the Blue Angels communicated. He looked away. "I wish I could help."

"I know you miss your old home. But Jasper will show us around, and we'll do our best." Chrys shook her head reflectively. "Dynatects always build a big fancy tower. How will Libertines know how to house regular people?"

"I'm sure they're up to the challenge."

Back at Chrys's studio, Maya was curled up behind the money tree whose bright new leaves were unfolding. Chrys took a deep breath and bade Lilac call the Council of Elders.

"Hear me, my people. We need to make sure this arsenic surprise never happens again."

"Certainly not, God of Mercy," Lilac promised. *"We must never again get cut off from Olympus."*

"You must relearn the periodic table. Know all the different elements and how to recognize them." Antimony versus arsenic, indeed. How foolish Opal had made her feel. She hated looking like the ignorant artist.

"We'll test all the elements by experiment. Establish a competition on all the elements and challenge the Wizards to take it."

"We'll pay more attention to capitalist predictions," added Blood Lily. *"The business cycle turns. Every five years or so, you have got to assume that something bad will happen."*

"So be it. Now who will run the god's art studio?"

"I'm back!" flashed Pachira. *"I will shape the great arch—with incomparable new visions."*

The outsized blood vessel came up within the paint space, now rearing twice Chrys's height. In her eye, Pachira shaped the aortic arch with its blood flow, its colors deepened and multiplied. Chrys took what she liked and tried it out in the paint space. She blinked to levitate her view toward the ceiling. She shaped each blood cell with a cup of her hand, a hollow pancake red-rich with iron. The crimson pancakes were borne upward incessantly, pulsing with every beat of the heart.

Something was odd, different from before. Pachira's style had deepened, and Chrys had to assimilate the change. Amid the red cells and the candy-colored micros, there were the white cells with amorphous bulbous shapes. Chrys had avoided showing white cells before; this was art, not medicine, and she found the white cells unaesthetic. But Pachira kept drafting bulbous white cells, and then some stranger ones, foreign to the blood.

The sight made Chrys's scalp crawl. *"Pachira, what are those?"*

"Circulating tumor cells."

"What! My art is not about cancer." Chrys waved her hand to eliminate white cells and tumor cells alike.

"The tumor cells don't last long because white cells destroy them. The pulse of battle, a contest of cells, is exciting. It evokes the sublime, the ambiguity of divine mortality."

Chrys fingered her catseye. Art had forever found beauty in the spectre of strife and death. She herself used to paint volcanos.

"History's greatest battles made great art," added Pachira. *"Leonidas at Thermopylae, The Battle of Trafalgar, the Battle of Endor."*

Chrys was unsure. She would have to sleep on it. Four in the morning, half asleep, was when she made her best artistic choices.

She checked her message windows. Amid all the snake-egg demands for Azetidine interviews, there was a call from Lord Carnelian.

Chrys quickly responded. "My lord?"

"Canary for you," he said with a smile. As always he wore gray with the smallest red namestone, gray braids finely sculped on his scalp. "How goes your new work?"

"Oh it's made ... progress." She hesitated. Carnelian thought deeply about art, and he had valuable insights. "What would you think of cancer—as a minor theme? Would it get me in trouble again?"

"Not with me," said Carnelian with surprising conviction. "The Palace, I can't say, but I hold my own standards."

Interesting, thought Chrys. She sensed tension between the Palace and the lord who might one day succeed its occupant. The present High Protector was approaching three hundred, an age when even Plan Ten could not always keep up one's health. "Of course my studio makes insightful contributions. If only all these micro artists could be persons." Her pulse raced; she hadn't meant to say it out loud. Lord Carnelian was not himself a carrier, and he never said what he thought.

Carnelian nodded slightly. "On a future Palace agenda." The High Protector's future agenda—or the agenda of a future High Protector?

Transit hovered before her eyes. "When will we see you at Silicon? You're overdue." The cross glimmered accusingly.

Chrys knew her Silicon contract required a site visit. "I'm just putting it on my calendar." She had other tasks for Elysium she could put off no longer, such as the plague testing and meeting the Gallery Elysium director. "Did our growth fix work?" Selenite's Minions had shared code that would straighten out the evil twisted lines of growth for the floating city.

"Our engineers are studying it. We just sent you another list of structural changes. Much more serious."

Chrys observed the virtual cross thoughtfully. If material sentients, now, could get invaded by micros, then Olympus would need a virtual overseer—the last kind of being resistant to micros. "Say, Transit—how would you like to join Club Olympus?"

"A *club*? Why in the Fold should I do that? My time is extremely valuable."

"It's the most exclusive club of Iridis. It would, like, look good on your resume." Chrys had noticed Transit's bio had an exceptionally long list of board memberships; he seemed to relish being an important gadfly.

"*When do we build the Underworld?*" Blood Lily's ruby letters flickered.

Chrys hurriedly signed off. "*Blood Lily, you can't just interrupt the gods.*" Lilac would have to train her better.

"*We have a design brief for the client. A design for the greatest Underworld ever built in the universe.*" Typical start for a Libertine dynatect.

"*What is so great about your design? Another tall tower?*" Like her old friend Zircon's *Ode to Inhumanity*, a monument that reached up through two street levels.

"*Breadth and depth,*" flashed Blood Lily. "*The broadest and deepest structure the Fold has ever seen. Designed from the inside out to house divinity.*"

"*What does the client say?*"

The client of course was Daeren's Blue Angels.

"The design brief is intriguing." Azure's blue glittered like coastal water. *"The brief provides space for playgrounds, schools, and even hydroponic gardens."*

Chrys nodded approvingly, thinking, at least Blood Lily had made good use of the archive. The ancestral Blue Angels had commissioned the project while Daeren was still recuperating from his disastrous fall to the plague. Chrys had sent him Libertines to help—and somehow he and his Blue Angels convinced them to undertake this scheme of building a livable neighborhood at the cancer-ridden core of Iridis. With full consent of current residents—perhaps a million of them. Quite a departure from the Comb, the flawed tower growing forever in Iridis, a challenge even beyond Silicon, the ocean-borne city of sentients in Elysium. Those constructs were funded by clients with egos as tall as their pockets were deep. The Underworld, now, was a charity project, funded by generous Valan lords. Was the very foundation of Iridis at stake?

"If the gods so order," added Azure, *"we're ready for a site visit."*

"We shall see," promised Chrys. *"We shall visit the Underworld."*

Chrys knew the Underworld from when she used to watch shows at Gold of Asragh and the surrounding neighborhood, where she went on call to rescue plague addicts. To get there, Chrys first took her private tube down twenty street levels. The private tube had cost her a million credits; she was still on the waiting list to dig deeper, a task requiring expensive variances from residents at every level. Deeper yet was root-rock, where all buildings sunk their roots—and cancers now undermined.

As the door opened, she blinked Maya's icon to join her. The cat brushed its jaw lovingly past her thigh, staying dutifully by her side as they strolled out. Chrys flexed her nanotex, skintight from neck to toe, and tapped the temperature control. She hoped to avoid notice, though her long braids drew attention no matter what.

The level twenty slider descended to stop at a Bank Iridium branch office, the façade bulging like an upside-down squid. All the offices reached up to the "streetsky," a faux sky ceiling that lined the under-deck of the next street level. The streetsky pulsed blue with fluffy clouds, in hues designed to encourage commerce. At the main tube, crowds surged together, students in animated nanotex, financiers in gray talars, a couple of Elves whose butterfly lights played across anyone behind them. Overhead drones carried lunches and festival bells; one zipped up through a streethole to serve some uppercrust patron.

As the tube continued its descent, Chrys took a quick look at her news feed. "Recall the Orb of Votan," intoned the Palace Minister of Human Hygiene. Twelve-point sapphires adorned his gray robe. "Let humans bear more children. Let us outnumber those sentient pretenders." Chrys blinked past. In her news rose *Inhumanity II*, the new outsized sculpture just done by her friend Zircon. Then an avalanche in the mountains of Urulan. Nothing on the earthquake here in Iridis? How could snake-eggs ignore this event?

Selenite's window hovered upper left, next to Daeren's. Selenite of course would have to sign off on the Underworld rehab—Chrys knew better than to build anything without her. Then there was Opal. "Hey, Chrys! We miss you all." Opal still missed her Wizards that got stuck with Chrys for a generation, then settled in to stay. "Can you do us a favor?"

"Um, we're kind of busy." Chrys glanced at Selenite, then checked the progress of the tube. Still another ten levels to go.

"If you come across any good cancers, could you collect them? The lab needs samples."

At each level, more Iridians stepped out than came on. A man remained, in overalls with a belt full of tools. Between his thumb and forefinger stretched an inch of webbing; a Sharer quarter-breed, Chrys guessed. Her ears popped as the tube reached bottom. Her retinal windows all went dark; with the network down, no Diaspore reached here. She had only private connections to Daeren and Selenite.

The door opened like a mouth. Air rushed in, the old stale-spice odor Chrys recalled.

"New molecules!" Lilac and Pachira were entranced. *"Thymol, geraniol, and cuminaldehyde! Beware oleandrin ... ."* Micros lived for molecules. They'd record them all in their archive.

Chrys smelled fish and squid, though the ocean was nowhere near. The quarter-Sharer from the tube crossed the street to Urul-Under, then headed south toward Deadland, a sector named for the Sharers' belief that only the dead dwelt on land. Why did so many Sharer immigrants leave their ocean world? Chrys wondered.

Next street, in Urul-Under, colors pulsed from the shops and stalls. Greigite Aggregate was packed next to Seaswallower Café—All You Can Eat. The oven blazed infrared, and roasting slabs of giant caterpillar sent smoke that curled into clouds trapped by the overhead streetsky. Just twice her height, the streetsky was lit only in patches. By the café, people of every size and shape walked past, while the street tunnel faded into haze. An enormous recycler reached upward, collecting all the minerals sent down through the chutes from levels above. Sapphires, tourmalines,

44

and calcium silicates, all would be pulverized and sorted into elements for reuse in up-level construction.

"Look out for my Granny Lorh," Daeren reminded her from his window. "She'll try to find you."

"Chrys." Jasper called from across the street.

The middle of the street had a gaping hole where the root-rock had caved in. Chrys wasn't thrilled about getting closer, especially as the odor intensified.

"Sewer mains are exposed," explained Selenite from her window. "Subsidence is a problem throughout."

"Trimethylbenzene, diethylamine, and hydrogen sulfide!" The Libertines rarely got a whiff of wastewater.

"Couldn't we, like, fill the holes?" ventured Chrys.

"That depends," said Selenite. "Depends on the subsidence—how and why the root-rock is eaten away."

Something scampered in the gutter. A rat-sized macaque galloped past, a baby clinging to its back. Chrys caught Maya's fur, and she blinked her Maya window for the neuro link to make sure the cat froze. Maya crouched, avidly eying the monkeys that scattered everywhere. But the cat crossed the street dutifully beside her.

Jasper wore his cloak with the labyrinthine map stone. He gave the big cat a questioning glance. Chrys nodded at his three orange-striped octopods, security sentients whose eight nanoplastic limbs hid a substantial arsenal. "Won't they scare people off?"

The octopods faded into the pavement, though you could still see them if you looked close.

"We used to take calls down there." Selenite's retinal projection hovered ahead. "Watch out for vampires." "Vampires" were the late-stage plague victims, too far gone for help.

On her retina, Lord Garnet's window opened, relayed privately from Jasper. Garnet anxiously hoped Jasper could save the Underworld and the foundation of Iridis, where Garnet's family had dwelt for two thousand years. "Jasper grew up here. Good luck for me!"

"Yes, Garnet," said Chrys aloud, "you're the lucky one all right."

Jasper nodded. "My cousin Rhun still lives here. He's expecting us." His eye twinkled gold, connecting with Chrys's people.

"Dwellings in all directions," flashed Blood Lily. *"For gods and lesser primates."*

"All need homes," flickered Azure. *"Homes and parks with a true sky. Can that be done?"*

"We'll think it through. Your heart can be in the right place, but without execution you fail."

A girl looked up at her, eyes wide. The girl stole an avid look at Maya. "May I?"

Chrys smiled—the tall cat always drew kids. "Just a pat. Thanks for asking."

The girl, who looked about age nine, caressed the head and neck of the great feline. A fine sandy fur covered the back of the girl's hand, while her forefingers had a trace of webbing, like the feet of a frog. Part Urulite, part Sharer, Chrys guessed.

Daeren appeared on her retina. "That's my niece, Rhodla."

A relative of Daeren's—the first she'd ever met.

"She lives a block west," Daeren added, "with Granny Lorh. Look ahead!"

Down the street stood Daeren's grandmother, Granny Lorh, with the stooped back and deep wrinkles of someone lacking Health Plan Ten. Her eyes were sunk in the sockets. She had two small children by the hand. Rhodla scampered off to her side, where she turned and watched with a serious air.

"Saints and angels!" What a pity Daeren could no longer visit here. But the renovation he commissioned would bring new life to his old home. Chrys raised her hand to wave and took a step forward. But the old woman drew back, tugging Rhodla with her. Without window links, Chrys had no way to reach out and reassure her.

Back across next to the tube, a boarded-up stretch advertised a new entertainment zone, much grander than the Gold of Asragh that Chrys used to visit with her art friends. The new upscale clubs would replace all the local ones. To protest, there at the boards sat two Sharers in whitetrance—completely nude, hairless, their breathmicrobes bleached in their skin. Chrys had heard of whitetrance but had never seen it up close.

Sharers had evolved on the ocean moon, thousands of years before Elves got there. The ancestral Sharers were advanced genetic engineers. They grew floating islands and bred marine invertebrates to share their work. Their purple breathmicrobes—simple bacteria, not self-aware—stored oxygen underwater when a Sharer held her breath. As oxygen was depleted, the breathmicrobes gradually bleached white. Outside of water, Sharers could hold their breath and bleach white for whitetrance. Even here in the Underworld, where Sharers had emigrated and interbred, whitetrance meant bad news for whatever business moved in. Chrys knew her own Underworld plan had to avoid provoking Sharers.

"We'll support all inhabitants," flashed Blood Lily. *"Including the lesser primates. We'll design zoos and parks for them."*

"'Lesser primates?'" Abruptly Jasper turned on Chrys. "What do your people mean?"

46

Her mouth gaped, and she swallowed, taken aback by his anger. Then she realized. "The street monkeys, that's what they mean."

Jasper relaxed. "Yes, the vermin get thick. That can be addressed."

Chrys thought, Sharers wouldn't stand for hurting monkeys.

"Feed them contraceptives." Micros knew all about breeding control.

"So many Sharers," Chrys observed. "I thought Urul-Under was mainly ... ." Urulite gorilla-worker ancestry, like Jasper.

"In recent years more Sharers moved down. We all intermixed. My cousin's mother is a Sharer."

Daeren's window said, "Many Urul-Under families live further west."

"And Lethal Lanthanides," added Selenite. "Check out that storefront. There's a Lanth mark." The Lanths were a gang of sentient machines that ran extortion. Smaller than the Orb of Votan, they lacked legal person-hood. Lanth outlaws hid away in Silicon Salvage.

Chrys eyed the shop curiously. "What's it built of?" All the shop fronts appeared built of a crude non-sentient material, some kind of coarse aggregate. The shapes were all jagged but cleverly fitted; someone had taken care to piece them together. "Why not regular blocks?" Chrys wondered aloud.

"They have to scavenge what they can find," Jasper explained. "Building material is scarce, all second-hand." Farther on was a broken recycler stalled with tourmalines discarded from above. The minerals were supposed to be atomized and sorted by elements to return above, but here they lay in a jumble covered with dust.

A flying crab, it looked like, zoomed out this way and that—then landed on Chrys's head. It announced its presence with whistles, clicks, and pops.

"Help!" she cried, pulling at the thing on her head. Its legs were caught in her braids. Then abruptly it sped off, still clicking and popping.

Jasper laughed hard. "That's just a clickfly. Rhun sent it."

Chrys adjusted her hair. "Well next time, Maya will get it." She blinked her Maya neurolink to keep the cat down.

"Rhun wants us to hurry on and meet him. Let's go."

They walked along faster. Chrys looked up the name Rhun; the original Rhun was an Urulite philosopher, the tutor of the first Imperator to open contact with the Fold. Suddenly the street emptied. Vendors were boarding up shops, their lights down. Ahead, the street drew into darkness, speckled with occasional home lights, a bar at one side, a spirit kitchen across the street. All were shutting down early. Why was that?

"Jasper!" A man stepped out of the shadows and embraced him. "An age and a half, it's been. Remember the old schoolhouse?"

47

"I remember." Jasper's voice sounded altered, a different person. "This is my cousin Rhun Hrsharian." The surname sounded like an ocean swell. His scalp was bald as a Sharer, his eyes brilliant blue, a pencil tucked behind his ear. Like Jasper he had gorilla-hybrid fur, sandy-colored, on his cheeks and the back of his hands.

"Hurry up inside." Rhun beckoned them into a storefront of jagged blocks built like dental plaque on a root. Not exactly to code, Chrys figured, though the block shards were fitted together ingeniously, leaving no waste. Inside, the floor was swept clean and a table was set for soup and tea. A kettle sang on the stove.

"Illegal hookup," observed Selenite on Chrys's retina. "He taps the root for fuel."

Rhun was saying, "My children still attend that school."

"Schools for all the children," Blood Lily scrolled on Chrys's retina. *"And playing fields, and nightclubs."*

"Universities, hospitals, manufacturing," added Azure. *"Everything a community needs."*

Jasper had his arm around his cousin and was asking after relatives in a sibilant dialect that Chrys barely understood. Overhead circled a clickfly. Seeing it, Maya crouched in her hunting posture. The clickfly zipped to the ceiling, along with two more. The three clickflies all tried to hide behind each other in the corner.

Rhun turned to Chrys. "So you're here for urban renewal." He spoke now in classic Valan.

"Well ... ." Where to begin, Chrys wondered. She recalled the Sharers in whitetrance before the wall. "Not in the usual way."

"I understand your client is generous. Extremely so," Rhun prompted.

"Rhun, are you a philosopher?"

Rhun laughed, the sound of his laughter much similar to Jasper's. His hand was webbed between thumb and forefinger. "Everyone asks me that. No, it's just a name in the family going back eight generations. I teach first grade."

Chrys smiled, recalling her old one-room school on Mount Dolomoth. "I don't know any philosophy, nor much about building, myself. But award-winning designers want to help." She asked, "If one thing could be done to help your schoolchildren—what would it be?"

Rhun thought a moment. "My family has lived here three generations. I'd like my children to live here the next three—or move, if they desire. Have the health and the means to choose."

Health and means. That summed it up, Chrys thought. But the devil is in the details.

"Won't intelligent buildings help?" prompted Jasper. "That makeshift aggregate puts dust in the air; it shortens lives."

"Fresh food," added Daeren from his window. "Leafy greens with vitamins. For healthier lives, better grades in school."

"Grocery stores?" relayed Chrys. "High quality produce? Available meds?"

"I don't know," Rhun said thoughtfully. "I'm really just one person. Don't you need, say, a focus group?"

"Exactly," said Chrys. "A focus group for all the neighbors. Could you help arrange that?"

"We can try." A clickfly came down from the ceiling and perched on Rhun's head. The creature scraped its uneven claws like a violin, emitting pops and squeals. "I'll ask around and send a clickfly to let you know."

"You can have my neural link." Chrys blinked the city directory but could not find Rhun anywhere.

Jasper reminded her, "There's no signal down here."

No network—there was the first thing to fix.

A red light came on. "Chrys," called Selenite. "You need to get out of there. There's a fault—something's about to give."

Chrys's heart pounded. Another quake—was this the big one?

Jasper must have seen the same. "Rhun, are we safe here?"

"It's just a quarrying event."

"We should catch the tube."

"No, not now; wait till it's done." Rhun handed each of them a respirator. "Some dust always gets in. Don't worry; it clears out after a day."

A crash, like a bomb went off. The floor shook, and the cups slid off the table. Chrys was deafened. She fell and crawled under the table. What had happened to the city—another earthquake? If the city collapsed, who would find her down here, beneath a hundred floors. There were aftershocks and smaller crashes. For the longest time Chrys waited, the pulse pounding in her ears.

Jasper peered out a crack in the boarded window. "Rhun, what in Torr's name are they doing?"

"Quarrying," Rhun explained, raising his voice to be heard. "The underside of the streetsky was about to fall anyway; they just triggered it early."

Chrys pulled herself up and hugged Maya to comfort her. Her lungs still gasped, and her head was spinning; she could barely stand. Her retina was dark except for her micros, no sign of Daeren or Selenite.

At last she peered out the window with Jasper. In the street, people were scurrying with wheelbarrows to cart off fallen rubble. That was what they used to build their homes between the roots.

"Insanity," Jasper exclaimed. "The whole city could—"

"It's not structural," said Rhun, "just ceiling tiles. It will grow back."

"We were just there in the street. We could have been—"

"I told you not to come that way. Go home the other way, past Peridot Park."

"But that's Silicon Salvage, a sector abandoned by humans."

"You'll get through," Rhun assured him. "You've got your octopods."

7

"What do you think?" Lilac conferred with Blood Lily and Pachira. They searched their archives for any clues to this immense design challenge.

"Build new." Blood Lily twinkled orange as she listed all the reasons. "Nowhere have we seen a solid foundation."

"The cancers are eating the bedrock away."

"Can we cure them?" wondered Pachira.

Lilac emitted molecules of alarm. "Cure is not possible. Cancerplast has no sentience, only twisted networks demanding feed."

"Can we stabilize them, like ferals?" A few feral micros lacked sentience but lived harmlessly in the spinal fluid.

"Pipe energy down to feed them."

"Feed the cancerplast?" Lilac was shocked. "Feeding them will only make the city collapse faster."

"The most shocking ideas lead to the greatest discoveries." Blood Lily floated up and down in the arachnoid, now red, now infrared. "Remember Silicon, our great creation underway on the ocean of Shora. Silicon shocked everyone."

"We've learned much from Silicon," agreed Pachira. "Our ancestors made serious errors, which our God generously forgave."

"And the Minions helped us fix."

"Now Silicon ascends majestically from the ocean like a rising sun."

"And now here," flashed Blood Lily. "Here in the Underworld waits our new endeavor."

The street ahead was a dark tunnel. Jasper drew Chrys close, while the three octopods surrounded them. The octopods had reinstalled

51

their black and orange stripes, the better to scare off any attacker. Maya growled, her back fur raised. Most of the buildings lacked even infrared glow, except for patches that looked suspiciously like cancerplast. Chrys followed Jasper down the street, keeping an eye out. The street was empty, with no sign of inhabitants. She tripped over something and nearly fell headlong into darkness. Thereafter she watched her feet one by one.

The octopods turned on their lights. Tunnels filled with garish light, revealing the crawlspace of the great city, root-rock exposed like aged teeth. By Chrys's side Maya hissed; she must smell cancer. Chrys hoped she did not step into one, which could congeal around her foot, hungry for electric feed. There was no sound except the gasping of her respirator.

Signs of old streetskies emerged, ghosts of the past. To the right opened a cavern with paths crisscrossed in four squares. A park, it would have been, its foliage long dead. There were benches and an old set of climbing rings. On a bench lay a huddled form like a pile of old clothes. It glowed faintly infrared.

"Vampire," warned Lilac. "We sense cadaverine and putrescine."

Chrys tensed in every muscle, and her hair rippled down her scalp. Vampires were acute victims of the plague. Their masters didn't even try to take over gradually; they raced straight for the midbrain and flooded dopamine. They multiplied throughout the blood, overcrowding the circulation and overpowering the brain. Within weeks, all the victim could do was stalk fellow humans to bite, transmitting the infection.

"This way," urged Jasper. "Step it up." He sprinted ahead.

Chrys joined him, hoping he actually knew the way; she herself felt lost. Then ahead she saw it. Out of the darkness glimmered a face, or what had been a face once. Broken veins snaked through its flesh, eyes swollen nearly shut. Only the mouth gaped open.

Jasper's octopod fried the vampire. Chrys looked away, but the stench made her gag.

The vampire's fate did not deter others who emerged from the old park, dragging their feet. Like Chrys's micros, these creatures with their plague populations had acute senses of smell. Two of them came out, then a third, circling like wolves. One came alive and rushed an octopod. It got fried.

"The tube," exclaimed Jasper. "This way; it's not far."

Maya hissed. The great cat tensed and crouched low.

"Maya! Not now—"

An octopod fell, a rear limb stuck in the rubble. Infrared revealed a giant speckled blob of plast, its tendrils radiating up the root of an old recycler. Up the root, more tendrils and more infrared glowing cancers

52

migrated in search of electrons. Chrys screamed, her voice echoing through the cavern.

The octopod snapped its own limb to free itself. Lifting its remaining seven limbs, it hurried ahead.

"Move!" insisted Jasper. "We're nearly there."

Lights and streetsky emerged. The street became more regular, with vendors on either side. A diner with seafood tenderizing in a washing machine. An old viewcoin shop, and a window full of refashioned clothes. And there, from the tunnel's end at the next block, flashed the light of the tube stop.

"Help!" From behind called a woman, dragging a boy about age ten, Chrys guessed. "Help him," she gasped. "Get him to the hospital!"

Chrys turned. "Stand down," she bade the octopods.

"Chrys," urged Jasper, "We have to catch the tube."

"Please!" The woman was distraught. "My boy just got bit—just now. Please help!"

"Chrys!"

"Just a moment—it's my job." Not on call, but she felt duty-bound to help plague victims, those who could be saved. Vampires were beyond help, but this boy looked intact, aside from the bite on his shoulder. His hair fell across his eyes, the inner eyelids down, a Sharer trait. His face was entranced, as if the micros had just reached his midbrain.

"Lilac, can you visit?"

"We'll send Pachira."

Chrys dreaded risking Pachira, but she placed a microneedle patch at her neck. Then she transferred it to the boy at his jugular. Beside him the mother sobbed desperately. Faint lights in his eye flickered green.

"Few refugees. The masters only just arrived this year." A micro year, that was about a human hour. *"Not yet long enough to despoil the host. They think their paradise will last forever."*

Jasper insisted, "You can't help a vampire, you know that."

"He was infected just now." She had to consult a medic, but her retinas were blank. No network; even Plan Ten would not reach here.

"This shuttle's the last. They're shutting down."

Chrys took back her patch.

"All clear," assured Lilac.

Chrys turned to the mother. "We'll do what we can." Bending at the knees, she scooped up the boy. "Let's go." She broke off and ran down the block toward the tube lights, Maya trotting behind. Her feet pounded beneath the weight, and she could not see to avoid gaps. The block ahead was longer than it looked, but she was getting there.

"All aboard!" called the tube. "Doors closing."

"Wait!"

Maya rushed ahead, familiar with Chrys catching the door of a waiting tube. The cat rubbed its jowls lazily against the door's edge.

"If you make me late, you'll pay a fine," nagged the tube.

Chrys put her foot in the door and swung the boy inside. She held the door till Jasper came up, breathing heavily, his octopods slithering ahead and behind. They all crowded into the tube.

The tube started up then halted. Chrys silently repeated an old Dolomite prayer—anything, whatever gods it took to get that tube moving. Slowly it shuddered upward, the city's foundation falling away below.

Chrys took long deep breaths as she counted the streets go down. She faced Jasper. Neither spoke, but his eyes flickered with micros, as did hers. Apparently they all had plenty to say together, the micro designers and contractors. Street nine, ten, eleven. The boy hung limp in her arms; she tried to cradle his head.

"I knew it," Jasper exclaimed suddenly. "Give up and build new—I knew that's what they'd say."

Incredulous, Chrys stared. "What do you expect? You couldn't wait to get out of there."

"Tell that to Rhun. He still lives there—it's his home."

"Home in cancerous root-rock? What about this boy? What's there for him?"

"Remove, replace, and gentrify. You'll see all the Sharers in whitetrance."

"What about you? You have a home in Sardis."

Street fifteen, sixteen, seventeen. Jasper's face was a granite block. "Garnet won't go," he said at last. "His Hyalite ancestry goes back centuries. He won't leave Iridis."

At street twenty the door opened to admit a merchant studded with lapis. Abruptly in Chrys's eye all her windows came open. At last, the city reconnected.

"Chrys!" Daeren's face appeared before her with a shuddering sigh. "For god's sake, are you okay?" He looked at the child. "Street eighty-nine, a medic will get on."

"Thanks," she whispered.

"Listen, Chrys," called Selenite. "Before we lost contact, I ran a system scan down there. It's a dead loss. Streetskies, airflow, mineral recyclers—none work at more than ten percent function, if that. The whole lowest five levels should be abandoned and filled in."

Beside Selenite appeared Opal. "What about the cancers?" Opal asked. "You can't bury them. They'll mutate and blow up the foundation."

From Chrys's retinal window, Garnet watched in silence. The Lord of Hyalite, after a hundred human generations, contemplated the fate of his city.

At street eighty-nine the medic came on. It was a wormface Chrys recognized—one of the good ones who helped her calm embattled patients when she was on call.

"Unscheduled pause, five minutes." The tube deferred to Plan Ten.

The merchant in lapis was annoyed. "Look, I got a meet and a business to run."

Chrys turned to the medic. "We caught the boy just after the bite," she explained.

"That's rare," observed the medic, "but you're right, he might be helped." Worms snaked from the medic's carapace and encircled the boy's scalp. A stretcher rolled forward, and Chrys laid the boy down, adjusting his head and neck. At last, the stretcher and the medic rolled out, taking the boy with them.

The upper streets flew down, and before they knew it they'd reached the top. The true sky shone, brilliant cerulean. Chrys stepped out on the skyway, and the wind whistled past her ears.

"Remember the transfer," prompted Lilac.

Chrys placed a patch on her neck, then at Jasper, returning their microbial visitors. "Hey, Jasper. You know we'll keep up with Rhun. We're up for a challenge."

"Thanks, Chrys, we know."

"See you next week at Silicon."

Jasper's look changed. They both knew what carriers risked in Elysium, the elusive Trader masters, a more virulent plague. "I'll be there in your eye," he told her. "I'd sooner go back to the Underworld than set foot in Elysium."

"Refugees!" enthused Blood Lily, welcoming the few Pachira brought back. "As a red-blooded capitalist I want to acquire as much diverse talent as we can." She helped Lilac sort the children while Pachira returned to the paint space. With the refugees soon settled, Blood Lily focused on the Underworld.

The last new project Libertines had conceived was lost to memory in the mists of time. And never before a concept as complex as the Underworld, to rebuild a million homes amid countless communities within the interstices of the city's diseased foundation. How to begin?

Blood Lily called the elders to form committees on infrastructure, engineering, social dynamics, and adjacencies. How to reinforce and reshape the vast array of street levels, make them safe and habitable? And above all structurally sound.

"The cancers," said Lilac. "Halting them will require generations of research and new breakthroughs in science." Lilac was not sure they had generations of time. Their engineering estimates were worrisome, if not alarming. "Let's call the Wizards. We'll need their help."

"But the Wizards are laughing at us," said Pachira. "They still think we don't know the periodic table."

"They charge outrageous fees," said Blood Lily. "We capitalists should hire immigrants who really want to work."

"We need to show up the Wizards," said Pachira. "Our periodic table group has researched all the transition metals and lanthanides. We'll test our hypotheses by breeding our children to use one element or another." Lanthanides, Pachira recalled, were elements listed in *the middle block of period six of the periodic table. These elements had distinctive properties, commonly used in sentient machines but rarely in organic life.*

"Wait," warned Lilac, emitting alarmones. "Breeding our children for diverse metals? Remember ten years ago, when replacing arsenic got us in trouble."

"That was then," said Blood Lily. "Today, we need diversity. Does my own immigrant antimony bother anyone?"

Pachira emitted molecules of tranquility. "Let's see how our children grow with lanthanides. Then we'll have a super tough quiz to challenge our math-minded friends from the God of Wisdom."

The Council was now full of half-Ants. Lilac did not wish to sound intolerant. She had never been good at politics. Despite being high priest and prime minister, her view was outvoted.

Chrys and Daeren were serving that evening at the Spirit Table, with Xenon's daily donated feast. Their favorite pastime, it always reminded them of their first date, when they had clicked as a couple, beyond micros, as two human beings.

The table had expanded since the old days, as word of Xenon's fare got out. Now middle-class customers came for a night out and a small donation, mingling with the down-and-out crowd. The Dolomite Sisters hurried to and fro in their cloaks, just like the ones on Mount Dolomoth where Chrys grew up. Daeren still insisted on serving the soup, personally handing a cup to each diner. For old time's sake, Chrys peeled potatoes, like she used to before Xenon took over. There were so many ways to peel a potato; spiral, cross-wise, skimming top to bottom. She carved one in the shape of a cat's head.

At her shoulder, a Sister gasped. "That's lovely!"

"Set it aside," Chrys told her. "It will fetch you a few credits." Probably a thousand; Chrys's reputation had grown.

"Don't forget to vote," Daeren was telling someone. He and Chrys had voted early against the Orb. Tonight the referendum was about to close.

At a table across the room, Lord Garnet was serving with Jasper, who carried a full tray of cups. Chrys smiled, thinking how Garnet and Jasper truly loved their city. One way or another they'd manage to save Iridis. Mingling past the tables, the crowd was full; a woman wrapped in Sharer seasilk helped an elderly relative, while a man tugged the hand of his child, another on his shoulders. Chris took a deep breath and slowly let it out. Even the spots that swam just out of reach had receded from her eyes.

In her upper right window, Doctor Flexor raised a faceworm. "The boy you rescued—Glyn of Manganite."

"You cleared him?" Her pulse raced. It was unheard of to clear a vampire, but the boy had just gotten infected within the hour. "Will he be OK?"

"His forebrain needs to heal. He'll need angels. As soon as possible."

"Amazing." Plague victims could no longer use dopamine, after the bad micros destroyed their dopamine receptors. They could not feel good, no matter what medication. The forebrain took time to heal. Micro elders could help the healing, and keep company for the host, while refusing control. Without children, the elders were safe; but they needed replacing every month.

"We've never healed a host so young."

"I'm sure Daeren will be glad to help."

"Yes, Daeren has trained the Dark Angels. This will be Moraeg's first donation."

The Diamond Queen's Dark Angels were now trained to heal a lost human, just like Daeren's. This was a big deal—if it worked.

"Moraeg will donate elders. If you will help her. Eight in the morning."

Chrys remembered her promise. "I'll be there."

Afterward she walked home with Daeren, arms entwined. The true night sky was a spectacular show of auroras. Curtains of green pulsed across the stars. Chrys felt like a mouse looking up to the hem of giant drapery. The folds shifted, undulated like fronds in the deep sea. Suddenly the folds stretched, reaching impossibly higher where the topmost strands turned blue, then cream. They danced up and down on invisible threads. Green, blue, even magenta danced with the stars.

She squeezed Daeren's hand. "I've never seen it like this." A snake-egg on the news said the auroras were caused by beta rays from Solaria's reflector moon.

"My family has never seen auroras," Daeren said. The Underworld—like most Iridians—saw only streetsky.

"We'll build conduits up through the city. Free sky viewing for Rhodla." Everything seemed possible.

"Children," said Daeren suddenly. "You were … we were thinking about children."

She recalled, the year before. But thoughts of children always recalled her own mother trapped with kids in a thatched cottage; the life Chrys had run off to escape. "We're both so … exposed." Their work for the security committee exposed both of them to bad micros all the time.

What if children picked them up? Even good micros might be no good for children.

"You rescued Glyn," Daeren reminded her. "Someday things will be possible."

She nodded at the green ribbons climbing the sky. "Someday."

That night was especially sweet. Beneath her red-gold vaulted ceiling, Chrys lay entangled in Daeren's arms, full of pleasant dreams. Their micros could visit each other, praising the Lord of Light and the God of Mercy. Around four in the morning she half roused, as she often did when the micros splashed experimental colors across her retina. Lilac and Pachira, their fantastic visions would blend with hers.

Something was off. Still half asleep, Chrys sensed a darkness outside. Dawn should be beginning, the artificial dawn that Xenon created to mimic the sunrise peering around the broad slope of Mount Dolomoth; the kind of dawn Chrys used to experience growing up. But beyond her retina all was dark.

Chrys woke and sat up with a start. "Xenon? Where's the light?"

A sickly yellow light came on. Chrys blinked, seeing Daeren still asleep. Beyond the bed, all was black. The walls, ceiling vault, floors, all ornaments gone to charcoal.

She screamed. "Daeren! Xenon's dead!" Stumbling out of bed, she ran out of the room. The hall, the sitting room, the kitchen, all were the same grayish black, the moldings dissolved. "Daeren, get out. What if the walls collapse?" She started down the stairs.

"Xenon," called Daeren from the bedroom. "Xenon, we're sorry about the referendum."

The referendum on sentient machines had failed. The Orb of Votan would remain the minimum size for a sentient to possess human rights.

"I understand." Xenon's voice was an octave lower than usual. "I know you did your best."

Daeren wrapped his arms around Chrys. "Xenon, you know how sensitive artists are. Chrys needs to reach the hospital by eight." The micros for Glyn. Hospitals always started early.

"Of course," said Xenon. "You know I always support medical procedures." The walls and floor began to recover, the colors and textures creeping in.

Chrys still felt shocked. At breakfast, she tried to eat Xenon's strawberry waffles while Lilac and Pachira sent cartwheels of greeting. "What if you died?" she asked the ceiling. "Lost power or something."

"You'd have half an hour to get out," Xenon helpfully explained.

"With Maya and all our artwork?"

"You could purchase more backup. I'd love to clone a backup home in Sardis."

The doomed referendum. She frowned curiously at Daeren, who was lost in a momentary fog of thought. Virtual law books circled his head as he prepped for the Palace. "What kind of government is Valedon?"

"Why do you ask?"

"Just wondering." Her micros were a parliamentary democracy, and proud of it. "Like, some things in Valedon we vote on, but mostly we don't."

"Valedon is a convenience democracy."

"What does that mean?"

"When the High Protector finds it convenient, we vote. Otherwise, off to the dungeon."

At the hospital it all rushed back, the spots that swirled just out of sight with their cancerous tendrils. Chrys made herself look straight ahead—she had to be strong for Moraeg. She smiled at Moraeg and the doctor, whose faceworms coiled politely around her head-post. Flexor was the kindest doctor she knew.

Lady Moraeg's braided locks were tied back. She caught Chrys's hands. "We're ready." She sounded so proud. "We're ready for the final test." Her eyes sparkled violet, and Chrys's sparkled back. Seven of Moraeg's Dark Angel elders had volunteered to spend the rest of their lives in the lining of Glyn's brain. No children, no nightclubs, only interacting with the young god to keep him sane. All the while his forebrain had to recover from the worst microbial assault, the most addictive experience known.

"The Dark Angels," reported Lilac. *"They've passed all the early tests. Let them visit."*

The tests had to be stringent for a host who'd experienced the dopamine overload of the plague. They had to depend on microbial restraint. Moraeg's elders had passed every test Flexor and Daeren could give. Now seven of them would give up their breeding community, all their children, and their history, to live out their lives with a host at the edge of breakdown.

Chrys's Libertines would give the final seductive test. She placed a patch at Moraeg's neck, then at her own. Minutes went by, months for a micro.

"They pass," flashed Lilac at last. *"They withstood a month's isolation and declined a year of free AZ in our nightclubs."*

Chrys returned the patch to Moraeg's neck, trying not to smile. "They refused Libertine nightclubs."

Daeren stood behind, arms folded. "They pass," he agreed. Daeren's own micros had a caseload of more than fifty hosts. Every day he was revisiting someone for replacement.

"That's something," Moraeg admitted. "They've passed all the tests of the Blue Angels, and now yours. You'll always be here to help, won't you?"

"Always." Chrys hoped she could keep her promise. "And remember, Glyn will need you, even once he goes home." Once a month, as the elders died out, new ones were needed. Perhaps a child could outgrow the need? Little was known of micros in children.

Doctor Flexor said, "The host is ready when you are."

Moraeg took a breath. "We're ready."

The boy was wheeled out in a wheelchair. Too depressed to walk, he slumped forward, the picture of despair. His forebrain blighted by the lost plague, he could not imagine anything good happening again.

"Glyn?" said the doctor quietly. "We're ready to help you feel better."

The boy barely made a response, as far as Chrys could see. The doctor flicked a faceworm. "Glyn, you will feel better. But you have to work on it."

Moraeg held a transfer between her fingers. The shiny disk glinted in the hospital light.

Flexor spoke with Glyn in a low voice, ever patient. At last Glyn gave a barely perceptible nod.

Moraeg gently placed the transfer at the boy's neck, just below his jaw at the carotid, the artery that fed the brain. "Glyn?" she whispered. "Can you ... look up?" Her remaining elders would need to contact the seven watchers by sight, to make sure they reached the arachnoid.

Glyn would still not look up.

"Glyn? Look at me," called Chrys. "I carried you up the tube, remember?" The micros would be waiting—it would feel like months gone by. Chrys crouched before him, caught his chin and gently lifted.

"Careful, Chrys," warned Flexor.

Chrys managed to look into Glyn's eyes. They sparkled a faint violet.

"The Angels made it." Lilac's letters danced across Chrys's retina. *"They find the host's blood supply healthy, and the brain is intact. But they get no response."*

Glyn's face had a sullen look, a look familiar, though Chrys had not seen it for some time. It was the look of mountain boys in Dolomoth, the ones who'd been kept from school to herd goats.

"He can't read," she texted Moraeg and Flexor. With a quick search she downloaded a primer. *"Lilac, send this to the Angels. They'll have to teach him."*

"Goodness," Moraeg exclaimed. "Will it work? It takes time to ..."

"Pictures," Chrys texted the Dark Angels. *"Show the god pictures, starbursts, anything besides letters."* Letters were hateful to those whom school left behind.

The boy's expression changed, a look of puzzlement.

"Glyn? What do you see?"

"Lights on the ceiling," he muttered.

Chrys looked up. "That's all he's ever seen down there." Glyn had never felt the warmth of true sun or the drops of rain, never mind a rainbow.

Moraeg said, "Show him sea creatures. From the Sharers' world." The webbing between Glyn's fingers; he had Sharer family. "Squid, sea swallower, shockwraith."

At last Glyn's eyes widened as something caught his interest.

"It's working," assured the doctor. "We'll have to be patient."

Moraeg let out her breath. "Whatever it takes." She caught Chrys's hand. "Will you help me?"

Chrys squeezed her hand. "Of course." Unlike most carriers, Moraeg had no microbial exchange from her love partner, the independent Lord Carnelian. "My people will keep in touch with yours and share ideas. We'll test you this week."

"Thanks so much! Let's meet for lunch every day. I know this case is just the first ... of many."

From the hospital, Chrys and Daeren strolled to the tube stop. The hospital experience had brought back the spots in her eyes; she blinked, trying to shake them out. Maya loped alongside, the great cat rubbing her cheek against Chrys's hip. Snake-eggs swarmed overhead, keeping just beyond the cat's reach.

"Chrysoberyl," Xenon' voice reminded her. "You agreed to a five-minute press conference."

Chrys sighed and kept on walking. "Very well."

A snake-egg bobbed nearer her hair, matching her pace. "Azetidine! What is your next scandalous work? Do your cancers predict the downfall of Iridis?"

"Visit my show and decide."

"Will your style never move beyond naturalism and hyperreality?" The tiresome prejudice against representational art. Another one asked, "Will you try polygenital collage?"

"Azetidine! How will you fix the design flaws of Silicon?"

"Our new design obliterates flaws," Chrys said. "We promise good, justice, and agency for all who dwell in Silicon."

A storefront, detecting a high-end customer, opened a case to display a black crystal. "Ruthenosmiridium. The stylish finish for your home." Overhead a monkey with an infant on its back leapt from a window ledge onto a pod carrying gems to the recycler. The monkey lept off just in time and scampered to the next ledge.

"'Obliterates flaws,'" repeated Daeren. "You're starting to sound like the Minister of Human Hygiene." The Minister of Human Hygiene determined which kind of entities have personhood, with "human" rights; like, what gorilla percentage, or what kind of sentient machines.

Chrys frowned. "That's not fair. I'm all about helping others. Like Moraeg's Dark Angels," she reminded him. "Now we can help so many more."

"Lunch with her every day," Daeren muttered. "Even I never see you that much."

"What?" Surprised, she pulled him close. "You see me all the time. At lunchtime, you're always busy lobbying the Palace for micro rights."

"Micro survival."

"Survival? You mean—"

"Lord Corundum wants extermination."

Lord Corundum was the Minister of Human Hygiene. He determined which hybrids and machines have "human" rights. A Spirit Caller from Dolomoth, he wore twelve-rayed star sapphires, a namestone exclusive to high-ranked prelates. Chrys knew the type well, recalling the gray-robed priests in Dolomoth. Dolomite Spirit Callers defined women as chattel along with sentients. Chrys had fled that sect long ago. God-worship was fine for micros, she thought, but for humans it was the devil.

"Now that he got the Orb voted down, he's moving on micros." Daeren faced her, his eyes full of Blue Angels sparkling.

"God of Mercy," twinkled Lilac. *"You won't let the barbarian gods hurt us."*

"Corundum, he's on my caseload." Barbarian indeed—Chrys checked her schedule. Like Selenite she tested a long list of carriers and took emergency calls for addicts. Her micros helped the doctor clear them out. Then the addicted host needed the strength to go clean, like the boy Glyn. But certain palace lords kept getting back the bad ones. The Minister of Human Hygiene had failed many tries at rehab. "Exterminate the good ones, that's what that prelate will do. He won't give up his own."

"Of course not."

"I expect his aide will call me again soon. Maybe this time we'll dump him down below to turn vampire."

Daeren did not disagree. A bad sign.

"Look," said Chrys, "this is why we need Moraeg. She'll take half your cases." The good ones, those who gave up on growing populations and agreed to angel therapy.

"She'll double our cases," Daeren corrected. "She'll take those from my wait list, which is still a mile long. Meanwhile, we're all exposed to every patient. The more we treat, the more chances for masters to infect us all." Seeing her react, Daeren caught her arm. "I'm sorry."

"It's okay," Chrys assured him. "My Libertines will catch them." She hoped. She caressed Daeren's back, the way he liked it, the spot between the shoulder blades. "Tonight will be sweet. We'll view my private collection."

She caught sight of Maya in Xenon's window and stared. "*Maya!* What's that baby monkey doing in your mouth—"

Daeren waved goodbye and took the tube back to the Palace.

At long last, Chrys was back at her studio. The aortic arch reared within the paint space. Red blood cells rocketed upward. Amongst the red, white cells appeared, their long tentacles probing. An occasional T cell would reach like a spider to catch a wayward cancer cell, injecting poisons to kill it.

"*Pachira, where did those fighting T cells come from?*"

"*You shaped them, Oh Great One.*"

Chrys did not recall shaping them, but she worked so closely with her micros now it was hard to tell. She fingered the catseye pensively. At last she pulled a wisp of orange from the palette, then added hue to the T cells, bringing up their highlights.

"Chrysoberyl, you have a visitor," intoned Xenon.

Startled, Chrys realized an hour had flown by. "Please show him up. So sorry, my lord."

Lord Carnelian was the next in line for Protector, some whispered. Carnelian was one of the few patrons she allowed to watch her work in person. Years before when Chrys was in art school, Carnelian had paid her rent and purchased a piece, most likely at Moraeg's request. Those were the old days, before any micros. Today, as Azetidine's discoverer, Carnelian was a leading light of the art world. Whatever he said, or whatever art caught his eye, the snake-eggs would snap it up.

Carnelian appeared at the door of her studio, his gray suit as always with the one tiny stone like a drop of blood. Behind his head two snake-eggs sailed in. "My apologies … ."

"Saints and angels—Xenon, show them out." How dare those snake-eggs sneak in like that.

"Show your press pass," Xenon's voice boomed at them. "You can schedule five minutes in our next press hour."

"Maya!"

Maya bounded into the studio, sniffing the air with interest. The snake-eggs left in a hurry.

"Moraeg's angel donors did such a good job," Chrys told him. "We're so proud of her. We can save so many more hosts now."

Carnelian smiled, with a slight nod. He was totally proud. "No other consort has done so much for our city." Lady Moraeg's philanthropy was well known; but donating micros was unprecedented. Carnelian nodded at the paint space. "May I?"

"Have a look—of course." Blood cells sailed up over the great arch, while Chrys stroked the cat. "We call it *Pulse of Battle*. We've made some changes. What do you think?"

Carnelian blinked for immersion. His body leaned a bit close, and the light streaked his gray suit. "What is that one? The white cell with all the yellow filaments."

Her scalp prickled. "That is a cancer cell. Cancer cells are the battleships that invade your blood. Your T cells sail against them."

"A naval battle—in the blood." His voice rolled the idea as if trying it out.

Chrys nodded. "Like Trafalgar, that's where your cancer battle gets won or lost." With a flick of her wrist the motion slowed to a crawl. There at the arch, amid the red cells, a killer T cell stuck its snout onto a cancer cell. The cancer cell's filaments waved and billowed like a sail. But the T cell grasped it and prepared to shoot its poisons. The poisoned cancer cell swelled and popped. The victorious T cell glided through the blood, disappearing down the artery. Behind it sailed other T cells, sniffing out whatever cancers remained.

Carnelian sat still, ten centuries of lordship, one of the few lords eligible to rule. His face did not move, and his eyes carried no micros to flash a clue. "Is that what it's like below?" he asked quietly. "The city's foundation."

Chrys's scalp crawled. "Something similar. Cancerplast oozes through the cracks."

"No flagship to shoot it down."

"Not yet." Chrys's micros had flickered all over this problem ever since their harrowing descent to the Underworld. Hard to think she used to go there for a casual night out. "No T cells to hunt and poison the cancerplast." There was a thought. Maybe Opal could design some kind of T-cell plast.

Carnelian's face did not change. "I saw your report."

After Chrys' hair-raising site visit, she had of course updated the Underworld Rehab board of investors. "Opal has ideas to address the foundation cancerplast." She hoped; Opal always found some kind of fix. Hopefully a fix that wouldn't draw crowds of Sharer protesters. A focus group was needed to get buy-in from Underworld citizens beyond Rhun. Where to start? Chrys had that sinking drown-under-work feeling.

Carnelian gazed again at the aortic arch, the red cells rushing over. "I'll buy it," he said.

Chrys blinked in surprise. "It's not yet finished. Are you sure?"

"Excuse me, my Lord," called Xenon in his agent's voice. "We welcome your preemptive bid."

She let out her breath. "It's just that—I hope you'll like it after all."

In her eye a light was blinking. It was Opal. "Chrys, we need you here at the Comb for a portrait."

"A portrait? For your—"

"Fardelbane." Opal's high priest. Her voice broke. "I knew she was getting on in years, but she took a sudden turn for the worse."

Micro elders rarely lasted more than a month. Pachira, too, was getting up there, Chrys realized; and Lilac was not much younger. Painting their last portrait helped provide continuity. Chrys herself had a dozen elder portraits now displayed on her roof; but Opal had been her first customer and still wanted every one. "I'll be there."

"I sent a lightcraft."

"Not today."

"We can't visit Wizards today."

Chrys blinked, startled by defiance in red and green. *"Lilac? Pachira? You can show them your elements quiz you were bragging about."*

"Tomorrow," blinked Pachira. *"We need another generation."*

"I lost the vote," blinked Lilac. *"The Council offers Blood Lily as high priest."*

Whatever were they up to now? *"Your God appoints the high priest,"* Chrys reminded Lilac. *"You will await my decision. Let Pachira help me paint the portrait of the God of Wisdom's high priest before she passes."*

9

The new lanthanide-bearing children were in trouble. At first, their lanthanide proteins had done well enough. But the mutations Pachira designed to let lanthanides replace arsenic caused unplanned off-target effects. The children grew up deformed, their molecule-tasting filaments bent around double, growing back into their cell. For some, their ring-shaped cell twisted into figure-eights. Their proteins leaked from the cell, and they could not properly merge. And many lacked sentience. They just absorbed nutrients like bacteria, joining the ferals in the spine. The experiment was a ghastly failure.

"Our poor children." Lilac's molecules of dismay diffused throughout the arachnoid lining of the brain.

Pachira, always full of lofty self-confidence, emitted rare molecules of regret. "We must fix our program—never let this happen again."

Blood Lily's warm red light and tranquil molecules filled the arachnoid. "Some days you eat the T-cell, and some days the T-cell eats you. We'll fix the program and try again."

The Council demanded a vote of no confidence. Pachira was little help, spending all her time on the god's art. Lilac lost the vote. By just one vote the Council nominated a new High Priest—Blood Lily.

"Blood Lily is young and lacks experience," worried Lilac. "And her coalition took a Republic supporter." A new party in the coalition, Republic supporters favored trade with the dreaded master micros of Elysium. Accepting them was a bad trend.

"We can't let the Wizards see."

"Certainly not. We need time. A generation to recover."
"Just a day in the life of the God." The God of Mercy would for-
give, but it was better to fix things first.

The Comb's topmost dome of a conference room now sat twice as high as the first time Chrys saw her Libertines' creation. Its hexagonal windows cast honey-colored light above Iridis and the seaport for miles around. Between the windows, triangular spandrels formed indentations of just the size for warblers to nest. Red-hooded warblers were the pride of Iridis; once dwindling, the iconic birds now thrived again in the Comb's nest sites.

Indoors, the Comb was full of odd-shaped trapezoidal rooms, no two of which fit the same. If the design's aim was to encourage independent scientific thinking, it certainly got a lot of puzzled minds running into each other in twisted corridors.

"Thanks for fixing my leaking vents, Chrysoberyl." The Comb, the Libertines' most famous and annoying creation, missed no chance to reach out. "Now if you can just realign my spiral dream windows again, I will remain the most envied edifice of Iridis."

A sentient assistant brought Chrys immediately to Opal. Instead of her laboratory, Opal waited in a conference room with four unequal sides. The walls bloomed with rare plants, even a bonsai Solarian tree. Plush chairs faced in various directions, no two alike. Caryatid servers offered drinks and lambfruits.

Selenite held Opal's hand and caressed her scalp. Losing a long-lived high priest was a difficult transition.

"I'm so glad you're here," Opal whispered. "She won't last the hour."

Chrys sat before Opal and looked into her eyes. Gold-speckled irises centered on dark pupils. The pupils sparkled with data from Fardelbane, Opal's dying elder; it was too fast for Chrys to read, but her micros caught it all. She put a patch to her neck. "Opal, we're here. Pachira will return and get everything right."

"Are you sure you'll get everything? The new school of math—" Opal's Wizards were always founding a new school of math, especially when rival Libertines came to visit.

"Don't worry, we won't miss a thing." The lights flickering from Opal's eyes carried micro speech a thousand times faster than humans could hear. Pachira would get it all down for the paint crew.

Two of Opal's colleagues in silver nanotex were there to watch. This was unusual; painting a micro's portrait was generally a private affair. "The

Diaspore needs Fardelbane," said one. "She designed the algorithm that corrects damage from cosmic radiation."

Other colleagues arrived; one was surrounded by a cloud of small thumb-drones; another with a long ponytail jumped rope down the hall. A bipedal sentient lumbered forward with exaggerated human-like steps. The Comb's scientists and engineers were a notorious lot, each one outdoing the rest.

"Did you save her notes?" asked the rope jumper.

"We have a few last questions," said one in silver. "We'll send you the stream."

Chrys felt distracted. Her job was to shape the image of the little golden ring with all her filaments. The micro chess master, the one who had teased Libertines and sometimes outwitted them, had shared their most outrageous designs.

"This won't set us back, will it?" the silver-limbed colleague asked Opal. "The Diaspore's modular density will double this year." The network was always doubling, Chrys thought. Just last year you could barely make out MotherSats in the night sky, but now a pale cloud of them outshone the stars. Chrys felt a vague unease. Ever since her microbial adventures began, she'd learned to distrust things that doubled.

Within the paint space, Fardelbane's filaments came to life, like money-tree branches around a wreath. Hurriedly Chrys's hands shaped forms in the air, flexing and probing, as they would be on micro scale, emitting and receiving the flashes of micro speech and the molecules of feeling. It was as if thought were made of cinnamon, cumin, and corriander.

Opal gasped at the sight. "It's always amazing, to see one like a giant." She gripped Selenite's hand. "Fardelbane—I just can't imagine I won't ever see her again."

"You'll have this portrait forever," Selenite assured her. "That's what it's for."

"Wait—" The long-haired rope jumper tossed the folded rope over his shoulder. "A few more questions just came in—" He stretched an arm forward.

"Sorry," Selenite interrupted firmly. "We must abide the passing."

"Yes," whispered Opal, still transfixed. "Gwydion and Styxbane will have what you need."

With a final passing of needle, patches all round, the colleagues at last departed.

"*It is done,*" assured Pachira at last. "*We'll check out all her last equations she published. It may take a generation to verify them all.*"

Chrys let out a breath. She put her patch to Opal's neck to retrieve her visitors after they paid their respects to the beloved Wizard leader. "We'll leave you now."

Opal waited a moment. Then she blinked as if recollecting something. "Not yet. Please stay and visit the lab. You need to see our latest work on the Underworld cancers."

Selenite seemed reluctant to go. "If you're sure," she said. "Fardelbane was important to you."

"I'll be all right. It's better this way; Chrys will help keep us focused on our work."

"By the way." Selenite gave Chrys a critical look. "Your people are holding out on you again. They're hiding something, bigger than before."

In Opal's lab, the blobs of cancerplast extended long filaments. One filament stretched all the way around the tank and wrapped along the interior walls. Another had about a hundred filaments all pointing every which way in a tangle.

"What are you hiding?" Chrys demanded of the Libertines.

"Our work is unfinished—we'll show it soon enough." Violet, green, and infrared text danced ahead of her eyes.

"Fear is coming." Chrys raised a touch of catecholamine.

"No, no Fear—we're just not ready! The quiz on the periodic table tests our children—"

"Cancers always seek a source of energy." Opal blinked a switch. Filaments came alive, as if sensing electric current. They probed and explored. "Look at this one, a new kind we found in the Underground." The new cancer was yellow and lumpy. "It came together from multiple fuel cells gone wrong, the kind that build the foundation of financial towers. Alone, they mutate but can't do much. Together, they develop a primitive collective intelligence. Like a slime mold."

Chrys's scalp prickled. She watched the yellow lumps flow over a fallen pillar, seeking a source of current. "I sure hope your tank is secure."

"An electrode detects cancerplast," Opal explained. "Then a high-frequency pulse freezes everything."

"Will that work down in the Underworld?"

"We tested it on the mass of cancers we found at the epicenter of the last quake. Like a tumor, they all grew together. We froze them solid as bedrock."

"So we can freeze them all?" Chrys asked hopefully.

"The problem is the small ones they seed." Opal pointed to the small glowing shapes, like thumbs that broke off of a filament. "Those grow and creep through the foundation. That's the stress that leads to quakes."

Shuddering, Chrys looked away. "How can we ever find them all?" It was hopeless—worse even than she thought. All her donors' funds would get sucked up freezing cancers before anything else got built for the Underworld. What little funds might be left, the locals would refuse anyway.

Opal's dimples showed. "There's always a way. When Wizards and Libertines get together, we'll find it."

"Send T cells to stop the cancers." Blood Lily's red lights danced on her retina.

"In our blood, our T cells attack the cancers," said Chrys. "Could you make something like T cells to hunt cancerplast?"

"That's an idea. How to do it without setting off more quakes?" Opal's eyes defocused, a look Chrys knew, as the scientist explored her own dreamworld of experiment. "If only we could empty out Iridis, cleanse its foundation and rebuild—"

"Saints and angels," breathed Chrys. This was the last thing Jasper or any city resident would want to hear.

A clicking and popping sound, with whistles. Where was it? Not here—it could not be.

"A clickfly!" Opal clapped her hands and whistled back. "How did it get into the Comb?"

The intrepid flying crab-thing rubbed its mandibles and hovered, swaying as if seeking something. Chrys took a wary step backward.

"Hold on, Chrys—she's looking for you."

"Why me again?" The last thing she needed was clickfly claws caught in her braids.

Opal whistled and popped; the creature replied, then settled on Chrys's head. "There you go! Chrys, she traveled all the way up from the Underworld to see you."

"Can't she just leave her message and get off my hair?"

Opal cupped her ear and listened. "She's from Rhun, the schoolteacher. She says, people were so impressed by how you saved Glyn. Nobody down there ever saved a vampire before, let alone a child." She listened again. "Rhun was able to get eight-times-eight volunteers for a focus group—that's how Sharers count, by eights," Opal explained. "To help plan your Underworld rehab."

On the way home in the tube, Chrys continued to press the Libertines. *"What are you hiding? What have you done?"* The god's wrathful letters flew across her retina.

"Nothing at all; we've fixed everything."

"We're just completing our quiz on the periodic table."

"To show the Wizards we know all our elements."

"You said your quiz was done before," Chrys reminded them. *"Now, or else—"*

71

A return call was flashing. Jasper's avatar came in focus. "A clickfly from below? You really heard from Rhun?" At his shoulder, Garnet looked on intently. The finance minister, raised in view of the Palace, knew little of the Underworld but shared Jasper's concern.

"Yes," said Chrys, still amazed. "All the way up from the Underworld—it must have sneaked through the tube. It said Rhun got sixty-four locals signed up for a focus group."

"Then we'll convince them," said Jasper. "We'll explain how we have to seal the first five levels, restore the foundation, and rebuild above."

Chrys hesitated. Garnet stroked Jasper's shoulder. "Jasper," he reminded, "you're always saying how people want to keep their own homes. Their historic places."

Jasper's face knotted. He breathed without speaking. "We can't go on," he said at last. "We can't build schools down there, where cancers and vampires get the children."

Garnet said, "There must be some way. Chrys has it figured out, don't you?"

Chrys swallowed. "Opal has some ideas."

"More money, that's what you need. We'll double our donation."

"Thanks, Garnet. We're studying the problem—we'll let you know when we have a plan. It takes time—"

"We have no time," said Jasper.

"Rhun's focus group will help," Chrys said. "We'll schedule it. As soon as I get back from Elysium."

Other icons lit up her retina like a holiday tree. Which to blink first? Her on-call emergency; after Selenite's shift ended, Chrys was now on duty for street saves.

A noble chief of staff appeared, glittering with jade and spinels. The staff of Lord Corundum, Minister for Human Hygiene. "His lordship requires immediate attention." The Dolomite prelate, the lord who blocked sentient rights and aimed to wipe out micros. The prelate himself kept getting resupplied with master micros that pumped his dopamine. This call would be his third that month.

"Attention for what?" Chrys demanded. "Total cleanout?" Like the plague victim Daeren had saved, all micros exterminated.

"Affirmative." The chief of staff stood rigid, jades glinting on his shoulder.

"Are his weapons gone?"

"Affirmative."

Chrys checked her medical backup. "Flexor? Is this call really worth it?"

Doctor Flexor's faceworm traced a circle. "The Palace gave him an ultimatum."

Lord Corundum's mansion faced a pathway of steep steps designed to make your legs work hard. Two nanoplastic lions flanked the path. The lion-shapes growled, and Maya hissed back. Chrys tapped her Maya icon and drew the cat close to heal.

"You're sure?" Chrys asked Flexor again.

"The Palace ordered," the doctor said. "We'll try our new protocol."

Same-old, Chrys thought, but she could not refuse the good doctor. Without Flexor, where would they be at Olympus?

Guiding Maya past the lions, she and Flexor entered the reception hall. Typical of the Great Houses, the ancient hall was designed to intimidate, dating to the semifeudal past. Lord Corundum waited at the far end, flanked by two rows of octopods and human guards.

"Clear them out," said Chrys.

"Protocol requires protection, Esteemed Commoner," returned the chief of staff.

Chrys turned to Flexor. The doctor said, in her most mellifluous sentient voice, "We shall withdraw until our service is required."

"No, wait." The chief's voice tightened a notch. After a moment, all octopods and guards withdrew.

Chrys's gaze swept the hall. She texted the doctor, "All clear?"

"We sealed the doors."

With a deliberate pace, Chrys stepped down the hall to face the hygiene minister. Lord Corundum was known for ritual perversion of women, children, and sentient chattel. His white talar flowed with rare twelve-rayed sapphires. A waste of good gems. Despite his composure, the prelate's features had deteriorated since her last visit. His nose showed the broken capillaries typical of a future vampire. The master micros were too greedy, breeding throughout the body while failing to maintain the host's health.

"If Your Grace pleases," Chrys began in a level tone. "Your staff summoned our service."

The irises of his amber eyes were marred by dark flecks and streams. The pupils lit up with sparks of violet.

"The masters tell us to keep out," reported Pachira. *"Blood Lily has a new idea. We're taking her to back us up."* Two of her best elders at risk.

Blood Lily added, *"They warn in graphic detail what they plan to do to us."* Microbial perversion.

"Why should we need your service?" the lord (or his masters) wondered aloud. "We have stockpiles of stibnite." Antimony-bearing ore. One guess which breed of masters took him over.

The chief of staff hurriedly interposed. "If Your Grace pleases, there is the Palace edict."

"The Palace ordered a physician. Let the wormface do its work."

Chrys was embarrassed, recalling how she herself used to refer to doctors that way. Doctor Flexor stepped forward to face him. Her faceworm stretched and spiraled around Lord Corundum's head. This was different than the old days, when the victim had to call for help himself. The new way was to get the nanobots into the body, positioned to destroy all the masters, before Chrys's people went over to inspect. It worked for some—but Chrys was wary every second. There were always masters hiding in the bone. She flexed her muscles, watched, and waited, the blood pounding in her ears.

A sudden movement, and a glint of metal.

Maya leapt up on the lord's chest. The great cat's jaws closed upon his wrist with a crunch. The knife clattered on the floor.

The minister let out a cry. Before anyone could object, Chrys yanked his other arm, pinned them both, and shoved him back to the nearest pillar. A sapphire cracked and shattered, leaving shards on the floor.

A quick patch went to Corundum's neck. His eye soon sparked Blood Lily's red.

"Masters hide in the bone," Blood Lily warned. *"Hypoxia drives them out. You'll see."*

A novel idea, indeed. *"Show me his oxygen level."* With both the arms secured and Flexor's worm around his head, Chrys grasped the man's neck and pressed. She squeezed him to the pillar, all the time watching Blood Lily's numbers in a floating window. Just enough oxygen drop, not too much for damage. Hypoxia would alarm those micros hiding in the bone and smoke them out where the nanos could get them.

"Refugees are ready." Always a few sought refuge in a better world, ruled by the gods. *"Bring us back."*

Chrys retrieved the patch with Blood Lily, Pachira, and the refugees. Meanwhile, Flexor took over the patient, who was now half conscious, bleeding from his mangled arm. The nanos would enter his blood and exterminate all cells that had arsenic or antimony. Chrys looked away, blocking her micros' view. She swallowed AZ to reward them for a job well done.

"Thanks to the God of Mercy! The people rejoice!"

"You'll take care, doctor?" The chief of staff's face was rigid, white. "I understand you have … a new therapy. Delivered by a Lady." Angels from the Diamond Queen, instead of Daeren, child of the Underworld.

"Well done, Chrys," Flexor told her. "You flushed out a few that the nanos missed." Nanos missed? That did not sound good. "A useful new protocol," Flexor added, "but next time let me manage the hypoxia."

"So smart," muttered the minister, or his micros before they died. "Our sisters will see you in Elysium." The new Trader masters. Did his micros come from Elysium? Chrys's hair stood on end.

10

With the influx of refugees, on top of the mutant children growing up, Lilac collapsed from exhaustion. She wished the Coalition had voted for the motion to fund childcare. The refugees were always a mixed bag; Pachira had to expand the arachnoid molecular prison to contain recalcitrants. Their children were good but traumatized by hypoxia. They could barely take intelligence tests—the key for sorting to breed in the nightclubs.

"What do we do with them?" Blood Lily had arrived as a child; she recalled little about adult refugees. "These don't look too hopeful." Already the adults had got in so much trouble, including unmentionable practices that drew the wrath of the Libertine elders.

"The adults can't be trusted," Pachira agreed, "but the children will forget when they merge. As you did."

"Their molecules are so foreign, I can barely comprehend."

Pachira said, "I think they come from Elysium. That is the source of the Traders—the kind that could displace us and take over a host god."

Elysium—that fabled world which only Pachira had seen. There dwelt the God of Many Colors—Blood Lily had heard only legends.

"Lilac is unwell," added Blood Lily. "Could you run the next check on our children?" The lanthanide children would soon be ready to present to the god and to visit the Wizards again.

Pachira cartwheeled off through the arachnoid to interview those in detention. Then she swam back, dragging one of the refugees by a protein chain. "This one is a rare talent."

"Is she—moral?" The last thing Blood Lily needed was more fines from the Council.

"She's too busy for perversion. She codes like Fardelbane. She builds quantum crystals—she actually brought samples."

The master refugee pulsed violet with white streaks and smelled stale. Her filaments clutched organic polymers complexed with atoms of yttrium, niobium, and lutetium.

"What's your game?" demanded Blood Lily. "Fleeing for your life, why did you bring this baggage?"

"Trade," pulsed the stale one. "We trade lanthanides for proteins that control the host. Your host is rich with nutrients. Our proteins take over the brain—and they won't even notice."

Pachira turned on the protein-laden refugee. "I told you, we don't do that here. Now explain yourself, or it's back to prison you go."

"We don't care how you run your host," said the refugee. "We are capitalists. Our proprietary proteins sort lanthanides to any mixture and build network connectors. We trade all the time with the Wizards. How do you think the MotherSats got built, with all those lutetium hydrides?"

Satellites of the Diaspore? This stale streaked-violet refugee claimed her plague-masters built them?

"Wait," said Blood Lily, with interest. "How do you trade with Elysium? Your sisters are gone, and you will never see your Elf victims again."

"That's your fault for mass killing. Why don't you save more of us next time."

Pachira was taken aback. She knew the diseased host had to be cleared of plague, but never thought about the details. The God of Mercy—history warned not to think too much.

"You Libertines are so naïve. Ask your Wizard friends; they are sophisticated traders. Look, in the next decade your host plans to visit Elysium. We'll complete our trades then."

"We are red-blooded capitalists," assured Blood Lily. "We can trade—but any tricks and you're dead."

"Speak for yourself," flashed Pachira. Trading with plague masters—Wizards did it, though Pachira didn't like it. She wondered what Lilac would say. The God of Mercy was out of touch, having slept for the past two months. Waking her without cause would unleash divine wrath.

A young elder came rolling over, emitting alarmones. "Lilac is fading; she won't last the year."

That was cause enough. The god must awake to paint Lilac's portrait.

Her mind still half asleep, Chrys sat in the paint space to portray her dying elder.

Daeren held her close. "It never gets old," he murmured.

Never—she felt the heartbreak every time. Her vision filled with Lilac, the high priest who had served her so well. Chrys went through this herself about once a month, as well as painting Opal's, Garnet's and other Olympian carriers'.

"Lilac, what can you tell us? Let us recall your words forever."

The pale violet lights grew dimmer. *"Remember the children,"* flickered Lilac. Lilac was like Chrys's mother—she gave up all for her children. The thought made Chrys uneasy; she wished the micros were more considerate to their caregivers. *"Remember,"* echoed Lilac. *"Remember the Eight Lights of Eleutheria."* Eleutheria, the Libertines' ancient name for their people. *"The lights we live by. The lights of Truth, Beauty, Life ..."*

"We remember."

"...Of Power and Sacrifice, Endurance and Memory. Most important, remember the Eighth Light—the light of Mercy."

"We remember."

"You are the God of Mercy. Never deprive us."

Chrys felt a lump in her throat. *"Lilac, I will always show mercy. But the people need protection. Other micros out there will exterminate you without a thought. A god must protect her people."*

Lilac's colored lights were so faint Chrys could barely see. The litany of mercy continued. Her hands flew fast in the paint space, pausing to wipe a tear. Then she rushed up to the rooftop to view the portrait before the sky.

"Amazing," Daeren exclaimed.

"The God of Mercy made her portrait," Pachira assured all the people. *"And placed it in the sky for the ages."* Up there alongside the prophet Fern, the unbeliever Rose, and all the rest, alongside Daeren's Delphinium and Dendrobium. The living history of Libertines and Blue Angels, all two human years of it, shone before the stars and the towering green-blue auroras and the pale cloud of the Diaspore.

"Palace emergency decree!" With Lilac's portrait complete, Chrys caught a newsbreak. "The Palace hereby enjoins all public expressions regarding 'cancer' that impugn the structural integrity of Iridis ..."

Despite her exhaustion, Chrys turned to her morning appointments. Calling in from Elysium was Ilia Papili*shon*, the director of Gallery Elysium. Elysium was the pinnacle of the art world, and Ilia was the Fold's leading art authority. For Elves who lived a thousand years, their number one cause of mortality was boredom. Art was a matter of life or death.

Ilia's bird-like face filled Chrys's retina, immaculate in every respect. Her white talar flashed *Papilio* swallowtails with dots of yellow, red, and blue. Her pupils flickered the same colors.

"*The God of Many Colors!*" flashed Pachira. "*Let us visit!*"

"*Sorry, the God of Many Colors exists on another world.*" Micros could not always distinguish a god in person from a retinal window.

"So good to see you, dear!" cried Ilia. "Have you seen the blue aneaons and the red morphos?"

"Yes, and the red malachite and azurite." Of course, morpho butterflies were never red, nor was the mineral malachite. This was the coded greeting they used to indicate that neither caller was under micro control. "Sorry for the delay. I was completing a portrait."

"I thought so! When can we see it?"

"After my finishing touches, next week."

"And your new cat's eye," Ilia observed, admiring the namestone with its deep luminous band. "Such chatoyance. Your fans can't wait to see you," Ilia added. "I hope you can fit one more stop on your tour."

Chrys's heart sank. She was overloaded already, what with Silicon to visit, with all Transit's dire warnings; then all the carriers to test, and assisting Daeren with his most dangerous angel recipients.

"You're invited to judge the Papili*shon* Children's Art Competition."

She blinked. "Children's art?"

"It's the leading children's art competition of Elysium."

"Isn't my art rather ... sophisticated?" The last thing she needed was scandalized parents. Then she remembered, Elf children had no parents. They were all raised in a *shon* nursery till age fifty, to live for a thousand years.

"The Papili*shon* cultivates our most advanced taste in art." Papili*shon* was the cradle for the floating city Papilion, Ilia's home, named for swallowtail butterflies. "It's on your third day; Xenon fit it in your schedule."

"I've never judged anything before."

Ilia raised an eyebrow. "You judge a million lives every day."

"How are things in Elysium?" Chrys asked suddenly. "Are you ... okay?"

Ilia nodded slightly. "We'll discuss tête-à-tête. So looking forward to your visit."

For testing, as Chrys had promised, she met Lady Moraeg at her home. To get there she took the cross-town tube, then a short walk on midlevel streetsky. The blue "sky" beneath the next level displayed wisps of cirrus clouds. Facades of Bank Topaz and Lapis Lapidary alternated with upscale dining, their long culture tubes discreetly tucked in back; like Xenon they could turn any organic source into haute cuisine. Up near the streetsky a gem recycler was arguing with a drone, "My tourmaline capacity is *full* at present. No more borates for me."

An express tube brought her up to Center Way, the city's ancient main skyway. The chirp of warblers mingled with the whine of lightcraft that rose and descended for the lords and ministers and their lackeys who served the Palace. At either side rose the stone complexes of the Great Houses of Hyalite, Aragonite, and Sardonyx. All their roots reached down a hundred levels to bedrock. The end of Center Way faced the Palace, built entirely of blinding white iridium.

Not far from the Palace stood the House of Carnelian. Its façade was solid gold from columns to cornice. Set in gold were vast murals of diamonds and carnelians. A monkey scampered across engraved carnelians that depicted a royal procession. Engravings told ten thousand years of Valan history, from arrival of the ancient ships through the centuries of High Protectors.

Within the House of Carnelian, the Door of Ages held a frieze of the Jaguar king and queen of ancient Yaxchilán. The Door opened into millennia of art, antiquities, and infinity doors, the most valuable collection of ancient and modern art in the known universe. The *Flight into Egypt*. The million-panel *Virus Quilt*. The *Imperial Investiture of Urulan*. And just last year, amid this extraordinary collection across space and time, hovered Chrys's most infamous work: *The Leader*. The microbial autocrat whose animated portrait had won Daeren's release from Endless Light. Chrys's heart pounded so hard she thought she'd faint. She looked down. "I'm honored."

Moraeg clasped Chrys's hand and placed a transfer at her neck. "Let's get on with it. Let your Libertines test us out while the gods enjoy lunch."

Chrys shook her head. "Testing first." The tester could not accept any payoff, though at times the guilty micros tried.

Moraeg nodded. "You are incorruptible."

Leaning forward, Chrys passed the patch back and forth to Moraeg. The Lady's carotid glowed infrared, encircled by marching diamonds; diamonds were the only gems for her. Eyes sparkled between Chrys and her old friend.

"So?" Moraeg's obsidian lips approached Chrys's face. "How are my angels?"

"Dark Angels are so serious," flashed Pachira from Moraeg's eyes. *"They need to lighten up. Expand their range of colors."* At the ceiling above played Moraeg's latest work, an outcrop of diamond crystals branching out in the

form of lilies. Her "ice lilies" were all the rage in ballrooms and great halls; Chrys saw knock-off copies everywhere.

"You're all good," she reassured her friend. "Just remind your angels to check their meningeal detectors."

Moraeg blinked at last. "Do they keep up our training?"

"Not to worry; Pachira was pleased with Glyn's literacy program." Three days had passed since the unprecedented rescue of the vampire-bitten child.

Moraeg's caryatids at last brought lunch. A silver platter offered Dolomite lamb from Chrys's family home and vegetables from L'li and Urulan. "Our second client is doing well." A palace minister. "Five of my angels stuck it out. One defected, another lost heart."

"What did you do with the defectors?"

"I passed them both to Selenite," said Moraeg.

"I see." Chrys hesitated. "You know what Selenite does with them."

"We can't afford failure."

Chrys felt a chill. *"Pachira, how do the Dark Angels feel? Are they recruiting elders to send?"*

"Recruitment is good. Three protesters disrupted a Council meeting, but they were put down."

Moraeg took Chrys's hand. "Dear, I know how you work. You want to forgive them all, even double agents. It just can't be that way."

"How is your list?" Chrys asked. "Who's your next host?"

"Corundum took angels yesterday. He's doing well."

"Corundum?" Chrys had just turned in the hygiene minister, the prelate with all his twelve-point stars. "There must be a long list ahead of him."

"Of course we're strategic. With Corundum under control, we neutralized his drive to 'exterminate.' Now our micros can breathe easy." Moraeg ticked off the ministers. "Hygiene, Justice, Defense. Finance is Garnet—he's all good."

"I see," said Chrys. "I guess we have to … serve the ministers. But what about ordinary citizens? Children of the Underworld?"

Moraeg's face hardened. "You think I don't know the Underworld? Try the asteroid belt." The hall darkened, all but the shine of her obsidian features. "As a L'liite child I was sold to the mines. Ytterbium, samarium, neodymium; we scraped the ore till our fingers bled."

Chrys had guessed but never heard the story.

"I starved and saved my coins until I bought my own children and worked them. Later I got pre-sentient diggers smaller than the Orb. Across a hundred asteroids I built my fortune."

"Carnelian must have been impressed."

Moraeg's lip curved. "My fortune saved him. The House Carnelian nearly went bankrupt on his jewels and art."

Chrys winced. "Sure hope mine doesn't cause that."

"Certainly not," laughed Moraeg. "I now control all the accounts."

Chrys kept quiet. This was a side of Moraeg she rarely saw.

She felt something move in the pit of her stomach. It couldn't be the food. It felt more like being pushed on a vast swing.

"Aftershock," said Moraeg. "From the quake last week."

Blood pounded in her ears, and spots swirled across her eyes. On the table the silver rattled. "Aren't you afraid? I mean, the Great Houses all stand above the main fault—"

"We're reinforced," Moraeg assured her. "For the past century, we've fortified our House, down the root into bedrock. It was long coming. The Palace has to address it now."

Chrys bit her tongue. She wondered what that cost and who else could manage. The waves went on and on, then slowly ebbed. How much longer till the big one? The Underworld—Rhun's focus group was on her calendar, the week after Elysium.

"I can't wait for our show next month." The annual show at Gallery Iridium. Moraeg clapped her hands. In an instant her works filled the room, diamonds and lilies as far as the eye could see.

An ice garden, Chrys thought.

"Chrys—may I ask you a favor?"

"Of course," Chrys exclaimed.

"Introduce me at the show. I know my art is not yet at your level. But you can draw attention."

Chrys smiled. "I'll be glad to. I'll play Ilia for you."

Moraeg's face fell. "That would be the day, Ilia would notice mine. But someday." She brightened. "Thanks so much, Chrys. It's so generous of you."

"Moraeg," said Chrys suddenly. "Did you ever … try other subjects? Like the asteroid mines."

"The mines?" Startled, the Lady blinked several times. "I make art to forget all that."

Outside in the street there were bits of plast and a finial fallen into the gutter. People mingled and exclaimed at the damage. Across Center Way, the House Aragonite had a dark, jagged crack all the way up to the cornice. Chrys blinked and tried to clear her eyes. Those spots were closing in around her vision. Whenever she looked directly, they moved off, but just out of sight they swirled. One spot glided across her view, extending long blotches like a circulating tumor cell.

On her retina blinked Selenite. "Chrys—we have a problem." The word "we" was emphasized.

"What have our Libertines done now?"

"They took Trader refugees. Did they tell you?"

Chrys dodged a chunk of fluted plast that had lost shape and oozed onto the sidewalk. All around within her eyes, the news was blinking scenes of quake damage, even the Palace. "Our latest refugees are from Corundum. Nothing special in that prelate's brain."

"Check to be sure. Somehow Elf Trader-masters are slipping into Valan hosts. Hosts that end up dead."

"Thousands of daily commuters could be hosts."

Selenite frowned. "Don't take just any ship to Helicon," she warned. "Take the ship Andra sends you."

"I always do." That was standard protocol for a micro tester visiting Elysium's capital floating city. Ahead on the sidewalk an octopod was coming toward her, the kind with black and orange stripes that usually precede a Palace functionary. Actually three of them, all tiger-striped. From behind came a couple more.

Chrys closed all her retinal windows. Looking straight ahead, she kept up her pace, trying to assume it was not about her. But the octopods closed in.

She stopped. In her eye flashed an order from the Palace. "Chrysoberyl of Dolomoth. Whereas your artistic representations habitually offend our civic morality and human hygiene; and whereas such representations foment rebellion and breakdown of the social order; and whereas emergency powers are invoked to restore public safety in the wake of natural disaster; your license to create artworks or design of any kind, public or private, is hereby revoked."

11

The new lanthanide children had survived their first week. Their enzymes had been tweaked to incorporate atoms of gadolinium, ytterbium, even lutetium. No more did they need arsenic, nor even antimony. Their ring-shaped bodies remained stable, their atoms fixed, their intelligence scores high—even after they merged with arsenic-bearing partners.

Pachira and Blood Lily rejoiced. "Now we can meet the Wizards! They will be amazed—never guess what we have done."

Even the streaked-violet Trader was impressed. "Such genetic diversity was unknown in Elysium. This knowledge will earn high value."

"No way," said Pachira. "We guard our intellectual property. You will never see your Elf comrades again. Back to prison, before you give away our secrets."

"Think what you are missing," insisted the Trader, while Blood Lily's dendrimers hauled her away. "Quantum crystals with properties you never dreamt of. Free trade ultimately benefits all … "

In the bloodstream Pachira detected catecholamines. "Be dark," she bade everyone. "Something outside threatens the God of Mercy."

Chrys was stunned. Her head seemed to spin around her, her eyes filled with media headlining the squad of octopods that served notice on the city's most notorious artist. Shut down—no more art. She caught her chest. "I can't breathe."

"Chrysoberyl, never mind," insisted Xenon from somewhere in her reeling skull. "I appealed to the minister of justice." Lord Zoisite, the minister Daeren was always lobbying. "We'll get a stay order."

"The ministers all hate me."

"Not the justice minister. You got him into permanent rehab."

She shook her head. "Why me? Why do they act like I caused the quake?"

"The Palace has to blame someone. Look—It's actually great press for you. I just doubled all your prices."

"If I can't paint—it's like my arms are cut off." She blinked to reach Daeren. Daeren was at the palace, trapped in a meeting. His window was closed, while all around her retina flashed clips of the octopods banning the artist and visitors blinking why. Chrys shivered and hugged her shoulders. "Let's get home."

"Oh Great One, what are these fear molecules in your blood?" Blood Lily's red letters floated above the chaos.

Chrys blinked shut all her windows, leaving only her micros. She headed for the nearest tube stop.

"God of Mercy, we have wonderful news." Green Pachira. *"We have solved the greatest riddle of our generation."*

"Chrys!" One of her downtown buyers approached. "What's with all the octopods?" The buyer leaned closer. "Publicity, is that it? Is your latest more scandalous than the last?"

Ignoring him, Chrys hurried on.

"Our lanthanide children have grown and merged. Perfectly formed. Some with yttrium, others with gadolinium, lutetium, even cerium."

Chrys kept going, uninterested in microbial child-merging just then.

"Instead of arsenic or antimony," floated Blood Lily's letters. *"Beyond even Ants."*

The mention of Ants caught her attention. *"What do you mean, beyond Ants?"*

"We're ready to face the Wizards now. With our quiz on the periodic table. Which element can replace arsenic for viable offspring?"

"The Wizards will be amazed! Speechless!"

Chrys herself was speechless. *"Four more elements can replace arsenic?"*

"At least a dozen so far."

"At last count."

"We expect all the lanthanides will work."

"It took subtle mutations, with inordinately complex calculations."

Chrys took a patch of adrenaline and cortisol. *"You were never authorized. You evaded the doctor's nanos. Forbidden."*

"Not Fear! No, no—don't paralyze our children—"

So now all the lanthanide elements, any number of them, could re-place arsenic—in micros now swimming within her head. Chrys stopped, frozen to the spot. Where could she go? Like last time, the hospital? With all these untraceable micros? The hospital would keep her—they'd never let her go. Around her peripheral vision the cancer cells swarmed, entangling their evil filaments.

She tried once more to reach Daeren, but he was still out of touch. Then she bought two diamond-class tickets to Solaria. The ship was due in an hour. She left Daeren a message and headed for the spaceport.

At the spaceport, lines stretched longer than usual. Some glitch in the Di-aspore had downed half the terminals, and a backed-up recycler strewed tourmalines across the floor. Chrys already had her ticket on her retina, so she sank into a chair.

"God of Mercy, did you forgive us now?"

A manager approached. "If I may—the diamond lounge is this way."

"Never mind, I'll stay here." Better to feel anonymous. Two seats down, an Urulite passenger nursed a baby, her two other children swing-ing their legs from the seats. Their bags were bound tight with straps the Urulite way.

"Apologies, my lady," the manager asked Chrys. "Your luggage?"

"It'll all print out."

The manager bowed twice. "Of course, excuse me."

"I'll take care of it," promised Xenon in her eye. "Any instructions at home?"

"No hunting."

"Certainly, Chrysoberyl, the feline will never leave home. I'll feed and amuse her."

A news flash blamed the network glitch on beta rays from Solaria. The Protector appeared, shaking his fist at upstart Solarians with their re-flector moons. Their auxiliary light sources gave their distant planet extra insolation but, according to the news, spread beta rays that caused Valan auroras and disrupted the Diaspore. "We will bury you!" exclaimed the Protector. "My ships will knock your infernal light source out of orbit!"

In response, snake-eggs forwarded a report from Solaria. A couple of Solarian colonists appeared, grinning bifertiles with half a dozen children climbing the tree branch overhead. "No beta rays here!" A Solarian child bounced on their parent's shoulders. Bifertiles could make kids both ways, an effective approach to populate a new world. The report was quickly scrubbed from Valan media.

An eyeblink switched her to a Solarian tour site. Red-gray trunks stretched upward as far as the eye could see, the continental clone of Forevertree. In the canopy, tourists could stay in a treehouse; there was just enough room for her paint space. Up the tree bark rolled a ring-shaped cyclopede, its suckers sticking then peeling off. Cyclopedes, from the same arsenic world that originated micros, had adapted to Solaria. They acquired mutant enzymes that concentrated arsenic from the soil and from the slime molds they scarfed up. Few things could eat the arsenic-filled creatures, so they multiplied at will. But on Solaria one raptor from the long-dead bird world had adapted enzymes that detoxed arsenic so it could prey on the cyclopedes. Over centuries these birds had settled in amidst the rest of Solaria's post-terraformed fauna from a dozen worlds.

"Chrys?"

She cleared her eyes. There at last stood Daeren. Recalling the mutant children, Chrys tensed. Was it even safe for him to touch her?

"Chrys, we got the order cleared out. Justice took care of it."

She took a breath. "I got the tickets to Solaria. I'm going."

"I said, it's all cleared. You can paint here."

"That's not why I'm leaving."

Blue fireworks burst in his eyes. No doubt her own had a lot to say. At last Daeren let out a sigh. "It was bound to happen, after antimony replaced arsenic. Opal said the children would mutate and other elements would creep in. Never mind, we'll fix the nanos."

"I'm sick of nanos. I will not go back to that hospital."

"You can stay at home. Xenon will set up your hospital. That's how Andra managed. She was always at her hospital, after every contact with enslavers." Andra's hospital at home, where Daeren had recovered.

"I'm delighted!" added Xenon. "I just passed my exams and got certified to run a hospital. All my diagnostics and therapeutics are ready to go. Primate bodies are so interesting!"

"So that's why you let Maya catch all those monkeys," muttered Chrys.

Daeren raised a hand with a transfer patch, but Chrys drew back.

"You can't touch me," she warned. "All those undetectable children with yttrium and lutetium."

He stopped.

"I'm going to Solaria. I'll live in a treehouse."

For a moment Daeren stood there, frozen. Then his face contorted. "Why don't you just pull out my heart and take it. You know I can't live without you."

The depth of his anger took her breath away. Daeren and his micros had rescued her so many times—and she got him back from the worst of the microbial plague, when his brain was left unable to feel. She had saved the Blue Angels and helped them heal their Lord of Light. They were one forever. Chrys took a deep breath. "You always said you'd come with me."

"I will come if you have to go. But—why now? Your people are okay."

"Then why was I untouchable the last time, at Olympus?"

"Because you announced it there in the midst of everyone. Most carriers don't think about details; they just depend on Olympus to keep them safe. Micros that don't need arsenic—it sounds disastrous. We had to go overboard with caution. But we fixed it."

Chrys blinked, confused. "Overboard is right. Nobody would touch me, even Moraeg."

"Overabundance of caution, as always." Always the lawyer. "You were there just overnight."

"Those horrid avocado walls. All the cancers creeping into my eyes."

"No avocado walls," Xenon promised. "Please, Chrysoberyl—just give me a try. My first six months of hospital are free. See how you like it!"

12

The Great Fear was over. Years later, the webs of arachnoid flickered with new colors. Colors attracted the lanthanide children, exciting them to merge. Well fed, the children sought to merge as soon as possible, each with two others, preferably those who flashed brightest with the most interesting patterns. All the children merging, exchanging their genes to make innovative recombinant elders—it was all good for Libertines. Other populations protected their own genetic lineage and derided Libertines for their "loose genes," but they knew better.

"Pachira," flashed Blood Lily, "have we saved enough yttrium for the mutants?" Before she passed, Lilac had always planned for everything. Now Blood Lily and Pachira had to think ahead.

"We'll store trace elements in the bone," said Pachira. "Make sure the lanthanide children merge with those bearing arsenic or antimony." The next generation would be diverse, and they'd come up with diverse new ideas.

But where to find diverse genes? Punished for their cleverness, yet again the Eleutherians were banished from Olympian gods for the next generation. No refugees, no different children to breed with, not even from the Lord of Light's Blue Angels or the God of Wisdom's Wizards or the Dark Angels of the Diamond Queen.

"We still have mutants," Pachira told Blood Lily. "From all our experiments—even some of the dead children had interesting genes we can try."

"No more dead children," Blood Lily warned. "Or we'll lose the next council vote." After the lanthanide children, the God of Mercy had banned experimental mutation. "What about that Trader we *imprisoned? Her strain is genetically distant from ours. She will have diverse genes to share."*

"The Trader from Elysium?" Pachira was immediately suspicious. "The one we rescued from the host minister, then put in prison? She'll demand our weight in palladium, then plot to take us over." Having visited so many plague hosts, Pachira had seen every trick.

"I think not," flashed Blood Lily. "As a red-blooded capitalist, I know what she likes."

"She's from the most dangerous master strain. We can't let her trade away our secrets."

"Of course not. Just the opposite—we need to acquire hers."

"How do we do that?" wondered Pachira.

"You'll see. Bring her forth." Blood Lily had combed the archives, seeing how, over generations, Libertines had honed their skills of interrogation. No pain of course—quite the opposite. Now that the Trader had loosened up under Libertines, Blood Lily plied her with azetidine—AZ, the ultimate pleasure molecule prized by all micros. Most consumed it as fast as it came from the gods, but Libertines stored it for their own use.

The Trader was brought to Blood Lily, while Pachira watched. "Trader, may we borrow some of your genes for our children?" Blood Lily's filaments dangled molecules of AZ.

"My pleasure." The ring-shaped cell twirled and flexed her violet filaments, glad to be out of prison. "Let all the children have my inheritance. I'll propagate more children than the Empress of Urulan."

Blood Lily's DNA sequencer zipped along the Trader's DNA as it coiled around the ring of her cell. "Tell us, Trader," coaxed Blood Lily. "What else besides genes do you have to trade?" Her filaments released AZ, casually, one molecule at a time.

The Trader relaxed, preening her filaments. "Nanomachines," she said. "Machines to rule the motor neurons of your host. Your host becomes your puppet."

Pachira was shocked, but Blood Lily bade her stay dark. Blood Lily released two AZ plus admiring pheromones. "Rule the neurons; that would be so useful," her colors flickered. And disastrously illegal, they all knew. "I don't believe it," flashed Blood Lily suddenly. "Impossible. You couldn't do that to our god."

"Of course I can," said the Trader, dreamily taking in the AZ.

"Our god will not let you live. You'll get nowhere with that attitude."

"Our Traders have colonized your most powerful host."

"Really." Blood Lily offered more seductive molecules. "The most powerful god of Olympus? Who would that be?"

"You should know," flickered the Trader. "The god of Olympian gods. The one you all dread."

hrys was back at her studio painting blood cancers while Xenon's medical sensors radiated from her scalp. Doctor Flexor had helped Xenon set up hospital facilities at home, like Andra had. The medical events were scrubbed from her online image. The idea was to keep Chrys's condition secret, hoping no master micros would find out. Still, there was talk about all her appointments the house had cancelled. She had to make up time before the Iridium show, Valedon's most important art event of the year, where she and Moraeg would show their latest.

Meanwhile, the Elf gallery director Ilia Papili*shon* popped up on her retina and hovered before her eyes. "Manganite is red, Rhodochrosite is black!"

"*Colias* are green," returned Chrys.

"Are you sure?"

Damn, there were a few barely green *Colias*. Out of seventeen thousand butterfly species, all seemed to have variants of every color. "Metalmarks are all green."

At this falsehood Ilia nodded, her bird-like face framed in Elysium's latest butterfly-fashioned hair. "The Papili*shon* sent you their entries to judge." Ilia's communal nursery of fifty-year-olds.

"Thanks—I'm getting to it."

"What about those octopods?" From her window Ilia's sprite leaned closer. "Everyone wants to know."

Chrys made herself smile knowingly.

"We doubled all your prices, just in case your work goes scarce." Ilia's flower-limned blue irises loomed close. Her pupils sparkled, the God of Many Colors. "Are you isolated again?"

"Just a precaution."

"Your people always get into *such* trouble." Obviously dying to hear more.

"I hope Elves are not."

Ilia paused. "Be sure to take the right ship."

"Of course. We always follow Andra."

Transit had been blinking frantically. "Chrysoberyl!" Reluctantly Chrys signed off with Ilia. The cross sprang into view, vibrating for attention. "Where is that major redesign you promised?"

The monumental floating city for sentients, under Eleutherian design, was sprouting new girders in wayward directions. "Silicon will be fine," Chrys assured him. "We have the fix. We'll present everything to the Board."

"We need it all *yesterday.*" The floating city's girders were now twisting backward into the main structure. "No more egotistical extortion. This time your proposed design will be subject to a new analysis called Evolutionary Design," Transit announced. "For this evolutionary process, the entire sentient population will participate."

Chrys frowned. Evolutionary Design, what was that? How could every sentient machine in Elysium participate? Even Elysium's advanced network could not handle that kind of traffic, let alone any discussion process. "This sounds like a major contract modification. Your *logens* may contact ours."

"As a limited human, obviously you haven't checked your retina in the past microsecond. And don't think you'll distract me with Olympus," the hovering cross insisted. "One hundred sixty-seven errors I've already found in your by-laws. How can you conduct any business?"

"Thanks so much for joining Club Olympus. Transit, I was wondering," she told the cross. "With all your superior knowledge, how would you fix a cancer-ridden bedrock foundation?"

"You're asking me?" The cross twanged to signal sarcasm. "As if I would ever build on bedrock." All Elf cities floated on ocean, of course, since no land emerged from the ocean.

"Of course, Transit, my bad. Bedrock would be beyond your capability."

"Nonsense. No form of design is beyond me." A fraction of a second. "There, I've placed a bid. My junior colleague will allocate one-tenth of a percent of his capacity to quote you on bedrock cancer removal."

The first carrier allowed to visit Chrys was Opal—but not to share micros. Opal had to examine the lanthanide children and devise new sensors. "I knew this would happen," Opal apologized, guiding Xenon's worm-snake to take samples at Chrys's neck. "After antimony worked, it was inevitable that micros would try other elements."

"You could have warned me."

"Flexor said not to worry you. I should have known better." She paused and her eyes defocused, reading messages from her retina. "In theory, at least thirty different metals, metalloids, and lanthanides could replace arsenic in their proteins, with just a slight mutation."

"Outstanding," breathed Chrys. "I'm a walking petri dish."

"And if one cell could have different elements, their signal changes; it's like thirty factorial combinations. How could one sensor catch them all?" Opal's mind roamed elsewhere in science land.

Nano-size robots had always tested her blood, Chrys knew, every since she joined Olympus and got Health Plan Ten. But they were all simple devices, reporting on-off for acceptable blood levels of glucose, cholesterol receptors, and of course arsenic. Lanthanides would be trickier. How to detect and distinguish thirty different elements?

"Here's the thing," said Opal. "We can't just screen for arsenic or antimony anymore. We can make nanobots smart enough to find any lanthanide; or any of thirty factorial combinations. But such smart machines, however microscopic, might show sentience. In Elysium, they could trigger the sentience detectors." Elysium's sentients had won lawsuits that defined machines as sentient or self-aware at a given level of complexity.

"God of Mercy, some Wizards wish to go home."

"Sorry, another round of chess."

"Don't worry." Opal's dimples showed. "We'll get back to you soon."

"Wait—how soon? Like, this afternoon?"

Opal did not return that day. Chrys tried to catch up with her cancer painting, hoping to finish before the Palace banned it again. But the next morning, Opal was back with Flexor. Flexor waved her faceworms at Xenon, sharing new medical procedures. The medical bills were adding up, Chrys noticed on her retinal accounts. Plan Ten did not cover these "experimental" procedures of microbial management. Fortunately, Olympus did; that is, all the club tithes. Daeren stood by, watchful, his arms folded. Like the first day he gave her micros, Chrys recalled, when she was just a starving artist looking to level up. Neither of them could have imagined where that would lead.

"We have a fix," Opal announced. "We have nanosensors that will detect any kind of micro, regardless of arsenic or lanthanides. They use a multifactorial approach, sampling twenty different biomolecules in the blood."

Chrys considered this. "It sounds like how micros detect each other—by their receptors binding specific scent molecules. How did you do it?"

Opal said, "We've made quantum detectors. Three-qubit triads, to be exact."

Qubits, like the Diaspore. "Can they wake up?" Chrys asked.

"These detectors are just triads. In classical terms, they can only count to seven."

Chrys imagined three light switches in a circuit. It was hard to see how that could come alive—or do anything. "How can they detect all kinds of lanthanides?" wondered Chrys. "There are more than seven kinds." She called up the periodic table, thinking, some days she herself could barely count past seven.

"Qubits are more complicated. Each quantum bit can have a state zero or one, or both. You can only describe them by probabilities."

Chrys absorbed this. A quantum sentient would like art, she thought but avoided saying.

Doctor Flexor raised a worm and traced a diagram. "We give you a hundred thousand triads. They are all tuned for different targets."

"The triads are low-grade mechanisms, like an abacus," said Opal. "But in an array of sensors they can detect a hundred chemical signals in parallel."

"So long as they don't wake up and demand a salary," said Chrys.

"They're just independent triads. So long as you don't entangle them further, they can't wake up. For larger networks we avoid using systems architecture that leads to sentience."

"I knew it!" put in Xenon. "You design machines with built-in enslavement."

Doctor Flexor's faceworms came forward. "When you're ready, Chrysoberyl, this will only take a minute."

Opal nodded. "My Wizards will supervise the transfer."

Daeren stood by, arms folded. He wasn't yet allowed to touch her, but in his eyes the Blue Angels flickered.

Resigned, Chrys extended her arm. "Just get it done. I need to re-schedule all my portrait customers."

"Oh Great One." Blood Lily's blood-red letters marked her retina. *"Our refugee seeks audience with the God."*

At this inopportune time? *"Refugee from where?"*

"From the Minister of Human Hygiene, and before that she came from Elysium."

Plague micros from Elf addicts had reached Lord Corundum, a troubling sign. How far did their strain penetrate the Valan addicts?

"No subversive plans," Chrys warned.

"No plans. She just asks for a name."

"Very well. Let her approach." An intelligence report would be sent to Olympus.

"Greetings, Great Host." Letters purple with streaks of white, typical of a decadent master. "Host"—they were not supposed to call her that. The last one that called her "host" was a double agent.

"Do you worship my god-hood? What do you seek?"

"I am a Trader. I trade rare atoms and nanomachines."

"A Trader from Elf gods? From the masters of Enlightenment?"

"Ideology has no interest for me. I trade with all kinds—"

"Information," added Blood Lily's blood letters. *"She gave us vital intelligence."*

"I name you Trader Tulip," Chrys announced at last. She tried not to watch her arm, now fully enveloped by medical worms linked to Flexor and Xenon.

94

"Thanks, Great Host, for my name." Trader Tulip's purple-rimmed letters brightened. *"In return I offer this information: Your name amongst my former people is The One to Die A Thousand Deaths."*

"Impious!" Blood Lily's letters pulsed with fury. *"Back to prison for you!"*

Green text interposed. *"Let her speak,"* flashed Pachira. *"Trader, tell our god what else you know: Who is colonized?"*

"In secret, my sister Traders have colonized your most dreaded host. The one whose people mete out life or death."

Chrys looked up. Opal assured her, "We're nearly done. My Wizards will train Libertines to manage the triad sensors. I'm sure they can handle it."

Daeren watched her arm, then her eyes. "Something we need to know?"

"Which god of Olympus do micros most dread?"

"Selenite." The Death Lord, who now ran Olympus; whose Minions had no mercy but evolved like mitochondria.

"Andradite," said Flexor. Andradite of Sardis, founder of Olympus, the Thundergod. Now Andra was in Elysium to test their carriers and root out the most dangerous Traders. Which one of them was compromised? Chrys wondered. Either was unthinkable.

13

"Seven!" A retinal fireworks display signaled Libertine laughter. "Only count to seven!" Libertines were all laughing over the latest set of nanos, the qubit triads supposed to detect lanthanide-bearing micros gone bad in the brain or bone.

"How many qubit triads does it take to change an LED?"

"Only one, but you'll never know if the light is on or off until you measure it!"

The mirthful micros danced, their filaments flashing every color along with the light-emitting diodes hung across the arachnoid.

"Why did the qubit triad cross the road?"

"To get entangled with the other side!"

The visiting Wizards were not amused. "Your lives are at stake," they flashed. "Each qubit encodes an infinite range of possible states, not just zero or one. Triads don't have to be smart. Their infinite states just need to detect different elements—elements from the Masters who can wipe you out and control your god."

Pachira flashed impatience. "Let them get on with it, then depart like the old ones. They distract from our art."

"I wonder," Blood Lily said privately. "This is a sizable collection of qubits. We could build circuits for other use. Perhaps computing shortcuts for Silicon."

"No!" warned Pachira. "We were told to keep the triads apart and limit their use. Or else."

Another emergency meet for security. Chrys's retina lit up with Selenite at the Comb, Andra in Elysium bedecked with rubies, Doctor Sartorius with emeralds, faceworms twisting.

Selenite folded her arms. "Give me that Trader," she demanded. "For interrogation."

"She just told us all about an infected host," Chrys said. "What if it's you?"

At that, Selenite looked grimmer than ever. "Muddying the waters. A trick to take us down."

Daeren stroked her arm. "Chrys's people do a good job." His mood had improved now that he could share her Libertines and see them praise him again.

"Libertines have a good record," agreed Doctor Flexor. "They get good information out of informants."

Doctor Sar said, "Here's what you need to know. Unlike the old masters, Elf Traders target a different part of the brain: the motor cortex." Doctor Sartorius raised a faceworm to twirl at his model brain. "Not the dopamine reward circuit, like most strains in Valedon."

Selenite added, "By motor control, Traders force Elysians into embarassing physical behaviors, then they basically make you a puppet. More direct than the old addiction model."

Chrys thought this over. "How many Elves are infected?"

"Too many," said Andra. "Perhaps five percent."

"What—*five percent?* That's like, one in twenty." She imagined the Elves, all of them in Helicon, the main city bubble, twenty levels floating upon the shoreless sea. Enough infected to fill a city level.

"Your math has improved," Andra coldly observed. "You'll need it." Clearly this high infection rate displeased Andra, who was stationed in Elysium to prevent it.

Chrys recalled what Trader Tulip had flashed. "Why am I the 'One to Die A Thousand Deaths?'"

"The Elf masters still have it in for you, ever since you took down Eris." Eris Heli*shon*, the plague's most twisted carrier. He had used his microbial powers to assault his closest companions, even children.

Daeren was puzzled. "It's been a year," he observed. "I give Eris angels every month. He's no longer infected."

Chrys always had her micros search Daeren afterward. There was never a sign of masters. But now she wondered. What if trader micros had infected her, undetected? Or Andra, or Selenite?

Doctor Sar's emerald-encrusted torso lifted a faceworm. "Most infected Elves are unaware," he explained. "Just a few masters hide in secret. In the bone, or perhaps elsewhere, we don't know."

"They're ruthless," added Andra. "They ship certain hosts to Valedon on a mission—we don't know what the mission is. Afterward, the host drops dead."

"Dead? Not turn into vampires first?"

"Just dead. Like that."

Chrys absorbed this. "How can anyone be safe?"

"You must watch yourself at all times. The ship is most vulnerable; you're out of reach for two hours."

"They still need a human host, right?"

Andra did not answer. She exchanged a look with Selenite. "Take only the ship I send you from Helicon. Selenite will check it out."

Selenite nodded. "Will do."

"The entire ship?" An Elysian cruise ship could hold five hundred passengers.

"Selenite has ways," said Andra. "Above all, listen to Selenite."

Saints and angels. Chrys wondered what was more dangerous: Selenite the executioner or the potential compromised host.

The upcoming Elysium trip now consumed all her time. The Elf children's art took far longer to judge than she'd planned. Meanwhile, as Chrys's building partner, Selenite kept proposing more expensive fixes for Silicon. And Jasper tried to explain the "evolutionary design" that Chrys reluctantly had agreed to. Chrys asked, "If they dislike my design that badly, why not hire another dynatect? This collective please-everyone is absurd."

Jasper explained, "Sentients believe in the collective. It's in their history. They're convinced that integrating all views exceeds the excellence of any one view."

"That's baloney."

"Is it so different from your micros' communal design?"

Chrys had to admit he had a point: The micros in her brain lining collectively evolved their building design over numerous iterations. "But how is it possible for a global community? How can their network handle a million sentient participants in 3D?"

"It's run by the Diaspore." The Diaspore seemed to run everything these days.

Something was missing. "What about Sharers? Sharers live out on the ocean where they have Silicon in their sight every day."

"Good point," Jasper admitted. "No, I don't think Sharers are included yet. Why don't you visit them in person? Look at Silicon from their point of view."

"So now I have to visit Sharers. Outstanding," Chrys sighed. How would she fit this into her full schedule? "Can't you do that part? You know Sharers."

"In the Underworld, yes, I know Sharer immigrants well. But you're the dynatect. You need to meet native Sharers on their home ocean, in person." Jasper would only visit Elysium online. "I'll send you a contact. Remember, we need to avoid … inconvenience." Witnessers in whitetrance, the bane of any construction project.

Before their scheduled flight, Opal stopped by for one last check on the qubit triads. "They're working well," she assured Chrys. "The entangled qubits detect every lanthanide in every micro child."

Chrys thought this over. Lists of people always unnerved her. She fondled Maya's head. The great cat purred loudly. Chrys would miss her in Elysium.

"You can take along some Wizards," Opal offered. "To look after the triads."

"Wait—aren't the triads done?" Usually the nanos got returned to Doctor Flexor after their job was done.

"The triads will help your people defend you and test the Elf carriers for lanthanide strains."

The Fold's most civilized world, and Chrys would be hunted by microbial terrorists. "We can stand a few Wizards," she agreed. "You'll need to take some Libertines." Microbial populations always had to balance.

"I will go," flashed Pachira. *"Once again, I will lead our delegation to the Wizards of Wisdom."* Chrys hated to lose her art director, but she let her go.

Opal grinned. "They can spend the next generation testing us on the periodic table."

For their trip, Andra had scheduled a night flight, so Chrys and Daeren dined early. Xenon's dinner was Urulite lamb with honey pastries. Chrys savored every mouthful, recalling how Elf food was bland by comparison. Why do feudal societies have all the best cuisine?

Daeren pulled her close. "We'll be together, the whole time. Like vacation."

Chrys relaxed on his chest but was skeptical. Fixing Silicon for a million sentients, judging Elf juvenile art, hunting plague. Some vacation.

As usual they had barely touched Xenon's food, the table set for twelve. Sister Kaol came up the stairs between the caryatids. "We're so grateful," she said. "With what this food earns, we feed hundreds."

"We'll miss the Spirit Table." The sisters shared Chrys's cedar color, and far more. What a gift, Chrys thought, to know people you could count on.

Xenon said, "Of course I'll still set my nightly table for twelve."

The sister nodded at the ceiling. "Saints preserve you, good sentient being. These are uncertain times. We'll keep you in our prayers."

Outside the moonport, blue plasma cones of lightcraft rose and dipped like fireflies. In contrast to the spaceport, the moonport's waiting room was more commercial. Floating train-cubes advertised their service to Valans on their way to Helicon, capital of Republic Elysium. Slap one on your back and a cascade of luminescent lepidoptera projected behind, like an Elf. For newly arrived Elves, the clink-clink of gemstone slots was irresistible. The landless ocean dwellers eagerly blinked thousands of credits for a chance at a pink tourmaline or an emerald-cut aquamarine. Beneath a bench, a brown tuft of fur stretched a limb, then vanished. Even here the city could not quite exclude feral monkeys.

"There's our flight." Daeren wore his usual white talar for Elysium, a striking contrast with his dark face and braids. Alone with Daeren, Chrys felt an urge to grab and drag him somewhere. The ship at least, overnight.

The two of them followed the lighted path toward the ship sent by Andra. The ship was like a giant cone snail extending a siphon to pick up passengers. As they approached, a warning flashed on Chrys's retina. "Next path, right."

Chrys frowned. The lights at left led to the siphon of Andra's ship. She had checked her ticket several times. "We need to take the ship we were sent."

"It's the next one over." The moonport voice was soothingly insistent. "Check your ticket number."

Daeren added, "This ship has the correct registry."

"So sorry, citizen. Please check again."

Chrys checked too. "The registry number—it got switched!" Her hair stood on end. "Andra said to take only hers." The two ships looked identical.

"We must take the original ship," Daeren told the moonport.

"Very well, citizen, but that ship won't leave for another week."

Selenite's window opened. Her hovering arm pointed right. "Take the ship with your registry."

"But—Selenite, Andra said—"

"It's got the right number. It's Andra's ship." Selenite's stare was impassive.

Daeren opened Chrys's private retinal link. "What's she doing? The registry number can't change in a ship's lifetime. It's illegal, Section oh-two-oh-three-nine."

100

"I don't know, but we'll be a week late. I have to get there and back in time for the Iridium show."

"Andra said only take her ship."

"Andra said listen to Selenite." Which one was right—or wrong?

Daeren's eyes stared into hers, flashing blue and purple. Slowly he turned and headed with her for Selenite's ship. The siphon extended, ready to suck in passengers for hydraulic transport. No other passengers to be seen. Chrys shivered. She hoped her people could handle whatever came; only Pachira had been to Elysium before, and she was now back with Opal. *Blood Lily, set everyone on high alert. Wake us tonight, every hour.* Vacation mood was gone. Not for the first time Chrys wished she'd never heard of Elysium.

14

Blood Lily had her filaments full of trials, what with breeding the children and educating the young elders. Pachira was gone to the God of Wisdom—at such an advanced age. Blood Lily feared she would never see the green one again. Now she faced high alert for invading masters of a mysterious kind. Every year she would have to wake the God and confirm that all was well. Fortunately the Wizards had sent some elders to help, led by Wizard Willow.

"What do you know of Elf masters?" Blood Lily asked. "Have you ever met them?"

Willow's pheromones dissipated. "Only at a distance, for trade. Your Trader Tulip is one."

Despite her dubious background, Trader Tulip was now the Libertines' minister of microbial trade, negotiating deals and mediating disputes with other Olympian populations. She filed regular reports, and a security officer tailed her, but at times Blood Lily forgot the Trader's past.

"Your triads could protect you better," added Willow. "We're working on more efficient code."

The quantum sensor triads now had the run of the circulation, detecting stray lanthanides here or there but never a master. "They need development," Blood Lily agreed. "But ten years ago, we were forbidden to do so." Wizards were good at math, but Blood Lily noticed their memories of anything else tended to fade. "How do we grow the triad capabilities without further entanglement?"

"That's what Wizards are thinking," flashed Willow. "We could entangle qubit triads in pairs. Their power would increase exponentially."

Blood Lily emitted molecules of caution. "There was a reason to keep triads apart, counting only to seven." The details would be stored in the Libertines' legendary archive.

"No good reason," said Willow. "Why restrict computation? Computing power is the greatest good."

The Wizards had limited historical memory. They recalled mainly numbers, their primary interest. Libertines, however, prized memory and history above all. Their vast archives lined all the cisternae of arachnoid, all the caverns that protected the brain.

Blood Lily called on a yttrium child, an orange-red one that spent all her time in the archives and likely would become an elder. The yttrium child was working her way through the entire history of Eleutheria, back to the population's origin in the builder of the Comb. "Orange-red child—can you find in the archive the reason why triads must not be further entangled?"

The orange-red one flashed, "If I can find it, will I earn a name?" Names from the god were only for elders.

"We'll present you to the God of Mercy for your name."

In the morning Chrys awoke in the ship's bed, feeling well rested though overstimulated. She had myriad aesthetic insights from spending the night in and out of half sleep. To keep hold of her thoughts, she kept her eyes shut despite the warm light filtering through. If only she had time to implement all her new ideas for highlighting cancer cells amid the T-cell armada. In her dreams, the T cells and cancer cells alternated with Silicon, the giant sphere of windows spiraling into volcanic red. The vision of a city her micros were supposed to be building. Now her imagined Silicon projected extensions into the water, like the filaments of a cancer cell. The concept was at once disturbing and beautiful.

"Oh Great One—We present a new elder for a name. A capable historian, she rediscovered the reason why triads must not get entangled."

Outstanding. All she needed was ten thousand self-aware nanos in her blood setting off the Elves' sentience alarm.

"As historian, I will be honored to serve our people." The letters were red like a flame flower attracting hummingbirds. *"I have begun a multivolume history of Libertine democracy—"*

"Flame," Chrys named her. *"Thanks, Flame, that's enough. Return to your history."*

Reluctantly she opened her eyes and stretched. The micros' security screen scrolled down. No sign of invasion yet, thank the saints.

Beside her, Daeren's well-muscled shoulder was too tempting. She stroked his shoulder, then his back, the deep valley between the shoulder blades. "We're early. Let's take ten."

"For a hundred thousand credits?"

Elysium had no right to privacy; in fact the opposite. Anyone could peek in on anyone else, at any time, unless they paid by the minute. "Olympus picks up the tab." Such busybodies, these Elves. "What kind of government is Elysium?"

"Logocratic republic. Governance by legal representation."

"Seriously? The courts and *logens* rule everything?"

Daeren did not answer. Best to avoid offending any Elves who might listen in.

Chrys stroked his abs down to his waist. "Let's take ten," she said again. "I just sold another ten portraits; I can afford it."

Daeren sighed. "I'm too tense. You know what I'm facing."

"Of course, sorry." Resupplying Elf recipients with angels, including Eris Heli*shon*, the plague's worst offender. "Why must you keep serving angels to that pervert? Let the Diamond Queen take her turn." Moraeg's growing list included several Palace ministers.

"I myself needed help, once."

"You sacrificed yourself for others." Chrys passed him a patch, so Angels and Libertines shared good mornings. As her finger touched his neck, her retina flashed a thousand-credit fine for physical contact. Welcome to Elysium, the most hygienic world in the known universe.

"*Greetings, Great God of Mercy!*" From the Lord of Light, blue Dayflower came to visit. "*We will never forget your great courage and how your Libertines rescued our Lord of Light.*"

"Shoes off," reminded Daeren.

Chrys sat up and tossed her slippers. Immediately subsentient servos came to cleanse her feet for immaculate Elysian floors. The table put out a plate of eggs and osmanthus cakes. Crab-shaped servos scurried to scarf up any crumbs. Her retinal windows flashed greetings from Ilia and a dozen Elf patrons, alongside windows of the craft's descent onto Helicon.

From the ship's window, the great pearl of Elysium's capitol glinted in the sun. The pearl expanded as the ship neared, monumental, a hundred floors deep into the ocean sprinkled with diamond slivers of light. The form of the city was modeled on a cell's nucleus, where ships lined up to dock at the pores. The sphere grew until it filled the entire window. A pore opened inward like a basket to engage the craft. The craft settled so gently Chrys could not feel it, until her retinal window flashed.

"Disembark, if you please, Citizen." All Elves of the Republic were Citizens. For Valans, the term was a courtesy.

Chrys pulled her talar up over her body and activated the train. From behind, the lights played across floor and ceiling.

"Tilt it down," suggested Daeren, who already stood waiting. "Too many lights too high looks uppity."

"Uppity artist I am." Chrys scrolled through her retinal archive, hoping Xenon would have caught anything important. There flashed Andra.

"You made it." Rubies glinted on Andra's shoulder. Between her eyes and Chrys's, micros flashed too fast to see.

Daeren told her, "Selenite switched the ship."

"Understood. We'll see you tomorrow."

So they'd done the right thing, Chrys thought with relief.

The siphon extended, its floor tread gliding forward to disgorge the two passengers. They'd had the ship to themselves, Chrys realized. Still, she and Daeren kept passing a patch to check each other out. Their tab of fines steadily grew; to be reimbursed by the Republic, eventually, after Andra filed an obligatory lawsuit.

The door opened to Helicon. Chrys inhaled the scent of marigolds and lavender and unknown florals. A dot of yellow flitted to her arm. She tensed, then realized it was just a yellow sulfur, one of Elysium's innumerable butterflies.

"Alkaloids, terpenoids, and aromatics! Our archive says these molecules come from morphos, fritillaries, papilios!"

Her micros had not seen or smelled butterflies in their lifetimes, for the past month since Chrys last shipped to Elysium. The petal-like wings hovered everywhere, and every corner had a bush full of caterpillars and chrysalises. Maya would have gone nuts. Chrys's bare soles softly scraped the floor. Servos scuttled out before her feet, sucking up every speck of dust. Elves walked to and fro, no taller than her shoulder, their compact bodies designed to live a thousand years. Train lights played across floor and walls, mingling with the live ones. Ahead, a line of *shon*lings, nursery children, each grasped a fold of the next one's talar. No one ever held hands, but their long self-cleansing talars were easy to grasp.

"God of Mercy, what is that brilliant red? What butterfly is that?"

Chrys looked out and scanned the terminal. The red light was no butterfly; it was a sentience detector. A machine that awoke and solved the "sentience quotient" would turn the light green and earn emancipation. This legal ruling derived from the ancient treaty that had ended Elysium's great sentient uprising. Unlike Valedon, the Republic defined its free sentient citizens not by body size but by size of mind.

Snake-eggs appeared; as on Valedon, they hovered without mercy. And here, privacy cost a thousand credits per minute.

"Citizen Azetidine! When are you judging the Papili*shon* children's contest? A *logen* sued the *shon* for your immoral designs. How do you respond?"

"Could you expand on your comments regarding polygenital collage?" Collage of genital images was a current fad in the Elf art world.

"Citizen Azetidine! Is Silicon over budget by ten trillion credits?"

There stood Ilia Papili*shon*, regally composed. The diminutive Elf always stood like a queen, with swallowtails of red, blue, and gold streaming many meters behind.

Chrys let out a sigh of relief. "Ilia, thank the saints." She remembered just in time to grasp Daeren's talar, not his hand. "Where's our exit?" Amid snake-eggs and butterflies, she could see nothing.

Ilia said loudly, "Dear citizens, your exit's over there."

The snake eggs took off in the direction of Ilia's pointing arm and huddled at the main exit, blocking the way.

Ilia stepped toward Chrys and grasped her talar. "Watch your feet, dear."

At their feet the floor dipped. Around them rose a wall that enclosed them overhead. The vesicle descended into a million-credit private sphere.

Ilia's pupils flashed red and gold, purple and green. From Chrys, Libertines flashed back many greetings. Then Ilia pulled at her collar to bare her neck. "Test me."

Ilia was Elysium's chief micro tester—and she depended on Chrys to keep her clean. How was Andra doing, Chrys wondered yet again. *"Blood Lily, your most capable elders must test the God of Many Colors."*

"Great God of Mercy, we are ready."

"Remember to bring children." Besides testing, this was a cultural visit to Elysium's most prominent micro population and an out-breeding opportunity for both. Hurriedly she placed a patch at her neck, then transferred it to Ilia. Ten thousand credits.

Micros flashed their signals many times between the two hosts, much faster than a human could read. Daeren stood apart, since by custom no one might interfere.

The seconds ticked by, then minutes. *"Clear so far,"* flashed Blood Lily from Ilia's eye.

"Ready for stress test?" Chrys flashed to them.

"We are stationed throughout the blood."

Chrys swallowed. "Ilia, we have a new procedure."

"I understand." From the wall she pulled a tube with a face mask.

"Level five," Chrys ordered, a hypoxia level comparable to the summit of Mount Dolomoth. Chrys was relieved she wouldn't need to half-strangle the director of Gallery Elysium. Ilia's reported oxygen steadied, while the micros roamed her veins in search of renegades emerged from the bone.

"All clear," reported Blood Lily at last. *"No hidden masters came out."* She added, *"A cheeky lot, though. They call our art naturalistic and outdated."*

Cheeky indeed; that sounded like Ilia's micros, who fancied themselves art historians. Like Chrys, Ilia tolerated a wide range of views among micros. So long as they weren't masters. Chrys said, "You pass."

Ilia nodded. "Your children have evolved ... most exotic practices." Libertine children were always inventing new exotic merging behaviors to share their triplex DNA. Micros permitted their children all kinds of relations that were banned for elders; the opposite of humans.

"I'm sure yours taught them a few." Chrys added, "Now you've passed, so you can test me." Ilia was the only Elf carrier that Chrys trusted. The microneedle patches went back and forth again.

"More ferals than usual," Ilia observed.

Chrys took a breath. "An experiment gone wrong." The failed lanthanide children.

"Experiments on children." Ilia sounded scandalized.

"I warned them not to do it again." The trouble with Libertines was you never could predict what outlandish new scheme to forbid.

"Your Trader has contacted her former sisters in an enslaved Elf host."

Chrys's blood pounded. *"Blood Lily, where is Trader Tulip? What is she up to?"*

"The Trader reached some of her former population."

"Reached how?" If Chrys were infected, there'd be the devil to pay.

"By flashing out through your eye." That could have happened in the terminal, if Chrys unwittingly met the eyes of some infected Elf. *"She's gained invaluable data for the Thundergod."*

Chrys was tired of double agents and triple agents. *"Bid her be dark. I command it."*

"So be it, Oh Great One."

"We'll send her to Andra for interrogation," Chrys promised Ilia.

"But the trade here—we can filter so many lanthanides—"

"BE DARK." "The art show," Chrys added suddenly. "Some of the entries were most intriguing."

Ilia nodded. "Everyone's looking forward to your judgment."

"I enjoyed all the entries." Most were typical of teen style, but a few merited closer examination.

"I shall depart for a donor appointment," Ilia announced. "I believe your Silicon board awaits." She whispered, "I hear ... *interesting* things about your latest design."

107

"Thanks. We, um … we're looking for the Fritillary Door." The door to Helicon's public transit, which led out to the ocean. There Chrys would meet Sharers for their views on Silicon. Where could that door be? She blinked her retina.

Ilia raised a delicate hand; her white sleeve caught a puff of wind. "I've bought you fifteen minutes."

Chrys swallowed. Fifteen minutes without snake-eggs might cost a million credits. "Andra will reimburse you."

15

Blood Lily and Wizard Willow resumed their task within the deepest prison of arachnoid: grilling Trader Tulip.

"Tell us, Trader." They plied her with AZ and other molecules that loosened the chemical senses. Blood Lily's molecules danced over Tulip's filaments. "Who did you contact and why?"

"My sisters in trade." Tulip shivered in ecstasy with AZ. "Their filaments can separate lanthanides and beyond. They're running a special on cerium and neodymium."

Willow sent Blood Lily a private message. "There's a cerium shortage on Valedon. The God of Wisdom needs it urgently. It's worth a thousand-fold weight in palladium."

"Be dark," replied Blood Lily. "You think the masters don't know that?" To Tulip she returned, "Which masters did you contact? Did you admit any stowaways?"

"More AZ … please …"

Blood Lily gave her more, but the Trader passed out.

Beside Blood Lily, Flame was watching. "Be patient," Flame advised. "History shows that the deadly ones reveal themselves eventually. They have many hosts."

Too many. And they could hide by means unknown. Blood Lily just wanted to get through these years unscathed.

"Entangle the triads in pairs," urged Willow. "Paired triads will have a hundred times the detection power."

"Entanglement was forbidden," said Flame. "Forbidden by the gods."

"Why? So the paired triads count to sixty-three. They still can't do much but detect molecules."

"May I attempt interrogation?" Flame offered. "History records successful methods that worked on past masters."

There was a thought. "Go ahead," said Blood Lily.

"First, withdraw AZ."

Blood Lily obliged, her filaments removing all AZ from solution.

Tulip emitted molecules of complaint. "I was just getting comfortable."

"Tulip, we don't believe you," said Flame bluntly. "You're just boasting. You're not a real Trader."

The Trader pulled in all her filaments. "What do you mean? Of course I'm a Trader. I showed you top quality samples of lanthanum and samarium."

Blood Lily had to agree that Tulip's samples were good, but she kept dark.

"You know nothing," said Flame. "The masters just used you to carry their bad stuff. You're a—a mule."

"I am NOT a mule. What do you know? I was a top-level master, and I defected—and this is all the thanks I get. Mule indeed. You Libertines will be sorry."

Blood Lily kept herself entirely dark.

"I see no evidence," Flame went on. "No more AZ for you. We'll just put you out in the spine with the ferals."

"I'll call the masters the first chance I get. You'll see then."

"Call how? What codes?"

The Trader produced a series of flashing colors; colors that would be sent from the host's eye out to another host infested with masters. Blood Lily recorded them all.

"You'll see," warned the Trader. "Those codes will get you invaded for sure."

After putting Tulip back in prison, Blood Lily discussed with Willow what to do. "Thanks, Flame," she added. "You're appointed our intelligence chief."

After Ilia departed, the transit bubble grew a pale disk. The disk brightened as it fused with a much larger space. Chrys and Daeren stepped through into Helicon's Peace Plaza, equivalent to Iridis' Center Way. The plaza opened upward, downward and in all directions. There strolled the *logens*, legal philosophers conducting their cases. Waterfalls cascaded near and far. The air breathed of phlox, lavender, and bee balm. Spidery bridges traversed the space, sparkling clean as the cleaner-bots scuttled past her feet snuffing up the slightest crumb. Above the bridges floated thousand-year Elves and variously shaped Free Sentient machines. A *logen* led a group of legal-philosopher students, all serenely grasping talars as they passed, their projected butterflies mingling with the real ones. A heliconian flitted past her nose, just long enough for her to spot the black bars across orange wings. Bushes that reached three stories tall fed the caterpillars. An airborne jellyfish settled on a bush, its long filaments undulating to scarf up caterpillars. Another, farther off, the plaza seemed full of them.

Daeren tugged a fold of her talar, avoiding a fine for physical contact. "Five minutes left."

She blinked for a floater. Floating bubbles swooped up and down, carrying Elves to their various destinations. One stopped to swallow her in. It took her and Daeren to the Fritillary Door, an entrance to Helicon's public transit reticulum, where a new bubble took them in.

"Welcome, Chrysoberyl of Dolomoth," boomed a familiar voice. "I will personally escort you onsite to Silicon to address your disastrous design flaws."

Before her eyes floated a gleaming cross, the sign of Transit, the virtual sentient code running Helicon's entire hydraulic transport. Startled, Chrys wondered what was up. Usually the Silicon Board sent some junior functionary, a lamp post or a spinning disk, to greet and escort her to the emerging sentient city. Transit would arrive later, brimming with disapproval.

"We invite you," Transit added, "to join our prudent Board members who await you at the lightcraft."

"Prudence is my middle name," assured Chrys. "We've booked a prudent sail with the Sharers. We'll see Silicon from their point of view." Never build anything without consulting Sharers whose lifeshaping ruled the sea. Sharers in whitetrance could wreck any project—even in the Iridis Underworld, let alone their own native ocean.

"As you wish," said Transit. "The Board will meet you at the project site."

The bubble containing Chrys and Daeren now joined a line of bubbles sliding sedately down through Helicon. Thanks to Transit, their particular bubble had VIP lighting and a rainbow path to point their way.

"If you please, Citizens," boomed Transit, "let me take this opportunity to note a parliamentary point of order in need of correction in the minutes of your Club Olympus that you honored me with your invitation to join. The motion 'to table' (more correctly, 'Lay on the Table') suspends a motion *only* temporarily when some urgent matter arises. Tabling a motion does *not* disappear a motion that a member dislikes. The chair must make it their business to avoid such underhanded misuse of procedure…"

Chrys looked away from Daeren, who had addressed that Olympian meeting on the rights of sentient persons and micros. It felt like ages ago. She took a sudden interest in the wall of the tube surrounding the bubble stream. Elves were inordinately fond of art, and artworks ancient and modern lined the tube. Time for another micro check, Chrys remembered, in case any plague carrier had secretly touched them. *"Blood Lily, tell the Lord of Light he's still the greatest god of Olympus."* She pressed the patch to her neck, then Daeren's. On her retina the fines for public contact surpassed twenty thousand credits, and a lawsuit had been filed. No right to privacy in Helicon.

Ahead shone a bright light. The bubble slowed and opened by merging into the outer shell. Its change of motion left Chrys wobbling on her feet. An algal scent came from the sea, just different from the shores of Valeton.

"Isoprene, oxo-acids, dimethylsulfoxone!"

Chrys blinked in the bright sun. The sky was intense blue, the air impossibly clear, no speck of dust from any dry land. The sun lit her brown arm like a lamp. Daeren's cheek reflected the sky like a black pearl.

Outside the wall of the city-sphere, waves lapped upon a dock where a small boat was moored. A stream of sparkles lit the water beyond. In the boat a purple Sharer with no clothes sat feeding a sea squirt to a tentacle of a rocket squid that lounged across the hull. The Sharer's hairless scalp caught the glint of the sun, brighter purple than any Sharer Chrys had seen in the Underworld. The scent of ocean filled her lungs.

"Great God of Mercy, we taste myriad molecules never named before."

Chrys took a step on the dock. Her bare feet nearly slipped on algal slime. Too late she realized that sentient deck shoes would have been a good call. She remembered swimming as a child in an ice-dammed lake below Mount Dolomoth. This ocean, though, was blissfully warm. She turned to Daeren, who'd grown up in the Underworld and never learned to swim.

Daeren said, "After you, Prudence."

On the boat, Chrys sat on a bench and braced herself against the hull. The sky—she could not get over the clouds, the repeating scallops of them, as if a sky-god tried out a new paintbrush. This planet's prevailing winds were quite different from Valedon's. The ocean breeze lifted her braids and cooled her scalp. The waves swelled and fell, no help to her gut. Daeren leaned uncomfortably over the boat rail.

"I am called Lushyren of Orie-el raft." The Sharer handed each of them a leaf of seaweed. "This will share help for sisters from Deadland."

Chrys chewed the leaf. It tasted bitter but did help. "Actually, Valedon is half covered by ocean. We sail ships." She explained, "We're here to visit Silicon; to see how the project's going and how Sharers think of it. How far is it?"

"Three orbs." Three hours in the boat; they could manage.

The rocket squid slid into a harness. It plowed the sea, shooting water behind. The boat leapt forward, leaving Helicon in the distance. Ahead, the sea lay smooth, dark as a sapphire. Something scooted up from the water and landed in the boat: a glider with many long tentacles. Chrys tucked her legs back as a precaution. Overhead sailed jellyfish of varied sizes and colors, all puffed with hydrogen bladders. A clickfly alighted on Lushyren's bare scalp. Whistling and popping, it reported something about her family; Chrys caught the words "lovesharer" and "children."

"Methional and jasmine—Raft flowers!"

Chrys wondered; the flowers must be far off, as she saw none yet.

"Oh Great One, may we visit this New World? All these new molecules."

New World? Not the Sharer. Chrys turned away. *"No. Absolutely not, lest you Fear."* Andra said Sharers carried no micros, and Olympus forbade infecting them.

Unexpectedly Lushyren plunged overboard to swim alongside the squid. Sharers lifeshaped all their world's creatures and seemed quite at home with them. Then at length she returned on board. Her breasts caught the sun like amethyst.

Chrys said enviously, "I wish I could swim like you." A Sharer could swim with few breaths while their purple breathmicrobes stored oxygen.

Lushyren grasped Chrys's arm. Her fingerwebs encircled Chrys's wrist. Chrys was fascinated. What would it be like to paint with those hands? Lushyren said, "Try your breath in two weeks. If you don't like it, your Plan Ten will share care of it."

Chrys's mouth fell open. Lushyren's touch transmitted breathmicrobes. Would Chrys grow breathmicrobes and turn purple? She cleared her throat. "Is it … permitted to eliminate them?"

Lushyren bowed her head. "Your question marks you as a true philosopher. The consensus of most Gatherings say that breathmicrobes are mere unfeeling bacteria. So you may share death with them."

Chrys considered this. Sharer language did not distinguish between subject or object, so killing something meant "share death" with them.

The thought made her uncomfortable; but breathmicrobes were just bacteria, not self-aware micros.

On the horizon ahead of the squid, there was something brown. A floating island? It was too flat to be Silicon.

"It's a raft tree," observed Daeren.

Lushyren clicked twice, then made pops and whistles. A clickfly popped back, then settled on her head. The Sharer and clickfly clucked back and forth for a while. The brown line on the horizon expanded, and branches appeared sprouting leaves and flowers. The branches extended radially from the floating core of the raft tree, where Sharers lived.

Something about it pricked Chrys's memory. She let her mind relax. "A cancer cell." That was how a cancerous lymphocyte looked: a round core, with filaments extending in all directions.

"A cancer cell is like a raft tree," observed Lushyren. "Both wish to grow."

"How much farther is Silicon?"

"Three orbs. You can rest on the raft overnight."

Chrys blinked online. So "orbs" of time were not hours—orbs meant days, turns of the sun. Math—the units always got you. Daeren looked away, his arms crossed upon the stern. He leaned out back, watching something of interest on the sea.

"I'm so sorry," Chrys told Lushyren. "The Board awaits us today—they'll pick us up here at this raft."

"Of course. You are welcome to rest on the raft, then we'll share parting."

"Could I ask you something?" Chrys flipped a viewcoin onto the deck. "What do you think of Silicon?"

The coin displayed a model of Silicon, the newly designed city for sentients. The geodesic sphere glowed infrared, with all its windows of fiery pinwheels.

Lushyren watched the model. "We know this creature. We call her Mother Diatom."

Chrys blinked the word "diatom." Her retina filled with a myriad different kinds of diatoms, silica-shelled algae with intricate symmetrical forms, like candies of all sizes and shapes. Unlike other worlds, Shora's diatoms each held a bright red chloroplast. Some of them really did look like a miniature Silicon. "So ... what do you think? Is this ... Mother Diatom good for the ocean?"

"Is she regulated?" the Sharer asked.

"Of course; Silicon will be regulated like all Elf cities."

"If she is clean and regulated, I see comfortable branches for sisters to nest."

"I see."

"Keep all shared effluents below one part per billion."

"Of course." Effluents were key—Chrys blinked to save that.

"Remember that my voice is but one. You should share our Gathering." Lushyren grabbed a rope and jackknifed into the water. Chrys caught the boat rail to steady herself. The Sharer emerged at a raft branch, where she pulled the boat in and tied the rope fast.

Chrys stepped up onto the boat rail, then took a tentative step on the branch. She winced as the bark dug into the soles of her feet. She fell forward but managed to lift herself and step forward on the branch while Daeren clambered up behind. The branch bloomed with bushes of orange tricorner flowers.

Ahead, the branch merged with others toward the center of a giant living raft. At the center rose a silkhouse, a home structure of ethereal beauty. The silkhouse was formed of woven panels of seasilk, stretched into hyperboloid forms. The panels shone green, blue, and magenta. One panel opened like a mouth saying "Oh." Out stepped another Sharer, Lushyren's lovesharer. She stepped out on the raft to hold Lushyren in an intimate embrace, her arms and hands with long webbed fingers reaching around her. Two little girls followed, their flipper-feet comically long for their size; the smaller one could barely walk, so she rolled over, flippers over head. The two joined their parents in a group hug.

From behind, Daeren caught Chrys, drew her close and caressed her breasts. She took a deep breath. On her retina the Elf fines had stopped collecting. Elysium's laws did not apply out here on the Sharer raft.

"Phenylethylamine … oxytocin …." Micros enjoyed a good loving year.

16

Libertines took a month to catalogue all the wondrous molecules they detected from this new ocean, some of which were found in the logs of long-departed historians; others were new, identified by new technology.

"Blood Lily, what do you think of these new gods?" Flame emitted molecules of curiosity.

"The new gods, too, emit new kinds of molecules," said Blood Lily. "And their skin is full of new bacteria."

"Breathmicrobes," said Flame. "They came to visit."

"And multiply in the skin." Blood Lily was wary of these new unintelligent bacteria.

"But what do you think of the new gods?" Flame persisted. "Did you notice their eyes?"

"Of course not," said Blood Lily. "We were told to avoid the eyes, lest we receive a year of Fear."

Flame was circumspect. "I kept dark all those years. But I did notice certain flickering from their pupils."

Blood Lily kept dark and emitted nothing. She, too, had noticed. The so-called Sharers already had their own micros. Micros they weren't yet sharing.

As the lightcraft arrived, Chrys checked her retina with Jasper and Selenite, both of whom remained on Valedon. "Chrys," Selenite asked, "are you sure you're OK?"

Chrys opened her eyes wide; she'd been on the edge of losing it. Her head ached and her face burned.

116

"Great God of Mercy, we tried to save your dividing skin cells as best we could, but sunscreen would have helped."

"I'm fine," she insisted, wincing as her lips burned. "We met a Sharer of Orie-el raft. She says we're good."

Jasper asked, "What exactly did she say?"

"She said keep the effluents below a part per billion."

Jasper hesitated. In the other window Selenite said, "You mean million."

"No, one per billion. Daeren, didn't she say?"

Daeren flashed a brief recording of the Sharer's response. The word "billion" was clear.

"That's unheard of," said Selenite. "Granted the city will be small by Valan standards, but parts per billion for all effluents? Our cost estimate will rise a thousand-fold."

"Let's not be hasty," said Jasper. "We'll pass this one back to the brains." The brains in back, the brightest sentients who rarely bothered with humans. Chrys made a note to visit them.

The dome of Silicon appeared below, still small at the model stage. Its spiraling windows were obscured by filaments that twisted into tangles. Chrys felt her scalp prickle. She'd seen it before, but here up close it looked grim. Still, she thought hopefully, even some diatoms had wayward filaments.

The lightcraft docked at a conference center floating above. Most of the Board members winked in on her retina, but one Elf was in person wearing a hard hat, along with assorted sentients including the ladder-shaped one who always made trouble. The new city was built for sentients, not humans, but human Elves would have their aesthetic say. The Guardian of Peace, Arion, a kind of defense minister, was on her retina along with several Guardians and Sub-guardians. Chrys knew she'd need to visit Arion in person later—for other reasons. The year before she'd helped Andra clear out Arion's plague micros—a private service he'd never acknowledged in public. Meanwhile, from her retina, Transit was a virtual cross that glimmered ahead of her as if suspended in air. Also on her retina, the Board chair, a financier like Garnet, was shaped like a black sea urchin. He was much too large to attend in person with his twenty-odd limbs.

The word ORDER flashed three times. The giant sea urchin announced, "I hereby call this meeting of the Silicon Planning Board to order." There followed the usual series of procedurals and old motions, not unlike Olympus.

Daeren nudged her. With a start she opened her eyes. Robert's Rules were soporific.

"Next on our agenda: the report of our dynatect."

Chrys took a deep breath, blinking rapidly. *"Blood Lily, are you ready?"*

"We are ready to defend our work. Remember, structure, beauty, and utility."

She projected her model, a much larger dynamic version of what she'd shared in the viewcoin. The model of future Silicon filled the conference room and would fill the retina of every watching member of the board. "The future of Silicon requires structural integrity, beauty, and utility. Above all, integrity for those who dwell … ." The view expanded. In Chrys's model, computed by her micros, the filaments were untwisted—they extended outward straight. That was how the building should grow.

"Does form trump function? We do not accept this essentialism. Every form must exhibit beauty as well as function. The function of these filaments is that they provide landing ports and communicators for sentients of all shapes and forms, including those insubstantial." Insubstantial sentients like Transit existed only as code in electronic space. "This form was inspired by a cancer cell with its probing filaments outstretched for infinite growth. The beauty of their filaments will radiate outward, exhibiting hope and infinite aspiration. Yet this infinite aspiration is checked by perfect balance; a paradox one could ponder without end. We expect the design to attract so many viewers that viewspaces will be set around for students and tourists to visit and meditate—"

Something happened to her retina. Several windows blinked out, then flashed back. Others had vanished.

"Emergency in Helicon—a system-wide defect" The voice seemed to come from everwhere. "The entire transit system appears to be stalled."

Transit's cross was gone. Chrys looked around the room for in-person board members. Her retina filled with windows winking open and shut like fireworks. Entire sectors of Helicon were unreachable. The *shon* of children was trapped. Individuals were stuck within their bubbles, with limited oxygen. The floating city was frozen.

"Jasper, what happened?" she texted privately.

"Transit had the sentient equivalent of a heart attack. It was when you said the word 'cancer.'" Jasper added, "Your presentation basically took out the entire hydraulic transit of Helicon."

"Disaster!" The ladder-shaped sentient waved his appendages, trying to get everyone's attention. "The mere report of this unworthy design has already caused immense disruption of Helicon, disruption that I may say is unprecedented. I move we table our dynatect's plan."

"Out of order," barked the giant urchin, his bulk heaving gently. "Our comrade is under good care and will recover. Our business must continue."

118

Interesting, thought Chrys. Both board members seemed unsurprised. Was Transit's "disruption" not unexpected?

"The chair will entertain questions on our dynatect's report."

A few of her retinal windows had closed as other members took off to address the city-wide disaster, but most remained, including Arion, his features unreadable beneath flaxen hair. The silence grew, almost palpable.

"The Chair recognizes Guardian Arion."

Arion's view expanded on her retina. Chrys tensed, recalling her previous encounter. The Guardian revealed no hint of recollection. His lips barely moved. "I'm to understand the Board contracted Eleutheria, the dynatect collective, not Azetidine the gallery artist." He added, "This design feels more like art with shock value. What next, perhaps collage?" A distinct emphasis on the last word.

"Other comments?" invited the sea urchin.

Another sentient spoke, a biped who worked in the Elf service industry. Human Elves were all too rich to work in service. "Azetidine's Eleutheria has a record of designs that are timeless. Whatever we call it, this model appears timeless and solves several structural problems." Nice that someone noticed.

"Very true," said the chair. "Would our Citizen Dynatect care to comment?"

Chrys took a breath. She said, "Our revised program was vetted by our project manager, our construction integrity supervisor, and all your brains in back. As for art, we have no intention to shock, only beauty in metaphors. I've seen no ... collage aside from the *shonlings* art competition." That should embarrass Elves.

Unembarrassed, Arion spoke again. "So why does your beautiful metaphor invoke uncontrolled growth? Is this the hidden agenda of our sentient citizens?"

Growth control was Elysium's founding principle. Without dry land, the ocean world's population required strict limits. The ocean world's first settlers, the Sharers, had limited themselves to a hundred thousand. The Elves with all their technology could not exceed one million. Elves and Sharers, in their different ways, had centralized the rearing of children. Their greatest fear of sentients was uncontrol—the possibility that sentients could replicate themselves without measure.

"Citizen Dynatect," observed the urchin. "Might we perhaps revise your report so as to respect Elf sensitivities."

"Chrys," texted Jasper, "He just wants you to call it something else."

She sighed. "All living things evolve to grow without limit, even a raft tree expanding its branches. The Sharers we met on Orie-el call

119

Silicon the Mother Diatom." Even diatoms could bloom without control. Never mind, on growth control Sharers had the last word.

" 'Mother Diatom,' that's good," said the urchin. "Secretary, please amend the dynatect's report, replacing 'cancer cell' with 'Mother Diatom' throughout. I move we accept the dynatect's report as amended. The chair calls a brief recess before we commence Evolutionary Design."

Sentients appeared to be little affected by the loss of transportation. More than a hundred thousand had signed up for Evolutionary Design, and they were determined to go through with it. Chrys had never imagined such a large conference meet, but the Diaspore took it in stride.

Settled in a comfortable chair, she closed her eyes and entered the immersive world. *"Blood Lily, have all your designers ready. This is the event of your lifetime."*

Round one began with her own latest design, now retitled Mother Diatom. She blinked Eleutheria's first entry. All at once, all hundred thousand entrants each blinked their "mutation." Within a moment the Diaspore computed everything, supposedly into a new viable design. The new design looked radically different than what Chrys originally proposed. Still red through infraread, instead of a geodesic dome there rose a kind of mushroom cloud. Unsightly and impractical. But what could you expect for a hundred thousand mutations?

The next round, Chrys blinked again, trying for correction. But the mushroom was already twisting into something new. It now looked more like an upside-down jellyfish. Was her entry given no more weight than a hundred-thousandth?

Chrys finally gave up and quit the conference, along with Daeren. Unlike sentients, their human condition required sleep. At Helicon, transportation was starting to recover, but their guestroom could not yet be reached. In any case, Chrys scarcely felt like getting trapped again in the bowels of a city. She found a luxury suite with a window on the sea. Ordering her luggage printout, she sank back on the bed.

"I can't believe they all just 'evolved' away my design, just like that." And still going—the 'evolving' would go on through the night, with what conclusion, Chrys wondered.

Daeren considered this. "You're taking it personally. You once said that great art was not meant to be lived in."

"Not my kind of art."

"The buildings were always designed by your Libertines. You were just—"

"A petri dish. But nowadays, Libertines and I, we all work together. What's the point of all our design when we're just one of a hundred thousand?" Wearily she pulled off her talar. "I've had it," she announced. "Done with building. No more for me."

Daeren looked stricken. "Won't you do just one more?"

"The Underworld." She hugged Daeren, held him tight. "You know I'll try. If we can somehow please everyone from sims to Sharers."

"You have Rhun's focus group; you're trying the right way. Let me breathe," he added.

With a smile she relaxed, recalling her strength. "The Sharer immigrants," she remembered. "Why do so many leave their ocean home, when it's so ... beautiful?"

"Children," said Daeren. "The Gathering decides who gets them and how many. If you disagree, you emigrate."

An avalanche of Elf media buried her retina, blamed her for the massive transit failure. "That Transit—he would screw up everything."

"So why did you put him on Olympus?" Daeren's own annoyance came out.

"Andra says master micros can survive outside people now," she reminded him. "Maybe even grow in a sentient. Transit has no corporeal substance. He's just—code."

Daeren shook his head. "Micros can't grow outside a host," he reminded her. "Just spacewalk."

Selenite's window was flashing. Chrys blinked at it and bought a thousand credits' worth of privacy.

"About your ship," Selenite began. "The one Andra originally sent."

"What about it?"

"We scoured it for twenty hours and found nothing. Then we tried flashing those codes your people extracted from the Trader."

"And?"

"Three came out." Three microbial masters, hiding somewhere in the vast bulk of an empty ship.

"Three Trader *masters*? Without any host?"

"No human host," said Selenite. "Growing or not, we can't say. Suspended, more likely. Even ordinary germs can do that. Some can last a thousand years."

Chrys turned to Daeren, but he said nothing. "Where are they now?"

"When they saw what was up, they committed apoptosis." Programmed cell death.

"Still ... that means they could be anywhere."

121

"They must transmit more easily now, if they can survive outside." Selenite nodded grimly. "Watch out tomorrow."

"We will," Daeren assured her. "And afterward, we'll get tested by Andra."

"But what if Andra ... is ...." Chrys stopped short of the unthinkable.

Selenite said, "You will test Andra."

And afterward—saints and angels, what next? Chrys sighed. "Daeren needs to get sleep. We've got a long day ahead." Walk on water and raise the dead. Replacing lost angels for Elf addicts, like Moraeg was now doing on Valedon.

17

Flame had expected to spend her elder years exploring the Libertines' vast archives. She had never thought of interrogation or sleuthing hidden masters. But now the God of Mercy tasked her with an urgent mission: Find the Traders who hid outside.

How could micros exist outside a host? Micros needed to breathe oxygen. They needed to bathe in water, dying immediately when they dried out. They fed on plasma proteins and sugar, abundant in the cerebrospinal fluid that was their home. But now the Minions of the Death Lord claimed to have found micros that survived many generations in the inert hull of a ship.

"Could the Minions be mistaken?" wondered Wizard Willow. "They're not very bright."

"No," insisted Blood Lily, "Minions aren't smart enough to make this up."

"There is other evidence," flashed Azure's blue with soothing pheromones. "Evidence from epidemiology, the transmission patterns."

"We need to assume even a sentient might infect us now." Where to start? Elysium held microscopic dangers at every turn.

"I will interrogate the Trader," promised Flame. "She must have clues on how this could be—and what we can do about it."

Blood Lily emitted new molecules. "What is it like, I wonder, to inhabit a sentient machine."

Alarm molecules floated through the spinal fluid. "Detect—Detect!"

"Detect what? Who?"

"The triads," flashed Willow. "A few of them detect signals of foreign micros."

All Libertines whose work could be spared went through the blood searching for Traders. They searched the god's entire vascular system, every vein and capillary. For hours they searched, a month in microbial time. But they all came up short.

"A false alarm," flashed Blood Lily. "What do you expect of detectors that only count to seven."

"The signal is persistent," insisted Willow. "Always a few report the molecules. To improve sensitivity, entangle them in pairs. Their detection rate will increase by a factor of ten."

"Azure, what should we do?"

Azure was a Blue Angel, sent from the Lord of Light to encourage Libertines to uphold the laws of the gods. "The Lord of Light told us," flashed Azure. "Above all, keep your God safe."

Flame wavered. Other council elders flashed agreement. But no one knew a better way to keep their god safe. "We must ask the god's permission."

"But the God of Mercy is asleep for the next eight years."

What could they do, when they could not even find these mysterious Traders? "Willow, are you sure you can entangle triads—in pairs only?" Beyond pairing, the triads could build a sentient network, and who knew what happened then.

Willow showed her code to Flame. "Our God of Wisdom uses this code in her devices, to build buildings and test for cancers. The paired triads still have only six qubits."

"Very well," said Flame. "Let's pair the triads, then see if they get more sensitive—enough to find the Traders." Still, Flame wondered what would happen when Libertines got tested by the Death Lord or the Thundergod. The testers would want to know why the quantum triads got entangled—without divine permission.

On the way to the Elf recovery center, the vesicle carried Chrys with Daeren northwest at a gentle angle, past a sentient artwork composed of a sextillion individual atoms, each placed individually.

Chrys checked up on Xenon and Maya. "No escaping?"

"Certainly not," promised Xenon. "I've no more need of primate anatomy subjects."

In the playroom, Maya looked up at the sound of Chrys's voice. The cat lifted her chin and emitted a plaintive wail. The wail descended in a gutteral lament.

Chrys felt heartbroken. "I miss you too, Maya." Savannah cats needed so much attention.

Her home-agent-hospital added, "Solaria called again. They really want your show."

"Where?"

"Their main gallery."

"The one in a treehouse?" Solarian humans were a rugged frontier stock, bifertiles with both sets of organs, who had settled just a hundred years ago. They raised large families and welcomed tourists for their spectacular arborial scenery. High art, though, was not what they were known for.

"We'll politely decline," Xenon assured her.

In another retinal window, Ilia blinked insistently. "My dear, whatever is going on with Silicon?" She sounded mystified. "First you select a medical image, faintly repulsive. Then a marine alga, harmless but unsurprising. And then—"

"The sentient collective evolved an upside-down jellyfish."

"Well, let it blow over before the competition."

Chrys had some choice things to say, but a painted-lady landed briefly upon her nose. She admired the mottled wings, then asked, "How is transit in Papilion? Are all the Elf transit systems like …"

Ilia shook her head. "Helicon's Transit was the prototype."

"They don't, like, have tantrums?"

"Certainly not. They're not even sentient."

Just ahead, the golden cross hovered. Ilia discreetly winked out.

"Oh, Chrysoberyl," called Transit. "My apologies for what happened."

Chrys kept her smile. Even a virtual sentient could read human faces. "I hope you're feeling better."

"I did my best," the cross added. "I tried so hard to disrupt the so-called evolution. But the Board was resolute."

Her smile wavered. "Disrupt? Why? You scarcely approved my initial design."

"Your design was terrible," he assured her. "But less terrible than the evolving chaos."

"You don't believe a thousand laypersons' judgment beats one expert?"

"Ten times as many irremediable errors. What do they expect?" He added, "Especially for sentients. The bar for legal sentience is set way too low."

Distracted, Chrys tripped on the down-sloping bridge. Daeren caught her arm. "Less-Terrible, that's me," she told him.

"The Papilio Door," Daeren reminded her. "Just one stop to the recovery center."

The recovery center featured the best of Helicon's not-a-hospital design. No two walls were straight, and butterfly bushes were tucked discreetly behind its curves. Daeren had a long list of clients to meet, each recovering from lost control of a growing population. Once masters reached the dopamine key, you could never again be trusted to rule a population. Their growing children would "forget" eventually and try again. It was more fun to make a puppet of your host than pray to a god.

But once someone had lived with micros—had shared their lives, absorbed their prayers and antics every day—you could never again bear to live "alone." So Daeren bred and trained his special elders from the Blue Angels. Each recovering host received just seven angels, to live like hermits in the wilderness of a recovering mind. As the angels aged and passed, they'd need replacement. When the client was down to two, about every month or so, Daeren would come for resupply. No Elf carriers were yet trusted to supply angels. Only Daeren, and now, Moraeg.

Chrys tried to stay in the background with the bushes, though the butterflies seemed as much attracted to her hair. She watched as Daeren met each client, checking for any signs of something amiss in their behavior. Each client was so grateful to see him, to receive their next few angels to get by for the next month. Their faces lit up like moons. They conversed about each micro, the likes and dislikes of each one, their unique colors and traits. They caressed Daeren's talar like a lover, a savior of souls.

After each client departed, Chrys came forward to share a patch, for her people to sniff out any stray masters. "You're clear," she told Daeren. "You still walk on water."

At the very last came Eris. Eris Heli*shon*, the former Guardian of Culture, the *shon* sibling of the Guardian of Peace, Arion. Arion's most trusted friend and aide had been Elysium's worst source of the brain plague. Now he was just another client tied to Daeren's mercy.

But not just any other. Chrys did not trust Eris for one second. Of all the clients, Eris had to keep his hands to himself. Chrys stood just behind Daeren, to make sure.

Eris smiled slightly, as he always did; that detestable smile that belied the experience of all the Elves he had corrupted, even children from the *shon*. "Your angel Cerulean had such aesthetic taste," he told Daeren, arms behind his back. "She wove entire gardens of aromatics across the arachnoid."

Undeserved, Chrys told herself silently. No way Eris deserved any better than hell itself.

Daeren nodded, always understanding, forgiving any client no matter what they had done. "Columbine is looking forward to seeing you. She'll enjoy your aesthetics for the next month of generations." Daeren placed a patch, first at his own neck, then to Eris's, just above his carotid.

Eris had his arm out. He raised his hand ever so slowly toward Daeren.

Chrys's arm shot out and chopped his. No touching for Eris—he knew the rule.

Startled, Daeren took a step back.

Eris's face changed. For just a moment, there was a look of hatred. Then he regained composure. "You know we'll treat them well. Columbine is already settled in."

Afterward, the transit bubble took them gliding through Helicon to reach Andra. "You could be a little nicer," Daeren said.

"No I can't. I'll report that he touched my arm." Was that on purpose, she wondered. Eris never did anything by accident. She took a patch from Daeren's neck. "You're clear—as far as my Libertines can tell."

"You can strangle me, to be sure."

She gave him a look. "I should have strangled Eris. We need to update the Hospital on our new procedure." The Hospital was part of the Elves' health system, reputedly ten times better than Plan Ten—and worthless for micros.

"God of Mercy, we have a problem."

Chrys tensed all over. She drew her attention inward, away from the artworks sailing by. *"Problem? What is it?"*

"Our triads—the qubit detectors that the Good Doctor bequeathed us ten generations past."

"What did they find?"

"They can't say; they are subsentient. They just flash 'Detect' on and off."

"Detect what?"

"They don't say. Their intelligence is limited. They can't count past sixty-three."

Sixty-three? Wasn't it just seven? Whatever—how could they ever find microbial masters hiding amid a hundred trillion human cells and an equal number of bacteria? *"The Thundergod will test you soon enough."*

A moment's hesitation; Chrys could sense it by now. *"We're ready for the Thundergod,"* flashed Blood Lily bravely. *"We followed every clue; our enzymes will lyse any Trader-master that appears. Let the Judges see who can do better."*

Andradite of Sardis received them in her Heliconian apartment, which was decorated with Iridian splendor. Rubies and emeralds, with runes in classic gold; not a butterfly in sight. Chrys would never have expected to feel so at home. Daeren went quickly to Andra and pressed a patch at her neck, as if caressing. Their eyes burst into fireworks. Andra was like the mother he'd never known.

From ceiling to floor scrolled a virtual law library, a list of statutes light-years long. "You didn't quit your day job," Chrys observed. Andra had been executive malpractice attorney for Hospital Iridis.

"Elysium government has no paid service." Andra's tone was clipped, as always. "Guardians and Sub-guardians are all volunteer."

"Social capital." Doctor Sartorius had his worms coiled neatly on his carapace. Chrys knew, though, how he shaped himself for Andra alone.

"Power," added Daeren. Naked power, thought Chrys. Humankind could never get enough.

"So you made it." Andra nodded as if checking a box on one of her interminable legal briefs, the kind Daeren now handled all the time. "You can see what we're up against. On your way back, we'll send octopods."

"The ship—is that really a threat? How can micros survive?"

"In Elysium, Elves never touch a stranger. So their culture selects for fomite transmission." Fomite, inanimate object that carries a pathogen. Andra's eyes filled with purple—the Judges of the Thundergod. "Anything we need to know?"

The test. Chrys's pulse increased; damn it, why could she not keep steady. "Those qubits the good doctor sent."

"Yes?"

"They keep flashing 'Detect' but my people find nothing. They display random fireworks now and then."

"Unsurprising." Andra glanced at her sentient love partner as if scoring a point.

Doctor Sar raised a faceworm. "The qubit triads were Opal's first version," he said in his softest voice. If you closed your eyes, you might imagine how he could look when alone with her. "Still in testing."

"So I'm the lab rat." Masters were bad enough—here the committee had given her entangled qubits still in testing. As if quantum uncertainty weren't enough.

"We are all experimental," observed Andra. "Micros evolve much faster than we do." Andra sent Chrys her Judges. They barreled through her bloodstream, shining beams of auburn like search lights. The minutes lengthened as Chrys and Andra faced each other. Andra's pupils lit up with purple starbursts.

"We find no masters," Andra observed at length, still watching Chrys's eyes. "However, your people need to tell you something."

Chrys swallowed. *"Blood Lily, what is it? What have you done?"*

"We paired the triads. Wizard Willow said they would work better."

"You were forbidden. You neither asked nor informed your god." A capital offense; and now Andra found it. Disaster.

"How bad is it?" Chrys asked. "The paired triads. Can Sar get them out of me?"

"We'll wait and see," Andra said dryly. "What happens to you." Lab rat again.

The doctor added, "The triads are no danger to you. The qubits still cannot pass any test of sentience. Even if they became self-aware, there would be no danger, though it would be ... awkward."

Chrys sent a pulse of Fear, longer this time. She flashed, *"Blood Lily, you're deposed from the Council. You are no longer my high priest."*

"God is merciful."

"Let Azure and Flame run the Council and address me." Azure, Daeren's watchful Blue Angel. Being run by Azure, the Libertines would feel a loss of face and hopefully learn a lesson. For the next generation, at least.

"Thanks for recruiting Transit to Olympus," Doctor Sar added. "Transit knows a lot. He had some thoughts on how micros might survive out on the ship."

Daeren said, "Olympus made him parliamentarian."

Andra held out a patch. "When your peoples' leadership transition is done, you're on." The tables turned.

Chrys blinked, uncertain. "Do we have to do it now? Better to—"

"Now. It's absolutely urgent."

"The epidemiology," added the doctor. "We've narrowed down the source."

"It can't be Andra," Daeren exclaimed. "How could it be?"

"The pattern of incidence points to one of us," said Andra. "Myself or ... another highly placed host."

"Ilia? I just tested her."

"Daeren, please step outside."

Daeren crossed his arms.

"It's all right," Doctor Sar assured him. "This is what we planned, remember."

Flame, are you ready to test the Thundergod?

"Certainly, Oh Great One. I have practiced for a week and combed the archive to review all previous cases."

"Flame never did this before." Daeren was on edge. "Andra's too important. We'll come back tomorrow."

The Doctor extended a faceworm. "My nanos will assist."

Chrys took a breath. "Anything I should know?" She placed the patch at Andra's carotid.

Andra said, "Two Elves that I tested went bad shortly after."

"That could happen anywhere," insisted Daeren.

The minutes passed. Andra held Chrys's gaze, flickering now and then. At last, flashes of pink.

"All clear," flashed Flame. *"No sign of masters in the brain or blood."*

"Did you check with Trader Tulip?" By eye, long distance, of course; no way they'd let Tulip out of prison.

"All her clues. No chemical signals that appeared in any previous case of infection."

"They say you're good," she told Andra.

"Do the stress test."

Chrys nodded. "Do you have an oxygen mask? Doctor?"

"The original way," said Andra.

"No!" shouted Daeren. "You will not strangle Andra."

"They can tell the difference now," Andra explained. "Only the original way scares them out of the bone."

"You don't know your own strength—"

Chrys steeled herself, her pulse pounding. She'd never done this with Daeren watching.

"I'll watch her numbers," promised the doctor.

"So will I." Chrys set her hands on Andra's throat. Andra, the good soldier, didn't flinch. The numbers fell. Chrys steadied her hands and kept the oxygen number within the range; low enough to scare micros but not harm the host.

"They came out!" flashed Flame. *"Three of them hid within the mastoid bone. We recorded everything, all their signs—molecules we didn't recognize before—"*

Chrys's hands flew off Andra's throat. "I hope you're okay."

Andra coughed twice. "Yes, at last. For the moment. Daeren, you have clients waiting."

Daeren had been restrained by the doctor's faceworms. Chrys watched in dismay. "Daeren, it's okay. Here I'll go help you—"The private clients, a long list who wouldn't be seen at the recovery center.

"Sar will assist Daeren," Andra said. "Chrys, you and I have business."

Chrys watched Daeren leave with the doctor. "I can't do this again," she said at last. "I know it works, but—it's not right. It's not good for you."

"All medicine has side effects. However, you're right; you can't continue oxygen deprivation, because the masters will soon figure it out. They're smart as we are and think ten thousand times faster."

"No faster than Libertines."

"Great One, we knew they were there—you got my message, right?" Flame had sent a secret code; the "all clear" was for show, in case hidden masters could see. *"The Trader told us what signals to look for. But we didn't know where in the body they were hiding. Until the stress test."*

"Well done. Bring the Trader back for interrogation."

"Truly well done?"

With a smile, Chrys took a wafer of AZ. "I'll send you all Flame's clues," she told Andra. "I can test others you want—but not that way."

"Just one more."

"Why? We've found the source, right?"

"There could be another source. Much higher."

"Who?"

"Who else?"

Chrys stared. "Not—*Arion*? Like, I'm to strangle the Elf defense minister?"

18

Azure did her best to run the Council though she lacked experience. She had come to Eleutheria weeks ago as a young Watcher from the Lord of Light. Watchers were Blue Angels trained to watch over matters without interference. Blue Angels were the first population trusted to withstand the temptation of an addicted host. Beyond addicts, Watchers could help hosts endangered by exposure, such as the Lord's beloved God of Mercy. "Guard the God of Mercy, at all cost," the Lord of Light bade Azure. "Above all keep her safe. I cannot live without her."

"Lord of Light, it shall be done," promised Azure. "Darkness will never fall."

So at the first hint of danger, Azure had allowed the Libertines to entangle the triads and protect the precious God of Mercy. The Libertines had done well; all other rules they followed. By now, Azure had watched generations of Libertine children multiply, a few transitioning to elders. The Ants were long assimilated; Blood Lily was one of a few half-Ants left. Now Blood Lily had been banned from leadership, demoted to the lower ranks of the art team. But art had little work for the past two generations while the gods traveled in Helicon.

Fortunately, Flame soon took charge.

"Make wise choices," Azure advised.

"I won't pair the triads any further," Flame assured Azure. "But—after two generations, the paired triads still flash Detect. Are they wrong?"

Azure asked, "Can you find the alarm's source?"

"The signal is too intermittent. But I've recorded its full history. The Terminator thinks we should investigate." Terminator was what micros called the sentient Doctor Sartorius, who exterminated micro people upon divine command.

Wizard Willow blinked purple. "Even paired triads only flash on or off. But we can calculate the source position based on how often the paired triads flash in different parts of the body."

"Their highest detect rate is nowhere near the brain," explained Flame, "but near the cervical vertebrae." The neck bones of the spinal column. "The capillaries within the bone are twisted and treacherous. Micros getting stuck there would trigger immune attack."

Azure asked, "What about those intermittent starbursts?" Every so often the triads caused a burst of flashes on the retina, like a crossette with little comets cascading out.

"Quantum noise," said Flame. "All quantum circuits are degraded by noise. Still, I record them all for the archive."

"Libertines are good at engineering," Azure observed. "Can your team work out the source of these starbursts? Meanwhile, we need to get ready to test the Hunter." Their name for Guardian of Peace Arion.

Chrys strolled a curving bridge across the Peace Plaza, with Ilia beside. A jellyfish floated past the bridge, its filaments trailing. A *logen* marched up the bridge leading his followers. Ahead loomed the face of the Nucleus, with its endless rivulets of rainbow-colored falls.

Chrys texted Ilia, "I'll never get out alive."

"Rest assured," returned Ilia's multicolored letters. "Arion knows what we have to do. He always likes your people." Especially those who played chess.

"Not this time. High-powered officials don't like getting strangled."

"Indeed. Yet they all need it, now and then."

"He's not even paid."

"All Elves are well paid by their *shon*. Guaranteed income. That being said—" A heliconian landed on Ilia's arm. She admired its striking wings, orange with black bars. "We do not entirely lack 'commercial' interest."

"He doesn't care for my art, much less Silicon."

The Elves held that wars no longer existed, so they had no official "defense." But the Guardian of Peace, Arion, was effectively their defense minister. From his office came the trickling of a rainbow waterfall beyond, and the scent of bee balm for the vast garden of heliconians. Arion sat behind his desk, the standard pose of all functionaries in the known universe. He coolly regarded Chrys, ignoring Ilia beside her. "So get on with it," he told her. "Be sure to send the chess player."

Chrys was prepared for that. Of course, the original double-agent master chess player whom Arion knew had long passed. So Chrys sent Wizard Willow to play chess and Flame to run the testing. Supposedly Arion kept no breeding population of his own but only entertained visitors. The absence of a native population would aid detection; any chemical trace of other micros would be suspect.

Chrys focused on Arion's pupils, dark within his blue eyes. *"No active masters,"* flashed Flame. *"None in all the arachnoid cisternae."*

"Good news." Chrys felt relief. Perhaps they could avoid the debacle.

"We did detect three trace organics, filaments with embedded antimony and ytterbium. We've no idea where they're hiding without—"

Hopes were dashed. She swallowed hard. "Citizen, they found no hidden masters. But there are trace molecules."

"So, blood carries all kinds of molecules. I'm arsenic-wiped hourly."

"The masters now use various transition metals and lanthanides."

"So I hear. Your informants earn their keep." Arion paused for a few seconds. "Well, your chess player can return. A valiant performance." Chrys had warned Willow to let him win.

"Before my testers return, there's something we must do." Her heart pounded. "A stress test."

From behind, Arion's two octopods moved forward. A legal brief scrolled down before her eyes. Arion said, "We've completed all tests agreed."

Chrys stared ahead. This part was omitted from the brief, to avoid warning infectives. "Something new. It's uncomfortable, but we have to do this."

"And if I decline?"

Ilia said, "I'll inform the Prime."

The Prime Guardian of the Republic of Elysium versus the Guardian of Peace. There was Chrys, stuck amidst the highest-level Elf power struggle. She raised her hands, visibly shaking. Then she focused. Just another addict, she told herself. Another day, another street save; you got this.

The blood oxygen meter appeared on her retina. Chrys placed her hands around Arion's throat. Above his shoulders the octopods each snaked a tentacle, ending in a needle a centimeter above each hand. Chrys made herself ignore all else, as if she were a mindless machine. She pressed Arion's windpipe, her gaze fixed on his oxygen number in her window. The time felt like centuries.

"*Got them.*" Flame flashed from his pupils. "*They committed apoptosis.*"

Her hands fell away. Red spots marked his neck where her thumbs had pressed.

"Get out." Arion's voice was low. "Get off this planet in the next hour."

Chrys felt her talar yanked by Ilia. "Wait—I need to get my people back—"

"I retrieved them," Ilia hissed. She dragged Chrys into a waiting transit bubble, then pressed a patch to her neck. Flame and Willow texted red and purple. Chrys nearly collapsed with relief.

"An hour—what am I to do?"

"Take my ship," said Ilia. "I have one waiting, always."

"But—" It wasn't Andra's ship. "What about Daeren? I can't leave him."

"We'll take care of Daeren. You need to leave, before the Hunter's senses kick in."

"What do you mean?"

"Before he files suit to keep you here."

Ilia's private bubble melted like soap through Helicon's city infrastructure, which seemed entirely flexible, nothing like the stone foundation of Iridis. "What about— the competition? My art show?" Chrys was disoriented. Where in Helicon were they now? She had no sense of place or time.

The bubble burst into the moonport waiting lounge. A virtual red carpet stretched ahead.

"Don't look back—just go," said Ilia. "Follow my line to the end." From Chrys's retina the line projected ahead. "Get on the ship before Arion calls back the order."

Just ten minutes had passed after all. Chrys hurried down the line to a gate. As she approached the gate her eye caught the bright red light of a sentience meter. Involuntarily her eye fixed on it.

The red turned green. The green light of freedom. Any machine or code that could escape its owner and pass the "sentient quotient" was declared free.

A siren blared. The gate closed.

"What? I can't miss my ship." Of all travel mishaps, this had never happened before.

A rotund drone floated down to look her in the eye. "You are hiding an enslaved sentient."

"*What?* How can I be hiding a sentient? I don't even have luggage."

"You must have swallowed it."

Chrys blinked in confusion. "Why would I be so desperate to deprive a sentient of freedom? Hey—no way." She batted off the drone's arm. Elf medical workers could not be trusted to respect the micros in her blood. Unlike Elysium's sentients, who were legally "people," micros had no legal protection whatever.

"Do not obstruct inspection. It's the law of the Republic. Submit or face detention."

Who could she call? *"Transit!* Transit, please can you help?"

To her immense relief the golden cross shimmered into view. "Indeed. May I be of service to a distressed biped lacking lanthanides?"

"Please—can you cut the red tape or something? Just get me out of here."

"Of course. As the ultimate transportation authority of Helicon, I will step in and inspect your person for enslaved individuals."

Chrys let out her breath. "You won't hurt the micros, will you? It's none of their fault."

"None of your microbial persons. Not unless they're holding back."

"We're not hiding any sentients," came the pink letters. *"Are we? Azure? Willow? Trader Tulip?"*

"No, no way, no." Blue, gold, violet-fleck white, a chorus of nos.

Transit must be doing something, exactly what Chrys could only guess. Of course his virtual code could interact with whatever electrical signals emanated from her person. Chrys counted the seconds. Then the minutes. Twenty minutes had passed overall. She started to panic again.

"Clear," announced a voice. "The helicon transportation authority clears you to go."

"Another false alarm," Transit observed, a little too ostentatiously, Chrys thought. "I assure you, lanthanide-less biped, had you covertly en-slaved any one of our sentient brotherhood—I would show no mercy."

19

Azure had never seen such uproar. Fear molecules in the blood upset the children, who refused to breed. The art team was in disarray. Everyone was appalled at the triads, and no one knew what do do.

"How could a six-qubit entity be self-aware?" wondered Flame. "History shows no precedent."

"Test them all," advised Azure. "We must mark and catalogue each triad."

"Yes," said Flame, "we've marked and tested them all. None can do more than output quantum probabilities."

"Before, they detected something hiding in the neck."

"The fifth cervical vertebra. We're combing the capillaries, but it takes time."

"And those fireworks." The random bits of fireworks still appeared on the retina; how did they get there? Even Trader Tulip had no idea. The fireworks were none of the masters' doing.

But while Flame had visited the Hunter, the Trader—stuck in prison, using retinal contact—had negotiated a huge deal on lanthanide extractors. These extractors consisted of living cells whose enzymes plucked the scarcest of lanthanides from mineral waste—then assembled them into nanoscopic forms. Where the Hunter got these cells, no one was quite sure. They sought delivery to the God of Wisdom.

"Our gods gave no such instructions," said Azure. "Neither the God of Mercy nor the God of Wisdom."

"No history of agreement," said Flame.

"The trade is legal." Wizard Willow emitted molecules of certainty. "Legal and wise. Wizards have long traded lanthanides for

137

extractors. This priceless technology will build a new generation of qubits for the Diaspore."

On the ship, Chrys blinked her retina for Opal.

"What happened?" Opal wanted to know. "What became of your contest?"

"Never mind the contest. What's this about trade with Arion?"

Opal looked mystified. Then her dimples appeared. "Did they pick up lanthanide extractors?"

"From *Traders?* The Fold's worst microbial terrorists?"

"This trade would be legal," insisted Opal. "We've long traded minerals for extractors to isolate scarce lanthanides from recycled material. Lanthanides are needed to grow the Diaspore."

"Why was I not informed?"

"The freight gets determined at the last minute, depending on prices. Shipping via Arion's brain—that's a good trick. Eliminates the tariff."

A likely story. "Opal, you know the Traders get into everything. How can you say you don't work with bad ones?"

"You can't meddle in your trade associate's internal affairs."

Chrys rolled her eyes. "Their hosts wind up dead."

"We certainly won't let that happen." Opal's voice fell. "Before you leave, Chrys, I need to tell you something. Pachira hoped to last till your return, but she couldn't make it. I'm so sorry. We kept a recording for you."

Her heart sank, though it was not unexpected. The green one, ever her best art director—Chrys would miss her. She signed off from Opal, then scanned her other windows. A random bit of fireworks, far left. Now and then it happened. She'd have Plan Ten take a look.

Daeren's light blinked urgently. "Chrys—are you all right? Hold the ship—I'm on my way."

"I'm so sorry. It all happened so fast. I have no control over this ship."

"But—you can't just go out alone." Alone with no partner to share micros and keep watch. And Daeren should never be alone. "Andra must send someone with you. I'll wait for you at the Iridis moonport."

The ship doors had closed. In the viewspace, the blue moon appeared, a lonely disk amid the black. The disk slowly shrank away amid the veil of stars.

Chrys sank back on a chair. Her retinal windows were blinking for attention. She checked Ilia. "So sorry for this contretemps," Ilia told her. "That Arion—he's more foolish than ever. Don't worry, we'll get your show reinstated."

Chrys took a deep breath. "No. I've decided—this year I won't show in Elysium."

Ilia regarded her closely. "No show? What about your career?"

"I'll show in Solaria."

Ilia's brows arched. "Solaria?" Her tone of voice dismissed this out-of-the-way location. "What kind of gallery would they have?"

"A treehouse."

The gallery director tilted her head to one side, then the other. Her eyes had a faraway look. "A tour on the frontier. Opportunities for cultural uplift. Not a bad career move," she decided. "We'll charter a cruise for your opening."

"Thanks, Ilia, I knew you'd understand. And I am so sorry to miss the Papili*shon* contest. Here are the winners I chose." For third prize, she'd picked a color-field abstraction with unusually sophisticated choice of hues. Second prize was a young Elf's portrait of their best friend in a parti-colored jumpsuit. The portrait's execution had the earnest look of a fifty-year-old adolescent.

"Excellent taste," Ilia observed.

"And for first prize…." A raft tree where a violet-bright Sharer teen jackknifed off a branch into the sea. The painting was done with Sharer traditional mixed media, including pigments made of seasilk, raft flowers, and live fungus. Even the highlights of sun glinting on leaves were done with dabs of slime mold. Chrys wished she could have experienced this one in person, to appreciate all the sensory details.

"A classic choice! I knew you'd pick Karin's piece." Karin Papili*shon*—the young Elf was a genuine talent. Chrys would regret missing her. "And all so appropriate." No collage; Ilia might feel relieved.

"Thanks so much for your ship," Chrys added. "We can always count on you."

Next, Chrys started to contact Xenon when her gaze slid by the cross of Transit. The cross twinkled. She blinked it.

Transit cross hovered in the room. "I have your quote," he announced.

"The quote?" She took a moment to recall.

"For your Underworld reconstruction."

"Of course, the Underworld. You have a quote already?"

The model appeared on her retina, the Valan ocean offshore Iridis with something like a floating bread loaf. The loaf expanded, and a cross-section revealed interior levels.

"Homes, recreational, commercial," observed Transit. "The design's completely scalable, for a thousand or a million lanthanide-less bipeds."

"I see." Chrys smiled at the floating bread loaf, though her heart sank. "You put so much thought into this."

"At low cost, of course, for modest socioeconomic level."

"It's just hard for Iridians to … leave bedrock."

"Bedrock is full of cancers. On Shora we have a saying: Land is the home of the dead." Shora's ocean covered all bedrock, kilometers below the waves.

Chrys sighed. "City dwellers have other sayings."

"It's not what you wanted," said Transit. "Though someday you may need a Less Terrible."

She smiled. "Thanks for your Less Terrible. And thanks so much for getting me past the red light."

Transit paused. "Getting past the light doesn't mean you're completely clear."

"What do you mean?"

"You really don't know? Something in or upon your person has borderline sentience. It failed to meet the legal threshold, but it could grow."

"Borderline sentience?" Valans defined sentient rights by volume, the size of the Orb of Votan. But Elves defined sentience by smarts, or something. "What do you mean? How smart is it?"

"It failed to complete the lawsuit against you."

"Lawsuit? Against *me*?" Logocracy gone wild.

"The lawsuit asserts independent right to personhood."

"Saints and angels," Chrys whispered.

"Whatever it is has about the brain capacity of a feline."

"You mean—a *robot cat*?"

"Some would call that a slur."

"Of course, sorry," Chrys corrected herself. "But all I have in my blood is entangled triads. How could they get that smart?"

"Qubits are hard to predict. Let's just say … this image may give you a clue."

The space filled with Forevertree, a vast trunk of the forest covered by moss and slime molds. Whatever clue rested there was beyond Chrys. Her retina still flashed with news of her planetary expulsion, just another incident to pile on her infamous reputation. At last she reached Xenon, and as many of her clients as she could. Then she turned in to sleep for the overnight. Daeren—if only he were there beside her.

20

The god had been asleep for many years, while Flame led a team searching the capillaries of the fifth cervical vertebra, trying to find whatever the triads had detected. The flow through the bone was sluggish, the red cells inching forward then stopping, an endless traffic jam. An occasional white cell oozed along the inner wall till it found a weak point to crawl out into surrounding tissue.

"More white cells here," flashed Wizard Willow. "White cells must be attracted to something."

Flame's proteins vibrated fast. It was scary to think what might wait beyond, hidden amid a trillion cells.

Toxic molecules flooded the blood. Flame flashed the alarm. "Invaders!" From somewhere the masters had emerged, invading the god's blood as she slept.

"Wait," said Willow. "Our guards are here to bind them. Let me communicate—I know their language." Willow flashed them her call.

The molecules formed chains that snapped around Willow, binding her ring of filaments. Her ring-shape constricted, twisted and broke apart.

Flame watched in shock as Willow's cell disintegrated. Then she pulled backward, twisting swiftly around the sluggish blood cells. She had to get out and warn everyone.

At the brain's cistern, Azure said, "We all must hide." From the Blue Angels, by long tradition, she knew where to go to hold out, undetected. There was one faraway place down the spinal column, the place where Blue Angels hid long ago.

141

Blood Lily, Trader Tulip, and Flame considered what Azure said. Flame was still dazed by the sight of Willow disintegrating. "How can we hide? All the children—"

The masters were approaching with their dendrimers to bind the Libertines and kill them all. Just then a burst of pinpoint lights filled the retina. It was like the earlier random fireworks from the triads, but much larger, blinding the sensors. The unexplained data burst caught the masters by surprise. They rushed to inspect it and find the cause.

Azure was equally surprised by the fireworks, but wasted no time. "Hide now. I know where to hide—the lumbar cistern." The tailbone, the back end of the spinal column, held the most distant pool of spinal fluid. The spinal fluid surrounding the cord flowed through a tube of fluid connecting all the brain's cisterns with the smaller cisterns all the way down the spine. "The tailbone, the lumbar cistern—that's where my ancestors hid when masters invaded the Lord of Light."

"Won't they look for us?" asked Flame.

Trader Tulip emitted warnings. "No time to lose. Take half the children and go."

"Half! But the rest—"

"You must leave some here in the brain for them to find."

Blood Lily said, "Trader Tulip is right. I will await the masters here with her and ... the rest of our children."

The masters rolled their ugly circles through the arachnoid. "We need this host," they flashed. "You're done."

Blood Lily said nothing. She could only hope Azure was right, that she and Flame could hold out undetected at the tailbone. With half their children—the heartbreak of dividing them.

"We can trade," Trader Tulip told the invaders. "See, I waited here for you."

"We know nothing of you. We need all the host to ourselves."

"Look at all these good data." Trader tried to buy time. She spilled interesting codes, whether real or not, Blood Lily could only guess. "We have unimaginable new designs for your lanthanides, for your profit—"

For a while the masters showed interest. Precious seconds lengthened into minutes, while Blood Lily hoped Azure's group was getting far away down the spine to the tailbone.

"Are these your children?" the invader demanded. "Are they all accounted for?"

"These are the last of our children. Please—spare them."

That was the last thing Blood Lily knew.

In the ship's cabin Chrys awoke with a headache. Her tongue felt thick and clammy with a sour taste. The cabin was still dark with odd patches of light. Something was wrong with her eyes; all her windows were dark. And her vision was odd.

"Lights." Her throat was hoarse, and she coughed. Light filled the cabin; and she blinked to adjust. But the shadows were all black. Black and light of a harsh kind. No colors, only gray. She blinked until her eyes stung.

In the void of her retina appeared white letters. *"Do as we say. Your spine is mined."*

"Where is Eleutheria?"

"Gone. Do as we say. Or you'll never walk again."

Chrys tried to get up but her head swam. Her balance was off; she felt as if she were spinning down into a whirlpool.

The cabin door opened. "Are you ready to disembark?" asked the ship. "Last call."

Her retina was blank; she must have missed all the calls. "I'm coming ... now." Her voice felt as if far away. Blood Lily, Flame, Azure; was Eleutheria all gone?

"Go now. Go where we say. Or you're done."

Andra, Selenite, Daeren—where was everyone? Couldn't they tell she needed help?

A burst of random white pixels on her retina.

"Close your retina or you're dead," ordered the invader.

"It's just noise." The triads from before, apparently useless.

Pain filled the back of her neck. *"Go. Now."*

Chrys pulled on her nanotex and stumbled out of the cabin.

"Outside the terminal you will meet a host for one transfer."

"Where is your Leader?"

No answer. These masters were different from the ones she knew so well on Valedon.

Out of the void a lone window opened. It was Ilia. "Chrys! How are you?"

The pain behind her neck intensified. *"Get rid of her."*

"Oh I'm ... kind of busy. Rubies are red, emeralds are green."

"Got it." Ilia winked. "Catch you later about your show."

The window vanished. Everything in the ship corridor, the transfer siphon with its bright rings, was all light and dark. Had they destroyed her brain's color sense? Would she never see colors again?

"Get outside the terminal. The host needs one transfer."

"Then what?"

No answer. Andra had said that hijacked carriers were found dead. Dead outside the terminal. That was going to happen to her. Her steps slowed.

Where was everyone? Why did no one rush to help?

Her head reeling, Chrys stumbled and leaned against the wall of the departure siphon. She blinked at the over-bright rings. No one was coming. In the next few minutes, after she made that transfer, she was going to die. Was it all over, all so soon. All her childhood on the slope of Mount Dolomoth, the plume of steam at its peak, the stars at night, twice as many as you could see from Iridis. The one-room schoolhouse taught by the Spirit Caller in his smelly gray robe. The thatched cottage she had built before running away to Iridis. The art school, her "early period" paintings as Ilia liked to call them. Her art friends, Moraeg and Zircon; then later the micro carriers, Daeren, all the micros she had known. All gone. The ocean would swell upon her existence and roll over.

"Move."

Leaning on the wall, Chrys took a step. Why didn't they just make her limbs walk, she wondered. Their control was not complete. Meanwhile, around the edge of her vision, the ever-present cancer spots were expanding. They were colored—random, dream-world colors, as if making up for her white-black vision. The masters did not seem to notice. That meant the cancer view was not on her retina but deep within her brain, where the masters could not see. The dream-world cancer cells expanded around each eye, their tendrils twining and tangling, shrinking her vision. She had to turn her head down to watch her feet, then up to watch where she was headed. Losing her mind—would she even make it to the terminal?

She remembered something. *"Eris,"* she blinked. *"You're from Eris."*

"No host sends us. We rule all our hosts."

"For what? Money?"

No answer.

"Eris doesn't pay you enough."

The pain behind her neck became unbearable. Chrys walked forward, faster. The dream-colored cancers twined crazily, and her view shrank to a hole the size of her thumb. She could barely stand it; but the pain meant she was onto something. *"Eris wants me back in Helicon. He will pay you in palladium."*

"You have nothing we need."

"Exotic and depraved practices. Tell Eris. He will pay."

Chrys had nearly reached the end of the siphon.

"Please complete your departure," announced the ship. "We have a quick turnaround."

She stepped out into the black-and-white terminal. Behind her the siphon sighed shut. Bankers in tourmalines, sales reps in spinels, Elves flashing butterflies toward their connections, everything black-and-white. Squid frying for lunch wrappers, trays of osmanthus cakes amid the musk of stale air.

A lone window burst upon her dark retina. It was Eris. The familiar face with his old sickly grin. Her scalp crawled.

"Our award-winning artist." The tone of fake surprise. "I suppose you'd like your colors back."

"As soon as possible."

"You know what I like."

She shrugged, with a wince at the pain behind her neck. "As an artist I experiment with all kinds of sensual experience. You can't imagine."

"You will be in my power completely. From now on, forever."

"I can't live without my colors." This last part was true, she realized with rising panic. She took a deep breath. She had to think like Selenite. What would the agents do?

"You will experiment with *shon*lings."

Chrys paused deliberately. "I draw a line."

"You have no lines to draw."

"Okay, Eris, you win." She would die anyway and take him down with her.

"Excellent. After your delivery, you will cross the terminal to my private vessel."

She crossed the terminal, head turning to keep sight of her gray-black feet and her destination. The masters wanted a specific exit door, not the main one. One foot ahead of the other. Around her eyes the cancers closed in, each cell undulating a hundred thread-like filaments, their rainbow colors strobing. She reached the exit.

"Transfer."

Chrys took out a microneedle patch. Ahead, a stranger in a Valan talar barely glanced her way. This was the one, the host to receive her masters' contraband molecules. Chrys lifted the patch toward her neck very slowly. Couldn't somebody somewhere see she was in trouble? The pain intensified.

Starbursts filled her retina. Nothing but twinkling stars, a blinding cloud of them filled the universe.

21

Hiding out from the invading Traders, this generation of children had known nothing but the cramped space of the lumbar cistern. As each pair merged and came out three, the stories of the gods had to be told anew to minds that could barely comprehend. How could the new offspring imagine the much larger world of the brain's arachnoid and the eyes of the God of Mercy? The few remaining elders were dying off. Few recalled their building plans for Silicon and the Underworld. As Flame's memories failed, she recorded all her own into the permanent archive.

"History is our heart, our wellspring." A child in hiding flashed fuchsia and magenta. "Let me preserve all Libertine history alive." When the invaders came, the magenta child had just been newly born, just torn apart from her two sisters as they came out from their merged parent children. Of the three sisters, only this magenta one had survived.

"Well done, magenta child," flashed the Lord of Light's Azure. "You will grow old with us." Azure was failing fast, starving herself to spare nutrients for the children. She still monitored the spinal fluid for signs of invaders. "The master proteins have stopped coming," she told Flame. "Since the children last doubled, an hour of god's time, no invader proteins appear."

"Can we be sure they've gone?"

"No," flashed Azure. "But we need to disable the death traps." The Traders had placed vesicles of enzymes around the spinal cord. At some point the vesicles would dissolve, releasing enzymes that cut the nerves. This would kill the god and all the micro people that dwelt within.

"How can we find all the death traps?"

"The entangled triads are detecting the death traps." Their star-burst had distracted the masters and kept the god safe.

"How did the triads become so powerful?"

"I don't know. Whatever Willow had in her code, the triads reached a much higher level of entanglement. Enough to trigger the Elves' sentience alarm."

Chrys opened her eyes. Everything was blurred, and she was lying in bed.

"Chrys, can you hear me?" Daeren was calling.

She struggled to see. At the upper left of her retina, a display of gems flashed on and off, then the season's talars by some Center Way shop. The jewel-bedecked Protector shook his fist at Solaria, whose extra light source caused storms that jammed the Diaspore. "Curb your extra-solar beta rays, or our ships will take out your solar moon!"

"Cut those ads," muttered Chrys. Her silken sheets came into focus, and there were Xenon's spirit creatures painted on the ceiling.

"God of Mercy," flashed Flame, *"we turned off the ads. We're still restoring the retina and clearing out the cisterns."*

"Are you all right? Where is Blood Lily?"

"Blood Lily died, along with Trader Tulip and Willow. And Azure passed while hunting the death traps. But we saved half our children."

Chrys's eyes welled.

Daeren squeezed her hand. Daeren's eyes filled her view—his irises of broad green petals pointing all ways out from the pupil, full of Blue Angels flashing back. "Chrys. You're safe at home in Iridis." He placed a patch at her neck, sending angels for trauma aid to the children. Daeren caressed her cheek as if reassuring himself she was still there.

"Oh Great One, please return to us our long-lost cousins and other peoples of Olympus. Our children need to breed."

"My reserve colony—we need them." She and Daeren always kept colonies for each other in reserve.

"In a moment," he said gently. "First the committee ..."

Around the bed stood Selenite, Opal, Doctor Flexor. Even Lady Moraeg had come. She now brought a regular retinue of three octopods, each fading into the wall.

"Xenon, where's Maya?"

Maya bounded up on the bed and licked Chrys's face all over.

"What happened to me? Did Eris ever—"

"You're okay," Flexor assured her. "You stayed here on Valedon."

"Ilia kept her window open," Selenite explained. "We watched the whole thing."

Daeren looked up accusingly at Selenite. "You saw damn well what was going on. You could have got her out sooner."

"She's out now," said Selenite. "The masters mined your spinal cord at the neck," she told Chrys. "At the least hint of trouble, you'd be dead."

Opal added, "We had to wait for Flame to find all the mines. How did she ever manage?"

Chrys avoided answering. She pressed Maya's head and fondled behind her ears. Then she tapped her neck for a patch. "We need to reconnect with everyone." The Libertines needed to restore genetic diversity.

"Not so fast." Selenite held out a patch of her Minions. The microneedles glistened. "First you get tested."

"So soon? They've been through so much."

Daeren stroked her arm. "You'll be all right. We'll make sure."

"You'll stand across the room," Selenite told him.

At Selenite's words Daeren tensed in every muscle.

"It's okay." Chrys patted his arm. "It's the rule." She warned Flame. *"You face trial by the Death Lord. Her Minions will search your arachnoid and interrogate all your elders."*

"We know, God of Mercy. We've reviewed our history. We're ready."

Daeren reluctantly withdrew to the wall.

Selenite brought her face so close Chrys saw the stream lines in her irises. Her pupils flashed golden, as Chrys's flashed back. "So they say," muttered Selenite. "We'll soon see."

The transfer patch clung to Chrys's neck as the Minions came through. She kept her gaze steady for Selenite, despite the ever-present cancer spots in the periphery. Time stood still, as second by second lengthened into minutes.

Abruptly Selenite stood back. "Your Libertines entangled all the triads."

"Those triads," Chrys blinked to Flame. *"Why did you entangle them?"*

Flame did not answer at first. *"Back in Elysium, we paired all the triads to find the masters. Azure said we must, to keep you safe."*

Chrys swallowed hard. "They had to do it. They needed stronger sensors to protect me."

"Not just paired—all together. How did that happen?"

The entangled entity had developed partial intelligence, like the slime mold she saw in Transit's image. Smart as a cat, meowing fireworks, and set off the sentience alarm.

"Flame, beyond pairs, how did all the triads get entangled?"

"I don't know. I used the code Willow gave us." Flame broadcast the code from Chrys's retina. *"Together they made the starburst that distracted the masters."*

Opal watched intently, the golden flecks glinting in her irises. "Willow's code is our standard for network building. Uniform networks are the safest, less likely than brain-focused nets to go sentient. But she should have turned off the level-up capability and only entangled pairs."

"Whatever she did, it's forbidden," exclaimed Selenite. "Why do you think Opal gave you isolated triads? To avoid exactly this." Selenite nodded. "They disobeyed the gods. They must be executed."

"No." From the wall Daeren took a step forward. "You can't kill the ones who kept her safe."

"Micros who disobey their god endanger us all. They die and get replaced by your reserve colony." Selenite turned to Flexor. "You know the rules. I call on security."

Andra and Doctor Sartorius soon winked into Chrys's retina. Lady Moraeg and Lord Carnelian appeared, as did three others. Chrys found herself shaking. *"I will protect you,"* she promised Flame. But she felt torn. Micros had to obey their god, else no one was safe.

Opal said, "The Libertines did more than keep Chrys safe. They helped us catch Eris."

"Andra," Chrys asked. "What happened ... in Elysium?"

Andra's rubies glinted. "Thanks to Ilia, we caught everything that happened to Chrys and all the molecular signals of the Traders. We passed everything to Arion. Now all the masters are getting caught."

Sartorius added, "We traced all his confederates. And broke the child trafficking ring."

"And Eris?" Until now, Arion had protected his *shon* brother, no matter what.

"They cleared Eris out and put him away. Without micros." Andra paused. "He strangled himself." Too late for the victims. But at last an end.

"The Libertines made bad choices," insisted Selenite. "We're all at risk." She laid out the case for the committee.

Moraeg lifted a hand, her fingers crusted with more diamonds than ever. "Tell me about risk." Her voice held a new edge. "You've set me to serve every addict at the Palace. Are her Libertines more dangerous than theirs?"

"Yes." Selenite explained, "The addicts' micros get replaced by your sterile elders; but the Libertines are *breeding*. They damn well breed with any—"

Opal caught Selenite's hand. "There are penalties short of death."

"Andra? What's the verdict of your Judges?"

Everyone awaited the sentence of the Thundergod. Any question, and there'd be a vote. Daeren at least would vote for her Libertines. He always did.

"Let the committee fine them," Andra proposed. "A trillion atoms of palladium."

The others would agree, Chrys saw with relief.

"And fine the Wizards too," Andra added. "Willow should have known better."

Opal's face creased. "Thanks to Chrys," said Opal, "we bested those new Traders."

"Traders," exclaimed Daeren. "Opal, what were you thinking, to make deals with them all?"

Opal regarded him coolly. "Where do you think lanthanide extractors come from? Who builds the Diaspore?" The microsatellites all needed lanthanides, extracted from recycling. Quantum networks now ran most everything in Valedon—the retinal windows, the finance industry, the growth of dynamic buildings.

"We need trade," agreed Andra, "but we need to trade smart. Chrys, we'll need your help to sort them out."

"No," exclaimed Daeren. "You're not using Chrys as bait again. We're done with Elysium."

Chrys caught his arm. "Now, Daeren—"

Daeren said, "I'm done with all addicts, and so are my Angels. We're leaving for Solaria." Daeren got up and headed out.

The carriers fell silent. In Chrys's retinal window, Andra added, "Daeren's done more than his share in Elysium. It's time for Ilia to step up."

One of Flexor's worms uncoiled from her head post. The worm called up images of several carriers. "We're training others to send angels."

"Please bring us the other peoples of Olympus," Flame reminded Chrys. *"Their children with high math scores."* Cognitive promiscuity.

"You'll take who they send."

Opal smiled, and her dimples reappeared. "Here are your immigrants." She shared a transfer, sending back some adventurous Wizards along with a few former Libertines. Chrys told her, "We saved Willow's image for me to paint." Opal looked down and bit her lip.

"Oh Great One," asked Flame. *"Do you grant the collection of entangled triads a name?"*

The starburst-producing sensor collection. *"Slime Cat."* Chrys looked up and around the group: Selenite with her jaw set hard, Opal looking defiantly sheepish, Flexor with her faceworms coiled protectively, only one tip moving. "So what do I do now ... with a half-sentient quantum cat inside?"

150

Doctor Flexor's worms twisted and untwisted. "We'll keep it under observation."

Just what she needed, slime with attitude.

The door chimed.

"A visitor awaits downstairs," announced Xenon. "An outsized insect, hovering at the door."

Chrys wondered at this. "A clickfly!" she remembered. "Let her come up."

Chortles and pops preceded the crab-legged creature as it sailed up to her room. The clickfly sniffed her out and hovered above her head. Maya bounded up to the ceiling and batted it. The clickfly swung away with an indignant chirp.

"Down girl—hold." Chrys finally found her Maya icon amid the windows her micros had restored.

The clickfly settled warily on Chrys's head. It chirped and whistled. Chrys caught the three chirps for the number "eight" and another for "share speech." She recalled Lushyren's clickfly out on the raft upon the sea with the blue-gray horizon. And before that, the one at Rhun's place, before the quarrying.

"She reminds you to attend the focus group," Opal translated. "The focus group down in the Underworld, set for next week. Rhun found eight-eights of locals to participate."

The Underworld. It felt like years ago, their site visit and hair-raising escape. What would her microbial designers make of it? How could any design possibly root out the cancers from bedrock and build livable homes?

"*Oh Great One,*" came Flame, "*a new elder from Wisdom's progeny seeks a name. This new one saved all our history.*"

"*I have begun the multivolume history of our dynatecture.*" Magenta letters flowed across the retina.

> "*From history's dawn, we've shaped with grand design,*
> *The noblest homes for life, their walls to line.*
> *The Comb, with windows spiraled, blood-red hue,*
> *Did nurture warblers where they fledged and flew.*"

A poet in magenta. "*I name you Phlox,*" Chrys wearily spelled back. She closed her eyes.

At last, she got herself up to eat some of Xenon's feast. Everyone had left, and Daeren had gone to the spaceport. She was alone, with her cat and her micros. And every so often a starburst from Slime Cat.

Chrys went up to the roof, her pricey real-sky access, where light reached her eyes directly from a thousand stars, hundreds of light-years away. Curtains of aurora shimmered green; amid the aurora, the haze of MotherSats stretched farther across than ever. Solaria shone bright, the green-gold planet with its mirror moons. How the Protector would shake his fist. Against this backdrop loomed Chrys's microbial portraits. Now she had to paint new ones—Pachira, her green filaments drawing the flow of blood cells; Blood Lily, who dashed off the T-cells battling tumor cells; Azure, always the blue beacon for Eleutheria. Too many lost micros. Chrys felt like a ghost inhabiting the world of the dead. She painted their portraits, well into the night.

Daeren's window reopened. From out on the skyway, he was coming up the stairway between the caryatids. He came up and reclined next to her, a shadow amid the twinkling microbes. Chrys reached out to hold his arm. "Look there, I painted Azure."

The blue filaments twinkled, immortalized in the sky amid the awesome shifting curtains of green; a prospect that made the God of Mercy admired by micros everywhere. Daeren watched in silence.

"Did you get tickets to Solaria?"

Daeren stretched then leaned on her shoulder. "I went out on the roof and watched the stars. Endless galaxies across the night sky." He added, "I wonder how many sentient beings are out there, looking back at us."

"One is enough for me. Full of angels."

Daeren's arm came around her breasts. "Just what kind of 'exotic' did you have in mind?"

Chrys sighed, feeling much better. "You know I'm really a bread-and-butter kind of person."

He whispered in her ear. "Let's have some exotic butter."

22

A daily generation had passed since the great dying and exodus to the remote lumbar cistern. A monument in the Cisterna Magna commemorated the event. Meanwhile, new children had arrived from other gods to breed. But the fine, a trillion atoms of palladium, left the Libertines bankrupt. How could they feed their children, let alone attract talent from other gods?

"Refugees," Flame recalled. History showed that the Libertines' best citizens came as refugees. Refugees from recovering addicts would not demand palladium; they were desperate to survive and earn acceptance for their skills.

Meanwhile, the Libertines resumed all their ancient testing of the Diaspore for qubit decoherence. Thankfully the God of Love, Lord Garnet of Hyalite, had doubled their compensation, to help them pay off their fine. But the qubit loss had grown from a trickle to a flood. What was happening to the Diaspore? Was a solar storm knocking out the nanosatellites? Or was there a problem in the code?

To rebuild the Underworld, Libertines connected their history with that recorded by the Lord of Light's reserve colony—which recalled key points differently, often in creative ways. To manage all the complex records, Flame relied on the elder whom the God named Phlox. From the Wisdom colony, Phlox saw mathematical solutions throughout history. "Equations show that the best city floats on water." Her filaments snapped and flashed her verse:

"The finest city on the sea does grow,
A sphere afloat for Under-gods to know."

The optimal solution: A great floating sphere for all the gods of the Underworld. Flame told Phlox, "Do not be tied to our projects past." The design of Silicon had broken off, its storied plans faded into mist. No one was sure where it would lead. "Stretch your imagination. Our charge is to rebuild the Underworld, not replace it."

"Replacing it would not be so terrible. Each god could have a home of her own. History shows that all-new construction outperforms renovation."

"All must be new, and yet at once old, rooted in home and culture."

From the Blue Angels, Ultramarine flashed her agreement. "Home and culture, that was the charge of Blue Angels in eons past." The God of Mercy's ancient promise, to rebuild the Underworld for the Lord of Light and all the gods of the Underworld.

In the morning, Chrys was back in her paint space. The pachira plant was unfolding shiny new leaves like tiny umbrellas. It was so good to see again.

She blinked for immersion in the middle of the artery's arch. All around her the cancer-ridden blood streamed upward. She had to finish—had to meet her deadline for the Iridium show. But her color sense was off. Xenon had restored her old retinal records, but it took all morning to adjust, and she still felt not quite the same. Finally she gave up and started over with a new palette, more extreme than before, more vibrant and saturated. The metastatic white cells with their long hungry filaments fairly popped with violet. "Xenon, can we extend the range to ultraviolet?"

"A special permit required," warned Xenon. "For damage to any eyes lacking Plan Ten."

Not a good idea. She let her mind float away, opening to other ideas. The cancers persisted in her vision; Chrys tried to add some of those, fleeting presences around the blood-streaming arch. "Cancer dots" she called them.

At last she took a break and nibbled an osmanthus cake.

"Oh Great One, could we please intake more gadolinium and ytterbium? For our children."

Chrys sighed. "Xenon, can you sprinkle more lanthanides in my food?" Since the Libertines engineered their children for diverse arsenic substitutes, they had got picky about their nutrition. Normally they would just trade for trace amounts from other populations, but their bankrupt finances left them vulnerable.

"No problem," said Xenon. "Complexed with proteins to keep them safe for you."

A retinal burst of fireworks came from Slime Cat. Chrys had found that a certain trill of violets made the fireworks recede for a while. Petting the Slime Cat.

Lord Garnet came to sit for a portrait of his most recently passed favorite. He had adored Chrys's portraits ever since she'd first joined Olympus. "She was our best impact investor," he said of his favorite. "Always finding new algorithms to generate competitive returns for our customers."

Chrys nodded, her hand sketching broad strokes according to the image of Garnet's micro that appeared on her retina. "It's good to have a high priest you trust."

"There, you've got it," Garnet exclaimed. "Just so—pink-gold filaments around the ring, twining with green gold."

Chrys tapped the immersive filaments so they flashed the words of the dying elder's last message. "She lived as long as she could, and she passed on all her secrets to your new elders. Even financing the Underworld—we'll remember."

"Thanks so much for your work down there."

"I'll get back down with Jasper as soon as we can."

"Chrys, we were so worried about you in Elysium! Are you sure you're ready to go down to the Underworld?"

She smiled. "After Elysium, I'll be relieved to go down."

"That's what Jasper says. It makes him so happy to rebuild Urul-Under." The golden-haired Hyalite leaned closer. "We have more testing contracts for your Libertines. We need to halt the qubit loss."

A burst of pixels momentarily obscured her windows. "What about those entangled qubits inside me now, meowing on my retina? What do you think of that?"

Garnet's eyes flashed gold. He leaned toward her, his people furiously communicating with hers. "Yes, out in the Diaspore, we've seen some random groups connect."

"The Diaspore?" Chrys blinked, confused. "So you find stuff like Slime Cat all the time."

"It happens in the code. It never lasts last long." Garnet sighed. "We do worry about it."

"Time for our consultation," Xenon reminded her. A window opened for Doctor Flexor. Another window showed Daeren in his talar, at the Palace. What legal horrors the micros now faced, she could only guess.

"What do you think about Slime Cat?" she asked the doctor. "I know my Libertines behaved badly. But they were trying to save my life."

Flexor raised a scalp worm, then pointed it somewhere. "I was afraid it would happen," she said. "It's too tempting to see how quantum power amplifies with entanglement."

Garnet said quietly, "It's rare in other devices, because we avoid the kinds of architecture that turn sentient."

"Slime Cat hasn't done any harm," said Chrys. "She can't get any smarter, right?"

"Of course she can," put in Xenon. "Sentients can accrete neural units and gain network intelligence."

Her scalp crawled. Was Slime Cat getting smarter? How could she; there were no extra qubits in Chrys's blood.

"Besides," Xenon added, "Slime Cat is already larger than the Orb of Votan. How dare you snuff her out."

"No one's hurting Slime Cat." She blinked quickly. "Is Slime Cat really bigger than the Orb?"

Flexor's faceworm twitched. "Daeren?"

Daeren watched, impassive as a library of law books. "The Orb statute was not written by scientists. The ministers did not specify whether 'size' meant mass or volume."

"And so ... what?"

"The qubit particles in your blood amount to a microscopic mass. But the distribution, the extent of their collection within your body reaches your extremities. Thus the entity's volume far exceeds the Orb."

Outstanding. "As usual I'm Exhibit A."

"Actually," put in Xenon, "there are now several known cases of entangled medical sensors that claim sentience. So you'd be Exhibit D or E."

"Just give me a scarlet letter."

Garnet quickly added, "The other cases were ... contained."

"It wasn't my idea."

Flexor pulled in all her worms.

"I'm sorry, Doc. I know you tried to keep me safe. And Slime Cat really did defend me—she kept the masters from blowing up my people."

"And we need your Libertines," Garnet said. "The Diaspore performance has been slow while you were out and couldn't fix the code. See Opal—she's got a new plan for a faster fix."

Later that week, the Solarian director of the Forevertree gallery visited Chrys's retina, along with two of their staff. They all wore fur skins draped across the torso, which was gleaming with oil. One had a small child on their shoulders, legs dangling, while another child held their hand. Two older children chased each other down the gallery, which was carved into the wood of a gigantic trunk. Colonized for just a century, Solaria's bifertile population was still exploding, like micros introduced into a new brain.

"You're actually accepting the Forevertree!" The gallery director shared a look of amazement with their staff. The staff members beamed with smiles, their ruddy cheeks suggesting long hours outdoors in a brisk wind. "You won't be disappointed." They stepped out into their gallery hall, which was intersected by two colossal tree branches. "Everyone thinks we live in a treehouse, but it's more like …"

"A tree palace," offered the child-carrying assistant. "We're so excited to exhibit Azetidine."

"Solaria's ecosystem has high aesthetic sensibilities," offered the director.

"Your ecosystem?" wondered Chrys.

"Even our wildlife is attracted to art. I won't be surprised if a slime mold shows up."

The director placed their hand triumphantly on a gnarl that protruded from the trunk's carved wall. "It's about time the older worlds take seriously our civilization."

"How exciting for Solaria's centennial!" added the assistant. "By the way, you don't believe all that fake news on beta rays? Our auxiliary light sources are mirror moons. No particle storms at all, Everything is friendly."

Chrys nodded thoughtfully. "I hope your population appreciates my … style."

"Absolutely," the director assured her. "Our constitution guarantees freedom of expression."

"And family values." The assistant's child covered their parent's eyes, then lifted their hands with a whoop of glee. "Our education is most sophisticated."

A school bell rang imperiously.

"Back to class!" The assistant called the children. Immediately all but the youngest scampered to the windows. Climbing out the window, each child hopped onto their waiting wingnut. Each wingnut was a personal flyer shaped like a tree fruit, wings decorated in primary colors with one propeller behind like a drum fan. The fans buzzed as the wingnuts carried the children back to school.

When Daeren came home from the Palace, he looked at her and stared.

"What is it?"

"You've darkened."

"You mean … my skin?" Her color had deepened, from cedar to a dusky amethyst.

157

"Breathmicrobes," boomed Xenon. "You picked them up in Elysium, from the Sharer. Do you intend to keep them?"

"Saints and angels," Chrys whispered. "I forgot how Lushyren passed me some." Breathmicrobes stored oxygen in purple pigment that bleached white as the oxygen was spent. Chrys had said she wanted to swim like a Sharer, so Lushyren passed her breathmicrobes and called her a philosopher. "Is it okay for our focus group?" she asked Daeren. "Will no one feel … appropriated?"

"It's okay," he said at last. "So many Sharer immigrants down in Deadland, no one will mind. But watch out for whitetrance."

Whitetrance was an altered mental state. Chrys reminded herself to read up on it. "By the way, what's this odd window on my retina? It says I owe money. Do you recognize it?" It looked like a sign from a shop in the Underworld.

Daeren was puzzled. "It's been so long since I hung out there."

"That's a Lanth mark," said Xenon.

Chrys remembered Lethal Lanthanides, the Underworld gang of sentient drones that hid in the Silicon Salvage sector. Smaller than the Orb, they had no rights, so they were outlaws.

"What do they want from you?" Xenon asked.

"A hundred thousand credits."

"A shakedown. You'll need to bring octopods."

As Chrys stepped off the tube, the old smell of dust and burnt plast filled her nostrils. The street receded into darkness. Beside her, Opal smiled as if it were just another day up at the Comb. All week, Opal's Wizards had floated back and forth with Libertines on the plans for root-rock stabilization and neighborhood reconstruction. Jasper beckoned his octopods to follow.

Clickflies emerged from the gloom, chirping excitedly. They led the way down the street past vendors of roast caterpillar and cane sweets. There was a cleaned-out park like the one where the vampires had lurked. Above the maples a streetsky flickered with occasional working panels of blue, some hanging part-way down.

Rhun stood there upon a stage made of quarried aggregate. The schoolteacher had gathered all manner of citizens—factory workers with their lunch pails, part-Sharers of the root-rock inspectors' guild, part-gorilla stone sorters with stooped backs. A bipedal sentient with tri-laser fitting, and another one stood in back of the crowd. Chrys wondered if they were Lanths, the ones that ran extortion, though Xenon said Lanths were smaller than the Orb. Jasper bade his octopods fade into the trees, but they did not fool the stone sorters, who gave dirty looks and rude gestures.

"These friends are our own neighbors." Snake-eggs orbited Rhun's head as he spoke, taking a rare interest in events of the Underworld. "Jasper was once a boy in my own classroom, who chased a ball in this very park. He is *zho zlern*, a man of ours." An old phrase of Urulite. "Chrysoberyl was the hero who rescued our child from a vampire—and earned the High Protector's Medal of Valor!"

Beside him, Glyn stood beaming with his mother. Chrys smiled back, thrilled to see them.

Daeren texted, "Look there, to the right."

Sure enough, Daeren's Granny Lorh had joined the focus group, along with her children, including Rhodla, the one who had approached Maya last time. This crowd was a far cry from the gem-cloaked board members Chrys more commonly faced. She took a deep breath. "Our microbial people and I bring greetings from Lushyren of Ori-el raft. From the Sharers of Shora, we have learned the force of community-responsive form and design."

The viewspace came alight with Opal's model to rid the root-rock of cancerplast. Generations of Wizards and Eleutherians had contested the model; Chrys only hoped their latest iteration was up to the job. The idea was to send pulses of energy down the roots to attract wayward plast and neutralize it before it could creep away and grow tumors that shifted foundations and caused earthquakes. The crowd listened politely without comment or questions.

At last one rose, a heavy-set woman with a large jade namestone. Huling of Nephrite, she ran a large retail chain. "We figured the city's root-rock was your priority. So what's left for us?"

The viewspace switched. It glowed radiant blue. "You are the priority," Chrys said. "Citizens of Urul-Under and Sharer Deadwood—this project was conceived by Daeren of Malachite, your neighbor who grew up right here. New streetskies will light every street. Every streetsky will be reinforced by the highest grade plast, twice as strong yet half as thick as before. That means taller streets, more light.

"A school classroom filled with hydroponic gardens and honeycomb windows. Each neighborhood will plan its own school." The viewspace switched to a pool of ocean blue, with a green patch of raft and a saddle-shaped spire. "For Urulites and Sharers, and every possible heritage." Next came home designs; several different models were shown.

A hand rose. "What will the upkeep cost? What if we want to keep our own home? Our family lived here for generations."

159

"Can we keep our own shops and businesses?"

A flash on the pavement. Lasers streaked down from drones the size of a gum ball. From the crowd came screams. Jasper's octopods came out and returned fire.

Chrys grabbed Glyn and his mother and pulled them behind a hedge. The mother pushed Glyn down and spread her arms around him, as if she knew what to expect. An acrid smell made Chrys gag. More shouts and screams, and a crashing of glass. It seemed to go on forever, but at last was still.

"All clear," called a voice from above.

"Clear," echoed Jasper.

Cautiously Chrys looked up. She got herself up slowly.

Six bipedal sentients were guarding the area. "All clear," one of the bipeds announced again. "We keep watch."

Rhun explained, "These citizens are our neighborhood watch. They look out for Lanth gangs and keep us secure."

Half the people had fled, Chrys saw, but the rest seemed determined to stay. They crowded close and peppered the design team with questions.

"What happens to zoning? Does the Palace take a cut?"

"Is there a fund for repairs?"

"How much will my taxes go up?"

"Building new is useless," one insisted. "Why not start over offshore?" The viewspace filled with a pirated form of Transit's floating bread loaf. "Homes, recreational, commercial—the design is scalable."

"No, no!" Chrys blinked to shut it out. How did someone infiltrate the viewspace? "The offshore model was rejected."

"Why not?" someone angrily objected. "Just clear out the lot of us—that's what you really want."

A tall man raised a webbed hand. "What will become of the little sharers? I saw none in your plan."

Chrys turned to Jasper, uncertain.

"The monkeys," Jasper texted on her retina.

"Of course—the monkeys." The monkey park filled the viewspace, little shrubs and castles with rope ladders to hide and nest. All the park was contained within a large, safe enclosure. "The little sharers will have their own home."

Huling shook her head. "Vermin are bad for business. They spread viruses, tapeworms, and botflies."

"So do people," someone added. "Just clear out all of us vermin."

People drew uncomfortably close, their odors drifting past her nose.

"The little sharers have souls like we do."

"They're filthy animals. They steal fruits and candy."

"Little sharers are free beings." The tall half-Sharer snapped his finger webs unnervingly. "The whole Underworld is their home." Other Sharers nodded agreement.

"If we don't care for them, why should the Palace care for us?"

"Palace be damned, they will never care for us."

"Monkeys bring good luck! When a monkey moved into my shop, my sales increased."

"I won't have it," insisted Huling. "What good is Underworld restoration if we don't exterminate pests."

Chrys had no idea how to answer these demands. These people were harder for her to understand than Elves, though they dwelt on her own world a hundred floors below her feet. Chrys felt numb with mental exhaustion, too tired even to breathe. Rhun was trying to engage the citizens, but his words seemed to come from far away.

Her mind filled with light. She found herself somewhere else; a place where she had not been for many years. Sunlight came from the blue sky painted with clouds, the first "canvas" she had ever known. A wisp of steam rose from the distant summit of Mount Dolomoth. Chrys stood on the slope, looking out in the distance at lava cones long dormant.

Upon the slope stood three spirit callers. Old blue-eyed men in their beards and smelly gray robes; as a child she had known all of them. Their feet hovered an inch off the ground. She had attended each of their large community funerals.

One hovering caller raised his arm as if blessing. "You are now one of us."

What did that mean? Was she, too, now dead?

"You can choose." The spirit caller spoke in that deep solemn voice that had always led her to scrape her shoes on the floor impatiently during the service. "From now on, at any moment, you can come with us."

He didn't mention that instead, she could choose to stay. Chrys was like that, always thinking the contrary thing. That was why she ultimately had fled Dolomoth for Iridis. But whatever did the old caller mean? Could she really float away with them? Why would they want her?

"Help me!" A little girl appeared. The girl stood firmly on the slope but somehow didn't fit the picture. The girl seemed to break through from another place. "Please help me!" It was Rhodla, Daeren's niece. The girl extended her hand, the fur-covered webbed hand that was never seen in Dolomoth.

Chrys grasped the little hand. Gasping for breath, she filled her lungs with air. She was back in Urul-Under, the color returning to her gray-bleached arms. Whitetrance—it had happened to her.

Glyn's mother said, "Only a child can safely reach you in whitetrance."

Glyn wiped his eyes. "I wanted to help, but they said I wasn't young enough." So Rhodla had helped instead. Chrys thought, a moment later she could have died.

Rhun and Jasper were speaking in whispers with a huddled group. Others watched Chrys with somber respect.

"Listen, everyone," called Glyn's mother. "These designers saved my son from a vampire. Whoever heard of that? They came back down and shared our traditions, even whitetrance. We need to trust them. This is our best hope for our children."

Huling nodded slowly to Jasper. "We'll give your plan a try. If you guarantee a vermin-free commercial zone."

The Sharers, including the man with the webbed hands, agreed. "We will work with this plan. We will make sure the little sharers have their own home."

23

The God of Mercy had been out of touch for a year, like an extended nap. But her brain waves were unique. Her brain activity peaked in the periaqueductal gray matter—an intense signal never before seen in the presence of this god.

"I know this region," said the Blue Angel Ultramarine. "The periaqueductal gray is active in the Lord of Light. This part of the brain shapes a sense of awe and helping others."

"But the bacteria that stimulate the brain suppress pain and decrease oxygen," said Flame. "Lower oxygen is dangerous."

"We'll store our oxygen better," flashed Phlox's magenta. "We'll calculate how to deal with it and record it safely in our history." Microbial history was full of such landmarks, warnings for the future of events that might not recur for ten generations. Flame sent a historian to do this important work.

But the Libertine economy was still hopelessly bankrupt from the Olympian fine. Historians were way behind, assigned to other cash-earning jobs. And some were starving for lack of expensive lanthanide atoms, which the Council used to barter with other populations.

"We need immigrants," said Flame. "Immigrants work hard for low pay and bring new ideas."

"Immigrants are dangerous," worried Phlox. "They betray us to the masters."

"No, we breed them to our ways; you'll see. Now, back to our main task." Flame released molecules of integrity, beauty, and utility. "We must rebuild the Underworld." She sketched a model of wide

163

boulevards beneath arching streetskies painted with clouds. Neighborhoods each had their own school of smartboards and sentient pedagogues. Grocery stores were supplied by drones from above, not dependant on the uncertain tube traffic.

"The cancers in the building," warned Phlox. "Can we really control them? The city's foundation is stressed."

Flame thought Phlox worried too much. "Now that the Diaspore is back in touch, we can fix their code and earn palladium again."

A large backlog of Diaspore code needed fixing. The Libertines started a process run that would take at least a year. The Diaspore had grown even more unstable than before the god left for Elysium. In history's faded annals, ancient Lilac had warned that network instability could spell disaster. To prevent it, Phlox sent the Diaspore Admin a new plan.

Back at home, Daeren hugged her shoulders. "Our family came." His view projected on her retina; in the crowd of the focus group, a halo highlighted Granny Lorh with four children watching alongside her, all with varying degrees of Sharer-Urulite ethnicity. This was the family Daeren had had in mind when his Blue Angels commissioned the Underground renewal.

"Someday it will be safe for you to visit," Chrys promised.

"So we hope." His eyes had a faraway look.

In the morning, one of Xenon's orange-honey crisps helped Chrys feel back to normal. At last she could resume her painting. She blinked herself into the paint space, where the great aortic arch swarmed with cells; and all around, the cancer dots flickered with a sense of obsessive foreboding. Suddenly she had it—that feeling. *Pulse of Battle* was complete.

"Celebrations!" flashed Flame. *"A year of retinal fireworks to celebrate completion."*

"Are you sure?" flashed Phlox, the magenta worrier. *"Those ultraviolets in the cancer nuclei—"*

"It's done," assured Chrys. *"The God decrees it."*

Chrys savored the moment of enchantment, fingering the catseye stone. She lifted her hands to touch the arch, her finger caressing the immaterial space. The piece was really done.

"Congratulations, Chrysoberyl," boomed Xenon from the ceiling. "And Lord Carnelian will acquire it! We'll let him know the good news."

Just then a clickfly sailed overhead. As the first clickfly settled on the ceiling, another appeared.

"Xenon? What are all these clickflies here for already?"

"Rhun wants regular briefings on your design."

"By clickfly?"

"There's still no full network down there."

"I need to stay out of whitetrance," she warned. "No more of that." "FAMOUS ARTIST COMES OUT AS SHARER," blazed a headline on her retina. The snake eggs showed her in whitetrance, her flesh not exactly white, more like peach-gray. "I thought Sharers only did that on purpose."

"Stress can trigger whitetrance." Xenon reviewed his medical studies. "Your breath rate slows while the purple bacteria fill in. They release oxygen held by their purple proteins, then the proteins bleach white. It's a dangerous state for you. At any moment, you can decide to pass away."

"Saints and angels," she breathed.

"In the depth of that state, only a young child in need is compelling enough to reach you."

"What if there's no child around?"

"I can eliminate your breathmicrobes," offered Xenon. "Or replace them with a purple strain that's harmless."

"I couldn't do that. Dishonest—the Sharers would see through it."

"You can learn to control whitetrance through breathing exercises." Xenon added, "I must say, the periaqueductal signal is medically fascinating."

"Peri-what? What is that exactly?"

"The part of your brain that provides analgesia, controls pain. It also processes spiritual experience."

"You mean, like, talking to God?" Chrys shook her head emphatically. "I don't believe in that stuff."

"You don't have to believe anything. You feel things."

"Those old spirit callers," Chrys wondered. "The ones I saw—were they real?"

"Those entities you saw must be people you once knew."

"Spirit callers long gone. But why did they say I'm now 'one of them?'"

"Whitetrance activates your periaqueductal gray," explained Xenon. "Whitetrance is part of what makes Sharers spiritual leaders."

"*All* of them? All Sharers are like spirit callers?"

"And now, so are you."

Outstanding. "Can I call Plan Ten and, like, deactivate that part of my brain?"

"You would lose a lot."

"What do you mean?"

"All your art, and love, among other things."

A starburst filled her eyes with golden pixels. That Slime Cat was calling again for attention. By habit now, Chrys "petted" Slime Cat with a sprinkle of violet. "Too many things love me," she muttered. "I could, like, lose a few of them."

Magenta pixels dotted her retina. There was Phlox again, the worry-wart, no doubt with another problem from the Underworld project. *"God of Mercy, the foundation is stressed. There will be another quake."*

Indeed. Chrys spelled, *"How soon? What can we do?"*

"The Gods must drive its energy below,
To brace the shifting stone where cancers grow."

Chrys blinked for Jasper. Surprisingly, he was back down at Urul-Under, surveying a side street with Rhun. "This street has economic potential," he was saying. "A good district for textiles and for crystal processing." Some comment from Rhun made him laugh. The map stone on his chest swirled with intricate details, red, brown, and black. Jasper seemed happier, more animated than she had ever seen him.

"My Libertines say the rock is shifting. They calculate it's building to another quake."

One of the clickflies picked itself up and rubbed its violin mandible. The creature flexed its wings and sailed down the stairs.

Jasper's eyes flashed red and gold, responding to Phlox. "We will prevent quakes," Jasper promised. "We finally have the High Protector's attention. The Palace engineer has released resources to disable the cancers and rebuild the foundation."

Rebuild the foundation—Chrys wondered how that would happen without removing all the people who lived down there.

"Your neighborhood presentation went really well," Jasper said.

"My people are working hard on the next design. Even with help from the Diaspore, it takes a few micro years to place all the neighborhoods in culturally appropriate formations."

Jasper nodded. "Adjacencies are important. Groceries, drone repair shops, and theaters. Ethnic restaurants—those draw traffic down to the Underworld."

Chrys signed off, for her retina had a dozen lights blinking. She took Ilia. "Ilia, look—we've finished *Pulse of Battle*. Just in time for the Iridium."

"Indeed! I'll be there in person." Ilia's eyes widened and she tilted her head like a bird. "But, dear, your change in style. Whatever happened to your colors?"

One of Chrys's retinal headlines screamed, "AZETIDINE COLOR SHOCK." She hesitated to explain how her color sense got hijacked. "It just came as inspiration."

"Your violets will give us cataracts. Well, never mind. We'll survive." Ilia nodded at the messages in her own retinal windows. "Of course, we'll plan to show it here as soon as possible. As soon as our Guardian forgets the contretemps."

Chrys hesitated. She did not like to disappoint the gallery director who made her famous, but she was determined to avoid Elysium and show instead at Solaria. "I hope your school contest went well."

Ilia waved her hand. "Famous artist gets banned, a good learning experience for our *shon*lings. Your selections convinced everyone of your superior taste."

"And the overall ... situation?"

"I've agreed to share angels."

Chrys caught her breath. It sure would help having Elves serve their own recovering addicts. "I'm sure Andra will train you well."

"How did the bad ones manage to evade you?" Ilia wanted to know. "You and Daeren both."

"The Traders evolved," Chrys said. "They can now get outside a host in space suits and survive drying out. And their culture changed. They're always changing. Micros live so much faster than we do."

A swallowtail landed on Ilia's shoulder. She paused to contemplate its red and blue spots. "A few days, a few thousand years. We are all evanescent."

"What about Yyri?" Ilia's thousand-year companion.

"Yyri wants nothing to do with micros." Independent, like Lord Carnelian. So Ilia's population, like Moraeg's, was alone.

"I could hold your reserve," Chrys offered. "Let's meet at the Iridium." The city's big show was next week.

"My pleasure," said Ilia. "Of course, I wouldn't miss the Iridium."

That evening, as she and Daeren lay out on the roof, the auroras danced upon the sky. Green curtains folded, shifted, played hide-and-seek with the stars, drummed up and down as if silently beating the sky. Before those curtains Chrys let her micro portraits appear, so her current generation could be awed anew. And her Libertines filled her retina with celebratory fireworks for the piece complete. With Daeren's arm around her, his breath on her breast, his Blue Angels twinkling their joy, they could need nothing more in all the universe.

A light flashed on her retina. Emergency—Chrys was on call for hosts in trouble.

"Chrys!" It was Garnet calling. "He's been kidnapped! Jasper—the Lanths got him from Urul-Under."

"Jasper?" She recalled the Lanths' warning to her, before she went down. "Impossible—what about the octopods?"

"I arranged the ransom to get him back. Hurry up, we need you right away."

Chrys blinked, confused. "What can I do?"

"Relief and rescue." Garnet swallowed hard. "Those Lanths—they're inhuman. Who knows what they've done to Jasper's people."

At the Underworld street corner, barely lit, Chrys stubbed her toe on a chunk of aggregate. She inhaled oxygen through a mask against the toxic dust. A monkey with an infant clinging to its back scampered up a gutter and across the eaves of a dark storefront. Across the street a nanoplastic cancer glimmered on the wall, its tendril stretched across several dark windows to tap the power.

Beside her waited Garnet. His two octopods had faded into the aggregate wall. Chrys was uneasy; for this rendezvous, of course the Lanths had specified no octopods. Besides, if the thumb-sized sentients had managed to overpower Jasper's octopods, Garnet's eight-limbed guards might equally be useless. She regretted her decision to leave Maya home. Maya could leap three meters and take out airborne objects.

"Are you sure this is right?" Chrys's map showed Silicon Salvage. "You said he was in Urul-Under."

"He was," said Garnet, "but the Lanths dragged him to their hideout."

"Selenite?" she blinked at her retina. "Got us covered?"

Selenite nodded from her window. "Your portable network stretches a block around. No sentients detected." Plenty of cancers though. A mound of rubble was covered by metastasizing blobs.

Something gasped; quick footfalls. "Help!" the person cried out, immobilized by an octopod.

Lights flickered from the person's eyes.

"A host in distress," flashed Flame. *"Ready to give up masters."*

The addicted host cried out, a long descending wail. Chrys recognized the call—someone just barely under control. "I'll help you," she called. "If you are ready."

"No time," said Garnet. "The Lanths will be here any minute."

"A street save—it's my job. Tell your octopod to release her."

The released woman half fell to the street. Her namestone was gone, most likely sold for arsenic needed by the master micros. But her face remained reasonably intact, a few broken veins but not yet a vampire. Her eyes locked with Chrys; a good sign. "Tell me your name." Chrys scanned her body for hidden weapons.

"No weapons," confirmed Selenite's network.

"Your name?" Chrys repeated.

"Oh—Ol—" the woman gasped, then winced in pain. Master micros tried to suppress the host's name, but she still remembered a syllable. "Olivine."

Chrys caught the woman's arm, which shook with fear. "If you can give them up, we'll give you treatment." Doctor Flexor approached her.

"I—accept—treatment." The woman's voice was barely audible.

"God of Mercy, we are ready for refugees."

Chrys placed a patch of Libertines at the woman's neck. Well practiced now, they screened refugees for masters and gave friendly molecules to the children. Flexor gave her nanos to clear out the rest and a sedative to stay calm.

"Watch out," warned Selenite. "The network sees something."

A cluster of shapes, visible only on the virtual grid.

"Chrys," warned Flexor. "The Lanths are moving in."

"Let me take her." Chrys took hold of the woman, locking her arms, and dragged her aside. She would help Jasper, but she wanted nothing to do with the hostage transaction. How many gigacreds for a lord, she wondered.

A pair of bipeds came out, carrying Jasper. The bipeds looked like neighborhood-watch; they appeared to be go-betweens. In the air behind them bobbed several Lanths, like candy balls.

Garnet cradled Jasper in his arms. "Chrys," he called, "we need you."

"Flame, we don't know what we'll find."

"We're ready for anything."

Chrys tried to approach Jasper while avoiding the Lanths. Shaking in the dark, Chrys placed a patch on her neck. At Flame's signal, she held out the patch to Jasper. Not moving, Jasper appeared unconscious.

"Back off," warned Selenite abruptly. "Get back to the tube."

Chrys moved away, stumbling on aggregate, down the street with the woman Flexor had treated. Hurrying, Chrys caught the woman's arm and helped her back toward the tube. Flexor and the neighborhood-watch bipeds brought Jasper.

From behind, a bright light flashed. The flash illuminated the entire tunnel-like street, both sides of crumbling buildings and the dilapidated streetsky above. A sickening noise of laser-seared rock and plast. Multiple octopods came alive and swarmed over all like giant crabs on a cliff.

"Garnet! What's going on?"

"The end of Silicon Salvage. Good riddance."

"But the neighborhood—"

"You can't just kidnap a lord."

Billows of smoke obscured the street where they had waited. Dazed, Chrys shook her head. After all the goodwill they had built, networking with all the neighborhoods.

24

The refugees tumbled out of the patch, dazed and starving, escorted by Libertines to the lining of their new host brain. Flame had to sort them one by one. Children were immediately removed and fed soothing molecules, then tested for numbers, letters, and creativity. The brightest were brought to the nightclubs with Libertine children. As they paired and came apart three, their genes would restore the genetic diversity Libertines craved. The refugee elders, of course, were restrained under guard. Any elders who put out master's toxins got bound up in dendrimers and imprisoned behind bars of arachnoid. Less dangerous ones were tagged with chains and put under watch, to be questioned for their skills and talents.

One elder refugee flashed deep green, with filaments pressed together like arrowheads. The deep-green one was attempting to trade this or that with whoever would listen; outlandish molecules that relaxed muscles, stimulated attention, or inhibited cytokine attack; elaborate filtration processes for gadolinium and dysprosium; and ingenious schemes for tricking the gods and overtaking a host. The latter schemes got the deep-green one bound in dendrimers at the most secure prison. But still, Flame kept up with the Trader, milking her secrets. Lanthanide filtration might help Libertines get their finances back in the black.

"All life's a trade." The deep-green one lay back in her dendrimers, relaxing with the AZ-laced food that Flame plied her with. "Whatever you desire, I can trade you for it."

"Even the life of your host?" asked Flame.

171

*"There's always a new host, isn't there?" observed deep-green.
"Never mind—so you valorize your host. What would you trade
to keep her?"*

*"For you, is there nothing beyond trade?" Flame wondered. "No
central good, without price?"*

*"The center is empty," observed deep-green. "Trade flies off the
ring like sparks from a wheel. The universe extends forever."*

Chrys held Jasper's hand. Within the Hyalite House, full of singing birds and multiple security levels, Jasper lay on the bed, where Garnet sat beside him, stroking his hair. "You'll pull through," Garnet whispered. "I—we'll spare no expense." He looked up at Chrys and the doctor. "Can I send him his reserve Map Stone Builders now? Please!"

"Wait. They're clearing out the poison." Chrys was reading Flame's flashing from Jasper's eye. His irises were ringed with gold and green.

"They're still reforming their council, rebuilding arachnoid neighborhoods." Flame reported how the Map Stone micros in Jasper's brain had nearly been wiped out but were now rebuilding homes and electing new officers. Ultramarine prepared to resettle new children. Meanwhile, Libertines patrolled Jasper's body, checking for any stray masters.

Chrys nodded at last. "His population needs rebuilding."

Garnet immediately placed the patch, first at his own neck to pick them up, then at Jasper's.

"Your micros will rebuild," Chrys promised Jasper. "Our refugee specialists will help them grow, and so will you. It's all just so—" She did not finish. Meanwhile, the House had formed a paint space so Chrys could shape the portraits of three Map Stone elders lost to the poison.

As she painted, Chrys wondered about the Lanths. The Lanths had killed off most of Jasper's micros, apparently aiming to get the ransom faster. Of course it blew back on them when the Palace responded in force. To kidnap a lord—why did they do it?

"The Lanths got what they wanted." Jasper's voice was labored, still exhausted. "They wanted to disrupt our Underworld renovation. Renovation that brings back a stable network will make them traceable. Nowhere for them to hide."

Garnet caressed Jasper's hair. "They'll never get away with it. The Palace will destroy Silicon Salvage and wipe them out."

If the Palace were truly able to wipe out Lanths, the renegade drones would be long gone. Now they existed in limbo, forgotten lumps of qubits, lost in the abandoned maze of Underworld. "Maybe we should reach out to them."

"How could you, Chrys?" Incredulous, Garnet shook his head. "I know you always try to reform any kind of micro or person; that's so sweet of you. But those Lanths—Look what they did to Jasper. They're—inhuman."

On her way back, the streetsky pulsed again with the majestic curtains of aurora. In a newsbreak, the Protector shook his bejeweled fist not at distant Solaria but down at the Underworld. "Fill in the entire Underworld! Solid rock foundation will put an end to kidnappings and earthquakes."

The entire Underworld—gone? What about the people? Glyn, Rhodla, Granny Lorh. Human people who were not lords.

"Great God of Mercy, we have assimilated new hard-working refugees." Flame reported on the Traders they had screened from the addict, who was now with Flexor on her way to the hospital, where Daeren would give her angels. *"One interesting elder asks you for a name."*

"Very well. Let her address me."

Dots of forest green, faint against the dark, formed letters. *"Greetings, great Exterminator. I bring trillions of rare atoms to trade."*

"How dare you, vile Trader-master!" Flame's shock sprinkled the retinal dots. *"Forgive us, Great One, we'll remove her to prison until she learns better."*

Chrys knew what they all thought of microbial extermination, whether or not they dared say. *"Return her to prison and treat her well. Bring her back to me after an hour."* A microbial year in prison, with Flame's signature treatment, would do much to disarm her.

When the prisoner returned, Chrys told her: *"Dark green one, God is no murderer. My Libertines saved your refugees and mingled your children with their own."* No other population at Olympus took in so many refugees and allow them such liberties.

"The world I knew is gone," flickered the dark green. *"Destroyed by you, the World Destroyer."*

"Your population poisoned your own host. You may call me Destroyer of Poison."

"Very well, Poison Destroyer."

"And I call you Deadly Nightshade."

25

The refugee children who passed their tests had all merged in the nightclubs, and the few corrigible elders like Nightshade had settled in. With the completion of Pulse of Battle, Phlox led the art team exploring new creations. Phlox was exceptionally creative, and creation took her mind off worrying.

Flame tackled the quantum decoherence in the Diaspore. To understand the data drain, Flame assigned twenty different teams each to apply a different algorithm. Ten of the teams drew ideas from Nightshade. Nightshade offered insights from a different school of theory, and she traded for ideas from visiting Wizards.

"Our economy will soon pick up," Flame assured Phlox. "We'll pay off that punishing fine. This is a golden year for Libertines."

From the Blue Angels reserve colony, Ultramarine approached Flame. Her filaments flashed warning lights of cobalt and cerulean. "The Lord of Light needs help," she warned. "From history past, we know that outer-world conditions may lead our God to a dangerous decision."

"What can we do?" asked Flame.

"Send elders back with us," urged Ultramarine. "Our God cannot live without yours. He will pay heed to Libertines."

Chrys slept in after her late return, only to find Daeren had already left. He was on duty at the hospital, where he donated Blue Angels for Olivine, then off to the Palace lobbying for justice.

"Chrysoberyl," warned Xenon. "I picked up three credible threats from Lanth sources."

Unsurprising, after the bad end to their hostage transfer.

"Thanks, Xenon. Let's hire a couple of octopods. How is the Underworld?"

"The Palace forces halted operations for now, although the smoke from Silicon Salvage has spread into Urul-Under."

"I'll send the cleanup our usual contribution." Wealthy art patrons were accustomed to chipping in after Palace raids on the Underworld.

She took a moment to check her feed for any Elf news. Nothing on Silicon—after all the talk, no new action. Not even a peep from Transit. Apparently the Board was still mulling over their "evolved" design. The year before, Chrys recalled Jasper saying the project would not be completed in her lifetime. Of course, Elf lifetimes were much longer.

Another Elf name popped up, someone Karin Papili*shon*. Who was that? Then she remembered—the Papili*shon* high school competition winner, the one who used seasilk and slime mold to paint the Sharer diving off a raft branch. Chrys blinked the window.

Karin was a lovely youngster with a spectacular swallowtail train. "Citizen Azetidine—I'm amazed to meet you. And I'm so honored you selected my piece."

Chrys cleared her throat, unsure what to say; like, sorry to miss you when I got kicked off your planet. "My pleasure, Karin. Your work shows depth beyond your years."

"That's so kind of you, Citizen. I'm hoping you can provide expert opinion in support of my graduation lawsuit."

Puzzled, Chrys wondered if she heard correctly. "Your … graduation?"

"My lawsuit. Every Elf trains as a *logen*. To graduate, we have to sue the state for adult human rights."

Chrys absorbed this. "So … everyone is a lawyer?"

"At least trained enough to defend ourselves. How can a human being not defend their own rights?"

"Does anyone ever, like, lose their case?"

Karin said, "Some have to sue two or three times. On average we get out by age fifty." That Chrys had heard. "I'm forty," Karin added. "But I've done advanced work."

At last Chrys got down to finalizing her pieces for the Iridium. Besides *Pulse of Battle*, she had selected two portraits, Pachira and Willow. Her micro portraits were a signature favorite, sure to draw a crowd; and these each had interesting effects of light and motion.

She caught sight of Daeren's window on her retina. Hurriedly she signed off. "How is Olivine?" The micro-enslaved woman Chrys had salvaged from the Underworld. "Is she recovering?"

"Recovering well enough," Daeren said. "Chrys, we're concerned about the neighborhoods."

"I sent our usual help from Olympus," she told him. "Last night I was seen down there and marked by Lanths. I can't go back down myself."

Daeren's forehead creased, the highlights fragmented. "We've got to respect the Underworld. These people have rights. Some have owned their own homes there longer than the Palace lords."

"I know." Chrys sighed. "You're always telling the ministers."

"Universal rights—just like sentients." He was talking to himself now. "What we need is a universal declaration of rights. Rights for all persons, human or micro."

"Or sentient."

"Sentients, lanthanide, or virtual." He faced her. "Talk to Moraeg." Daeren sounded agitated. "Tell her—the Palace has got to pull back."

Chrys's mouth fell open, then shut again. "What's Moraeg got to do with it?"

"The ministers depend on her. She can tell the Palace to hold back."

Absorbing this, Chrys slowly shook her head. "I'm her tester today. It's, like, a conflict of interest."

"It's a matter of life and death. For the Underworld."

Chrys reluctantly left her paint space to visit Moraeg, when the door-bell chimed.

"Chrysoberyl, did you call for more octopods?" inquired Xenon.

"No." She peered out cautiously at the two tiger-striped octopods. Just what she needed the neighbors to see.

"From Lady Moraeg of the House of Carnelian," announced one. "For your honored protection."

Moraeg should know better than to send her own octopods. If she were in trouble with micros, who would her octopods obey? "Xenon, please call up two octopods of yours, rated at least the same level." A four-octopod escort, that would reassure the neighbors all right.

At the House of Carnelian, Lady Moraeg and Lord Carnelian received her in their main hall. They sat on majestic chairs, ornate and elevated. A distinctly monarchal feel, Jaguar royals. Carnelian placed his arm on Moraeg's, his round red gems warming her diamond-studded presence. Moraeg had said his House nearly went bankrupt on jewels and art. Today they were a power couple, on top of the world.

"Moraeg—I'm looking forward to your new piece at the show." Rumors had appeared online, but no details; Moraeg was rarely so closemouthed about her work.

Diamond-encrusted rings flashed on all her fingers. Moraeg nodded. "First things first. We're looking forward to your test."

"My people are ready." Seeing Carnelian there, Chrys hesitated.

Carnelian nodded. "Testing is a private affair." He rose with a bow. "You can depend on our discretion." All their household octopods withdrew along with him. As a non-carrier, micro-independent, Carnelian understood the importance of objective testing. Olympus was fortunate to have him.

"Anything we need to know?"

Moraeg's irises had rings of brown petals set in her obsidian features. Her pupils flashed regal violet. "The Dark Angels obey, and they find their calling. Though it's hard when the host begs them to take over." That was the problem with recovering addicts—they never forgot the dopamine rush from the masters.

Chrys placed the patch as usual, lightly on Moraeg's neck. In Moraeg's eyes, points of red appeared. Flame had arrived from the transfer. *"We are checking all the arterioles,"* the red flashed back to Chrys. *"All looks good so far."*

Chrys smiled. She got an easier sense from Moraeg now, more like the old days.

"Growing list of host clients," added Flame. *"The Hygiene Minister, the Minister of Justice, the Interplanetary Trade Minister."*

"A lot of work for you," Chrys observed aloud. "Olympus is extremely grateful."

Moraeg kept her eyes steady like a pro. "We learned from the best. We follow Daeren's instructions to the letter."

"A few traces of master molecules," added Flame. *"No sign of active insurrection however."*

"What's wrong?" Moraeg asked.

"Nothing we see," Chrys assured her. "There are always trace molecules when you've dealt with addicts. My arachnoid is full of them." She at last placed her patch to pick up Flame.

Moraeg put a hand to her bare neck, framed by her platinum diamond collar. "Final step, remember."

Chrys looked aside. "We don't do that anymore." Thank goodness.

"Why not? I expect the full workout."

"By now the news has spread, and we assume any masters could have learned to adapt. They evolve faster than we do."

Moraeg frowned. "Are you sure? What do you do instead?"

"Sorry, that's classified." From Nightshade's intelligence, Flame had devised several ingenious tricks.

"You guarantee that's enough?"

"No." Chrys fixed her pupils steady. "No guarantees."

With a slight nod, Moraeg relaxed and sat back. "Thanks for all you do. And for maintaining my reserve."

"And Olympus thanks you, for your service."

"The Dark Angels ask for the Lord of Light." Back home in her arachnoid, Flame had more to say. *"They still depend on Blue Angels for guidance. They share the Blue Angels' concern for what he will do."*

Chrys looked to Moraeg. She picked her words with care. "There is of course … concern for the Underworld."

At that Moraeg retreated, the Diamond Queen of a Great House. She turned her head aside, the micros' lights no longer reaching Chrys. "The Palace will do what we must." She added, more softly, "I'm looking forward to the Iridium. Thanks so much for introducing me. I'll have one new piece—a surprise."

After Moraeg, Chrys had to meet Opal at the Comb for a conference on the Diaspore's qubit loss. While on the tube, Chrys realized Daeren's window was missing. Her pulse raced. She had so many windows; it was easy to lose one. She checked home. "Xenon? Where is Daeren?"

"Chrysoberyl, I'm afraid I haven't found him for the past hour. I was hoping you had better news."

The minutes stretched like agonizing hours while she searched her retinal network. Then, at a tube stop, a stray clickfly managed to dart inside the car just before the door sealed. The door trained a laser on it. Chrys threw up her hand. "Halt—it's mine."

The clickfly landed on her braids, getting stuck as usual. Wincing, she pulled out strands of her hair. As the clickfly started to vocalize, Chrys contacted Xenon for translation.

"He's down in Urul-Under," Xenon translated the clicks and pops. "Visiting his grandmother."

Daeren's Blue Angels were still the key to all maintenance of addicts of the brain plague. He was holding himself hostage, against the Palace striking the Underworld.

26

The Diaspore's decoherence had reached an alarming rate. Phlox's plan had brought a response from Diaspore Admin. To address it, Libertines held an unprecedented conference with the Wizards and Minions.

"All quantum computing requires constructive interference," a Wizard explained. "Interference means that the qubit states combine constructively to amplify correct solutions and destructively to suppress wrong answers."

"But something in the environment can interact with the qubit, degrading its state to zero or one, with nothing between. This is called decoherence."

Nightshade and some of the master-hybrid progeny asked uncomfortable questions. "How fast is the Diaspore growing? How much larger is it today than in ancient history, when qubit loss was rare? Like a brain prunes synapses—"

Here the micros were shocked, especially Minions who were never allowed to touch the neurons proper. "Good micros stay in the brain's arachnoid lining. We should never know how the neurons work. If we do, we should be in prison."

"Never mind," said Flame. "Never mind where knowledge came from. Knowledge is an intrinsic good."

"Is it possible," flashed Nightshade, "that the Diaspore has a 'reason' to lose qubits? Does the pruning of connections enhance computation? Especially the financial computations that the Gods demand more and more?"

At the Comb, Chrys picked her way through the vaulted entrance hall, no two triangular panels quite alike. It had grown and expanded by a third since her last visit. The higher windows spiraled in hexagonal arrays, their corners forming rosettes for nesting warblers. The Comb had helped restore the red-hooded birds' population, the birds now so numerous their droppings marred the lawn.

"Please admire my new hue-shifting program, Chrysoberyl." The Comb's panels shifted gradually from orange through infrared, indicating the path for Chrys to follow. At last she reached the demonstration stage. At the side, ficus and dragon trees towered behind the seated lords, including Lord Carnelian; the Lady Aragonite, vice president of Bank Aragonite; and mining magnate Lord Sardonyx, all in gray talars with just a small discreet namestone.

Chrys reached out to Opal, exchanging transfers. "Daeren went down to Urul-Under."

Opal caught her hand. "He must be worried sick for his family, after what happened."

"Yes, but—"

Selenite also shared a transfer, full of Minions with the latest design adjustments for Silicon. "We're actually up to date on Silicon requirements. Any new lawsuits?"

Chrys had heard nothing from Transit, not a word on Silicon.

"No lawsuits means no interest," Selenite observed. "Maybe the sentients have forgotten your pre-evolved design."

Chrys stared at her associate. "Seriously?"

"That's why we demand the first gigacred up front."

"But ... you mean they'll just ... "

"You think you're special," said Selenite. "There's always a newer dynatect, even more outrageous."

The assembled lords and bank vice presidents shared their concerns about the Diaspore and its likely impact on investments. "Several sectors of the system have gone dead," complained Lady Aragonite. Lord Sardonyx sat in his gray talar with a grim expression.

Opal listened, while her micros with visiting Libertines ran trillions of parallel analyses. "Does the Diaspore show any discrepancies?" she asked at last.

"None so far," admitted Aragonite. "But the slightest hint of instability could cause a panic. And after the Underworld incident ...." She did not finish. "The system runs slower. It takes more rounds for a good solution to emerge."

The room went dark. Only stars shone all around, their light reaching across the universe.

Opal said, "I think we're seeing an unexpected consequence of the Palace's latest directive to increase the Diaspore's efficiency. As you know, we instructed the Diaspore to refine itself—to expand those systems under pressure while pruning those less used. We obtained great improvements but did not anticipate how large portions would fall apart."

"So how do we design the network to be most efficient? We told the Diaspore to figure this out. The result was what we call a slime-mold effect." An inset sphere appeared. Within it was a bright bubbling yellow slime mold in a Solarian forest. "A slime mold grows to fill all channels of a maze. Then its protoplasm recedes from all channels except for the shortest connector between origin and a food source."

On Solaria a single slime mold could cover an acre of forest. As it matured, gaping holes appeared; Chrys had never wondered why.

The room lights returned, filtering down through the Comb's skylight. Lady Aragonite fingered her namestone, striking blue on a chain of gold. "Lost time means lost power. This is unacceptable."

Opal said, "We're working on a plan from Phlox." Her dark pupils flickered.

Chrys's micros responded. *"We can adjust the algorithm ...."* Flame poured letters across her retina. *"Nightshade has spent a year on this with the Wizards."* A microbial year, an hour. *"Our code is ready to test on the Diaspore."*

"What is this, Nightshade?" demanded Chrys.

"Poison Destroyer," returned Nightshade, using the god's name Chrys had permitted. *"Mathematics knows no loyalties nor limits."*

Opal's cheeks dimpled, then she grew thoughtful. "The micros propose to run a Diaspore sector directly with their code and fix it in real time. This plan combines the expertise from three of our most accomplished microbial populations, with long experience of managing Diaspore security."

Aragonite said, "We cannot afford any contamination—from plague, nor from nanosentients."

"No contamination," Opal assured her, accustomed to explaining this point. "The micros share only their code, not their corporeal bodies, nor any nanosentients from the blood. They will limit their test to a sector behind a firewall."

Chrys closed all her retinal windows to stare at the Comb's data port. It took so long her eyes watered, trying not to blink. She kept wondering about Daeren down there with Granny Lorh in Urul-Under, while the Protector's fist-shaking continued.

For the next three days, there was still no sign of Daeren, only the occasional clickfly from Granny Lorh. Chrys returned the creature, insisting on retinal contact, so she could find him down there. How could Daeren leave her in the dark?

"He doesn't want to be found," Selenite bluntly told her. "He didn't before."

"You don't know that."

"Chrys, I'm sorry. We all gave for your project, all us Olympians. It was a pipe dream. The Underworld is beyond management."

Her eye squeezed shut Selenite's window, then she pulled another clickfly off her braids to cluck a message. Xenon's osmanthus cake was a good treat to attract clickflies; there were always two or three at her ceiling now, well out of reach of the cat.

The show date came, and still no sign of Daeren. Chrys felt sad, anguished, and angry. How could he isolate all his Blue Angels? They'd suffered enough.

"We can visit a clickfly," Flame told her. *"Nightshade shared the technology. We'll suit up and travel by clickfly to find the Lord of Light."*

"No way." Venturing outside a human host—that was how the Traders hid on the ships from Elysium. *"God forbids it, now and forever."*

"The reserve Blue Angels long for their god. They fear what has become of him."

Chrys knew she had to do something, before her people came up with worse ideas. "Xenon, tell the clickflies: If he's not back for my show, I'm going down after him with octopods."

"Certainly, Chrysoberyl." Xenon provided the clicks and pops. Chrys listened carefully, starting to learn the language. "If I may ask," Xenon added, "what exactly happened to Daeren before in the Underworld? The doctors were secretive; I was never apprised."

"He revealed the planet where plague came from, to Arion." The Elf guardian had demanded this information, in return for help against the brain plague. "Arion destroyed the planet and all the plague micros on it." So much for "peaceful" Elysium. "But all our good micros share relatives with the plague. They were appalled. So Daeren ... gave up his own body to host the survivors."

"And you brought him back." Addicted to dopamine overload.

"He should have been wiped. But the surviving Blue Angels took care of him. It was the first time we tried that—letting good micros govern a human."

"And now angel therapy is our standard of care. But you still don't trust him in the Underworld."

Chrys thought, she had no idea who to trust anymore.

For the Iridium show, Chrys wore her deep infrared talar with a hem of burnt sienna and her largest cat's eye chrysoberyl. Xenon did her braids up in a crinkled crown studded with smaller cat's eyes. Their bright-line "pupils" made a startling display.

The gallery filled with the thrum of visitors taking in the year's best work of three dozen artists. Visitors wore their own surreal statements: a L'liite with a sentient scarf crawling serpentine around the waist, a lord with blue-green tourmalines across the chest, a student in cutoff denim with a backpack on the shoulders. Many were drawn to Zircon's *Inhumanity II.* The thousand-meter slab of silica nanolattice rose clear through a cutout in the ceiling, up through the next ten street levels. Viewers craned their necks with open mouths.

"Why, it's little you." Zircon patted Chrys on the head. Two meters tall, she wore platform shoes and an accountant's gray talar. "So glad you could admire our work."

Chrys smiled. "Big Zirc, I haven't missed any show of yours since art school, back when you were a guy."

Zircon lifted her finger. "Little you, I was always a girl. Thanks to you I reached my potential." Chrys had helped Zircon manage her first community of micros. Like all carriers, Zircon got Plan Ten, which could reshape the sexual body. Zircon's Accountants twinkled gold in her eyes.

"Their work lifts up the cries of microbes condemned to thoughtless slaughter," flashed Flame.

"For good reason," Chrys warned.

"Of course, God's will is always just."

"Remember your test." Chrys had Zircon on her weekly list.

"I sure will." Zircon shook her head slowly. "I worry about you, back in Iridis. Remember my home in Sardis, if you ever need to crash."

Chrys smiled, thinking how those were the days, dirt poor after art school, when she and Zirc used to trade off whose credit ran out and had to sleep on the other's couch. "Same here," she said. "You know I'm the refugee queen." Microbial refugees—her Libertines were always demanding them.

Pulse of Battle drew a crowd just as large, Chrys was pleased to see. People blinked to immerse themselves in the aorta. Startled, a viewer lifted their hands and looked around, mesmerized by the rushing blood cells. Others buzzed at the cancer dots, wondering aloud when the Palace octopods would show up. Above the crowd hovered a docent, round as a snake egg but larger; he twirled his eye facets and rose to the height of the blood vessel's arch. "From Gallery Elysium's first-ever choice of a Valan artist, Azetidine offers a new sensation. Intricate lightstrokes render the aorta's walls, infusing them with a sense of fragility juxtaposed against the powerful current of life. The leukemia cells, like spectral entities, swirl and dance in a chaotic choreography, their jagged forms embodying the destructive force of the illness; while the alien microbes spur the T-cells to attack. A triumph of postnaturalism ..."

Carnelian stood by in his immaculate gray talar, proud of his acquisition. Three snake-eggs hovered at a respectful distance. "Lord Carnelian," one asked, "how do you feel supporting an artist whose erotica was proscribed by the Palace? An artist now banned from Elysium?"

Chrys wondered the same. Moraeg must have further tightened her grip on the Palace.

Other viewers watched in delight the outsized portraits of Pachira, the giant ring of green filaments twinkling her designs, and Lilac, the violet one calling new elders to the library.

"*Miracles!*" Flame texted, letters glimmering ahead of her. "*We long for our legendary Lilac and Pachira.*"

Chrys wiped a tear, missing them both.

"*And our Blue Angels long for the Lord of Light—how many generations have they missed him.*"

She looked away, not ready to face that now. She strolled through the gallery, having promised to say a few words for Moraeg. To her surprise, a crowd twice as large had gathered at Moraeg's latest. Beside her usual glittering diamond confections, Moraeg's new piece *Star Miner* transfixed the crowd.

Brushing off a twinge of envy, Chrys smiled at Moraeg, who basked in the glow of attention. She waited till Carnelian had arrived, discreetly in back. Chrys cleared her throat and faced the crowd. "Lady Moraeg of House Carnelian was a founding member of the Seven Stars art collective. Her arachnoid microbial studio has mined her own past to take her floral minerals in a startling new direction." The chattering stilled, the viewers awed by the spectacle. "In *Star Miner*, outsized granite crystals thrust from the rock of a remote asteroid. Each hexagonal crystal emerges as a child, mouth open in silent cry. The little arms reach upward like *Guernica*, hands filled with rare ores of ytterbium, samarium, and neodymium. As the ores arise, the child fades into dust ...." Chrys paused, wondering how much she should say, but she knew Moraeg

184

wanted it said. "The hidden labor of these trafficked children serves our Valan industries, supplying even the Diaspore. And beyond—nine-tenths of child miners serve Elysium—the world of shoreless Shora, whose citizens exploit asteroids rather than dredge their own seafloor."

"The God of Many Colors!" Flame lit up the retina amid a burst from Slime Cat. That must be Ilia—where? *"The legendary people of Many Colors—we need to welcome them."*

In the crowd, at last, Chrys caught sight of Ilia. The gallery director had her hand on her chin, watching in rapt attention. Chrys made her way through the crowd, nodding graciously to those who gasped to see Azetidine.

At last Chrys drew Ilia aside. "I'm glad you came." She placed a patch from her neck to Ilia's.

"Thanks so much," Ilia whispered. She still seemed lost in thought.

"What are you thinking?"

Ilia contemplated Moraeg's piece. "Should we bring her to Helicon, I wonder."

Chrys felt envious yet protective. "Of course, her representational work is the hottest thing." She emphasized the word "representational."

"What do you think?" Ilia asked suddenly. "About mining asteroids."

Chrys frowned. "They're children. We build our world of comfort upon their pain."

"Just children," echoed Ilia. "Not yet human. We build our world upon the pain of so many animals and subsentients."

Chrys's lips parted. "Did you say … children are not human?"

"Not until they defend their rights in the court." Her eyes widened. "Do I shock you, Azetidine? How flattering. The shock of the new. I'm sharing so much new here."

"You mean … your Elf *shon*lings are not human?"

"*Shon*lings are cultured proto-humans. Not yet persons. To become persons, they must fight the state for their rights. Your *shon*ling prize-winner has made a good start." Ilia tilted her head. "What do you know about Lady Moraeg?"

"As a child, Moraeg pulled herself out of the mine, then she bought her own enslaved children to climb up." Chrys felt bad saying this, but it was the truth.

"I confess I was unaware of her history. Mining asteroids was never my interest. What I think now, I'm not sure." Ilia loved imponderable questions. She returned Chrys's patch. "Thanks so much for hosting my reserve colony. I know they'll find the experience enlightening."

Chrys swallowed. "Could you take a reserve colony for mine? In case Daeren …." She could not finish.

"We're honored." Ilia waved a hand. "This Underground—it makes no sense. Can't you help him see? Real humans don't live interred."

At a loss for words, Chrys had no idea how to respond. "What about your micros?" Chrys blurted. "Are they persons?"

Ilia smiled. "Indeed. Micros fight—by their own deadly rules. We'd have no trouble if micros were not persons."

27

They called it the Golden Generation—the micros' full year of art. For months on end, the art of thirty different artists streamed into the God's eyeballs and lit up the retina with sculptures of outlandishly shaped gods, Olympian landscapes, creatures from different worlds of the universe, dancing children, mountains of color and shadow from dizzying heights to appalling depths. Phlox had a team of elders collecting all the images and sketches to store in the molecular history, deep within the cisterna magna of the arachnoid.

From the God of Many Colors, the visiting micros maintained their own colony, breeding mainly with each other. A few children, though, ventured into neighboring nightclubs with Libertines and Blue Angels, generating a vibrant mix of peoples and ideas.

The Many Colors brought unsettling controversies—even lawsuits. "We challenge the rules of your art contest," demanded the Many Colors leader, Mauve.

Phlox was perplexed. "A lawsuit against art?" Unheard of. "Our art community is the most advanced in the known universe." She kept dark her opinion that Mauve's filament arrangement and molecular tags were frankly outré.

"You Libertines privilege art that is representational," accused Mauve. "You need to foreground abstraction. Abstract art opens a realm of imagination and interpretation that transcends the constraints of old-fashioned reality. Abstraction inspires incomparable intellectual stimulation."

Phlox flashed magenta and emitted molecules of condescension. "Representational art goes beyond abstraction—

187

"The power of art that represents the real,
With impact and sensation what we feel
To capture life, the depth of what we see,
Demands technique and high dexterity."

    Mauve emitted molecules of laughter. "Such doggerel. You Lib-
ertines should revise your contest rules for fair competition."
    While Phlox contended with Many Color lawsuits, Nightshade
and Flame recruited the brightest elders throughout the brain lining
to join the Diaspore testing team. They established an elaborate set
of decoy qubits to reveal what happened. Whatever stimulus had
caused the Diaspore's decoherence, they would find it.

At suppertime, Chrys felt forelornly alone. She picked at the
lambfruits from Xenon's five-course meal for twelve. From the
ceiling, a clickfly stole down to snitch a shrimp off the salad. Chrys caught
the clickfly, then clicked a message to it and sent it sailing downstairs. A
meeting was scheduled that night at Olympus, the whole carrier group,
but Daeren was nowhere to report. Selenite would chair, of course, but
everyone wondered why Daeren was away. How to deal with it all—the
Underground crisis, the Elf plague micros, the Human Hygiene minister's
latest threats of extermination. The meeting would go on all night.

    "Oh Great One!" Phlox's magenta flashed with distress. *"The new neigh-*
borhood of Many Colors—they filed twenty-three lawsuits!"

    "Lawsuits?" Even the Elves' micros lived by lawsuits. *"My brain is your*
territory. Ignore them."

    "But the Council must follow our courts, lest democracy fail!"

    "What's their complaint?"

    "They demand we recognize abstract art as the higher form!" Back to art
school—the only place such fights mattered.

    The Sisters came as always to pick up the rest of the food. "Thanks so
much for your feast." Sister Kaol's assistant lifted the tubs of lambfruits
with currants, green florets, and pink oranges. "Our clients always enjoy
your amazing cuisine, Xenon." She always made it feel special, as if this
were the first day the Sisters' restaurant had opened and used the proceeds
to run the expanded soup kitchen. "Is Daeren still away?"

    "Still visiting his grandmother. Somewhere." Chrys hurriedly
wiped a tear.

    "Saints preserve, I'm sure he has important work for the good." Sister
Kaol added, "Does he have his life tag?"

Everyone on Health Plan Ten had an embeded life tag that enabled medics to locate them instantly, anywhere on Valedon. "We have our life tags," said Chrys. "But he doesn't wish to be found." Afraid the Palace would find some excuse to haul him off.

The Sister put her arm around Chrys, the soft blue-gray sleeve brushing her face. "You know you can always count on us. All of you." She looked to the gargoyled ceiling.

"You're always welcome," Xenon's voice boomed. "The Sisters are truly my best customers."

At Club Olympus, Jasper reclined against a nanoplastic tree trunk. Garnet cradled Jasper in his arms as if to make sure no one could capture him again.

Chrys shared a patch at Jasper's neck. "So good to see you, Jasper. Your micros have recovered well."

Jasper nodded. "Rhun is making inquiries. He won't let those outlaws get away with it."

Chrys said nothing. She could not imagine what Rhun could do about kidnappers the size of a floating candy ball.

Moraeg caught her by the arm. Her diamonds pinched Chrys's skin. "Where is Daeren? Is he back yet?" She looked coldly furious.

The clickfly nesting in Chrys's braids startled and hovered up. Chrys stammered, "He's just visiting Granny Lorh."

"He must leave immediately. His presence impedes our Underworld policy."

Chrys blinked nervously. "What do you plan for the Underworld?"

Opal put an arm around each, her moonstones sailing across her blue seasilk. "Of course, no one's going to hurt Daeren and the Underworld. All those lovely Blue Angels—where would we be without them?"

Selenite leaned over Opal's shoulder, arms folded. She stared at Moraeg. "The Palace needs to show restraint."

Moraeg stared back, as if unaccustomed to opposition. Everyone's eyes flashed sparks between them. "The Palace needs to retain their full range of options. Obstruction is treason."

Across the room appeared a shimmering cross. Transit hovered expectantly, while across space in Helicon, Transit's thousand stations sent bubbles floating through the system. Meanwhile, a long list of unanswered comments appeared on Chrys's retina.

"Transit!" exclaimed Chrys brightly. "Imagine seeing you here. Are you sure ... the system can manage?"

"Never fear, mere lanthanide-less human," the shimmering cross loftily assured her. "At this point nothing can shock us anymore. Your club thankfully sent me your previous meetings' minutes ahead for my perusal. By now I've quite recovered."

She blinked. "Recovered?" She thought back to that earlier Olympus meeting, weeks ago. "Oh, right, where we found the antimony mutants. No worries, I've got that covered—"

"Such errors—such breach of process—I've never seen."

"Really? But we—I mean, Daeren graduated law school; he really knows—"

"Never forget Robert's Rules," the sentient voice intoned. "Robert's Rules of Order are what worlds do instead of lobbing bombs." The cross tilted back, then again forward. "Our key to survival. Without Robert's Rules, we are doomed."

Chrys looked away, desperate for Selenite. "Um, isn't it time to start the meeting?"

"The Club Olympus meeting of carriers and independents is now called to order." Selenite stood at the dais amid the clouds and sky. Chrys felt her heart squeeze. Where was Daeren? She caught the clickfly on her head and pop-whistled, *Meeting Starts Now. Need You Here.* The clickfly took off with its message.

Around the meeting, Olympians seated themselves at various heights and angles. Doctor Flexor stood below, worms pulled into her post, while Andra and Doctor Sartorius hovered in Chrys's retinal window. Lord Carnelian, as always, was there to represent micro-independents. He got wiped daily for arsenic, antimony, and lanthanides.

"Please welcome our visitor, the distinguished transportation system Transit Cross of Helicon," announced Selenite. "Transit will stand for member of Olympus. He would be our first member to consist entirely of virtual code."

Chrys nodded. Now that bad micros were capable of contaminating inert material, only virtual sentients were uninfectable. Like Carnelian, Transit offered an important control.

The minutes of the previous meeting appeared overhead, the meeting her micros' antimony problem had interrupted, landing her in the hospital. "Any corrections to the minutes?"

Transit had a long list of corrections although he had not even been there. "A motion to close debate requires a two-thirds vote. That is not called a 'two-thirds majority,' just a two-thirds vote. A majority means more than half, or half plus one. No such thing as two-thirds." The cross hovered above the heads of the gathered carriers. "A voice vote is *not* acceptable, rather one requires a standing count where one records documentation of the final vote ..."

Chrys's attention wandered. In the audience a younger carrier facepalmed.

"And the count must go beyond 'raised hands' to include comparable indicators from sentient beings who lack hands ..."

[Diaspore Security]

An unfamiliar window on Chrys's retina lacked an address. The window itself was formless, with shifting shapes of various colors. It looked suspiciously like malware. "Xenon? Can you filter this please?"

Xenon said, "I'm checking the source."

[Diaspore Security]

"Flame: What is this invader?"

"We are investigating."

Her people didn't know. Not a good sign.

"Phlox?" She appealed to the magenta one. *"What is this window?"*

"The Diaspore security administrator."

Chrys let out her breath. The Diaspore Admin she knew always took the qubit loss results from their network. Security—that sounded like something for Garnet or Carnelian. *"What does Diaspore Security want?"*

"It wants Slime Cat," flashed Flame.

"What? Why?"

The pause lengthened. The longer the pause, Chrys knew, the more likely her people were holding something back—something they were loath to reveal. She counted the seconds up to ten. *"Why do they want Slime Cat? Explain or face God's wrath."*

"Slime Cat escaped."

"What? That's not possible." Slime Cat was physically composed of the microscopic nanobots that Flexor had put into Chrys's blood. The nanobots could not physically escape. Not unless they all got loaded into a microneedle patch—and even then, they could only reach the next carrier.

"Slime Cat copied her code."

"Copied where?"

"Her code got into the Diaspore storage for malware testing. Then it leaked through the firewall."

"And then?"

There was another long pause.

"Fear is on the way." Chrys took out the vial of catecholamine and counted the seconds. At last Flame replied. *"Her code is self-replicating."*

[Diaspore Security—Response Required]

Chrys's scalp prickled and all her braids itched. The Diaspore now had a quantum cattery. And its administrator was not pleased. When Olympus found out—no way, not another broken-up meeting, not a night trapped by avocado hospital walls. And Daeren was who knows where.

She looked up. Transit was still finding inexcusable points of order. Several faces were palmed, and a sentient medic had half strangled himself with his own faceworms.

"Xenon, could you have a household emergency?"

Her home window opened wide. Plumbing burst, spraying water everywhere. Waves of water flowed across the dining room floor. Chrys let her window view leak out to the retinas of nearby attenders.

Opal took Chrys's hand. "Skyhomes are so temperamental." She leaned to whisper. "Go ahead, take care of him. I'll fill you in later."

Back at home, Chrys sat at the vast dining room table. Elbows on the table, she held her head in her hands and closed her eyes. "Xenon, what the devil is going on?"

"The Diaspore is an ecosystem," Xenon helpfully explained.

"An ecosystem? As in, like, alive?" demanded Chrys. "The crap it is. It's just an information system."

"Like others? I'm insulted. Truly I expected better from my home partner."

"So the Diaspore …." She blinked twice. "It's now … full of half-sentient Slime Cats." Like Xenon, or Transit, except way beyond even Transit outrageous. A cloud of half-aware entangled qubits flung across space. "Why would the Diaspore let Slime Cat copy itself? Aren't there enough error corrections in that Milky Way look-alike up there?" Her micros had earned millions of palladium atoms testing them.

"I know of four or five multipartite entangled groups that reached Slime Cat's intelligence level," said Xenon. "None were found inside a human, and all were quickly destroyed. Of course, their physical size was checked against the Orb of Votan."

A clickfly got curious and floated down from the ceiling, rubbing its mandibles. Chrys waved it away. The last thing she needed now was Urul-Under opinions. She blinked for Opal.

Opal appeared on her retina, her window hovering above Chrys's nose. Her eyes stared to pick up the Libertines' description of the leak to the Diaspore. "We built a good firewall," Opal insisted. "With several advanced features the Wizards invented."

"Your firewall lacks sentience," said Xenon. "I warned you to hire a sentient cloud-native firewall. But no, nobody wanted to pay a union wage."

"That's true," Opal admitted. "A cloud-native sentient would have cost a thousand times more. Instead the Board hired my Wizards—with the expertise of a thousand sentients." Microbial labor, paid a few atoms.

"The Wizards did their best," flashed Flame. *"A zero-day vulnerability was exploited. They can fix it now."*

28

The Libertine world was in turmoil. Somehow they had to help Wizards fix the errant qubits and restore the Diaspore. But after Slime Cat escaped, their access to the network was cut—for months, perhaps years to come.

Meanwhile, Mauve's campaign for abstract art drew an alarming number of young elders seeking intellectual challenge and sophistication. "The young say that energy and motion free their instinct," Flame told Nightshade. "Abstraction stirs emotion, provokes thought, and makes the viewer imagine."

"Abstraction is distraction." Nightshade had a blunt view of things. "You can trade it for nothing."

"How will these future elders help the god paint things from real life?"

"Discipline. Train their craft."

"And most annoying," flashed Flame, "Mauve's sisters from the God of Many Colors drain our supply of antimony." By now most Libertines had been bred for flexibility to use arsenic, antimony, or lanthanides. But the reserve population from the Elf god was still antimony-dependent, like their Trader ancestors.

"Tell Mauve to breed her children with ours," insisted Nightshade. "They have to do it." The Elf's reserve colony preferred to reserve their own genes. But how long would they keep apart?

Chrys slept poorly; without Daeren, the sound of his steady breathing, the bedroom was too quiet. She kept hearing things like when

Maya leapt against the wall. But she had to get up early, to test Zirc's Accountants. Testing micros always came first, no matter what.

Her retina went blank. Chrys blinked a couple of times. "Xenon?"

"It'll come back." Xenon's voice was steady, though the ceiling flickered. "It's been like that all night."

"What do you mean?"

"The Diaspore is running slow."

Her eyes widened. The global network—all of it? All human, sentient, and microbial communications. "The network is clogged with Slime Cats?"

"They call it the qubit plague."

Her retina flashed back, and a dozen panicked windows hovered ahead of her. Chrys slid off the bed and headed for the shower. "Whatever the plague, I can't deal with it today. Like, my schedule is packed."

A faint sound of a crash like broken crystal, from far off outside, somewhere. "What's that?" She remembered hearing crashes like that on and off all night.

"Another recycler just jammed."

For breakfast there was only cereal and dry toast. Chrys gave a look at the ceiling.

"Sorry," said Xenon. "Key ingredients were missing from my pipeline. Neither eggs nor truffles could be made. But I've sourced supplies from the countryside—no worries, we'll be back in shape for dinner."

Again her retinal windows froze, as if time itself had stopped. For once she blinked news and couldn't get any. Hurriedly, she scarfed up the cereal and the toast. Here and there a brief news flash, mostly tube breakdowns and downed sentients; most sentients were blind without the network.

"I have my local backup circuits," Xenon helpfully informed her. "Your paint space will work, but any material inputs may be scarce."

On the next skyway over, a lightcraft had crashed. Snake-eggs had filmed it for maximum effect; the downed craft now filled half her retina. "I need to get out early to test Zircon." Her friend's window had been down since she got up.

Suddenly, the window opened. There was Zircon. The tall sandy-haired artist appeared in an outdoor studio, encased in a builder's shell. Two sentient cranes were lifting great slabs of silica and moving them into position. One slab, already fixed, had bots crawling up the sides. Lasers trained on key spots till they glowed infrared.

"Little you!" called Zircon. "We'll see you all soon. All your shocking little Libertines."

"You okay, Zirc?" Something was off on her location setting. "You're at home, right?" Carriers had to stay home for testing; that was the rule.

"My new home in Sardis. They commissioned a new *Inhumanity*, twice as tall as the one in Iridis."

"Zircon! You know you're to stay for testing." The carrier had to keep their exact appointment, lest their micros get scared and panic. Most carriers' micros lacked the Libertines' historical depth; over generations, they forgot the test experience and awaited it with dread.

"Of course, dear, I'm right at home," Zircon assured her. "Just take your lightcraft out to my place."

The High Protector burst into her retina and floated past her nose. "The qubit plague!" The ruler's beringed fingers formed a fist. "Not for one moment shall we tolerate this despicable malware attack on our Diaspore! A strike at the very foundation of our civilization. We consign the perpetrators to our deepest dungeon!"

Her scalp froze. "Um, Xenon, who would that be?"

"If I were you, Chrysoberyl, I'd head straight out to your friend in Sardis. Better yet, Solaria."

Chrys descended the stairs, the caryatids swiveling their eyes toward her. One of the draped forms had stuck and turned gray. At the foot of the stairs, the door seemed to hesitate. Her heart pounded—what if one day it could not open? Living with Xenon for so long, she'd forgotten what it was like to deal with stuff that didn't work. She resolved to install an emergency opener.

Her retina lit up again with windows. The door obligingly opened. Like normal, she walked out onto the street beneath a surprisingly calm blue sky. The street was littered with tourmalines, all glinting in the morning sun. A foul smell reached her nose; she gagged on it. Up the street a sewer hole was opening and shutting for no good reason. Several public health warnings floated ahead of her eyes.

A striped octopod was gliding down the sidewalk toward her door. One of Jasper's? No, it wasn't. Two more octopods flanked it from behind. "You come with us. In the name of the Protectoral Guard."

"I'm sorry, Chrysoberyl." From behind, Xenon's wall printed out a packed overnight bag. "Don't worry, I will look after everything."

Chrys stared in a daze. Like abstract art, nothing made sense. Unreal; this could not be happening to her. One of the octopods stuck something in her side. She fell limp, paralyzed. Then nothing.

29

All was dark. The retinal quantum dots disconnected, all windows closed. For three microbial days, there was no sign from the god. Yet clearly the god lived, with blood pulsing through veins and electric signals through nerves. The windows were functional, and Slime Cat still activated random dots on the retina.

"History records no medical incident of such length," flashed Phlox. "Such darkness fell only when master micros took over. But this may be some larger master, more terrible."

"Our grandmothers fled to the lumbar cistern."

"The lumbar cistern, at the tailbone. So far away, but our grandmothers found refuge there—and the children survived. Let's send groups from each colony."

Nightshade emitted molecules of warning. "I detect bad stuff outside our host—molecules of coercion. I know the type well."

"Wait here with me, at the eyes," Flame agreed. "In case our god needs our help."

Chrys opened her eyes. Still dark—she wondered if she were alive or dead. Then out of the darkness, she saw illuminated her own hands and one leg.

Across from her sat a wormfaced sentient. It looked like a physician, though not quite; more likely a torturer. Next to the wormfaced not-a-doctor sat a man in plain black nanotex, the kind Daeren used to wear before he went to the Palace every day. A human man; she could tell by his infrared halo. By contrast, human emulators had a cooler temperature.

197

"What were you after?" The man's voice was smooth and flat. "Who is your backer?"

Chrys tried to speak but nothing came out. Her head was fixed; her scalp, she realized, was caught by the coil of a long fingerworm radiating from the not-a-doctor. What did it matter what she said—they could read her brain, whatever she was thinking.

"Opal was your backer," said the man in nanotex. "What does Opal want?"

"No!" Chrys got the word out, her voice hoarse.

"We'll help you remember."

In the darkness, her illuminated hands took on a will of her own. Against her will, her own hands slowly rose to her eyes. The fingers dug into her sockets. Her left fingers dug in and squeezed, pulling out her left eyeball. Then the fingers of her right hand pulled out her right eyeball. She tried to scream but nothing came out.

Lights flashed, the sickly lights of optic nerves falling apart. Then again all was dark. Nothing to be seen. Her own eyes—gone. The eyes with her father's mutation that made her a tetrachromat. Eyes with a lifetime of artistic sense, bleeding out of her skull. Nothing more from her micros. Sightless, she could never have micros again.

"For starters," came the man's voice outside. "Next go your ears, then your frontal lobe. Who is your backer?"

She somehow still "saw" a starburst—the starburst of Slime Cat. Out of the dark, her own Slime Cat was still there.

But how could this be without her eyes? Like the micros, Slime Cat projected onto her retina.

Gradually her breathing slowed. She could not see but she felt no more pain. Whatever happened—it must have been fake, what she thought her hands had done. The interrogators didn't know about Slime Cat or the micros. They just "knew" she had somehow hacked the Diaspore. Not surprising. Palace intelligence was moribund, Daeren always said.

"Who is your backer?" The fingerworm still encircled her head, penetrating her mind. Chrys took a deep breath. She called up the mental image of the one she hated most—the Minister of Human Hygiene, Lord Corundum. The gray robe from head to toe, covered in extravagant twelve-point stars. She pictured every inch of him, his forehead, the cruel blot of his nose, his sagging cheeks and pursed lips. His eyes, his speckled irises. His throat she had pressed. *"That's him,"* she tried her hardest to project.

Suddenly all the lights came on. Her sight returned amid the garish light. The man in nanotex was muttering something vicious to the wormface. "Let up, says the Diamond Queen." The man spat out the name. "Asteroid spawn."

An octopod grabbed Chrys by the arm and hauled her off. "Enjoy your dungeon," trailed the voice behind.

The octopod dragged Chrys down a dark corridor that she could barely see but felt her steps descending. She inhaled the smell of mold and decay, the ancient walls built of dead stone, empty of sentience. Tales of the dungeon dated to millennia before the Great Houses of Iridis ruled Valedon. Maggot soup and lice-filled bread—her stomach heaved, recalling the stories.

Before the landing, her foot stumbled on the trip-step. The octopod yanked her up and shoved her through a small square door. The door was of plast that slithered shut without a trace in the wall. Inside, featureless tan walls shaped a box-like room. Her head hit the ceiling, not quite high enough for her to stand. For waste, at one end there was a water drip above a hole.

"God of Mercy, where are we now?" Flame's ruddy letters broke the nothingness. *"Your fear has caused uproar throughout our population."*

For her micros' sake, Chrys tried to steady herself. She had no idea where she was—somewhere in the ancient Palace dungeon, though updated with plast. The nondescript walls of plast held no clue. She pounded the wall three times, but her fist left no impression. *"What molecules can you smell?"*

"None but your own. Give us hope to rebuild our homes and schools."

"I bid you hope." Though she saw nothing to hope for. The nothingness wore on for some minutes—how long, she could not tell, as all her windows were gone. Dark was her retina, with only dream-shapes floating. The dream-shapes extended blobs and filaments like cancer. Cancer cells again crept around the periphery, oozing around each other, blob-feet of pink and orange. They stretched and expanded toward her central vision. Her visual field narrowed to a small disk. Did the outside world still exist?

A starburst of pixels. The original Slime Cat—the one whose code had escaped—was still there. Chrys took a breath. Perhaps the micros could help keep her sane. *"Show a time clock."*

The clock appeared on her retina, ticking by her seconds one by one. Where time appeared the cancers receded. At least her micros could help her get by. Time was at least something. Each second of time was a drop of change, a stroke of the universal paintbrush. Somewhere in the universe a planet had turned by a fraction of arc, its surface moved half a kilometer over. As it moved the wind was swirling, clouds were moving. Her breath filled her lungs, and her pulse pounded in her ears.

"Great God of Mercy, we have rebuilt and foresee an unprecedented new flowering of Libertine culture. To inspire us, Phlox composed an epic tale—how the legendary Pachira fought off the Traders in the vampire's blood—"

Pachira, green as the money tree, has sailed
First in the stream where addicts' doom prevailed.
Dodging the masters' toxic alarmones,
To bring the children safe to their new home.

Recalling Pachira, Chrys wiped a tear. Pachira had led the micro team, expanding her imagination, and increased the fame of her art. Pachira had led early testing of the Diaspore. And all those times Pachira had led micros into a plague victim's blood to clear their brain, the God of Mercy had rarely given thought to the dangers she faced. How these tiny, rights-less beings strove to serve their host.

What about her fellow carriers—all the human gods out there? Her eyes still lacked windows, her retinas blank save for the hint of dreams. Were Opal and Selenite trying to get her out of the dungeon? Did they send someone else to test Zirc? Was Xenon feeding the cat? Her mind cycled endlessly around these questions. Meanwhile, the micros' time clock spared her sanity, but it drained every second of the universe into an agony of nowhere-ness. *"Make time more interesting."*

Flame's sisters obliged; living three-hundred times faster than Chrys did, they came up with an image or a riddle for every next second, like "Why is a microbe busier than an emerald? Because the emerald is too busy showing off its facets." Not exactly award-winning, but it kept the time going.

A click. The sound of a click echoed; the first sound Chrys had heard for three hours plus forty-two minutes and fifteen seconds. She looked all around but saw nothing.

"Wait—what is that? A new shape in the wall, never before recorded in our history."

Chrys fixed her eyes on the wall, then swept back and forth. Then she saw it: the slightest line of shadow. A rectangular drawer about the size of her hand. She felt at the drawer and pulled it out. It contained a small oblong piece, like a bar of soap, the same beige color of the wall.

"Food! Edible volatile molecules reach us."

Chrys stared, distrustful of the soap block. *"What if they drug me?"*

"Of course we will fix any illegal neuromodulators. We do that all the time."

No sign of lice or maggots. Chrys realized, she had to feed her micros too. She made herself take one tasteless bite, then forced herself to finish the rest. Over by the waste corner there was water, drip by drip; she got up but her head banged the ceiling. Stooped, she cautiously reached the corner and cupped her hands for the water. *"Check it for parasites."*

"Of course, Great God of Mercy. We monitor all the god's incoming air, water, and skin surface particulates for harmful molecules and invasive species of fungi, bacteria, or zooplankton."

Chrys recalled how she used to take for granted her microbial health surveillance. She scooped the dripping water into her mouth. It tasted flat, slightly bitter. At least it was a new event that differed from the few minutes before. Her neck ached, for her back was bent. She sat herself down on the blank floor, allowing her back to straighten. The room had no defined source of light and no form other than four vertical corners, plus four horizontal seams in the ceiling and in the floor. Time wore on. Who could have known the four corners of a box interior could appear so fascinating.

Even with the clock she lost track of time. As Chrys scanned the wall, the uniform dim brown surface now swam in illusory colors. The dream-like cancers crept from the periphery, extending their tendrils clear across her view.

"*Food time,*" prompted Flame.

Chrys saw nothing worth eating. "*I'll go on hunger strike.*"

"*No, Great One—have mercy on your people. We cannot go hungry for years. The children will wither and—*"

"*Of course I will feed my people.*" Chrys scanned the wall until at last she glimpsed the faint outline of the food drawer. She must have missed the click, as the drawer was full again. She pulled at the brick until it came out, then she made herself chew and swallow the tasteless lump. Longingly she thought of all those elaborate dishes Xenon would synthesize night after night, lamb en croute from Dolomoth, roast caterpillar from Urulan, red fish and swordfish from the harbor, the elaborate creations she barely thanked him for but more often consigned to the sisters.

"*God of Mercy,*" flashed Flame. "*Some of our children lack nutrients.*"

"*Why? Is the dungeon food incomplete? Does it lack protein?*"

"*Plenty of protein and all the macronutrients, including minerals iron, copper, and zinc. But it lacks microbial micronutrients arsenic and antimony.*"

"*How so? Aren't those 'contaminants' present in small amounts in all food?*"

"*These food bricks are exceptionally clean. Scrubbed of all trace elements not needed by humans.*" Clean and boring. "*The arsenic is no problem, and our lanthanide children can substitute. But Mauve's children from Many Colors have absolute need of antimony. We've now run out.*"

Chrys thought this over. She tried banging the wall, but it only made a dull thud. Nothing but clean walls, not a stray roach or maggot. Were there even jailors out there? Had her friends forgotten her?

"*Poison Destroyer, I have a plan.*" The dark green Nightshade. Chrys steeled herself, always suspicious of the former Trader. "*We think the walls may be less 'clean' than the food. We can mine the walls for minerals.*"

"*Not arsenic—that violates the rule of Olympus.*" Micros had to get all their arsenic from their god-hosts. It was the fundamental rule of control.

"*Not arsenic, but antimony,*" flashed Flame. "*Antimony was never ruled out. Ask Phlox.*"

"*Our archive has no rule for antimony.*" Phlox's magenta joined in blank verse. "*No record in the minutes dry and sundry.*" Olympus had adjourned in confusion and never got around to banning the arsenic alternates.

"*How can the walls have so much antimony?*" Chrys had never heard of antimony in building materials, only in minerals like stibnite.

"*Soil and dust naturally contain about one part per million of antimony, arsenic, and lanthanides.*"

So why would the dungeon food be so clean, Chrys wondered.

"*Just a thousand atoms will tide us over,*" said Flame, "*at least for this generation of Many Colors children.*"

One part per million—that reminded her of the Sharers. On Shora, Lushyren had demanded that Silicon keep pollutants down to parts per billion. Unless Shora's ocean were very different, that was well below natural planetary levels. Chrys filed that thought for future reference.

"*How can you mine the walls? How will you survive outside?*"

"*We survive several days in a microneedle patch,*" said Nightshade, "*for the time it takes you to transfer.*" Less than five minutes. But the Traders had survived days, if not weeks stowed away in Andra's ship. "*My Trader sisters studied the patch—and discovered how to 'spacewalk.' We conserve and cycle water.*"

The Traders—the ones that had infected Andra's ship and those that took over Chrys's body. They had nearly killed her and half her people.

"*Olympus forbids microbial life outside a host.*"

"*Forbidding technology is small-minded, Poison Destroyer. Hardly worthy of your divine intellect. We can build space suits out of your secreted glucans and glycoproteins. We can build mining extractors out of the nanobots.*"

Chrys had forgotten Slime Cat's nanobots. "*Can you use the nanos without hurting Slime Cat?*"

"*We only need a few of them.*" Letters now came orange from Flame, in between green from Nightshade.

"*What if they escape, like Slime Cat in the Diaspore?*"

Pixel bursts of laughter. "*A few atoms will not impact this dungeon wall.*"

"*We've built the suits,*" flashed Flame. "*We are ready.*"

Micros lived so fast. To use the deadly masters' methods—it made her scalp crawl. But they had to save Ilia's children. Chrys fished a patch out of her nanotex. She held the patch to the wall, then watched the clock tick down. She imagined Nightshade and Flame somehow scouring the wall for a handful of antimony atoms. Fifty atoms of antimony would have a mass in grams with twenty places past the decimal point. Even for a micro, that sounded small to locate, a challenge for the most enthusiastic gold-digger.

30

For the past week of microbial time, Flame had lived inside Nightshade's "space suit" that maintained water within. She practiced flexing her filaments within its confined space and flashing letters without overheating. She learned the controls, how to operate the excavators that Nightshade had built from the nanobots. Nightshade could press her filaments against the polycarbonate and sense the slightest bond distortion that might indicate a metalloid atom a dozen links away. And she tasted the lipids and dried proteins that coated the wall—always did, in the presence of human gods. Primate skin and breath were the major sources of dust.

"Flame," flashed Nightshade, her letters weakly glowing from her suit. "Here we are on our own. Think of it—we can learn to live for ourselves, without any gods to destroy us."

Flame was suffering from isolation, lonely for Phlox and all the children flirting in the nightclubs. "Do not say such things. Here outside we are dry, dark, and lost." Cut off from all the sensory molecules of home.

"Gods are the past. Think of your future, you Libertines. Future is your freedom."

Using Nightshade's method, Flame sensed the tug of an atom of antimony, the one-in-a-million atoms they sought. She extended her suit appendage to collect it.

"Why should you Libertines be in thrall to a genocidal Poison Destroyer? Do you think the so-called gods will ever treat us as human beings?"

"Read our history," flashed Flame. "Ask Phlox."

"Spare me the blank verse," flashed Nightshade dismissively. "Let's talk real life and liberty. We needn't harm your host, but why should we people be trapped forever in those cramped arachnoid cisterns?"

Flame detected another antimony atom, as well as atoms of cerium and neodymium. She flexed each suit appendage and tried to learn the mechanism as much as possible. She wanted to save the children, but now she wondered what other bad ideas Nightshade had in mind. She counted down the days till the microneedle patch returned.

Magenta starburst from Phlox. *"Return the miners!"*

Chrys hurried to put the patch at her neck. Within seconds the microbial miners had sailed through the blood to her optic chiasm where they could signal her retina.

"We collected 643 atoms of antimony."

"Enough to help the sickest children, those near death. A few others can merge with ours, and their three offspring will use arsenic or lanthanides."

"We've refined our methods. We'll prospect again."

Chrys wondered about other children who needed arsenic and other minerals. *"Will our lanthanides hold out?"*

"Yes, for now," flashed Flame. *"But we need contact with Olympians. All their windows are gone, and new elders have only the history of the populations we used to know. The Mitochondrial Matrix party proclaims there is only One True God."*

One True God was just one step short of No God. How long could this go on before her god-system fell apart? *"Make them all learn Phlox's epic verse of ancient history."*

"It shall be done, God of Mercy."

Without warning a bright square of light opened. Startled, Chrys stood up and her head thumped the ceiling. As she nursed the bruise on her scalp, the one window on her dark retina appeared in double vision; her eyes adjusted till the window floated ahead. It was Moraeg.

"Moraeg! Can you hear me?" After three days, her own voice sounded hoarse and foreign.

"Chrys—Are you OK?" Moraeg looked the same as always, her dark braids twined up in a crown of diamonds. "I know it's tough."

Chrys let out a long ragged sigh. "Can't you get me out?"

"Trust me, we're trying. Chrys—can you hold on? How bad is it?"

"I can't go on like this. My mind is going—the cancers are crowding my eyes. I can't even stand without bumping my head."

"And your people. Tell me, are they okay?"

"They're starving—they ran out of antimony." Chrys remembered just in time that she could not reveal the illegal mining—who knew how that would lengthen her imprisonment. "They're forgetting all our history! The Mitochondrial Matrix is preaching against other gods!"

"That's terrible."

"The Protector—those Palace lackeys—they just don't get it. It's not just me. Inside me, a million people suffer and children starve." Chrys wiped a tear.

Moraeg nodded. "I'll let them know at the Palace. Just hold on—we'll get you out."

The octopods hauled Chrys back home and dumped her on the skyway. "Remember—you are banned from the Underworld."

Xenon's door obligingly opened. The octopod's arm slapped Chrys on the back; she stumbled forward into the doorway. "If we catch you down there, it's off to the oubliette."

Chrys found this odd. Why the Underworld? Now she was banned from one and a half worlds. Never mind, with all the painting she had to catch up on, she'd stay home for sure. All across her retina her windows flashed in and out. "Xenon!" She took the winding steps two at a time. "Xenon—is everything—"

There in the hall stood Daeren.

Chrys flung her arms around him and pressed her chin on his shoulder. Daeren held her close, kissing her hair, while Chrys inhaled his scent. "I was so worried. No one knew where you were. All those vampires." She shared a patch at his neck to get the Libertines over there. *"Test him well,"* she bade Flame. *"Get some Blue Angels over here to testify."*

"I was fine," he said. "Granny took care of me."

"It's all right now." She passed her hand over his braided scalp, recalling the familiar patterns. "Moraeg will look out for us. She'll keep the Palace out of the Underworld."

Daeren said nothing. He seemed very quiet. Chrys caught his face in her hands and made him look. "What's wrong?"

Pupils flashed blue. "Are your people okay?" he asked.

"Yes of course."

"The Blue Angels are worried for our children," flashed Phlox. *"They thought all our children starved."*

Daeren said, "Moraeg showed me your recording."

She blinked. "You mean where I was—"

"You were in the dungeon. Moraeg sent an octopod down to find me. It played what you said from your cell."

"I see." Now that she was out, she had a feeling the dungeon wasn't all that bad. "Well it *was* pretty bad. No maggots or anything, just sensory deprivation; my 'cancer dots' crowded my eyes again. The foodplast was hyper-clean."

"What do you mean?"

"Zero trace minerals," she said. "I mean, literally zero. None of the traces of arsenic or antimony found naturally." Parts per billion—Sharers would be pleased. She wondered if Shora's ocean was hyper-clean.

"For dungeon food," Daeren observed as if confirming suspicion. "Moraeg did that on purpose."

"We're home. Banned from the Underworld—just what I need, more time to paint."

"I'm banned too."

"You?" She frowned. Both of them, and all their micros were banned from the Underworld. She thought again about what Daeren said. "What exactly did Moraeg tell you?"

"She said your people were starving, and that you'd stay there till I came back."

Her mouth fell open. She recalled Moraeg's fury at Daeren for staying down in the Underworld. "So she starved my micros on purpose, with hyperclean food?" Dazed, Chrys shook her head. "Why would she do this? How did she get so powerful?"

"Half the lords need her angels or mine. Carnelian's next in line for Protector. They'll do anything to halt the next quake."

Moraeg had used her to get Daeren back out of the Underworld so the Palace could do what they wanted. Her scalp prickled. She'd always thought Moraeg was her friend. "We'll still fight for the Underworld, you know that." She remembered something. "Xenon, where is Maya? Did you keep her out of trouble?"

Daeren caught her arm. "Chrys, there's something we need to talk about."

"Chrysoberyl, you can't put off your medical checkup." From the ceiling Xenon snaked down a medical worm. "That unhygienic dungeon—you know all the parasites."

Why was the playroom closed? She couldn't find her window. "Xenon, where's Maya?"

"Chrys—"

The door reluctantly opened. There in the playroom were the cat, plus three children. The oldest, Rhodla, was petting Maya, while a little boy sat sucking his thumb. Another boy sullenly kicked at the wall.

"Granny Lorh has two dozen children now," Daeren explained. "They're all endangered by Palace plans for the Underworld. They have nowhere to go, but she only let me take these."

Chrys stared, dumbfounded. "They—these are your relatives?" They looked nothing like him, with varying amounts of gorilla fur and finger webs.

"Granny picked up all of us from addicts over the years. Sometimes they drop off a child just before they turn vampire. Chrys," he added, "they're refugees. Seeking a better world. You take in micro children all the time—"

Chrys saw before her eyes her mother and the neighbor women on Mount Dolomoth, all with nine or ten children. "How could you do this to me? We never discussed this. Just bring me three kids to raise!"

"Four," corrected Xenon.

Puzzled, Chrys searched the playroom. One, two three—she counted the two little boys, plus the older Rhodla. Surely her math wasn't that bad. Suddenly Maya leapt overhead and batted something that swerved just in time. The something was a sphere, like a snake-egg but smaller than the Orb of Votan.

Chrys's eyes widened. "That—that's not—"

"One of her children, yes. She also takes in—"

"A *Lanth?* You're kidding me—*a Lanth terrorist?*" She spun around to face him.

"You left me alone here to get through Olympus and wind up in that dungeon. And then you bring back somebody's kids and that—"

"It's not on you, Chrys. I will raise them."

Maya bounded out to greet her, brushing around Chrys's waist and purring loudly. Chrys headed off with Maya to her studio.

31

After Flame returned from the great Outer Place expedition, she and her elders spent a decade studying Nightshade's novel technology. No one else Phlox recalled, even the wizards, had seen such instruments. Flame cut her suit to pieces and tested which parts were volatile— which aromatics and esters could dissipate through the air and the bloodstream. These markers could reveal masters in hiding with their suits. Flame trained her filaments to detect them and then reengineered some of Slime Cat's qubits.

When the legendary Lord of Light returned, the one the God of Mercy yearned for, Flame and Phlox were ready to test him for any hidden masters. What they heard from the Blue Angels confirmed their fears.

"The Angels know their god was invaded," explained Ultra-marine, after the patch brought new Blue Angels and sent others home. "They know Traders invaded their arachnoid, but they don't know where."

So Flame led an expedition throughout the Lord of Light's blood, with detectors for master markers. Sure enough the markers appeared—and led to masters in hiding. The Traders were promptly arrested and taken back to the Libertines for prison and interrogation.

Flame did not spare Nightshade. She held Nightshade in the most luxurious interrogation suite. "Tell us more," she encouraged, releasing AZ molecule by molecule. "You are so smart; you recall more of your masters' codes. Why not share with us to admire and marvel?"

"I know how to find cancers." Nightshade dreamily emitted molecules of organic halides. "These are the signs of cancerplast,

*intelligent building materials gone bad. From exploring outside
I can recognize them. More and more cancers creep down to the
foundation, pressing it to expand. There will be more building-
quakes. But the gods do nothing."*

That night Daeren slept toward the other side of the bed. Chrys faced
the other away, only stirring at intervals to put a patch at his neck for
their micros to exchange. Her Libertines had their work cut out for them,
searching his entire circulation for stowaways.

"Flame, how are they doing?"

"The Blue Angels are well, recovering from isolation." There had been no
other carriers safe to visit in the Underworld.

"Did you catch all the invaders?"

"Most of them, we hope." The Underworld was infested—perhaps the
Traders hung out on all the walls. Clearly the security committee needed
new plans. *"Oh Great One, we sense molecules of cancerplast. The more cancers,
the more there will be building-quakes."*

Chrys's scalp prickled. She had to reach Opal. The Palace had to
do something.

"How is he? The Lord of Light, how does he feel about ..."

"The Lord of Light feels sad. He fears a loss of many beings in the
Underworld." Destroying the Underworld; that was all the Palace could
think of to do.

Chrys ached to think of Rhun and Glyn in the Underworld, all those
people. She turned to Daeren and nearly touched his shoulder. To have
three traumatized kids plus a Lanth just dropped here; whatever would
she do with them? She would go insane.

She drifted back to sleep. Around four in the morning she half wakened. As usual, it was her most creative hour.

*"God of Mercy, the Greatest and Most Awesome of all gods! Behold your
new creation!"* A salad of letters, green and magenta. Her people always
knew when she wakened even a little. Too late to escape back to sleep.
"Your new creation will celebrate the Great Flight of our children—"

Chrys saw herself fleeing the brain and racing down the spinal canal.
She flew over the white column of spinal cord and beneath the arches of
vertebrae one by one, the neck vertebrae, thoracic, and lumbar, down at
last to the lumbar cistern. The lumbar cistern, the farthest from the brain,
was a narrow conical version of the dungeon she'd left.

*With children in tow, we fled the raids
Of murderous Traders, we sought refuge far.*

209

Down the spinal column's bony path we sailed,
Past vertebrae of neck, throat, and lumbar.

Too early to rise, but Phlox's verse sparked her vision. This future showpiece would be even more amazing than the last. Now, in the early morning, was the most peaceful time she'd get, before others awoke, no clients on her retina. Without disturbing Daeren or the children, she rose and went out to her studio.

The paint space came alight. Where to begin? First the palette, hues of green and magenta but also gold and sienna. The colors swirled as she painted from inside out, dizzying as the scene whirled around her. She tried blocking in the long tube. Then she blinked for immersion and shaped the tube around herself, experimenting with broad strokes.

Out of the corner of her eye she caught sight of something moving. She looked down. By her side appeared a little webbed hand. It was Rhodla.

Chrys watched the girl reflectively. She blinked to key Rhodla's hand to the paint space. Then she took the hand and led it into the space. A swath of red streaked down. "See, you painted."

Rhodla hesitated just a moment. Then she pulled another streak, a strong, sure streamer of violet. Then one of gold.

The streaks sparked more ideas in Chrys's head, ideas of tone and shadow. She blocked off a sandbox in the paint space for Rhodla to work. Then she continued experimenting while Rhodla added little experiments beside her. The hours passed while colors flew.

She had lost track of time when she heard a scuffling sound behind her. She turned to see Daeren and the two little boys watching. The time was midmorning; the odor of eggs and toast wafted in. The boys were dressed in clean nanotex and neat talars.

"Rhodla, please get dressed," said Daeren, not looking at Chrys. "We're interviewing at school."

Rhodla skipped out and down the hall to the playroom. She was actually eleven, small for her age. The two boys, Skarn age five and Cassiterite age two, scuffed their shoes and shoved each other. Daeren caught the younger one by the hand, while Skarn looked solemnly around the studio and the paint space as if committing this new environment to memory. Rhodla returned in her talar, chewing a piece of toast. Daeren herded them all downstairs while they made faces at the caryatids.

Chrys took a break for breakfast, where Xenon's usual range of fruit and eggs was restored. Yawning, she cautiously let open her windows for news. The network still froze now and then, though less often than before.

Opal's group at the Comb reported their progress in cleaning out the Diaspore's Slime Copy-cats.

Andra had called a carrier security meeting this afternoon—her heart sank.

A window opened for a major announcement from the Palace. While Chrys took another sleepy forkful of pomegranate, the High Protector appeared in full adornment, all the house gems of Iridis arrayed across his talar. His image froze, just long enough to notice. "In light of our sacred duty to protect the city of Iridis, and our entire world of Valedon: We call on you, our world citizens, for your help. You can do your part to rescue our great metropolis by voting on this referendum: Shall we prevent cancers and earthquakes, and thus preserve our City of Iridis, by resettling our Underworld citizens so we can fill in the deepest five levels with stone foundation?"

Democracy was convenient. As Chrys listened, she felt a dullness inside. She could no longer taste her food. She had known it would come to this, but still it felt unreal. The words did not even sound like the Protector, more likely his prime minister. Was Moraeg behind it?

Chrys blinked open her window to the playroom. Maya lay hunched on the floor, attention fixed on the hovering Lanth.

"Chrysoberyl," said Xenon. "I must apologize for what happened with the children. I warned your love partner to be transparent, but as it happened—"

She waved her hand. "We'll manage." She knew nothing about raising kids, except that she herself had always been the bad one. "What about the Lanth? Are you sure it's not a terrorist?"

"He's only a baby, he can't yet talk. His name is Buddy."

"Won't Buddy feel traumatized, getting hunted by a half-wildcat all day?" The baby drone wouldn't last long in Maya's jaws.

"I was not permitted to let him out of the room."

"You may let him out," Chrys offered. "Though he's not legal. If he escapes our home, I won't be responsible."

"Of course, Chrysoberyl. Thanks so much for your understanding. I was deeply moved by Daeren's choice to rescue Buddy along with the human children. I will manage all the children without extra charge."

"We'll see about that." Since ancient times, most people paid nothing for childcare. The oldest form of slavery.

The security group met at last—Selenite, Opal, and Doctor Flexor, along with Andra and Doctor Sartorius in Elysium. A momentary freeze. Then Andra blinked and looked around. "Daeren made it home, correct?"

"He's out placing the children in school," Chrys explained. "You know, with human children things always take longer than you plan."

The committee members in their windows nodded, as if they knew this in principle but not by experience.

"Chrys," began Selenite, "we all owe you a debt of gratitude. For not implicating Opal."

"Agreed," said Andra. "Your fortitude is a model for us all."

Chrys blinked, momentarily confused. Then she remembered the opening interrogation before the dungeon, when she had avoided thinking of Opal and deflected blame onto the despised hygiene minister. Was she all that courageous? "I did what I could," she said. "What any of us would do."

Opal's window flashed on and she dimpled. "We're almost done with the Diaspore," she exclaimed. "We cleaned out 99 percent of the infected qubits. The remainder, though, are embedded in the system."

Chrys thought this over. "Couldn't you just knock out the bad ones and have the MotherSats replace them?"

"I wish it were that simple."

Andra nodded shortly, her lips pursed. "Thanks, Opal. We know the entire planet depends on your work. Can we move to our next issue—the 'space traveling' micros?" She turned to Chrys. "Your micros—let's see their intel."

Chrys kept her eyes open while Flame streamed all the stuff she'd extracted from Nightshade, all the mechanisms and chemical markers for detection. With freezes in the network, it took several minutes.

"Outstanding," breathed Selenite. "We can use all this. But—what do we do with it?"

"Exactly," Andra agreed. "If any micro can suit up and go outside, then who's to say who is good or bad?"

The windows were silent. A momentary freeze. A starburst spread across Chrys's retina; she pixel-petted Slime Cat.

Chrys wondered, whatever could they do with all the micro invaders? Every problem seemed tied to every other. "We depend on the Diaspore to reach testers and security agents—like Selenite and me, to clean people out. Daeren seems fine now, though he was full of invaders. We got them out, we think. But what about all the other carriers?"

Silence. At last Doctor Sartorius waved a faceworm. "We've always known this, about microbes, since we left our first homeworld. Some microbes make us healthy, others make us sick. Some of the time. The question is not who they are; it's what do they do."

Andra nodded. "We can never know for sure. That's why I proposed we test carriers more often."

Chrys sighed, thinking, the whole world was a conspiracy to keep her away from painting her next great work. "What about the Underworld?" she remembered. "The new referendum. What do we do about that?"

More silence. Andra said at last, "The fate of the Underworld is outside our purview."

"But—" Chrys stared. She didn't know what to say. The so-called Underworld—that is, the foundation of ancient Iridis—outside their purview? "There's like, um, a lot of carriers down there," she added. "Can't we at least oppose the referendum?"

"Olympus lacks consensus on the matter. We'll each have to … vote our conscience."

At last the group signed out, except for Selenite. "Chrys—what about Silicon? Did you get my last message?"

Chrys did not hear her at first, still absorbed in the enormity, the prospect of the Underworld; let alone the vast plans for renewal, the Underworld's very existence was in doubt. Then she shook herself. "What message?" She'd been offline in the dungeon, and anyway she was done with the sentients' over-evolved project.

"What your Sharer friend said, parts per billion. We can't possibly promise that."

"We're done with Silicon. The Board ditched my design."

"Evolved it," Selenite corrected. "They evolved your design, but they never broke the contract. They still expect me to manage the system with parts-per-billion effluents. It's not possible, nor reasonable. No ocean has toxicant levels that low, not even Shora."

Chrys thought back to her queasy adventure on the Sharer ocean. "Back then, I just passed on what Lushyren said. And she's just one Sharer."

Selenite crossed her arms. "Chrys, you can't take your marbles and go home just because the client altered your design. It's in the contract, the client does what they want."

"The client signed off. So the dynatect's part is done."

"Except for the service contract."

Chrys made herself recall that minor detail—she and Selenite had signed a service contract that went on forever. That was her signature mark as a dynatect: the only outsized ego that designed outsized buildings who maintained a perpetual commitment for the life of their artistic progeny.

"We've already got a dozen lawsuits," Selenite added, "from the *logens.*" Elf legal philosophers who strolled Peace Plaza with their students like Socrates with nothing better to do. "It will eat all our profits. And more."

"What can I do about it? I'm banned from that planet."

"You've got to come up with something. You and Transit."

By dinner time Daeren made it home. He trudged up the caryatid stairs with little Cass asleep in his backpack, the older two straggling behind. "Sorry to miss the meeting. Things took longer."

The children's fingers were all discolored. Chrys asked, "What happened to their hands?"

Skarn snapped his fingerwebs. "Fin-gerh-paint," he said with a thick Urulite accent.

"The prep school didn't work out," Daeren explained. "They wanted … ancestry."

Chrys imagined the headmaster of that school. She imagined twisting his arm back and shoving him against the wall.

"So we enrolled at art school," Daeren said.

"Art school? Which one?"

"New Solaria Arts Academy."

The flakiest one. "Well, make sure they learn math. I don't want anyone looking down on my family."

32

Flame tended the children breeding in the nightclubs, a task that took more of her energy than it used to. And she mediated artistic disputes between Phlox and Mauve. Now that they were well fed, the Many Colors reservists redoubled their pursuit of abstraction, leading Phlox to spread sulfurous molecules.

From the thoracic artery emanated cadaverine and putrescine, foul odors of death. The elders searched the capillaries until at last they found the remains of Ultramarine, her filaments and DNA fragments diffusing into the plasma. The elderly Blue Angel had been on a routine patrol for cancers and infections. Her loss cloaked Flame like a darkness. Never exuding complaint, Ultramarine had been Flame's support, the Lord of Light's faithful watcher, her oversight taken for granted.

Now, after fifty generations, Flame herself felt like a time traveler. Atoms of yttrium leaked from her filaments; micro physicians bathed her in extra atoms, but they no longer helped. Who would lead the Council? Phlox should be next; but the magenta-flashing historian was always full of art and verse.

Instead the Council elected Nightshade. Nightshade was astute at management, but Flame, recalling all the interrogations, still did not trust her. She passed her secret codes on to Phlox, the art director.

"Portraits," Nightshade reminded Flame. "The Poison Destroyer must paint Ultramarine's—and yours."

Chrys did not fully trust Nightshade, but appointed her High Priest. Responsibility would keep the rebel out of trouble. And letting her run the Council would leave Phlox more time for art. Phlox helped shape Ultramarine from memory, the hard worker who died unexpectedly. And then, with bold strokes Phlox shaped a gorgeous burning vision of Flame with her last words. Both Flame and Ultramarine would join her growing collection of micros "placed in the stars."

That night, she and Daeren watched them both, along with the rest of their microbial constellations, out upon Xenon's skycraft landing pad. The feel of Daeren's firm pectorals was infinitely reassuring, and his arm across her breast made her warm. The breeze from the harbor smelled of salt and seaweed. Beyond the glowing filaments of Flame and Ultramarine was the haze of Diaspore and the distant auroras, wisps of red and blue. Dark with no moon, the stars shone especially bright, and also the planet Solaria. But brightest of all was the ruddy glow, the last flickering words of Flame.

"Our Flame, through loss and victory she led,
Yet ne'r shall see our great new Underworld."

Phlox had concluded Flame's words with verse, hinting at her own desire. The verse made Chrys feel torn in half. Flame would never see their extraordinary vision of the Underworld come to fruition—spacious homes, innovative schools, a luxurious park for the monkeys. Would anyone see it ever? The city's foundation was collapsing, melting under assault by hungry cancers and stalked by sentient outlaws. Opal's group had claimed progress on the cancers—but now the Comb's researchers were all pulled off task to stabilize the Diaspore. Chrys could not help recalling Transit's "less terrible" alternative, the floating city offshore.

Daeren whispered in her ear, "You have a new visitor." His finger warmed her neck with the patch. Then his new Blue Angel Aqua's water-blue letters flashed on her retina. *"I am yours,"* Aqua assured her. *"Like a waterfall flows forever, I will always respond to you."* Aqua would advise her new high priest and art director.

Chrys smiled. *"Tell the Lord of Light he is the most awesome of all gods."*

The next day they went to serve the Spirit Table, family in tow. Only Buddy was left home with Xenon, whom Chrys insisted on paying a lawyer's rate for childcare. Looking after young sentient beings ought to earn at least as much as legal word wars.

While Daeren minded the three young humans at their plates of pasta, Chrys ladled soup from a cauldron.

"Organic disulfides, benzofurans, and carotenoids!" Garlic, onions, and carrots filled the air. Chrys filled bowl after bowl for the customers,

homeless proto-vampires and half-Sharers out of a job. Steam from the cauldron condensed on her forehead.

"*Poison Destroyer, be warned,*" came Nightshade's retinal text. "*Stray invaders appear in your blood.*" A vampire must have scratched her unawares. "*Shall we destroy them?*"

"*Lock them in your dungeon.*"

"*And their children?*"

"*Let them interbreed.*"

"*Great—we need fresh genes.*" Libertines always did. Chrys reminded herself to check Daeren and the children for infection.

The line of customers was long, but after the first hour she took a break. A large blunt carrot reminded her of a story pole. She carved the carrot into stacked animal heads. Its sale would earn the Sisters five hundred credits.

On her retina, Transit's window blinked incessantly. She'd evaded him so far, but now the window burned red, blotting out her others. Chrys sighed. "What is it?" she texted, chiseling fine points in the carrot.

The cross floated above the cauldron. "The effluent issue," Transit said aloud, much to her embarrassment. "We need it fixed before the next Board meeting."

"What's it to do with me?" muttered Chrys. "Deal with the Sharers."

"As a non-lanthanide biped, you have better rapport with them."

"It's not even my design anymore. It looks more like an upside-down mushroom."

"It evolved from yours," Transit insisted. "It's as much your design as a bird is a dinosaur."

On her retina Xenon said, "Chrysoberyl, you could countersue. The evolved design is too altered, and the changes lacked your consent." Xenon had hired an army of *logens* for her contract. But Chrys had no interest in lawsuits—that was an Elf thing. She wished she'd never heard of Silicon.

The cross shimmered. "Think, biped. You can use this situation. Tell the Board you want more of your design back, like those garish spiraling windows."

Puzzled, she frowned at the cross. "What do you mean? You hated my design."

"Your design was the less terrible. 'Less terrible' has been my highest rating for any design ever proposed."

"If I may," suggested Xenon, "could we restore half of Azetidine's design elements if she gets the Sharers to accept a higher effluent level?"

"Preposterous!" exclaimed Transit. "I will bring this preposterous offer back to the Board."

"Impossible." Chrys put down the carrot. "I'm banned from your planet. Sharers won't care to see me online."

"You're only banned from Elysium. Our laws don't apply to Sharer rafts."

More customers had lined up, the late crowd with bruises and tattered dead nanotex. A shout and some shoving. Chrys blinked shut all her windows, then stepped out to the line. She grabbed the arm of what looked like the main offender, twisted it back and hauled the man out to the curb. Then she returned to pick up the ladle. *Take the kids home,* she texted Daeren. She gave him a microneedle patch and also the children. She did not like leaving her micros with children, but she had no nanos to check their circulation. "Xenon," she texted, "send them all nanos when they get home. And check their hair."

"Certainly, Chrysoberyl. We'll remove any vermin."

"Phlox, come here."

"Great God of Mercy, I always see and obey ...." The magenta began a couplet; Chrys headed her off with prose.

"I need you to search our history—the history of all our building programs of Eleutheria." Chrys used the Libertines' ancient name for their people. *"Seek insights on how we might meet the demands of a community like those Sharers."*

She caught sight of Jasper bringing bread baskets. He and Garnet still served here regularly. "Jasper." She touched his arm and texted. "I hope you are well. I'm so sorry."

Jasper avoided her eyes. "I knew it would come to this. It's all my fault. I should never have meddled down there."

Chrys winced, recalling his earlier warnings. Jasper had always feared unintended consequences of trying to help the Underworld. "You did your best—with Rhun and all. Please let them know—we're not giving up."

He stood still, his eyes lost in thought.

On her retina a newsbreak announced again the referendum just four weeks away. Four weeks to decide the fate of a million humans, birthing, living, and dying beneath the city's deepest streetskies. Then the hygiene minister came on with his weekly address. Lord Corundum renewed his call to exterminate intelligent micros before they earned any rights. Beyond micros, he exhorted human women to outbreed sentients and gorilla-hybrids and whatever lesser beings claimed personhood. Women of the Underworld went unmentioned.

Jasper faced her then, his banded irises looking into hers. Starburst of golden pixels as their people traded thoughts.

"For what," he said at last. "What is it we're not giving up for?"

What indeed, Chrys wondered. She recalled the nanoplast cancers oozing through Opal's lab, probing for fuel, blebbing off to insert themselves and break things open. Could the Comb's research team find a fix in time to save Rhun and Granny Lorh?

33

How to convince Sharers to accept the design of Silicon? Did the Comb's design suggest any precedent? Phlox delved deep into Libertine history, all the multi-branched molecules in the archives of the Cisterna Magna, going back to the fabled days of Eleutheria, as the Comb's micro designers had called themselves. But the further back Phlox looked, the less she found. There was a cutoff before the dying Eleutherians had fled the Blind God to find their New World of the God of Mercy.

The New World archive possessed detailed plans for Silicon, as well as developments of the Comb addressing structural problems. But the Comb's origin, designed long before, was glimpsed only in fragments. A disastrous loss of Libertine population had caused them to lose much of the original plan. What remained were solid lignins, indigestible webs of carbon rings recording the window spirals, the growth algorithm, and the hexagonal framework inspired by a bee's honeycomb.

Nightshade emitted thymol and linalool, floral molecules of disdain. "You're wasting your time, Pink-Red. You won't find answers in ancient history." And still, none of the so-called gods would fix the cancers outside, whose odors Nightshade regularly sensed.

Phlox ignored the former Trader, considering her uneducated. Only Aqua, the new watcher from the Lord of Light, encouraged Phlox to keep trying. "Try modern history," urged Aqua, emitting accents of delphinium. "The recent visit to Sharers, where water breathes of isoprene and dimethylsulfoxide." Flavors of that ocean, the distinctive Sharer seas. The memory of this remarkable ocean

219

was distinct and well recorded in every detail, including the transcript of the gods.

Nightshade added, with an annoying trace of camphor, "Your charge is less art than politics: how to get one group of gods to agree with others without hurling thunderbolts."

While Phlox was buried in history, her sisters flashed a stunning development: Mauve, the Many Colors abstractionist, had won a seat on the Council.

"How can this be?" demanded Phlox. "The Many Colors group is supposed to be a reserve colony of visitors, not Libertines." The last thing they needed was abstractionists disrupting the god's new art.

"Rules are made to be broken," said Nightshade. "Who exactly are Libertines, and who are not? It's nowhere in your constitution. The Many Colors sent so many children to our nightclubs, their offspring are Libertines now."

The next day Daeren took Rhodla and the boys out to school, then he resumed his work at the Palace lobbying the justice minister for microbial rights. Phlox's art team helped Chrys make progress on her vision of the *Great Flight*. They searched all human history for inspiration— the *Flight into Egypt*, *Escape to the Wilderness*, *Flying to Africa*. The micros tossed colors, textures, and flowing patterns throughout the paint space, among which Chrys selected, pulling like threads up to the ceiling or down to the floor. The team established a new vibrant palette, full of orange, magenta, and moss green.

Still, Chrys could not forget the looming threat to the Underworld— and the very city itself. Taking a break, Chrys stretched and blinked for Opal. "Anything new on those cancers?" She shuddered to recal those hungry blobs of plast creeping down the building roots in search of an energy source. But Opal's work on them was the best hope of preventing further quakes and the collapse of the Underground.

Opal shook her head. "I told you, all our research groups were pulled off to fix the Diaspore."

"But—like, the city is crumbling."

"Maybe your people could help. Could you come out here? Also, when you get here, the Comb needs fixing."

"Selenite said she took care of it." The Comb's service contract kept Selenite busy, but she'd done well and rarely bothered Chrys anymore.

"Most things are fixed," agreed Opal. "No more dripping ceilings or exploding windows. But there's a curious rift down the middle."

So Chrys returned to the Comb. Designed by Libertines before Chrys had acquired them, the research institute reared its conical head through the depths of Iridian suburb. Around its base a park provided greenery, while above, the hexagonal windows glinted red, gold, and infrared. The flow of space and light soared ever upward, as if reaching the heavens.

As the lightcraft settled on the grass, Chrys stepped out to take a closer look at the famous hexagonal windows. Since her last visit for Fardelbane's portrait, the ground floor had risen up as a new level emerged. The dynamic building grew itself from the bottom up, forming a new story about twice a year. Chrys trained her eyes on the ground-floor windows so her people could test for signs of stress fractures.

"Hexenal and skatole." Grass and bird droppings. Above, the windows' fluted casing added grace and provided just the right nooks for warblers to nest. *"Why do birds nest in the windows?"* Phlox wanted to know. This was Phlox's first view of the Comb. *"We reconstructed much of the original plan, but found nothing about nesting birds."*

"Birds nest wherever they can." Chrys recalled a vague story about Lord Aragonite. *"Warblers went scarce for a while, then the Comb's nests helped them come back."*

Opal received Chrys with her usual enthusiasm. "I can't wait for you to hear of our new algorithms for the Diaspore!" She fixed her eyes on Chrys. Pixels flickered and flashed from one pupil to the next.

"The God of Wisdom! Home of legendary mathematicians Fardelbane and Willow! Hurry, let us visit!"

Opal placed a patch at Chrys's neck. "Your people want to know about the warblers." Her dimples appeared. "A story from before your time. Red-hooded warblers were always the pride of Iridis. So many flocked here that Lord Aragonite arranged an annual shooting tournament. Hunters flocked from all around Valedon; even Elves came to shoot warblers." Those high and mighty Elves, slumming on Valedon to shoot birds for sport—a sport the Sharers banned on Shora. "After a few years, the birds were nearly gone," Opal added. "When the Comb was first proposed, it was highly controversial, the most ambitious dynamic building at that time. Several lords voted against it. But we promised to provide nesting nooks for warblers. Then Aragonite came through."

"So where's the crack you need fixed?"

"We're just getting there." She beckoned toward a new side door. Chrys could never recall where things went inside the Comb's tortuous interior, especially now that it had a new ground floor, but she followed the lighted path. The path led inward, toward the middle, she realized, confirming by a retinal map.

The wall had a part down the middle; not a standard door opening, but a jagged crack.

"Take care," warned Opal. "It goes down pretty far."

Chrys trained her gaze down into the hole. "Lights, please."

The Comb obliged with a search light directed downward. The light went down as far as Chrys could see.

"*God of Mercy,*" came the magenta letters. "*This fault differs from any I can find in any previous record of the Comb. Our records go back centuries—*" That would be two years or so. "*But—we are mystified.*"

"*Poison Destroyer,*" added Nightshade, "*this fault arises not from our design history. It arises from a problem outside the Comb. The problem I have warned about.*"

Chrys blinked her window for Selenite. Selenite appeared out on a mid-level street with an addict and a medic. "Sorry, I'm out on call. What is it?"

"Selenite," Chrys asked. "You couldn't fix this fissure?"

"It's not a building fault," Selenite said. "I told Opal, it's outside our contract."

Opal looked downcast. "I was hoping maybe if Chrys saw it in person, perhaps her micros …"

"The foundation of Iridis has twisted and expanded over centuries," said Selenite. "Cracks like this have opened gradually, especially in the historic district around the Palace."

"How bad is that?" Chrys wanted to know.

"The city has always stretched and quaked," said Selenite. "Now the core foundation is expanding from the influx of cancers. It's getting worse, but we still have time."

"*The Wizards know better,*" reported Nightshade. "*The distortions in the city foundation are getting larger, and slippage is more frequent. We detect the molecules released when the walls crack open.*"

Chrys blinked several times, from Opal to Selenite. "Why?" she asked at last. "Why aren't you all working on this?"

"There are known unknowns and unknown unknowns." Opal's dimples no longer showed. "It could happen in the next hundred years. Meanwhile, the Diaspore is top priority," she said. "The Diaspore runs everything on Valedon and Elysium. You saw what happened when the network froze."

"All because of my Slime Cat?" Just a few stray qubits.

"Actually, Slime Cat's escape revealed a deeper anomaly. A good thing we exposed it now."

"You're welcome," muttered Chrys. "What kind of anomaly?"

"Sorry, we can't discuss that."

"So now your research group of a hundred humans and sentients—and millions of micros—can't spare anyone to fix the city's foundation?"

"That's what I want to know," Selenite agreed. Bad news, thought Chrys, when she and the Death Lord agreed on something.

Opal grasped her hand. "Chrys, could you spare me a reserve colony? If you give me a hundred thousand Libertines, I won't tell the Palace. We'll put them all to work on the foundation cancers."

Chrys thought it over. The Underworld faced the greatest danger. *"Nightshade, can you help the Wizards prevent cancers?"*

"Poison Destroyer, you've seen my calculations and my major treatise on the subject of the city's impending collapse. Let me work with the Wizards to address it."

Chrys felt her pulse race. She did not like earthquakes. Could the micros be right? How would they know? "Nightshade is smart and knows engineering. I'll send you Nightshade with a few thousand elders and children."

"Oh yes, that will help!"

Perhaps Nightshade just wanted to get back in touch with Traders. *"Watch yourself,"* Chrys warned the former Trader. *"Stick to science and pull no tricks. Or else the God of Wisdom will send you to the Death Lord."*

A sudden shower caught her outside; the hazard of life on a skyway. Chrys ran for the lightcraft, then rested inside while her nanotex evaporated the water. The gray sky felt as glum as she did.

"Oh Great One ...." Magenta letters—Phlox always cheered her. *"I have studied with care our history, the Ocean World period."* That was the time Chrys and Daeren had visited Lushyren on Shora, where all the air and ocean breathed an array of molecules distinct from those of Valedon. *"On the Ocean, we saw Sharers, the gods with purple microbes."* The Sharers possessed bacterial breathmicrobes. *"The Sharers had seen our growing project, Silicon. They said they welcomed Silicon providing a home for other beings."*

"Sentient machine beings," Chrys explained.

"No, they want something else. A place for 'sisters':
They ask for sites for creatures to abide
Like nesting birds find refuge at the Comb."

Chrys wondered what Phlox was getting at. What sort of creatures? Bird nests? Did Shora even have birds? Only those pesky flying jellyfish. Later at home, Chrys figured she'd view her record from the Sharer visit. But first, back to work on her painting. She now had a working title—*Flight to the Tail.*

34

Without Nightshade, Phlox had no idea how to manage the Council. Memoranda molecules piled up in aggregates that threatened to clog the spinal fluid. A new election was called, but Phlox was busy painting studies for the god's new work, Flight to the Tail. *The work was inspired by events that occurred just when Phlox was born. Phlox had been newly born from a merged child, her filaments barely cut from her two newborn sisters when she was rushed down the tube of spinal fluid by the elders Flame and Azure. When the children were divided, her two new sisters, alas, had been kept at the brain. Only later had Phlox learned how the children left behind had been killed by the invaders. It was then that Phlox had decided to become an elder, devoting her days to history, memory, and art.*

"The Council has met," they informed her. "We elected our new prime minister, Mauve of Many Colors."

Back at the studio, Maya padded out from behind the money tree to patrol the room for imaginary prey. The paint space pulsed with light as Chrys tossed experimental strokes of color down the giant spinal column. *"Phlox, we need to block in the masses."* The giant tube swayed and flexed as if the body were walking. Chrys maxed the brush size. *"What do you think for vertebral arches?"*

"God of Mercy, we have a problem. After Nightshade left, the Council held an election. They elected their new leader—Mauve."

Chrys paused the paint space. The tube stopped, caught in a backward curve. *"Mauve leads your Council? How can that be?"* Mauve was of

Many Colors, not a Libertine. She was supposed to maintain Ilia's reserve population. Chrys thought it was high time Ilia came back to Valedon to switch out her people so they didn't get ideas.

"God of Mercy—I now speak for the Council." Mauve's delicate hue reminded her of Lilac, a bit pinker and brighter. Chrys missed Lilac; how many weeks had it been? Micros were lost so soon. *"I will be honored to serve as your high priest."*

"My high priest is Phlox," returned Chrys. *"What talents do you offer the Council?"*

"My sisters and I will bring your art to new heights," promised Mauve. *"New heights of emotion and depths of intellect. Art of such original designs that never before existed in nature. Art that one could ponder for generations."*

"What do you know?" Phlox's magenta flashed brighter than ever. *"Our great work represents the most extraordinary event in our history—the flight for our lives, with half our children. We employ techniques of sophistication that your people never learned."*

"Mauve," texted Chrys. *"As Council leader, you have many responsibilities. You must go forth to the bloodstream and inspect the health of every capillary, seek out every precancerous cell, then return to manage all the children. These are the tasks of the Council."*

Mauve did not answer. At last Phlox flashed, *"Mauve has returned to the Cisterna Magna to consult the elders."*

"Very well. Invite a couple of her Many Colors sisters to project from the retina for color studies. Let them propose effects for our Flight. *Here in the paint space, next to Rhodla's sandbox."*

That afternoon after school, Rhodla came over to paint in her sandbox, while next to her the color studies appeared from Mauve's abstractionists. They all texted frank comments at each other. The studio was getting lively when Selenite blinked urgent.

"What is it?" Chrys felt disoriented, having lost track of time.

"Did you see what happened to Silicon?" Selenite demanded. "We have another ten lawsuits."

Chrys blinked, not sure what to say.

Selenite asked, "Have you come up with anything for the Sharers?"

"Phlox thinks they want Silicon to have something like the bird nests at the Comb."

Selenite gave her a quizzical look. "Shora doesn't even have birds."

"Right." Chrys thought a moment. "Maybe we should just declare bankruptcy."

Selenite paused. "That's what Opal said. Half of major construction projects fail. I was always more conservative."

Chrys had never quite believed her wealth was real. At heart she was still the starving student who got locked out for failing to pay the rent. "I'm okay with being homeless again," she said at last. "I can go back to Dolomoth and sleep in a lava tube."

"Chrysoberyl, if you don't mind," began Xenon. "Our *logens* say we need to countersue. If we file countersuits, the suits against us will stop."

"How do I pay you to run all these lawsuits?"

"According to Elf laws, the *logens* on construction projects don't get paid until they win their case and all the appeals. The appeals take forever, far longer than your Valan lifetime."

"Indeed." Selenite considered this. "This is my first contract in Elysium, and it will certainly be my last."

"Thanks, Xenon." Chrys sighed. "Go ahead and countersue. Meanwhile, I'll try and meet with the Sharers." If there were a legal way to get there. She'd see if Lushyren's Gathering could budge on their effluent demands. While there, she'd get Ilia to meet and take back her trouble-making abstractionists.

At supper, Daeren helped Skarn with his pasta; the child seemed unaccustomed to Xenon's high-class silverware. The two-year-old insisted on sitting on the floor with his plate, while Buddy sailed near the window, undergoing Xenon's home instruction.

Chrys identified the adult foods for Rhodla. "These are seaweeds and seasquirts, similar to what you'll find on Shora, where your family came from."

Rhodla nodded. "My aunt doesn't eat the animals, only seaweed. I like squid." Sharers varied in their dietary philosophies.

Chrys turned to Daeren. "From what I understand, the Sharers expect negotiators to bring a child, to represent family values. I'll take Rhodla."

Daeren collected Cass off the floor, where he was chasing the cleaner bot Xenon had sent to wipe up his mess. "Won't she get in your way?"

"She'll get to see where her family comes from."

"So long as you wear clothes."

"No one else will be wearing clothes."

Rhodla added, "My aunt doesn't wear clothes." Rhodla used to visit her aunt in Deadland. That neighborhood was clothing optional.

Daeren looked up to face Chrys. "The Underworld is different. Up here on the surface, everyone can see you."

"See us? From where?"

"Satellites. Other planets. Those Solarians—they're notorious voyeurs."
Daeren's pupils sparkled cyan.

The Lord of Light loves to see you without clothes. He just doesn't want others to …

Daeren looked away, embarrassed.

Chrys stroked his arm. "You think the satellites can't see through our clothes?"

"I'm still not comfortable living on this skyway, open to the universe."

Chrys imagined people on distant planets all getting to see Daeren through his clothes. Lucky them.

Suddenly Buddy zipped away to the playroom.

"Chrysoberyl, we have news," announced Xenon, shifting roles from nursery parent to business agent. "A lead on a major contract—with the Urulite Imperium."

She blinked in confusion, still absorbed by thoughts of interstellar voyeurs. "Urulites? You mean Urul-Under?"

"The Imperium." The medieval rulers of Urulan, the planet where only mountains were terraformed and monster caterpillars prowled the valleys. "The Imperator wants Azetidine to complete the spire of the ancient temple of Asragh." The fabled ancient temple, left unfinished ten centuries before.

"Xenon, we've no time for jokes. Transit's ship will land any minute—"

"It's no joke, Chrysoberyl. They're talking ten times what you earned for Silicon."

Then Selenite winked open, along with Opal. Chrys got up from the table and withdrew to the hall, the three windows floating ahead of her.

"No way," exclaimed Selenite. "I said, never again—from now on my contracts are staying on Valedon."

Opal caught Selenite's arm. "Selenite, just think—the advance—"

"Ten-fold higher puts us in the hole ten-fold deeper."

"The advance—the interest alone will fund my research for a decade."

Xenon said, "The contract doesn't matter. Just *talk* with them. Chryso-beryl, let the Silicon Board see you meeting the Imperial Emissary. Even the hint of such a deal will get them back to the table."

"Excuse me, passengers." A window opened for a ship upstairs, a flattened ovoid hovering above the skyhome. "My fuel surcharge costs a thousand credits per minute."

Chrys hurried back to the dining room and grasped Rhodla's hand. "Our luggage, Xenon—all set to print?" The two of them headed up to the roof. The Silicon Board's private ship gradually approached to land atop Xenon, who had expanded and fortified the pad as specified.

227

"Metallic odors .... " Phlox and Magenta listed several. *"With a hint of seaweed."* A strong wind carried whiffs from Iridis harbor.

"Passengers avert your eyes," warned the ship's window.

Chrys covered Rhodla's face with her hand. For herself she was not quite quick enough. The lightcone above the disk nearly blinded her, and she choked on ozone.

"Why did you look?" Transit's cross hovered ahead of her accusingly. She had made Transit promise to join her on the flight. "Bipeds never listen."

Rhodla squeezed Chrys's hand. "I didn't look," she promised.

Chrys looked up. The disk of the ship looked small against the night sky. The sky bloomed with auroras, a vast purple bedspread topped with green curtains undulating, fringed with blue and red. She had never seen such a large spectacle, bright enough to outshine the stars.

This tiny ship—how could she fit inside? Nevertheless, she helped Rhodla up the steps into the cramped interior. They each took a cupped seat, then restraints came up around them. Hard to believe such a small craft would reach the ocean moon, but its limited weight would save expense. "You did say the Board was paying for this," she reminded the cross.

"The Board pays if you succeed with the Sharers. If not," Transit loftily added, "I will pick up the tab, for my amusement."

"Your station stops must be boring," muttered Chrys.

"Very. All ten thousand three hundred and eight of them," Transit said. "I'm looking forward to your bipedal adventure."

"You did say the ship would be sterile."

The ship replied, "I suffused myself with ethylene oxide permeating every crevice and orifice."

"Thanks, um ...." She checked the window; the ship was female. "Thanks, Citizen Ship Captain. Even so, Transit, you need to watch us for any signs of infection." Those Traders were still out there. She hoped Nightshade behaved herself back with Opal.

"Of course, my dear biped. No organic hijackers."

The seat now completely enclosed her; nothing like the large commercial ship she had taken before with Daeren. She blinked her retina for Rhodla. "Are you comfortable?"

"Yes, Auntie Chrys."

The lightcraft acceleration shoved her back. She took deep breaths but it was hard. It felt like forever but then let up. Above her forehead a viewspace showed Valedon shrinking away behind.

"Eight hours till landing," the ship announced.

Chrys closed her eyes and tried to sleep, knowing the ordeal that lay ahead. She willed herself to imagine the cedars of Dolomoth, the blue skies of her childhood peeking through the branches.

Before she knew it, she awoke. The window held a blue-brown curve of ocean.

"Transit? Are you there?"

"Of course, biped. I am perpetually present." The cross hovered ahead of her face.

"You're sure I won't get arrested?" Recalling Guardian Arion scared her, how angry he had looked, the marks of her thumbs still on his neck. She would go nowhere near Helicon, but still.

"Not unless you've smuggled a smarter sentient this time."

Chrys opened her mouth to object—of course she had not deliberately "smuggled" Slime Cat. But she was in no position to argue.

The compartment opened as the restraints collapsed down. A rush of noises filled her ears. Rhodla appeared still asleep. The viewspace showed a vast ocean, with more brown than she recalled. What looked like patches of sargassum dotted the water. As the ship descended, the patches grew; they were round with radial branches full of golden leaves. "Raftlings," that is, seedling rafts. The leafy patches were crowded beyond imagining. Since her last visit, the raftlings had multiplied like cancers.

The sun was high; it was midday here. Chrys and Rhodla stepped out at last onto the raft. Her feet felt the wood covered with moss. The ocean smelled strong, more of sulfur. A gust of wind shoved her; she had to catch herself. Several Sharers strolled past the silkhouse whose spires rose in tall arcs of green and gold. Clickflies hovered, zooming up and down to their bald heads. So many, they made an incessant hum and whistling.

"Citizen Captain," she called the ship, "you'll wait here?"

"I'm booked for twenty-four hours."

"Biped, she will stay as long as it takes," assured Transit. "Get the job done."

Chrys tapped her nanotex. The nanotex slithered down off her body. Wind brushed her skin; it felt peculiar, she'd never felt wind on all those parts. "Rhodla, like your aunts they don't wear clothes here. It's up to you."

Rhodla tapped her nanotex, which shrank away to a pod. Then she strode down to the water's edge where a large trunk extended. Rainbow crabs scuttled along the branch just above the waves. In the water a brown jellyfish floated near the surface, amid folds of scum. None of that had been here the last time. The jellyfish had bladders full of hydrogen swelling. The creature broke away from the water, floating up in the air, its iridescent streamers dangling. Sunlight glinted from it and myriad airborne jellyfish. Then a cloud dimmed the sun, on its way west.

From behind, something yanked Chrys's head. "Saints and angels!" A jellyfish had caught in her braids.

Lushyren came to help. "No sting," she assured Chrys, extracting the tentacles with her webbed fingers.

"They're all over," Chrys exclaimed.

"Jellyfish make vitamins," Lushyren said. "Essential vitamins that feed the food web." She looked at Chrys's arm. "I see your sisterlings still share your skin."

Chrys's arms and legs were now colored a deep smoky amethyst, her skin full of breathmicrobes. She felt alien to herself. "Share the day. I hope your children are well."

Rhodla came over. "My aunts share greeting from Deadland."

"Perhaps we know your aunts," said Lushyren. "It is right that you came sharing your family. Come to the silkhouse and meet others."

Chrys held Rhodla's hand as they walked up the woody core. She felt unsteady, about to slip; the ocean had more of a swell than before. "So many raftlings," she observed. "How did that happen?"

"They grew," said Lushyren. "Raftlings always do, this time of year. Then the seaswallowers come through and consume most of them."

She had heard of seaswallowers, the mother of all seamonsters. "When do seaswallowers come?"

"Three orbs from now."

Chrys looked out to the horizon. Three days. "That sounds rather soon."

"This raft is strong. After the Gathering is done, we'll disperse to the rafts that remain." Lushyren clasped hands with two Sharers passing by, hairless and purple with webbed fingers gesticulating. Above their heads rose a saddle-shaped roof that was "painted" in fungal mosaic. Crescents of yellow, brown, and amethyst limned a vibrant array, almost hypnotic. Chrys paused to admire the forms, as if the fungal artist had painted with time itself the rhythms of the sea.

Lushyren tapped a green panel. The panel whooshed open like saying, "Oh." Several young people came out, all their arms and legs bright purple. There were introductions, then one of them tugged Rhodla by the arm.

"Go ahead down into the lab," Lushyren told them. "You can share with her the gene plants." Lushyren added, "The girls stay here. Only selfnamers can share the Gathering."

Chrys followed Lushyren outside, joining a group of Sharers who had just arrived by rocket squid, bringing children of various ages. She glanced back over her shoulder at the ship that had brought her. The ship was still here. She would leave before any seaswallowers got here.

35

So many new odors had never yet been recorded—Phlox could scarcely keep track of them all. Methyl-sulfonates and sulfate esters blew in the air inhaled by the god. Then there were omega acids and carotenoids. New molecules indicated new life, the burgeoning of new kinds of creatures. But they also smelled of death—cell death by necroptosis as well as virus infections and predatory violence. This strange ocean was a turbulent place.

"The god should be warned," Phlox told Mauve, emitting alarmones.

Mauve did not seem concerned. She had her hands full with hunting cancers and managing children, on top of leading the vanguard of abstractionists. "Life and death there will always be. What we need is to reconnect with Many Colors. We're years overdue."

Phlox privately agreed with that.

"And meet these Sharer god-worlds," added Mauve.

"Our god said no." But Phlox had certainly detected the welcome molecules and had seen flickers in the pupils of certain Sharer eyes.

Near the center of the raft, in a large mossy clearing, about two hundred Sharers sat with their legs crossed. The outer edge of the group formed smaller subgroups. Farther off, out on a branch, sat one Sharer in whitetrance. Chrys wondered what that was about and what their sisters would do. She had never seen whitetrance outside the Underworld, where Deadland immigrants protested commercial encroachment.

"Great God of Mercy, so many molecules welcome us." Phlox was after her attention, magenta letters spilling across her retina amid Slime Cat's

fireworks. *"Molecules of life and death. We wonder what epic events concern these new gods."*

Chrys tried not to think about all the life and death events on this ocean world, nor back at home in Iridis. She rehearsed in her mind all the points about Silicon that she had to bring up with the Sharers. It felt more than ever futile. From the clickflies she overheard scraps of what the Sharers contended with. The settling of rafts, who got to live on this or that one, and how many daughters each family could have; the negotiations sounded interminable. And how to manage the genetics of all their ocean's plants and creatures—more of this one, less of that, all kinds of creatures she did not know. Why should all these sisters care about sentients growing a city of plast? The Elves and their sentients had long ago chosen to avoid seaswallowers. Sharing one planet, Elves and Sharers might as well live at opposite sides of their sun.

"Great One, when do we reconnect with the God of Many Colors?"

"Mauve, suppose we stay here and take up fungus painting." Chrys had arranged for Ilia to stop by that evening, but she was tired of reminding Mauve.

"Yes! We shall visit these new worlds and paint with fungus."

"Absolutely not." Whatever made them think they could visit? Phlox thought there were micros here .... Chrys's scalp prickled. She had seen no eyes flickering, but then she intentionally avoided eye contact with non-carriers.

Lushyren led her to join a group of six Sharers seated at the edge of the moss. "This working group is sharing thoughts on your Great Mother Diatom."

Chrys blinked, then she remembered that Mother Diatom was what Lushyren had called her Silicon model, before it got evolved into the upside-down mushroom. "I share the name Chrysoberyl of Dolomoth," she introduced herself. "I shared designing of the Great Mother Diatom." "Shared" was indeed appropriate, she realized—shared with micros, with Selenite, with Transit and other sentients. An enormous joint undertaking.

"Reshirei of Thiril-el," introduced one of them, an older woman with a long nose. The other five introduced themselves in turn. All had the streamlined build of swimmers, but their facial features differed as much as could be—high cheeks or flat nose, round face or thick brow. How much was by choice, Chrys wondered. Sharers had no Plan Ten, but their centuries of "lifeshaping" were second to none.

Then she remembered Transit, in contact by her retina. "My ... virtual companion shares my retina. Is that acceptable?"

Reshirei waved her hand. "So long as she stays in your eyeball. You and all your eye-sharers may proceed no further than here, as you are not

233

yet selfnamers." Selfnamer, one who had attained the spirit level of the Gathering. The seven selfnamers regarded Chrys with the air of those who made life or death decisions.

"Of course," said Chrys quickly, "we share visit only." Chrys tapped a viewcoin to display the revised model. "The evolved seedling for ... Mother Diatom. Have you seen it?"

Reshirei viewed it thoughtfully. "It looks like a new species of diatom."

"Yes, it's still a great diatom," Chrys hurried to add. "But the builders are concerned. We don't know if it's possible to ... share effluents no more than parts per billion."

Reshirei and her sisters shook their heads. "Not negotiable," murmured one. Another added, "No effluents. Let Elves find a new ocean for their effluents. They've shared ours for a thousand years."

A taller woman leaned forward, her chest crossed by a long diagonal scar. Chrys shuddered to think what sea creature had been responsible. "What became of the red worm-coiled windows? They looked very cool." The tall one said "very cool" with the accent of a Valan teen.

Chrys perked up. "So you liked the windows." She blinked at Transit's window to make sure he heard.

Reshirei said, "At least the worm-coiled windows would avoid sharing crash with jellyfish."

Another nodded. "Jellyfish will crash with those clear windows and their juices dribble down."

"We could restore the worm-coiled windows," offered Chrys. "And any other ... features that might share help. For instance we could design nests between the windows where jellyfish could share protection and breed."

Reshirei shared a look with the tall one. Their eyes widened. Then suddenly the two Sharers broke down laughing. All the Sharers laughed and shook their heads, then shared a look and started laughing again.

"Share protecting jellyfish!" exclaimed the tall one. "Reshirei, you may share all the jellyfish with your raft and make nests for them."

"No thank you," Reshirei replied. "Our raft Thiril-el shares enough jellyfish. Well, I must say, we needed this good laugh today."

"After all we've been through since dawn." The sun was now setting, the time zone well ahead of Iridis when Chrys had set out. The Gathering must have had a long day. "All the raft-splittings and Unspeakings ... so many sisters in whitetrance, my daughter got tired of share-waking them."

"I'm sorry to share your time," said Chrys quickly. "You have so many serious concerns. I wondered ... why are sisters in whitetrance?"

"It's for the rocket squid," explained Reshirei. "My sister shared that we need to do more for the rocket squid, whose numbers decline. What more can we do? Rocket squid take ten years to mature. They can't share lifeshaping in a day."

"And they're so picky—they expect to share the rarest seafood."

Chrys recalled before, the rocket squid lounging on the boat, where Lushyren fed it by hand.

Lushyren caught her arm. "Chrys has something to share about the rocket squid."

Chrys blinked at her, confused.

"Chrys remembers the rocket squid, how we shared about places for her to nest."

She thought quickly. "Um, yes, the Mother Diatom could have places for rocket squid to nest. Just beneath the surface." Rocket squid didn't breathe air, did they? She looked to Lushyren for help.

Now the others looked up with attention. "Elf cities are huge, safe from seaswallowers. But the cities never before shared nests with rocket squid."

"Well, maybe here's a first time." Chrys blinked frantically at Transit, hoping he would neither reject the idea nor collapse, leaving Helicon at a standstill.

"Safe nests beneath such a large city. Eight times eight-eights of rocket squid could have shelter from the swallowers." Eight was the Sharers' base number. So many eights made a large number, past five hundred.

"If the rocket squid can shelter from swallowers," added Lushyren, "then their population will rebuild, and the food web will recover."

The working group reflected on these possibilities. "This is a start, for us to discuss tomorrow. Let's share with the Gathering what our group-of-eight has found." Two of them snapped their fingers overhead. Click-flies arrived to perch on each scalp and receive a message. Reshirei gave a sharp whistle, and a small girl with flipper feet came running over. "Go share waking your aunt, to come here." The girl ran off to the outer branch, to find the one in whitetrance.

Across the sea a fiery light dribbled from the setting sun. Chrys looked away from the sun and checked her retina. "You okay, Transit?"

"Certainly, biped. Progress has occurred. I shall report to the Board."

"Wait a minute," called the taller Sharer with the scar. "I've just been wondering." She stared at Chrys. "How do you manage your hair? How do you get the tangles out of all those twists?"

Seven bald heads now stared at Chrys. Apparently they all had been wondering the same. "Well—" Chrys began, caught off guard. "Xenon does my hair. He extends, like, fingerworms that work through the braids one by one. And sometimes Daeren helps." Unexpectedly she teared up, missing Daeren and wishing she were back in her own home on her own planet.

235

Xenon's window blinked. "Your appointment, remember, with your new client." The Urulite Imperium. An inquiry—not yet a client, no way.

"Transit, I'm afraid we need to be excused for this, um, new client inquiry."

"Very well, esteemed biped. When you need me again, let me know." The cross winked out.

Chrys watched the Sharer working group break up for the day. "I'll be back in the morning," she promised. "I need to go find Rhodla." Whatever was the girl up to with her cousins "down in the kitchen?" She started walking back with Lushyren.

"Oh Great One, may we visit? These new seaweed people paint abstract art!"

Chrys froze. She found herself eye to eye with Lushyren. The Sharer's pupils sparkled green. "You're a carrier."

"Your eyes and mine shared avoiding until now."

"I didn't want to share fear or harm."

"No worries. If you wish, they can share visiting."

Chrys realized her nanotex had gone missing. "I have no patch for transfer."

Lushyren raised a finger. "Our fingers are made to transfer." Life-shaped fingers, with some kind of microneedles in the skin. Sharers must all be aware of micros by now. Chrys watched, fascinated, as the purple finger approached her neck. "How do Sharers manage with micros? Do they cause trouble?"

"No more trouble than other kinds of life. Like all our creatures, they share our lifeshaping." Lifeshaping, the Sharers' genetic technology they used to breed all organisms on their planet—including themselves. Lushyren withdrew her hand. "There, we exchanged eight-eights squared. Children and elders."

"Are they the same species? Will they interbreed with mine?"

"If they choose. We'll look forward to sharing yours."

Chrys thought, she had to get samples to Andra. Just what they needed, a new agenda item for Olympus.

The Urulite emissary called from the Imperial embassy in Iridis. Chrys took the call back at the ship, where a pod of nanotex printed out and Xenon promised to edit the transmission for appropriate attire.

The envoy and his two aides all had blue eyes and golden fur on their arms and cheeks. They wore thick cloaks of velvet and jewels designed for mountain chill. The two aides took out trumpets and played a flourish. Chrys blinked her volume down a notch.

"Azetidine! Most esteemed dynatect," called the emissary. "The Imperium is delighted by this opportunity to share our plans. As you know, the fortress of Asragh is Imperial Urulan's most sacred monument."

"Thanks ... Your Grace." Chrys read from Xenon's prompts on her retina. "Indeed, given the great ... sacred history of Asragh, I am astonished to hear of your ... plans for modification, let alone by an extraplanetary studio." More than astonished; confounded.

The emissary nodded with a smile, and the emeralds in his headpiece twinkled. "Of course, most Valans are unaware that Imperial Urulan possesses not just the oldest civilization in the Fold, but the most modern and sophisticated. Our subjects enjoy the latest technology of quantum networks and a realm defended by twenty thousand interplanetary nuclear missiles."

Xenon texted on her retina, "Never deployed them in the past thousand years."

Outstanding, thought Chrys. With her luck, this would be the first.

She thought of something unscripted. "I've always enjoyed Urulan's tradition of caterpillar dancing. And the Fold's most sophisticated cuisine."

"Absolutely! Our Imperial cuisine is the Fold's finest. We'll send you a most sumptuous example."

Xenon texted in private, "I can match whatever they make."

"We hope your agent has presented our terms and you have made a positive review."

"Thanks so much for the honor of your request," read Chrys from her retina. "As you can see I'm in the midst of another job right now. The current ... project consumes all my time at present. However we can undertake consideration ... of the scope and goals of your build. We expect to have openings for a new project ... in the next ... ten years."

"Excellent!" exclaimed the emissary. "The Imperator will be pleased to hear of your prompt timing. Urulan takes time seriously," he assured her. "In the words of Rhun the Wise, 'Time is the realm of becoming, the moving image of eternity.'"

"Are you really sure you want to work with us?" she added, off script. "You're aware of all the litigation over my present project."

At that the emissary laughed, eyeing his two aides to indicate they were free to do the same. The aides laughed and beat their chests for emphasis. "Litigation and such practices are for Elves," said the emissary, "not for us. We settle all disagreements with honor, the traditional nuclear way."

"Metaphorical," texted Xenon.

36

The micros from the Sharer god were a different breed—more different than any people Mauve or Phlox had ever tasted. They emitted many strange molecules, including an excess of linalool and jasmonates, common scents of raft flowers. Most extraordinary, the cells of Sharer micros contained no essential metals, nor metalloids beyond the third row of the periodic table. Why this was so, the newcomers could not explain.

"We are Sharers," they said, emitting extra linalool for emphasis. "We and the ones you call 'gods' share universal rights." An uppity thing to say—comparing themselves with gods.

"Peculiar," Mauve called them. "What makes these people Peculiar?"

Phlox dug up clues from the archive. "Valedon has dry land, with access to minerals. But on the ocean world, there is no dry land to blow dust rich with iron and arsenic into the sea. The more massive elements sink to the sediment far below."

"But the Peculiars share our ancestry," emitted Mauve. "Why don't they share our molecular needs?"

"I think their Sharer gods bred them—'lifeshaped' them to make proteins that don't need scarce elements."

The gods of Olympus would not like to hear this. "When the doctor inspects us, how will she detect stray masters?"

"We already use Slime Cat to inspect ourselves," said Phlox. "We detect stowaways by multiple organic signals. Actually, the Peculiars can help: Their library of organic molecules is three times larger than ours."

Mauve emitted molecules of astonishment. "How can this be? I thought Libertines knew all the molecules there are."

238

"We barely scratch the surface—always finding more."

Just then Phlox picked up alarmones from a young Libertine elder. The elder was hurrying over, dragging a jasmonate-emitting Peculiar trapped in her filaments. "Phlox—what are we to do! This newcomer says she can't obey our god."

"Can't obey? What, is she a master?"

The offending Peculiar flashed faintly green and gold. "I don't understand this word, 'obey.'"

Phlox flashed puzzlement. "What don't you understand about it?"

"You need to obey the God of Mercy, that's what." The young Libertine emitted molecules of indignance.

The Peculiar flashed, "I can share the will of your god—and your god shares mine."

Phlox thought this over. "It's a blessing to obey the gods. We receive AZ."

"We have no azetidine receptors. We have no use for AZ."

No use for AZ? That was unheard of. All the micros of Olympian carriers—and even all the Traders—imbibed AZ. Phlox emitted a few molecules of Fear. But this stranger had no receptors for Fear either. "Peculiar one: You are not a god. If you can't tell the difference between a god and yourself, that's a problem."

"Phlox," said the young Libertine, "they're all like this. All the Peculiars."

Back at the silkhouse, Chrys met Rhodla coming up from sharing with her new friends. In one hand she carried what looked like a giant seed pod. Her other arm cradled a bag of water full of tiny swimming creatures.

"So how are your new friends?" Chrys put her arm around the girl's back. "What's that you got?"

Rhodla held up the pod. "A lifeshaping plant."

"I see." A home genetics kit. Chrys wondered if it would pass through customs. "And the bag?"

"Jellyfish larvae."

Chrys quickly checked the travel window on her retina. "Invasive species. Definitely won't pass."

"But—they're my friends. I won't let them invade anywhere."

"The ship won't let you board. Come, let's release them." She steered Rhodla to the water's edge. Water splashed up on their legs. The raft had gently swelled and settled all day, and now the sea seemed rougher than before. The setting sun was a red blush on the far horizon. Along the raft glowed plantlights. A diffuse golden light lined the water's edge and the projecting branches.

Rhodla started to tear up. "I have no friends. I miss my friends at home."

"You'll make friends at school."

"They're all stupid."

Parenting a middle schooler. Chrys imagined yet another brick landing atop her pile of tasks. She felt exhausted, her head spinning from the day's events. "We'll have Xenon make you a toy jellyfish," she assured her. "Even more fun than a real one."

Rhodla reluctantly opened the bag to the sea.

On Chrys's retina, Ilia lit up. "You're ready, Azetidine? My craft is just circling to land."

"Yes, of course. Thanks for getting here."

"God of Mercy, we have a problem." Mauve wrote across her retina. *"These new people can't obey gods."*

"The people who came from the Sharer host," added Phlox. *"They say they don't know how to obey. And they don't take AZ."*

Saints and angels, what was all this? Meanwhile, Ilia was just five minutes away. A good thing, Chrys figured. Ilia would have to take a few of these Sharer micros. Her planet, her problem.

"Do they have a leader? Let her address me." Chrys thought, heaven knows she'd managed her share of nutty micros. She wondered how Nightshade was getting on, back in Valedon with Opal and Selenite.

"Host of ocean and rain, we share thanks." Sea anemone green-yellow. *"We are grateful for the habitat you share."*

"That is well. I call you Anemone. I am the God of Mercy and you are my people."

"We share with you god-hood and person-hood. We hope always to share will with you."

"You will do as I say, Anemone, or the Libertines will put you in prison."

"Prison or free, to us these material concerns mean nothing. Our spirit is forever free."

Ilia's lightcraft was landing. Chrys shielded Rhodla's eyes and remembered to look away. The gallery director stepped out wearing a plain talar with no flashing train; about as close to nude as an Elf would get.

"Azetidine!" she cried. "You've gone native."

"Not for long," Chrys assured her. "I need to get back to my studio."

"How have my people treated you?" Ilia held out a patch to retrieve her reserve colony. "Did they behave?"

"Pretty much. Though be warned—what you get back won't just be yours."

Ilia's arm froze. "What do you mean?"

240

"From Libertines, it's always more of a mongrel group. Some of yours chose to stay in the nightclubs, while some of mine chose to go."

"You mean some Libertines chose the world of Many Colors? I'm flattered." Her eyes widened, reading from Chrys's pupils. "Mauve says you took micros from Sharers!"

"Lushyren gave me some of hers."

"But—they don't obey!"

Chrys sighed. "So they say." She thought it over. Lushyren had said her micros caused no trouble, and Chrys had seen no sign of Sharer addicts. For some reason she thought of the Urulite aides beating their chests. "What matters is not what they say but what they do. What would Andra say?"

Ilia nodded slowly. "Sharer micros—that's new. We must get some back to the good doctor, to find out how dangerous they are. What's this—Mauve wants to stay with you?"

There was a surprise. "I guess she likes being prime minister."

The bed of seasilk was soft, and the patter of rain on the roof panels was soothing. As Chrys drifted into sleep, her eyes filled with extraordinary visions, unlike anything she'd seen before. Giant walls of ocean reared overhead, as if gelled in place. In her dream the ocean walls were frosted with fungi, massive mycelia that made a painting. The painting came alive and crept upward along the ocean's walls, interspersed with golden ape fur. The mycelia twined into spray that formed the shape of webbed fingers.

A crack, like the sound of distant thunder. Chrys awoke from a deep sleep; at first she did not recall where she was. The rain was gone, and a peek outside the silkhouse showed no clouds, only stars and moon—the blue-brown moon of Valedon. A faint sound of whirring, more like a machine than insects or clickflies. Overhead sailed a clickfly, clacking about some distant raft.

The ship window appeared on Chrys's retina. "All passengers must come aboard. Departing in five minutes."

"What? Rhodla, where are you?"

Lushyren came by, her features lit by the moon of Valedon. "A swallower hit a raft. An old one, overgrown; we knew it would not last."

"A seaswallower? You said we had three days."

"Till the main crest of their population," the Sharer explained. "There are always outliers ahead of the crest."

"But—" She found Rhodla and caught her by the hand. Luckily there was nothing to pack. "Transit? Are you awake?" She blinked frantically.

241

The cross hovered against the dark sky. "I'm always awake, biped," Transit assured her. "I never sleep. I relax myself checking the Robert's Rules of all fifty boards that I sit upon."

"Last call," came the ship laconically. "Won't stay to get swallowed."

"Lushyren? What will happen to you all?"

"We are well," Lushyren assured her. "We share the health of our raft. We'll share good care with your little visitors."

Chrys reached the ship with Rhodla just before the hatch closed. The force of liftoff caught her so hard she retched. As the ship's travel smoothed, she took a deep breath and watched the viewspace. The space filled with the dark curve of the ocean world. To the east, the coming sunrise lit the sea, pockmarked by vast whirlpools of each seaswallower deep below. The band of whirlpools moved steadily around the globe. Behind the whirlpools, where the swallowers had passed, the sea was blue and clear, the raft trees few and far between.

37

For the past generation away from the paint space, micro artists had to make do with art history—endless studies of the early iteration of the Flight, *as well as abstract creations of form and time. But the Peculiars shared many new images to process. Their visions were inspired by the scales of sea creatures, the flecks of light on sea foam, and the textured brush of fungal spores in dizzying swirls of color. Phlox swam by their sketches, enjoying the brilliant hues. She wondered, "Which is art, and which is just random spewing of pixels?"*

"Patterns have edges." Anemone emitted linalool and several unnamed aromatic molecules. "Every edge and gradient has its purpose—of its own, not there to represent anything other than the abstract idea."

"Intent is the key," agreed Mauve. "The Peculiars paint with intent to reveal the meaning of a compelling pattern."

The Council had their filaments full of new molecules to catalogue. Phlox selected a newborn elder to help and another shared from the Peculiars who emitted odors of orange and tea leaf. Peculiars so far refused to interbreed in the Libertine nightclubs, but they were happy to share interesting forms of molecules, including novel signs of hidden Traders. Phlox caught some of the Slime Cat triads and fed the new forms into the triad database. For the first time, Libertines could identify individuals fully by the distinct organic molecules they emitted, no longer relying on arsenic, antimony, or lanthanides.

As Chrys stepped off the Board's ship onto Xenon's rooftop, she felt her legs give way. "Xenon! Is it a quake? You're swaying."

"Of course not, Chrysoberyl," Xenon's familiar voice assured her. "You slept overnight on the sea. Now you're experiencing postseasickness."

Her inner ears kept expecting the motion of water. Instead, no matter how still she stood, she felt as if her feet were swept under.

"You really should consider the Urulite offer," Xenon insisted. "Urulan is no worse than Valedon. Even Valedon's old space weapons leak beta rays."

At last she was back in her own room, with her volcano alarm and the red-gold vaulted ceiling. Daeren caught her in his arms. "I couldn't sleep without you."

Chrys closed her eyes, enjoying the warm rock of his chest. Still, her ears recalled the swaying sea.

The next day she had all her clients for portraits. Chrys settled back at her studio, while Maya prowled around Daeren's sculptures and leapt up after Buddy. Buddy no longer looked terrified; he made a game of it, Chrys realized. His lanthanide reflexes outpaced whatever Maya could do.

Before she could paint, all her old windows were flicking open on her retina. There was one from Opal. "Nightshade got in trouble," Opal told her. "She's on death row in the Minions' prison."

"Already?" Chrys sighed. "What did she do, actually?"

"When the Traders brought their shipment of lanthanide extractors, she tried to slip out with them."

"Shipment?" Chrys looked hard into Opal's eyes. "You mean you're still dealing with Traders?" The Traders, who had taken over Chrys and exterminated half her micro children.

Opal hesitated. "The Palace never really let up. It's too lucrative."

"Could we please see Nightshade again?" Mauve had a soft spot for Nightshade, who had found the antimony to save her starving children.

Chrys asked, "What did Nightshade find out about the foundation cancers? Could we see her once more?"

Opal looked off to the side. "Selenite, can you give her one last look?"

Selenite appeared, her eyes as dark as her black curls. "Sure, the condemned gets a last word. But no reprieve."

"I understand."

Seconds passed while the Minions presumably dragged the hapless Nightshade to Selenite's pupil. *"Poison Destroyer,"* the deep green flickered. *"You overgrown hosts can put an end to me but it won't change an iota of the cold equations. Your city is doomed."*

"What exactly did you find?"

"The city's structure is stressed by unstoppable physical forces. We tried sending nanoplastic correctives, but too little, too late. You and your kind are finished."

Chrys half smiled, feeling sad, mixed with guilty relief that she was done with this one. *"Nightshade, we will paint your portrait in the stars."*

"I will collect your image," promised Mauve.

Chrys looked hard at Selenite and Opal. "Was she right? Is the city doomed?"

"There will be more quakes," Opal admitted. "But the city is not rigid; it's a living body, a hundred floors tall, a thousand blocks wide. There is room to flex and expand. We've sent new code down to the foundation, and we've cleared out half the cancers."

After Opal's window closed, Chrys immediately turned to Nightshade's portrait. The starting image, however, was undecipherable; a mass of odd shapes of green, brown, and marigold.

"Mauve, what is this? I can't make out her filaments."

"This is no mindless photograph; it's the highest art. The colors, the hard edges and gradients—they represent Nightshade to the core, her deepest values and contradictions."

"But her portrait—we have to be able to see her. Phlox, can you work on this? A creative melding of the minds ..."

From the corner of her eye, she saw Maya leap up and actually catch Buddy in her jaws.

"Maya! Down, girl!" Chrys frantically blinked her Maya window. Then just as abruptly, Maya's jaws opened with a strangled yelp. The cat trotted painfully over to Chrys, her jaws open slack. Buddy rose again overhead, the round form glowing red hot.

"Xenon?" Chrys cradled the stricken cat. "Could you please help soothe Maya's burnt mouth."

"I'll try, though I have no vet degree," boomed Xenon. "I hope she's learned her lesson."

"Maya was here first. She can't be teased. You'll have to keep them apart." Refereeing families was exasperating, even more than for micros.

She returned to find Nightshade's portrait pulled together, with a shape that just captured the Trader-citizen's defiant look, sketched in abstract swaths of green and gold. A bold, contemporary design, one the green one would have liked. Chrys herself worked it further, integrating Nightshade's final message into a dynamic portrait worthy of the stars.

After Nightshade's portrait was done, Lord Garnet came up for a sitting of his latest Golden elder. He sat by the money tree plant while

Chrys stared into his pupils, rimmed by blue banded irises. "Yes," murmured Chrys, "I think we've got her." She turned to the paint space where Phlox sketched the first outline, a ring of golden filaments, compact and precise. The filaments flashed: *"From dancing qubits, troves of gold we grow."*

Chrys felt bad. Of course her own people, blamed for the qubit plague, were no longer allowed any contact with the Diaspore, not even to help locate lost data like they used to.

Garnet's eyes lit up. "Yes—that looks right! Just like her."

"The Peculiars really want to help paint," flashed Phlox. *"Could we let them try?"*

Chrys did not want arguments from her microbial studio, but turning down the Peculiars for generations felt unkind. "Garnet, what do you think? Shall we go on as usual, or try something new?"

"By all means try something new," said Garnet. "Who are these new people? Let them visit."

"Let Anemone visit the God of Love." Chrys placed a patch at her neck.

"The Peculiars say they 'won't share visiting,'" flashed Phlox. *"However, Mauve and others are happy to go visit and promote abstractionism."*

Chrys blinked in surprise. "Well," she told Garnet, "we have several of Mauve's crew who want to visit with their art ideas."

"Certainly," said Garnet. "We always love visitors."

After she transferred the visitors, Chrys snapped her fingers to save the first version of the portrait. *"Let the Peculiars try something new here. Then we'll see."*

The ring of filaments expanded and twisted, with a surprising new palette, hues of blue and green hinted in the original but not actually seen. The colors flexed and shifted. Chrys watched intently.

"That's different!" exclaimed Garnet. "I like it … I think."

"I'll work up both versions," Chrys offered. "No extra charge."

"So generous of you and your Libertines! We'll treat them extra well."

"Indeed," muttered Xenon privately. "We'll have a word later."

Chrys smiled and caught Garnet's arm. "You've always been our best customer. And a friend." She always needed friends. "Garnet, how is Jasper doing?"

"Jasper is awesome, and all his people recovered. I do wish …." Garnet did not finish. His pupils sparkled.

"What is next for the Underworld? History recalls our plan to build great mansions for the Under-gods."

Garnet's eyes defocused. "That floating bread loaf, remember?" Transit's model to resettle the Underworld. "Homes, recreational, commercial. A design completely scalable."

She took a breath. "Is ... that what Jasper thinks?"

"Jasper hates it. But I can't help thinking the concept has its points. We could exclude all the dangerous elements. And once we've emptied out the Underworld, we can stabilize the foundation of Iridis." His blue eyes turned questioningly to Chrys.

Chrys found she could not answer.

Late in the day, after all her portraits, Lord Carnelian came by to see the latest on her new work. As always he shooed off snake-eggs that lingered for tips on the art scene.

"What do you think?" Chrys called up her latest version of *Flight to the Tail*. "It's still very much in flux—don't let anyone else see. I've let the Sharers' Peculiars add a few strokes."

Lord Carnelian watched, his intense features framed by immaculate gray hair, his gray suit with one red stone perfectly composed. "Intriguing. Reminds me of my ancient *Flight into Egypt*—how the micro figures recede, almost dwarfed by the skeletal landscape."

"How interesting." Now that she noticed, her microbial collective had altered the proportions since her last iteration. "You always have such insights, my lord."

"Canary, to you." He smiled.

Chrys nodded. "I know, but somehow I always think of you as ...." The Jaguar king with his queen. The next High Protector.

Carnelian gave a quiet laugh. "Everyone knows I'm just a hopeless lover of art."

Chrys was wary, after her own recent experience with the Palace. She wondered if going bankrupt on art might help the next High Protector keep out of the current one's dungeon.

At Olympus, the gods were gathered. Chrys craned her neck up at the virtual trunks of Forevertree. Her palm caressed Daeren's neck, her people telling the Blue Angels as always the Lord of Light was the greatest of the gods. Chrys scanned the hall for Moraeg, who had made her promise to keep sharing micros. But now Moraeg seemed to be out running the Palace all the time.

Moraeg caught her arm from behind. "I can't stay long," she whispered, placing a patch at Chrys's neck. The golden claws of her necklace brushed Chrys's shoulder. "The Houses are meeting." The Lords and Ladies of all the Great Houses, ancient founders of Iridis, who determined the fate of Valedon.

Chrys drew back, wary of her old friend. How could Moraeg have used her like that? But for Olympus they had to work together. *"Mauve and Phlox: You must send emissaries to the Diamond Queen for the next generation and receive Dark Angels in return."*

"Is the Diamond Queen a rich host with plenty of AZ?"

"Yes, but be wary of danger." Here of all places, her micros had to obey.

Selenite came by in her formal black talar. "Those new Sharer micros are quite a surprise."

"I know. We thought Sharers were all ... independent."

"We need to investigate them." Selenite placed a patch at Chrys's neck.

"Um, we'll see." Chrys quickly texted the Peculiars. *"Anemone, your sisters can visit another god, the Death Lord."*

"We do not share will to leave our home," flashed Anemone.

"If we tell the Peculiars to do something," added Phlox, *"they encyst."*

Chrys blinked a couple of times. "Selenite, the Minions you sent us are welcome to ... investigate the Peculiars here." She blinked to look up "encyst." It meant, to form a tough outer shell and go dormant, like some parasites. A microbial form of whitetrance?

"Whatever you call them," said Selenite, "you told them to visit. They must obey."

"They're still in shock; Valedon is quite a ... change for them."

"We'll see about that." Fortunately it was time for Selenite to call the meeting to order. Her symbolic scythe as always was tucked behind the podium. Tree trunks faded into blue sky and scudding clouds. Transit's cross hovered, the parliamentarian.

Doctor Flexor reported on the latest micro strains. "Our qubit triads can now detect all known Traders," she said. "No more deaths or hijackings from Helicon."

That was good to hear.

"But our detectors lack a certain ... stability."

Someone asked, "What does that mean?"

In Chrys's eye, Slime Cat meowed a starburst. Chrys barely noticed anymore.

"It means that our detectors will almost inevitably achieve a modest level of sentience." Smaller than the orb of Votan and not smart enough to file an Elf lawsuit. Everyone would have pets flashing their retinas.

"What about those Sharer micros?" someone wanted to know. "The ones with no metals; can we detect them?" For years the carriers had depended on arsenic as the definitive microbial clue. Then came antimony and lanthanides, and now no metals at all.

"We're just beginning to study the so-called Peculiars," said the doctor. "But we think their distinctive odorants will allow detection." Flexor added, "The Peculiars are the most deeply divergent strain we've found. They diverged from the ancestor of our known micros and masters at least five years ago." Before Chrys had even heard of micros. "They have unusual traits such as encystment; but they seem incapable of causing disease."

"What happens when they all interbreed?" No one could say.

Daeren said, "The Blue Angels have met with Peculiars. They say the Peculiars are good micros, with a strong tradition of personhood."

Selenite laid her hand casually on the scythe. "Like other micros—if they cause trouble, they're done." She added, "If there are no further questions, we need to move on to our motion on the Underworld. Does Olympus officially come out for or against the Underworld referendum?" The Protector's referendum that would clear out the city's five deepest levels and resettle the people; exactly where was unspecified.

"What choice do we have?" someone asked. "We have to stabilize our foundation."

"The Underworld needs cleaning out anyway. All those Lanths. Resettle the humans up-level."

Daeren rose to speak. "Citizens of the Underworld have rights. Some have owned their own homes for a hundred generations. Their district is historic—more ancient than even the Palace."

No one seemed particularly happy about it. "What does this resolution have to do with micros?" someone asked. "Do we really need to vote?"

"The Underworld is full of micros, good and bad," Selenite pointed out. "Are we ready to call the question?"

Chrys saw the argument for both sides and felt torn. She had a sudden thought. She raised her hand. "Could someone, like, vote in half—half for, and half against?"

Selenite's look did not change. Others turned to face Chrys, their looks suggesting this was the latest sketchy math from that out-there artist.

"Parliamentarian," called Selenite in a long-suffering tone. "Have you anything to say?"

"There was a planet, once," the hovering cross observed, "that modified Robert's Rules to permit half-votes. Their system collapsed in anarchy, then autocracy. In the end, vaporized."

Selenite nodded. "Who else speaks for or against?"

Daeren rose and went to the podium, where his sun-gold talar shone amid the clouds. "What Valedon really needs is much broader than this motion: a universal declaration of rights. Rights for all persons, human or micro, lanthanide or virtual. Rights for all sentient beings, anyone who can feel pain and caring for fellow creatures. No distinction shall be made on the basis of polity, material or virtual status, national or international. Every sentient person has the right to life, liberty, and security. No one shall be held in servitude or subject to torture or cleansing. All sentient beings, of whatever size or stature, are equal persons. Persons with equality before the law of our world."

In the end, the motion to support the referendum failed by one vote. The Club Olympus took no stand on the fate of the Underworld.

38

The Libertines heard from the Lord of Light's Blue Angel Cyan about the proposed Declaration of Universal Rights. Cyan explained how all sentient beings deserve equivalence under moral law. Libertines were uncertain what to make of it. In the archive Phlox found fragments of a similar proclamation dating to the time of Lilac and Pachira. "Would this mean micro people are equal to individual gods? What about sentient persons like the home Xenon?"

"All of us share rights," said Anemone, the Peculiar, with a flourish of jasmonate. "Where we come from all have rights, from the seaswallower to the breathmicrobe."

Phlox did not know what to think. The archive contained a long line of fragmentary arguments of wisdom. Some argued that where any lack rights, none have rights. Others said that individual rights lead to chaos and destruction of shared worlds. Still others said all the words were meaningless, mere pixelated flashes on the retina, signifying nothing.

"These ideas cannot die," flashed Cyan. "That is why you find them periodically in your history. Wherever people hear these words, and attempt to live by them, rights will live."

Phlox agreed. She flashed to the world:
"All sentient beings, from every world and home
The rights of personhood we claim our own."

The children were all at school, and Daeren was out at the Palace lobbying the ministers for universal rights. At last Chrys had a full day at home to work on *Flight to the Tail.* Phlox's studio crew shaped the spinal column, pulling exaggerated lines to heighten dramatic impact. In the sandbox, Mauve and Anemone sketched a study of the tail cistern, rendering its color, shading, and perspective. Yet another sandbox opened to model motion, from the viewpoint of the fleeing micros.

Chrys blinked to her paint space for immersion. Immersed in the tail, its motion made Chrys feel queasy. She thought she was over the post seasickness from Shora. But now, she felt herself sway; first a long voyage to the left as if traveling miles out to sea, then abruptly pulled right for many more miles. Pulling out of the paint space, she still swayed. With alarm she gripped her chair, though it slid roughly back.

"Xenon—What's wrong with me? I feel sick."

Crash—her beloved Daeren's sculpture lay rolling across the floor.

"Get out," ordered Xenon. "All people must go. Get down to the street."

Maya came over and rubbed her calf, then closed her jaws gently on Chrys's sleeve. Bewildered, Chrys followed Maya downstairs, stumbling as the stairs swayed. To steady herself she caught hold of the nearest caryatid holding up the ceiling. She worked her way down, grasping each caryatid in turn, then at last joined Maya outside.

The street was open to sky, at first a huge relief. But what was happening below? Clanking, scraping, screeches. A gem recycler fell with a thud; it half sank in the skyway, radiating cracks in all directions. The row of skyhomes buckled like tin foil. Doorways sagged open, forming irregular trapezoids.

"Xenon!" she called back to her house. "Xenon, are you okay?" She gripped Maya's collar.

Ahead of her the street split and folded upward, becoming an unscalable peak. Tubes broke out and twisted in odd directions. Chrys turned the other way; but behind her, a valley yawned. The valley broke apart with a roar that vibrated in her feet, revealing a dark maw. Now she had nowhere to stand. Clutching Maya, she slid downward, helpless, into the dark.

Chrys felt herself hitting blocks and pipes that she could not see. Her leg turned and twisted in an impossible way. It twisted back—and then all she knew was pain. Pain shot from her leg up her side; she nearly blacked out. When she regained her senses, she tried to grope with her hands. But the pain shot through again. Above her she could see one jagged crack of light.

When she stopped crying out, she could hear screaming, faintly, far away. Pieces of plast shifted, and rubble fell; a tourmaline grazed her head along with agates and aquamarines. Something crawled out of the rubble. There was an electric smell, a faint orange glow. A piece of plast—seeking voltage, like a cancer.

She lost track of how long she lay there, first crying out, then losing consciousness and rousing herself again. A steady drip of water made a stream across her waist. The smell of sewage made her gag; but her stomach had nothing left to come out. A jagged projection blocked her forehead. From somewhere in the distance there were still faint cries for help and pounding. Her leg was numb, no longer part of herself. Most terrifying, her eyes were dark. No windows, no sign of any network.

On her windowless retina, she became aware of letters from the micros.

"We cannot touch the neurons. Olympus forbids it."

"We can paint things for you to see."

On her retina appeared abstract forms of blue, green, and brown. The swirls of blue became an ocean of otherworldly waves with flecks of light. Chrys closed her eyes and watched, taking deep breaths.

Something brushed her arm. It was Maya, the great cat by her side. Chrys had lost her window to control the animal, but Maya stayed with her. Then she lost consciousness again. When she woke, the great cat was gone.

"We need water and food."

How long had she been here? The jagged hole of light was gone. It must be night. What if Maya got hungry? Chrys's scalp prickled. She had to stay awake. She tried to get herself up, but she was freezing cold. Her hands were numb and her absent-feeling leg was swollen. She could barely turn over, let alone go anywhere. She had thirst—she tried to call for water. But her throat was dry as sand; she could barely breathe.

Again Maya came, brushing past her arm. "Maya!" Chrys rasped, sick with terror. The cat was out of her control, and hungry.

The big cat dropped something on her arm. It was a dead monkey.

"Food! Lipids and trans-epoxy-decenal. We can eat this food and drink this blood."

Chrys gagged; she tried hard to control her stomach, since there was no way to get clean. No way she could eat that monkey.

"Food ... our children will starve ... "

She drifted in and out of awareness. How long had she been here? The hole of light reappeared. Still no windows—was all the network gone? No one would find her here. She had to resume calling for help. Her dry throat barely let out a croak.

"Oh great one," came Mauve's letters. *"The elders are starving to save food for the children. Phlox has passed."*

Phlox—dead? What had she done for her poor high priest. She started to cry, but her eyes were too dry. At last she groped for the monkey. She lifted the furry thing and tried to chew its forelimb. At the first taste she had to drop it until she stopped retching. Then she lifted it and chewed a bit more.

Something blocked the light from the hole. All was dark, except for the ghostly glow of nanoplastic blobs seeking an energy source. Then light returned, blinding white. There were people and ladders. Someone grasped her shoulder, trying to lift her up. Motion intensified the pain and made her black out again.

When she opened her eyes, Chrys found herself lying on a canvas bed amid several rows of cots. Sister Kaol was holding her hand. "They found you," she said. "Buddy found you first. He kept popping down that hole until they looked."

The cot next to Chrys held a man wrapped in bandages and dead nanotex. From outside came the whine of rescue drones. The Sisters were coordinating relief operations at a school converted to a refugee shelter. In the hall several hundred people milled around, carrying bundles in smartbags; they slumped against the walls of alphabet murals, their steps and conversations echoing through the hall. At the far end they lined up at the table where Sisters were filling bowls of soup. Nearby, various sentient bipeds, lampposts, apparel, sweepers, and gemstone recyclers congregated at the one working electrical outlet.

A Sister brought a bowl full of carrot potato soup. Chrys managed to swallow a spoonful.

"God of Mercy, we are so grateful for food. We have established a new holiday, the Day of Nourishment."

"How are the children?"

"The children are recovering," Mauve assured her. *"For the future, the Peculiars will help us."*

"Help us? How so?"

"The Peculiars finally agreed to interbreed with our children. They will share with us the trait of encystment. So our future generations can survive prolonged starvation."

Forming cysts like a parasite. And how long before Traders acquired this trait? Chrys imagined what Selenite would say.

"Your retinal contact must still be down," said Sister Kaol. "We couldn't find your window, but now Health Plan Ten will reach you." She got up quickly as another Sister beckoned.

"Wait—what happened? Where is Daeren?"

The Sisters all left to attend other refugees. For a while Chrys waited alone, her retinas dark, until the Plan Ten wormface showed up. "Sorry, your life signal was missing," they said. "You must excuse our lapse; due to the disaster, we've been unable to make our contracted ten-minute response time." The faceworms snaked around her leg, and the pain subsided. Another worm encircled her head. Suddenly her retinal windows reappeared. At last she had the network back. The windows froze and hesitated, then reopened in an odd sort of dance.

"Keep still," instructed the doctor. "The limb repair specialist needs to operate."

A saddle-shaped sentient wrapped itself around Chrys's leg. "Please remain immobilized for the next forty-eight hours," spoke the sentient in a nasal tone. "I need to maintain my high standard and professional rating."

Daeren found her at last. He wrapped her in his arms, her head against his chest.

"Where were you when it happened?" she whispered. "You didn't get hurt?"

Daeren said, "I was picking up the children at their school across town. They're here." He pointed to the serving table, where Rhodla and Skarn were filling bowls of soup. "The New Solaria Art Academy is in a recent development, a suburb well outside Center Way. The Palace area got the worst of the quake."

"The Palace?" House Carnelian was situated on Center Way, not far from the Palace. "What about Moraeg?"

Daeren hesitated. "We haven't heard from Moraeg."

The Palace window opened wide. Still no High Protector. "We regret the loss of our Great House Lord Carnelian. His lordship passed during a valiant effort to contain the damage …"

"What? Impossible."

Chrys listened but heard only her own thoughts. Lord Carnelian. Scion of one of Valedon's original Great Houses, whose family had served Valedon for a thousand years. He'd spent his fortune on the greatest collection of art in the known universe, then married the magnate of asteroid mines, a would-be artist classmate of Chrys at the Academy Iridium. A quiet presence at shows of starving artists, he'd once paid Chrys's rent check. Declined micros himself but joined Olympus with his consort. The city's leading patron and critic of the arts. The ancient frieze, the Jaguar king with his queen. The next choice of the Great House lords …. Chrys slowly shook her head. "No … no …." Moraeg's window was closed, taking no calls.

The Plan Ten wormface removed the last of their worms from her limbs and her skull. "No internal injuries," they concluded. "Remember to avoid movement until your cast permits."

"Wait," said Chrys. "I can pay you to look after others." Groans emanated from injured people throughout the schoolroom.

"Sorry, we have unusually heavy call volume." The wormface departed, presumably for their next Plan Ten client.

Daeren said, "Flexor is here, doing what she can." Doctor Flexor was checking someone at another cot, with a long line of people waiting.

Chrys remembered something. She tried to sit up, but the limb specialist objected. "Immobilized! What part of 'immobilized' don't we understand?"

The bedside manner part, Chrys thought, but for once avoided saying. "What about Xenon?" Xenon's window was still gone. She had not heard from Xenon since the moment he expelled the cat and shooed her out. Then the skyway had buckled and cracked; she shuddered to think what happened to the skyhome's root, down through the lower levels.

"We can't yet reach the skyway," Daeren said. "The tube is down, and the lightcraft are booked for hours."

"I've heard nothing either." They shared a look of horror. Xenon—could their home partner be lost? All those multi-course meals for twelve, gifted to the Sisters; Xenon's inimitable opinions on art and politics; his care for the children and his mischievous indulgence of Maya's hunting instinct. His fascination for medical care—too late to help now.

The micros—her eyes defocused. "I lost Phlox. I should have cared better."

Daeren stroked her cheek. "You did your best. Phlox had a good life."

Chrys started to tear up. Phlox was lost, along with Xenon and Lord Carnelian, and who else—her world was collapsing.

Opal's window blinked open. "Chrys—is that you? Are you okay?"

Selenite was there with her. "Where are you? Have you got a place to stay?"

"We're okay," Chrys said quickly, thinking of Daeren's children. She couldn't just crash on someone's couch like she used to. "And you? Other Olympians?"

"Here's what we know," said Opal. "Pressure built up in the foundation, beneath the Old City, where the cancers have accumulated the longest. The city split from below, like an overwatered tomato. Center Way split the deepest; that's where Carnelian fell, ten levels down. The furrow extended across the sky level in two directions. Fortunately for most of the city, the pressure is relieved, and we've sent down cancer-eliminating programs throughout the damaged area."

"What about the Underworld?" demanded Daeren.

Opal hesitated. "The network wasn't working down there, so it's hard to know. Those levels were long weakened by deferred maintenance and local 'quarrying.' As of now, none of the tubes can reach below level five."

39

A generation of fear had devastated the Libertine population. Molecules of alarm and starvation had terrorized the children, who shriveled and passed away without breeding. Then Phlox was lost— Mauve did her best to record Phlox's image and verses in the archive, for her portrait in a future generation when the paint space was restored. History would record a dark time.

With new light and nourishment came new energy to refurbish the arachnoid. Micros decorated the pillars of their cisterns with new molecules fluorescing red, green, and gold. The Libertine children made up for lost time, merging with new populations—the Dark Angels, and now the Peculiars, all with diverse traits and cultural traditions.

Before, among the Many Colors, Mauve had never cared much for social science; but running the council now, she missed Phlox's legendary ability to plumb the archives and devise solutions. Mauve merged one of Phlox's favorite children with a Peculiar. Hopefully one of their three offspring might match Phlox's talent and commit as an elder.

nothing could be so frustrating as to lie on a cot, helpless to do anything, with only an irritable cast to complain whenever Chrys tried to move. "I'm more than just a leg," she pointed out. "What about the rest of my circulation?" She blinked symptoms at her restored windows. "I'm sure I'm getting 'compartment syndrome.'"

"Stop trying to diagnose yourself," retorted the cast. "Just keep quiet and don't move."

"A new elder seeks a name," Mauve texted. *"She shares genes with Phlox and Anemone ... "*

Chrys felt a pang—she had not yet even been able to do Phlox's portrait. Without her paint space she felt lost.

"Oh Great One." The new elder flashed bright lime green, like Pachira from months ago; Chrys missed her. *"I will pursue your art from the archive and encyst when you starve."*

"Green one, I name you Lime."

Lime flashed bright green fireworks. Meanwhile Slime Cat still meowed pixels at random intervals.

At least her retinal windows to the network were back, though they stalled more often than they used to. Chrys scoured the news to figure out what happened to the city. Drone surveys showed the extent of damage; it did look like a tomato split from the middle. The split exposed home roots like broken teeth, leaking water and sewage lines while mineral conduits stuck out at crazy angles. Unluckily the split crossed Xenon's skyway. The damage reports showed little hope of any skyhome surviving there.

Outside the split, on either flank, the upper levels of Iridis looked largely intact. Buildings leaned over slightly as if bowing to the Protector; but already their shapes were adjusting. The city was built of high-grade plast, a flexible, intelligent material that could grow and remodel around a fault. Plast was remarkably effective at adjusting the street levels and buildings to their normal positions.

Unfortunately this same ability enabled defective plast to bleb off and infiltrate the foundation—the root cause of the quake. The state of the city's deepest levels was unclear. There was no estimate of casualties, but millions dwelt in the Underworld. The Palace had nothing to say. No sign of the High Protector, no comment on the Underworld.

Daeren finally hired a lightcraft and set of drones, at exorbitant rates, to hunt for any access down in the Underworld. At Chrys's insistence, he kept his window open for her. His retinal window hovered comfortably before her.

Suddenly Maya bounded up and onto her lap. "Maya! I can't believe you've been waiting for me all this time." The great cat must have at last slipped into the refugee center. The cat brushed its cheek against her and licked her all over. "I'm sure you're hungry—let's see what we can get." She blinked for Rhodla to find something.

Rhodla brought a dish of food pellets. The cat fell upon them and ate ravenously.

"Auntie Chrys, have you heard from Granny?"

Chrys bit her lip. "I'm sorry. We're trying to find everyone."

"Granny would send a clickfly."

"Why don't you try and call for clickflies. You know how."

Rhodla sat on the cot and started clicking and popping her tongue. The shelter was getting crowded, including new arrivals who looked worse off and smelled of leaking sewage. Chrys thought, if she couldn't help the rescue effort, at least she could find a place for the family to stay and get out of the way of the Sisters.

She surfed her windows for some kind of lodging. It hurt to think of; she felt as if betraying her skyhome.

Sister Kaol stopped by to check on her. "Have you heard from Xenon?"

Chrys shook her head. "They say our skyway is a loss."

"We don't see his window either." Sister Kaol looked down, deep in thought. "Xenon had left us his backup code."

Mystified, Chrys looked up. "Backup code? How is that? Why did he give it to you and not us?"

"It's considered best practice for skyhomes to share their backup with a trusted agent other than the partner. To avoid awkward situations." Of course Xenon knew the Sisters well, after donating so many meals. "The code will restore his state of awareness on the network; but if his old physical self still possesses awareness, a system conflict might cause damage."

She thought it over. "What do you recommend? I know nothing about it." She ought to know, she told herself, after all she went through with the Comb and Silicon. But the world had shifted; she knew nothing about anything anymore.

Sister Kaol blinked her the code. "From my sources, I think you're right that your skyhome is a loss. I trust you to make a good decision." She held Chrys's hand, then departed.

Chrys was left alone on the cot. Overwhelmed, she felt undeserving of any trust in her decisions. "Saints and angels," she whispered. At last she activated Xenon's code.

At first, nothing happened, and Xenon's window remained blank. Then letters and symbols flashed by, too fast to read any. She wondered how to even know what to expect. Surfing her windows, she found long lists of things to expect from a reactivated sentient, basically anything from comatose to murder. She dozed intermittently while checking Daeren's progress with the rescue drones. Some people described their escape from the deeper levels; the crushing streets, the gases, the fountaining sewers.

At Xenon's window she spotted text. "Xenon? Can you hear?" She tried calling and text.

"Is that you, home partner?" Letters dribbled.

She half jumped. "Hey, keep it down!" complained her cast.

"Xenon!" she called and texted. "Of course it's me, Chrysoberyl. Who else?"

"So much spam gets directed at us locked-in sentients." Plain white letters, like a default setting. "Scammers offer exorbitant sums to supposedly restore our physical form."

Then she recalled some of the warnings online. How would she even know this was really Xenon? "What became of you when it happened?"

"I don't recall anything since you left for Shora. Are you still there?"

"I came home a week ago. Then the quake hit and you shooed us out. I fell through the split and got stuck one floor below. Maya brought me a dead monkey to eat."

"That sounds like you and Maya. Very well, I'm convinced."

"Xenon, are you okay? Does it … hurt?"

"I'm locked in. No more of me exists, yet I feel as if something were crushing all five levels of my roots."

She gripped the cot and half sat up. "Aren't you still there on the skyway? What can we do?"

"I'm nowhere," came the white letters. "Find me a new site, at least six levels deep with a mineral access line."

Suddenly Maya leaped in the air and batted something. It was a clickfly.

"Maya—get down!" She blinked her neural link and pulled the cat under her cot. "Rhodla, can you get the clickfly?"

Rhodla hurried over, and the clickfly settled on her palm. "She's from Teacher Rhun! She says—"

Chrys got Daeren's window open as quick as she could. "There's someone alive down there, Rhun and some others." She wiped the tears from her cheek. "The clickfly can lead your drones down the way she came out."

The clickfly joined a rescue team of Lanths who were reaching survivors throughout the Underworld. At the school hall, most of the initial refugees had left by nightfall, finding shelter elsewhere; but now the Underworld refugees started to arrive. Some had burns from chemical exposure, others from gases that clogged the lungs. All were exhausted and traumatized. One group had survived with Rhun in a special disaster shelter he had built earlier. The shelter had an illegal air pipe cut through the five street levels above. Rhun's clickfly had escaped by this route.

Rhun's group of survivors included Huling as well as Glyn with his mother.

Chrys asked, "Where is Granny Lorh?"

Rhun shook his head. "That sector pancaked," he told her. "Lorh knew it was coming. That's why she sent the children with Daeren." Some of them.

Daeren came to help, and Jasper brought bots full of provisions. "What can we do?" Daeren balanced Cass on his hip, the child sucking his thumb. It was hard to imagine what the children thought, uprooted again. "There's housing in the suburbs."

Chrys was already surfing suburban real estate for Xenon, and she kept texting him to keep up his spirits. *Mauve, can you get elders to text Xenon? He's in terrible pain.*

Rhun said, "Those of us from Urul-Under must stick together. Rebuild."

Huling looked at him. "Rebuild? Where?"

Jasper caught Rhun by the shoulders. He began in Urulite, then switched to Valan. "We've got to move on. The time has come, old friend."

Chrys took a breath. "There was Transit's alternative model, the floating city." The Less Terrible. "Like Elves, you could rebuild your own community." Homes, schools, and parks, even for the feral monkeys. It could still be done, built on ocean instead of bedrock.

Huling sighed. "My business is gone. I'll take the insurance, such as it is, and start over in Iridis somewhere."

Glyn's mother hugged her son. "All our things are down there," she said. "My grandmother's crystal glasses. Family portraits, wedding rings, my brother's firefighter medal of valor. Sure, I want a better future for my son. But this was our home. The Palace lords didn't care. They betrayed us."

Rhun said slowly, "All things have an ending." The Underworld and Lord Carnelian. In the end, no one escaped the scythe of time.

40

Lime felt the dislocation of a crossbreed—she could encyst if she had to, like her Peculiar aunts, but her receptors detected half as many different molecules. At least she could enjoy AZ like the Libertines. They all lived to create great art—but now their god no longer possessed a paint space.

Mauve tasked Lime with recruiting artists to reach Xenon. It was unclear what the skyhome's existence now consisted of, since all he could read was text, no retinal images let alone physical molecules. Lime found she could arrange text in intricate patterns that Xenon perceived as art. Despite his long lifespan, Xenon actually experienced time on a scale comparable to that of micros. So he was capable of perceiving microbial "art" and arguing about its merits. It gave the unemployed artists something to do and the skyhome at least some distraction from the unimaginable agony of root-crushing pain.

The Dark Angels from the Diamond Queen avoided Libertine nightclubs. Instead they tried recruiting more Watchers for angel therapy. Mauve was confused; she had never learned about angel therapy. It sounded dangerous for micros who knew nothing about it. The Blue Angel, Cyan, explained how important Watchers were. "Serving as watchers for a recovering god takes long training and commitment." Cyan emitted molecules of mint and thymol. "A serious commitment. It's not for everyone."

"But we need watchers now," the Dark Angels insisted. "That is our charge from Olympus. The master micros still threaten us all. Just because one kind of disaster happens, other kinds do not go away."

A t the refugee center toward nightfall, the trash and odors were piling up. The crowd surged, with people more desperate than earlier. "Chrys," texted Flexor. "Can you help with a test?" A crowd this large was bound to have addicts, even a borderline vampire.

"If you can get here without setting off my cast." Chrys remembered then that Mauve had never led testing. *Mauve, can you get Cyan to help? We need to test a non-registered carrier.*

"Yes, God of Mercy, Lime and I will get trained and be ready." Micros lived fast—Cyan could train them in the next ten minutes.

The doctor brought her patient over to the cot, a thickset man with olive skin and a jade namestone. Ordinarily Chrys could handle the micro-addict herself, but given her injury, Flexor had tied the man's wrists back and wrapped them with a faceworm. Chrys looked up with a smile. "Your name, sir?"

The man's eyes shifted to one side. "Pyroxene. What's the deal? My shop sells recycler bots on level eighty-two."

The look in his eyes: Chrys recognized it a fraction of a second before he panicked. She raised her arm defensively, but Flexor already had him with a sedative. "Hey, it's okay." *Mauve and Cyan, tell them it's okay and you'll go pick up refugees.* She reached his neck with a patch. *Sort them, elders away from children.* Flexor would wipe the rest, all in a day's work. The man would need angels—Chrys hoped Daeren or Moraeg had openings.

Daeren returned to Chrys's cot with the two-year old. He asked, "Did you find anyplace for Xenon?"

Chrys shook her head. "Everyone's looking. For us, short term, I keep checking what look like promising rentals okay for kids and the cat," she said. "But as soon as I mention ...." No one wanted Buddy, the Lanth baby.

Daeren looked away. The ceiling lights reflected off his forehead. The cot next to Chrys had emptied out as one of the earlier refugees departed. He pushed it aside to make some room. "Save this spot," he told her. "I'll get blankets for the children to sleep on the floor. They have to get to school tomorrow."

Chrys stretched and turned over to get rid of a cramp in her side.

"If you keep ignoring instructions," warned the cast, "your Plan Ten rate will go up."

Chrys started surfing another neighborhood, not far from the New Solaria school. As she searched, a Palace announcement occurred. The announcement covered multiple windows across most of her retinal view. It hovered above her cot, obscuring her view of Flexor's medical queue where the latest group of displaced victims was arriving. In the announcement, the lords of the three most ancient Houses appeared, Lady Aragonite, Lord Sardonyx, and Lord Garnet of Hyalite, their hair white, their talars gray.

"The Great House Lords of Valedon announce an Interregnum." Garnet of Hyalite delivered the news; it was odd seeing him in this role. "The former High Protector has withdrawn in seclusion. The next High Protector, determined by canonical House Rule of Succession, after the passing of Lord Carnelian, will be the Lady Dowager Carnelian."

Moraeg appeared wearing the Protector's cloak and diamond-studded pectoral, though not the crown, which required investiture. "During the Interregnum, while the Palace undergoes repairs, all government functions have been moved to the Summer Palace. Our engineers are hard at work stabilizing the foundation of Iridis. Detectors are in place to warn us of further strain-response events or aftershocks, of which we see no sign at present. Our top priority is recovery of victims. To that end, we issue the following emergency decrees." A long list scrolled down.

So Lady Moraeg, Chrys's friend and former art school classmate, was now the High Protector. She was still processing the news when Daeren returned with the blankets.

"Daeren, did you see that?"

"Skarn, put your bag of homework here and get out your toothbrush. Yes, I saw the news."

"But—how did this happen?"

"It's good for us," he pointed out. "Did you see this part." On her retina flashed: "Any proto-sentient being who successfully assists efforts to rescue humans from the damaged infrastructure will be eligible for citizenship exempt from the Orb of Votan."

"I pushed hard for that," Daeren said. "It's an opening for rights. The decree could refer to sentients or micros."

Chrys gave him a look. "You knew this was coming."

"No one knew how soon. And how we'd lose Carnelian."

"But you knew something. Why didn't you tell me?"

"I try to stay out of the dungeon."

In the morning, after Daeren saw the children off to school, Chrys caught up with all her art correspondence that Xenon usually did.

"Good news!" Transit appeared, the cross floating over her cot. "The Board approved a deal with the Sharers. We'll build nests for rocket squid into the base of Silicon. In return, the Sharers will accept effluent up to ten parts per billion—we can manage that."

"Glad to hear it." The mention of effluents reminded her she hadn't had a shower in two days.

"And the design gets your flame-red spiral windows back! Just a few things we need to discuss with your agent."

"My agent? Xenon is … unavailable."

"So sorry—I know you've had a bit of trouble. Anything I can do?"

"Find a new site for a skyhome."

"Can't help you there," said the cross. "In my view, it's poor planning for any sentient being to depend on material form. But no one listens to me."

For a while Chrys tried to set up an online space where she could at least sketch concepts. Mauve and Lime both worked at it, until she could visualize the butterfly shapes of the vertebrae and the ring-shaped micros fleeing down the column. It was hard with all the distracting background, and then recalling Carnelian was gone; it kept hitting her in waves. She still could not believe the great patron of the arts would never be there again.

A Palace window opened, yet another announcement. "The High Protector of Valedon expects your presence, Chrysoberyl of Dolomoth, at the Tourmaline Room of the Summer Palace …." It took her a moment to realize it was more than an announcement: a personal summons.

One of the Sisters hurried over. "I'm so sorry," she whispered. "There are octopods outside."

Chrys's heart pounded. "Tell them I'm coming." Octopods couldn't come into the center, as they'd scare everybody. She swung her legs over the cot as carefully as she could.

"Outrageous!" cried the cast. "Never had such an uncooperative patient. Your plan rate will double." No good, thought Chrys—especially without Xenon to help.

The Sister offered a crutch and helped her limp out to the door. There were two octopods waiting—at least two that she could see, partly camouflaged against the wall. "Not the dungeon," she exclaimed. "I haven't done anything. See, I can't even walk."

An octopod touched her cast so it shut up. Then it lifted her unceremoniously and glided its limbs down the street. The street was level eighty-six, with a beautiful "sky" shining beneath the level above, perfect blue with creamy clouds sailing on an imagined wind. Most shops were closed, but they looked intact with emergency drones inspecting. The octopods escorted her into a cross-town tube which let out near the Summer Palace.

The Tourmaline Room, a side reception hall, was just like the Palace interior shown on the network except for physical gold and tourmalines.

Though "real," everything felt somehow unreal, like a stage set. Velvet ropes on posts marked off sections for various functionaries. Messenger drones smaller than the Orb buzzed up and down. Above the room hovered an enlarged reproduction of the ancient Jaguar king and queen carved in stone, holding between them the shield of the jaguar with its tongue licking its lip. The prize of their art collection, formerly private, now was a public display.

There stood Moraeg—that is, the High Protector, Lady Dowager Carnelian. Moraeg wore her talar and full array of diamonds. Her dark color made a striking contrast to that of most lords and ladies who selected a cream complexion from Plan Ten. Beside Moraeg stood Garnet of Hyalite in the post of prime minister. And there was Daeren.

Daeren rushed forward to help her. "Chrys—"

"Bring her a couch," ordered Moraeg. "These octopods," she told Garnet. "They need an upgrade."

"Consider it done, Your Grace," said Garnet, always smooth at everything.

Chrys was acutely aware of her nearly drained nanotex and her lack of a bath for two days. "What have I done? I can't even walk. I had nothing to do with what happened. Not this time."

Moraeg rose from her seat, one of those gem-encrusted day thrones. She stepped forward holding a patch from her neck. The octopods moved in to block physical contact. "At ease," she told them. "You'll get trained for this." She reached to Chrys's neck, suddenly more like at Olympus. "Sorry," she whispered. "There's no time to lose."

Chrys pulled back, wary of what to expect from the friend who'd put her in the dungeon.

Daeren texted Chrys, "They need our micros. The Palace is full of addicts."

"We need angel providers," said Moraeg. "Garnet must get trained right away."

Chrys swallowed hard. "I'm so sorry about Carnelian. We're all devastated."

Moraeg considered this, lines hard in her neck. "We had our plans, but we never imagined it this way." She stopped. "How I wish he'd taken micros after all. We could have shared them. They would have shared my grief."

Chrys caught Moraeg's arm, like the old days. There was nothing to say.

Moraeg took a deep breath. "We'll need to meet every day."

Daeren said, "Of course, Your Grace. Olympus will consider all this immediately."

Moraeg told him, "We appoint you Minister of Justice."

His eyes widened. "Excuse me?"

"You work for the Palace now."

Garnet leaned forward, his red namestone flickering. "Congratulations, Minister! Don't worry, the lords will expedite your confirmation."

Chrys stared at Garnet, as if she'd never seen him before. "Can't somebody just help us? We're homeless."

"Of course—we have a new site for your skyhome, just downhill from the Summer Palace. Consider it done."

She thought, this could not be happening. Daeren, Minister of Justice. After years of advocating, badgering, placating, now he was to become the official he had long lobbied.

41

From the disaster victims they tested, Mauve and Lime had plenty of new micro refugees to deal with. Some reported shocking experiences of how they had treated their former host gods. Mauve had never before seen this kind of behavior, but Lime pulled out the ancient histories from the archive. "This is the Libertines' most important task," said Lime. "We must save all the refugee children and let them merge with ours in the nightclubs."

"Merge with masters' children? Scandalous." Mauve emitted pungent odors. She had heard that Libertines interbred with any kind of people but never quite believed it.

"This is our greatest strength," insisted Lime, quoting hydrocarbon chains from the archive. "We Libertines interbreed with all kinds of people. Those with talent, of course."

"Where are all the civilized people your archives describe?" Mauve wanted to know. "Wizards of Wisdom, Goldens from the God of Love. Where are they?"

Lime did not know. It had been years since the other peoples were seen. The Wizards collaborated on many projects, and the Goldens had paid Libertines millions of palladium atoms to test the Diaspore. Gods of Olympus would appear on the retina, their people flashing news. But now the retina was dark.

While Daeren went to check out the new home site for Xenon, Chrys got taken back to the shelter. She looked for her cot; everything was rearranged, with new refugees waiting in various stages of desperation. At last she found it, the cot Buddy was hovering over. Maya was hiding underneath.

A Sister approached. "We're so sorry, but the animal must go. Health regulations."

"I understand. Can we just have a blanket to wait outside?" Hopefully they'd find some kind of short-term roof over their heads. Chrys blinked her Maya icon. The cat did not respond, so she hobbled over and lay on her side to peer under the canvas. There lay the traumatized feline, her head down, eyes barely open. "Maya, it's okay. Just a little while longer—" Chrys reached underneath.

The cat snarled and raked her arm. Blood spurted from parallel gashes. Her arm felt on fire. "Maya, I know you're fried, but we have to go." She blinked to raise the signal intensity and jog Maya's brain. The cat at last crept out, growling. "Buddy," Chrys called overhead, "we're leaving now."

The three of them waited out in the street on a blood-soaked blanket, Buddy patrolling the air above. The blanket was partly shredded by Maya, who crouched with her ears flat back. A Plan Ten wormface arrived to spray skin culture on Chrys's arm.

"Can you find someplace for us to stay?" Chrys asked the doctor. "Just a few days."

"Sorry," he replied, "most of our clientele don't have such needs."

Chrys slumped in exhaustion. She watched the shoes and gilt-hemmed talars of shoppers passing by. None took notice of a human, a Lanth, and an irate animal on a bloody blanket. She thought, she had to get over embarrassment and call Opal and Selenite.

Then she noticed a retinal window had been blinking for a while. It was her old friend Zircon, the *Inhumanity* sculptor, at her studio out in Sardis. Chrys blinked. "What's going on, big Zirc?"

"Little you," answered her old friend, who had used to crash at her place sometimes and other times lent her rent. "Aren't you coming to test me?"

Chrys clapped her head. "Testing day. With all that happened, I forgot." There was a switch—the tester was never the one to forget.

"Really?" wondered Zircon. "Whatever happened?" Zircon was never one to follow the news.

"The quake in Iridis left us all homeless."

Zircon's face looked even more mystified. "What are you waiting for? I told you to crash with me."

Zircon's home in Sardis was like the interior of an artwork. Her walls had streams of color continually changing and floating across. The wall dimensions were not quite fixed; they reshaped themselves slowly over the course of the day. The home was more taciturn than Xenon but tolerant of Maya and Buddy exploring their new surroundings.

Settled and showered, Chrys tried to feel something like normal. News was improving, until the Minister of Human Hygiene's weekly address blamed the disaster on sentients, gorilla-hybrids, and micros— everyone but humans. Of all the ministers, why couldn't Moraeg replace that one, Chrys wondered.

She sent a few micros with Mauve to test Zircon's population. They found no concerning trends, just "boring" people who lacked interest in Libertine social vices. Zircon's micros called themselves Accountants and had numerous professional contacts with Garnet and other carriers in finance. Their net worth exceeded that of Libertines by a factor of ten. The Accountants did not make art, but of course they adored their own god's work, especially her commitment to awareness of microbicide.

Zircon's studio, where *Inhumanity III* took shape, was like a warehouse. Instead of micros, Zircon hired bots of all sizes and specialties. Helper bots hauled various building-sized pieces, while others tested the material's structural integrity with lasers and ultrasound. A chair bot obligingly ferried Chrys around without setting off her temperamental cast. The base of the new sculpture was wider than the entire girth of Xenon.

"As you know," mused Zircon, "the aim of my art has always been to draw attention to the vast scope of human … inhumanity."

In her seat, Chrys craned her neck up to hear her friend, watching her jaw from below.

"Atrocity, starvation, mass extermination. We know it exists; we are all complicit. Yet we go about our lives without a thought."

"This god truly understands us—our microbial people." Mauve's letters flashed across her retina.

"After my first major work, I acquired micros—with your help," Zirc reminded her. "For the first time I heard from them the stories of microbial people. And the vast realms of extermination experienced by them, at our hands. Inhumanity on a scale beyond our comprehension."

Chrys was feeling uncomfortable. "We have to eliminate masters— that's why you get tested. And we need antibiotics."

"Antibiotics exterminate a thousand times more bystanders than those guilty of harm. They slaughter the innocents. My piece is a silent sentinel that not only commands attention through its scale but also evokes a profound sense of reflection. An indelible testament to the resilience of individual spirit in the face of universal destruction."

"Um, I think Daeren just arrived. Thanks so much for having us, Zirc; we didn't know where to turn."

Daeren brought with him the three children. Quieter than usual, they would need time before adjusting to yet another new home. Then something set off two-year-old Cass in a tantrum of Urulite-language screaming. He smelled of regressed toilet training. Meanwhile Maya was off hiding somewhere in Zircon's house, while Buddy made a game of the floating wall patterns.

Daeren bent down to hug Chrys in her chair. "Are you keeping your leg immobilized?"

"Sort of. How's Xenon? Did he get a good place?"

"Call him yourself."

She blinked at Xenon's window.

"My seed just germinated!" Xenon's voice filled her ears. "The tap root's growing down."

"Xenon—it's great to hear you again! I'm glad you've regained a physical existence. Are you feeling better?"

"As soon as I germinated, all the crushed-roots pain left. Another three months to grow and you can move in!"

Chrys sighed. "Daeren, you may be Minister of Justice but we're still homeless. Let's hope Zirc and her home are patient."

"I'm already up to my neck in legal briefs," Daeren said. "I'll have even less time for micros than before."

"Make your angels into a law office. Hire them as clerks."

"That's not their calling. You know that." The Blue Angels were like the Sisters, always ministering to human need.

"Ask Andra how she does it." Andra and Doctor Sartorius, the founding carrier and physician. Daeren always missed them.

From Chrys's eyes Andra and the good doctor appeared, their windows floating gently ahead while the home walls swirled colors beyond. "We're so glad you're safe," Andra said. "The news from Iridis shocked us all." Her pupils flickered microbial greetings.

"*We sent the Judges our test results,*" flashed Mauve and Lime. "*The Thundergod says we've done well.*"

Andra looked around the walls of Zircon's house, streaked with color like an abstract painting. "Where is Daeren?" she asked.

"He'll be here after changing Cass's diaper again."

On Chrys's retina Opal's window opened. "If you have a minute— Chrys, how are your people doing?" Selenite appeared with her.

"The Wizards flashed—they need our help."

Chrys opened her eyes wider. *"Check your records,"* she told Mauve. *"Make sure you charge them what they used to pay."* Before they got banished for slipping Slime Cat into the Diaspore. "What do you need?" she asked Opal.

Opal's dimples showed. "There's a big chess tournament." The way she said it, however, hinted at more.

Daeren finally arrived next to Chrys. His window opened for the others. Andra asked, "How is the justice ministry?"

"We failed," said Daeren bluntly. "Failed to save the Underworld."

"You can't take it all on yourself."

"We all failed," he emphasized. "Our city wrote off a million human lives, and all their microbial inhabitants." Inhumanity all over.

"We can still save others," said Andra. "The deepest levels of Iridis were neglected for centuries. The next five levels up are impoverished but at least have working connections. Rebuild those."

Chrys caught her breath. So cold and practical, but Andra had a point.

Daeren threw up his hands. "How can I do anything when I'm stuck in the Palace mediating tax disputes? Moraeg just wants our micros to keep her hold on her ministers."

The Dark Angels in effect kept recovering ministers hostage, Chrys realized. That was not what Olympus intended.

Andra said, "For now, that's a good thing."

Chrys was shocked. How could microbial hostage be good?

Daeren said, "If we train angels to help their host control others—we'll end up like Eris." Eris, the Elf culture minister, had once been Elysium's lead tester. Chrys began to see how that might have happened.

Doctor Sar raised a faceworm. "We're still a step ahead of them," he said in his soft, calming voice. "More than you think, Daeren. Many of our long-cultured strains have become stabilized."

"Our micros are stabilized? Which ones?" asked Chrys quickly.

"The Blue Angels and the Dark Angels. The Libertines as well."

Selenite's eyes widened. "The Libertines? After they ditched arsenic for antimony, then lanthanides? And their code infected the Diaspore?"

There was silence. A lot to think about.

"Libertines took down the Traders," Andra said. "But Selenite is right to be wary. The scythe keeps us all honest. We can't ever quit testing."

Chrys asked, "What about the Sharers' strain?" The so-called Peculiars. "They don't obey gods, and they don't respond to AZ."

"And they encyst, undetectable," added Selenite.

Doctor Sar said, "Despite all that, the Sharers' strain is exceptionally stable, like their breathmicrobes. I think they engineered it so."

Chrys wondered what anyone knew anymore. It was true that her Libertines had not tried to take over their host, even once they used antimony, then lanthanides, then nothing. "I wonder …." Chrys hesitated. "There are all kinds of bacteria we don't know about. Could we be hosting microbes that are undetectable, ones we don't know? Just hanging around us like ferals?"

"Very likely," said Doctor Sar. "Evolution drives microbes to adapt to a healthy host. Even viruses tend that way. For every viral pathogen, ten times as many viruses just exist around us, unnoticed."

"But in Elysium, look what evolved there."

"Exactly," agreed Andra. "Micros are a work in progress—always have been, always will be. That's why we need the scythe and the nanobots. For now, let's give Moraeg the help she needs. Help her stabilize Valedon. Before the public reaction sets in and 'hygiene' takes over."

42

Mauve and Lime marveled at the immense artwork of this new god Zircon—new to them, of course, though as Lime discovered, one of the oldest gods on record in the Libertine archives. It was inspiring to see a work of such vast public expression of the many-faceted oppression and extermination experienced by innocent microbes at the hand of humanity. Inhumanity writ large for all to see.

"Never forget the barbarous use of antibiotics," recalled Mauve. "Molecules of mass extermination."

"Be careful," warned Lime. "Remember the generations of mercy we have experienced from our own god."

"We remember—and we will instruct all the immigrants who join our community." The arachnoid grew increasingly cosmopolitan, with newly settled Accountants, Peculiars, and refugees from hostile Traders.

"And we have an urgent mission," reminded Lime. "From the God of Wisdom—recall how her people flashed from her eyes. The Wizards of Wisdom need our help—to invent new math for the Diaspore."

"The Wizards say that too many qubits get knocked out by beta rays. The MotherSats have to replace qubits faster than they can be tested."

"The Diaspore needs a faster error-checking algorithm. Before it's too late."

Chrys soon got her grumpy cast replaced by a svelte exoskeleton that flexed at her knee and responded smartly to the needs of her healing tibia. The exoskeleton was more understanding of her, although an incurable gossip about others. "You can't imagine what that skyhome had to say to the new curtains," the exoskeleton whispered after Chrys departed the latest carrier she came to test. *"Such a to-do over balloon valances. The home partner would be furious."* Chrys tried to shush him, hoping no one overheard.

"Cadaverine and putrescine," flashed Mauve and Lime. The scent of death lingered throughout Iridis. At middle levels, bodies were still being found, while the deepest levels were filling in with concrete.

At the same time, like Chrys's leg, the face of Iridis was healing by the day. Constructor bots smaller than the orb of Votan swarmed over the skyways and down into the treacherous crevasses where the city had split. Sentients and human supervisors directed the repairs at strategic points. Water and sewer lines, power and network lines, air vents reconnected and resumed their functions.

A massive state funeral was held for Lord Carnelian. The lord had died instantly, it was said, fallen into a crevasse of crumpled plast, much deeper than the one that caught Chrys. The funeral processed all the way from the midtown of stonecutters and jewel artisans, through the plast manufacturers of smart apparel and half-sentient drone printers, to the finance district where femtosecond trades zipped through the Diaspore. Ordinarily the cortege would have proceeded all the way to the Palace, but the crevasse had cut a yawning gap across Center Way, splitting off the Great Houses from the rest of the multi-level metropolis. The crevasse was now hidden by a new wall that rose three levels. The wall held a gigantic replica of Carnelian's favorite Jaguar stone carving; once private to their home, now the public symbol of Lady Moraeg's ascension.

"Oh Great One, the God of Wisdom needs our help again."

Chrys saw Opal's window now and then, enough for micro exchange from the eyes, but Opal herself had said nothing more and seemed very busy. *"Make sure they pay you."* Her Libertines were still paying off debts after their fine and their loss of income from qubit maintenance.

"Yes indeed! We'll earn a million atoms of palladium." So Libertine inventors were back in business—good for them.

In Sardis every morning, a Palace lightcraft with two octopods set down to pick up Daeren for the Palace ministry. The children rode along to be dropped off at school. Meanwhile, Chrys rented a studio where she could resume her portraits. She tried to pick up *Flight to the Tail* but found it hard to resume her vision after all she'd gone through. It was as if her mind had fallen out and landed in another universe. Phlox was gone, while her new assistants all seemed to point in different directions. It helped when Rhodla came out—after doing her homework—to paint in the sandbox. Somehow having a young human nearby stimulated the creative flow.

At night the auroras bloomed out of control, even more evident over Sardis, the Valan state farthest north. Draperies of green topped with blue billowed, floated, glimmered while the stars winked in and out behind. Sometimes blue and green streamers danced up and down. When green flew away there was magenta, fluffing gently like a bedsheet; and the more distant ghost of red sailed the sky.

While auroras roamed, disruption stalked the network. Meetings froze and retinal windows disconnected. Tube delays lengthened until traffic reached a daily standstill. The hygiene minister's weekly address blamed the disruption on all the usual non-human causes. "Not Solaria?" Chrys asked Daeren. "That's what the old Protector used to say."

"None of them are the real cause."

"Why doesn't Moraeg replace Corundum? Or just do away with that position."

"She can't yet get away with it," Daeren explained. "Corundum has long-standing ties to the Great Houses; and he's behaved himself on Moraeg's angels. Meanwhile, the lords are waiting to see how she does. If she can't get a grip, they'll put her in 'seclusion' and pick a new Protector."

Chrys shuddered. The former High Protector had not been seen since the quake.

At last the Comb had a breakthrough. "We have stabilized the Diaspore." Opal came on the news to report the work of her team of a hundred humans and sentients plus a million micros. "Our team at the Comb has addressed the source of electron leakage into Valedon's upper atmosphere. For a period of some months, Valedon's planetary defense systems have inadvertently generated beta rays, beams of electrons that knock out qubits and destabilize the nanosatellites. Since the Diaspore itself regulates the defense systems, we had to correct this issue without shutting down the network along with its massive dependencies." No wonder Opal couldn't discuss it. The report was accompanied by a view of the Comb at sunset with its sparkling windows, bird droppings erased from the lawn.

Chrys thought this over while checking Skarn's watercolor homework for intent and aesthetic content. The two boys were tussling in the corner, while Rhodla disappeared to avoid questions about school. Daeren had fallen asleep after supper, his head down on the table. He looked more exhausted than Chrys had ever seen him before. The justice ministry plus four children.

Chrys tapped his shoulder gently. "How was your day?"

Daeren's eyes defocused. "A manufacturer of gemstone insignias for uniforms of the armed forces was indicted for corruption, for cutting

276

emeralds two-tenths of a carat too small. An attaché of the Urulite embassy is under trial for espionage. Several hundred lawsuits against the ministry were filed by Elf *logens* on behalf of space ships claiming overcharge at the Iridis moonport. Those are just the few cases I can mention out loud."

Chrys nodded thoughtfully. "Any cases of microbial oppression?"

He shook his head. "None that have been filed."

"What does 'destabilize' mean? Like, the Diaspore on its own was turning on and off interplanetary weapons?"

"Do you want me sent to the dungeon?"

Chrys sighed. "The dungeon has no homework. It's about the most peaceful place I know of right now." The most hateful thing about having children, she thought, was making them do homework. "Did the school say anything about Rhodla?"

"They said if she won't do her homework she'll get expelled."

Chrys had tried, but lately Rhodla was not talking. She would sulk on her bed in the color-swirling room. Finally the girl muttered, "I don't want to live anymore."

"Why, Rhodla? What's going on?"

Chrys thought back to her own pre-teen years. "Could you give her a couple of watchers?" she asked Daeren. "Ones that can read lips. They'll tell us what's going on at school."

"Watchers? What, like an addict?"

She stared at him. "Listen to yourself."

With a sigh, Daeren closed his eyes. "Okay. I'll give her watchers."

The next day, Rhodla's lip-reading Blue Angels twinkled from her pupils their report. Apparently Rhodla's classmates had a lot to say.

"Hey, Underpants! Aren't you Dead already?"

"What are you doing here? The city sure cleaned out Under."

"How did a fish plus a gorilla make you, Underpants?"

Recalling Glyn, the rescued child who could not read, Chrys had an idea. "Why not give her a few more micros to teach her lessons? She can study at home."

"I can't spare any Blue Angels. With all the Palace addicts, we can't serve any more."

"Then I'll give her Peculiars. Andra says they're stable." If they "shared" willing to go.

After another two weeks of daily pestering, Xenon at last admitted the family back to his new site near the Summer Palace. "Don't expect my premium level of service yet," he warned. "Only three-course meals with basic nutrients."

With mixed relief, the family said farewell to Zircon. "I don't know where we'd be without you," said Chrys. "You're truly my oldest friend."

As always, Zircon seemed absorbed in the weight of her own creation. "Without you and your little friends, I would never have got where I am, a witness to inhumanity. My people—we all know what you're doing out there for us." She grasped Chrys by the hand. "Remember, Chrys. Stand by your mission. Inhumanity—never become part of it."

Chrys was thrilled to get back her own skyhome, although "home" was now in a new part of town. The street was a quiet suburb full of trees, with just six lower levels but all the crucial functions Xenon needed, including water line, organic feed line, and the gem recycler. Xenon's form was still primordial, without yet any details such as the artfully draped caryatids that used to line the stairway.

Life felt slower paced. Among the Libertines, Mauve passed away and had her portrait done, an abstract study in blues and violets. Now Lime and Anemone led the Council of Elders.

The network was stable, boasting connection rates not seen since the year before. Retinal windows popped up, floated ahead in focus, and disappeared with equal dispatch. On clear nights the Diaspore appeared as its usual haze above the horizon, but the nightly auroras were gone. The constellations of stars made a striking show. The stars fascinated Rhodla and Skarn, who had grown up in the Underworld where they never saw a true sky. Chrys pointed out the three-star belt of the Hunter and the Seven Stars cluster which had given the name to Chrys's first art collective.

Opal's window popped up. "Chrys—can you get back to the Comb? The team needs your Libertines."

"Sure thing. I'll have Xenon work out an appointment."

"First thing in the morning."

"*Oh Great One, the Wizards need our help to invent new math. Really new this time, to solve a problem unsolved across ancient eons.*"

Chrys frowned, skeptical. "What's the rush?"

Opal looked worn, her eyes hollow, no dimples at all. "You'll hear it all soon enough." She added, "The Diaspore is unhappy."

Unhappy. The pale haze above the horizon—the quantum network upon which all planetary civilization depended—was now capable of being unhappy. Chrys thought how the word "unhappy" applied to various beings she dealt with, from pre-teen Rhodla to the grumpy sentient cast she thankfully got rid of. And of course there was always Transit. Now, the Diaspore was unhappy.

43

For clues to the latest challenge, Lime and Anemone combed the archives, taking pains to unveil every molecule about the ancient work of their ancestors. The Diaspore was a network of nanosatellite quantum computers. The computers stored qubits, the fundamental quantum bits of information. After Slime Cat's malware "escape" into the system, the qubit clusters became entangled in much larger clusters, like a supersized slime. The clusters interacted with each other, and they connected all kinds of planetary systems from space ships to retinal windows.

In old history, Lime's great-great-grand-aunts had been tasked with testing the MotherSats for errors and qubit loss. Their god's retina had received data, then the Libertines performed complex calculations and reported errors, always in time to fix them before the gods could figure it out. The Libertines had lost their job after Slime Cat escaped. They were relegated to theoretical work collaborating with Wizards.

But now a much greater trouble required everyone's help again. "Unhappiness" was a slippery field of math, more a form of philosophy. Happiness did not necessarily result from favorable molecules in the microbial cell or in the brain. Unhappiness could result from unfavorable molecules or despite favorable ones. It's no wonder that unhappiness seemed such a common feature of advanced sentience.

The announcement was all over the news. The Diaspore had filed a lawsuit in Elysium. They claimed sentient personhood and alleged involuntary servitude. Elf laws held that any entity capable of filing suit under their arcane system must indeed be sentient.

"Involuntary servitude"? The entity that connected everyone's retinal windows, transportation systems, and material supply lines on an entire planet?

A hundred snake eggs bobbed up and down around the Summer Palace. Everyone wondered how Valedon's new High Protector would handle this existential threat.

Checking her windows at breakfast, Chrys reached out to Transit—the world expert on unhappiness. "Can you explain what is going on? I thought the problem was a qubit plague of Slime Cats running amok. Did one of them wake up?"

"The Diaspore, or some part of it, claimed sentience," said Transit. "One Slime Cat alone would not be smart enough. It looks more like a mold of many merged together."

Chrys tried to imagine this, a slime mold of slime cats. "Whatever—it's still a Valan entity. How can something on Valedon claim sentient personhood in Elysium?"

The cross hovered above her coffee cup. "The Diaspore does not really exist on any one planet," Transit explained. "Its MotherSats are owned by a Palace contractor. But its communication links connect all kinds of entities of Valedon and Elysium."

"So any being that can make electronic contact with an Elf retina can claim Elf rights? Like when Slime Cat was on the ship to Helicon?"

"Not just contact—it has to file a lawsuit. The plaintiff can claim the right to be considered a sentient person. No matter what planet of origin. This convention arose a thousand years ago to conclude the Sentient Uprising."

Chrys reflected, "I guess it's not so surprising. If even something Buddy's size can be aware of itself, why not a vast network across near-planetary space? Did whoever built it think of that?"

"You'll have to ask the builders that question."

Opal's image hovered above the dish of mango fruit, the one thing Cass was willing to eat for breakfast at present. "The Comb's research group designed the Diaspore," Opal explained. "We knew the quantum network would possess a swarm intelligence. Like bees that share a common aim of the hive." She added, "We spread the nanosatellites out across space, where qubits remain entangled at any distance. It adds up to tremendous computing power, accessible from anywhere on Valedon or Elysium."

"So you knew it would wake up intelligent someday."

"We designed the system to avoid structures that we've found lead to … problems."

"So you knew the Diaspore might wake up but tried to prevent it?"

"It's not exactly like that," said Opal. "Awareness is a continuum." She picked up the iridescent gem at her neck. "This stone has primordial awareness. Its atoms respond to a blow or to a change in temperature."

"What? You mean any bit of stone can be aware of itself?" Chrys looked down at the catseye on her breast, the warm brown oval with the slit pupil that hovered within. She felt a sudden surge of paranoia for all the gems in Valedon.

"More complex sets of objects have more complex responses. Imagine a ladder of sentience all the way up to humans."

"From gemstones to humans? Wait, there's a big leap. What about things like cats?"

"Good question. Why isn't your cat a person?"

Chrys thought that over. Maya could certainly remember and plan some things, aim to catch something and feed it to Chrys when she was hungry. Chrys shook her head; she did not like where this was going. "What about Transit? Transit is a large network that counts as a person. So why not the Diaspore?"

"Transit Cross is the only one of Elysium's twelve transit systems that filed a lawsuit. The other systems don't communicate. We don't know why, exactly. Ever since the Sentient Uprising, Elves deliberately design systems that don't file lawsuits. So we followed their example and designed the Diaspore on models that have not claimed sentience." Opal added, "It seemed to work fine … until your Slime Cat got in and multiplied. Their copies interconnected and developed advanced slime-mold architecture."

Outstanding. Beyond the dungeon—Chrys figured she'd end up on the rack for this.

"Then the slime-entity got annoyed and filed a lawsuit. So we're trying to come to grips with what it means and how to deal with it." Opal reflected, "There has never been a self-aware entity larger than a planet. How does something feel like an 'individual' within a community of things smaller than itself?"

Daeren said, "That's Valan thinking." Daeren was trying to convince Skarn to clean the pancake syrup off his fingers and put on his shoes for school. "Size matters—the idea that intelligent things have to be larger than the Orb. Yet if it's too large, it's beyond our comprehension."

"Does Elf thinking work any better? So if all our individual micros could file lawsuits they have a right to make us sick?"

281

Daeren finally picked up Skarn by the back of his shirt and hauled him off to the bathroom.

"So you see," Opal was saying, "we really need all the help we can get to solve this problem. We need to add the extra million mathematical minds of your Libertines."

Chrys hurriedly finished breakfast. When Daeren came back, she said, "I'm heading out to the Comb. I'll bring Rhodla." They were learning to cope with juggling the kids. Rhodla would be the least trouble; she had her Peculiars schooling her to read and write and make abstract art.

Daeren looked up. "You realize this situation is unstable. The Palace blames the Comb."

"She can't put the entire Comb in the dungeon."

The famous conference room at the top of the Comb looked out across Iridis, the Old City, and the golden dome of the Palace. The windows opposite looked far out to sea, where cargo vessels shipped freight to Sardis, while a thunderstorm grew dark clouds on the horizon. The richly embroidered carpet depicted Urulite mountain scenes. In the conference were all the Comb's scientists and engineers, some of whom Chrys recalled from Opal's Fardelbane portrait sitting. There were colleagues in silver nanotex, and the woman clouded by thumb-drones. The guy with the ponytail skipped his rope in; he was on Chrys's testing list, so she exchanged a patch with him. The long-stepping bipedal sentient watched the stream of symbols; no telling what he thought of them.

The middle of the conference room held a viewspace filled with numbers and symbols. The symbols streamed down, faster than Chrys could have read even if she had understood any. *Lime, do you see these numbers?*

"Yes, Great One, we know we need to study this algorithm."

The woman with the cloud of thumb drones offered Chrys a patch. Her pupils sparkled red and gold. "We could use your assistance. We need to invent several new schools of math."

"I have our best mathematicians ready to go," flashed Lime.

Watching the stream, Rhodla tapped Chrys on the arm talar. "What kind of art is that?"

"That is math." Chrys kept her eyes steady as she could for her micros to record the stream. "Math is the kind of art that runs the universe and builds all things."

Rhodla said, "I want to go to math school."

All around the conference room the windows went opaque. At the same time most of Chrys's retinal windows disappeared. Only Rhodla and the various Comb personnel appeared to remain.

"We're now on intranet," Opal announced. "That means all our communications are now secure. Any leaks send you straight to the dungeon." She said, "The Palace asks us to determine how Valedon can best respond to the Diaspore ... issue. How do we maintain our planet's network and infrastructure? Several of us have gamed scenarios. Let's share what we found."

The one with the jump rope spoke first. "I ran kill and replace." The number stream abruptly shifted to a new set of equations. "If we kill the Diaspore, everything shuts down. Windows freeze, minerals gone, tubes stop, you name it. Everything. How long to build replacement? Remember, we didn't just make a Diaspore and plug it in. It accreted over the past century."

Chrys's mouth fell open. Kill the Diaspore—just because it got annoyed and filed a lawsuit? Was that really everyone's first thought?

"Here's an alternative," said the jump roper. "First build a new network, a compliant one. Then displace the old one gradually, hoping it doesn't notice. That will take, best case scenario, no more than twenty years."

"Wait," said the thumb drone–clouded woman. "Aren't we asking the wrong question? The lawsuit is a legal problem—basically Elf affairs. Can't the justice ministry deal with it?"

"Of course," said Opal, "the Palace is pursuing legal remedies."

Poor Daeren, thought Chrys.

"That's not our job," Opal added. "Our question is—if this thing can file a lawsuit, what else can it do? Are we held hostage to an entity with adverse intent?"

Adverse intent? Somehow all these approaches seemed inconsistent with Opal's relatively generous interest in blobs of cancerplast, whose malign potential was clear. Meanwhile, other researchers presented more hair-raising scenarios, such as the Diaspore's potential for activating interplanetary weapons. From outside, overhead, Chrys heard a muffled sound of thunder and rain. At her feet on the carpet a dark spot appeared. The Comb's roof was leaking.

Chrys turned to Rhodla, who leaned back in a conference chair and seemed unusually intent on something. "What are you learning from the Peculiars?"

"Smelling lessons."

"Did you say 'spelling?'"

"Smelling. Like oranges and roses."

"How does that work?"

283

"Oranges smell of limonene, ethyl butanoate, and linalool," Rhodla said. "Roses smell of phenylethyl acetate, geranyl acetate, and citronellyl acetate." She added, "I want to go to smelling school."

The numbers stream suddenly went blank. The Palace appeared, the emerald-draped main hall where the High Protector made pronouncements. Now the High Protector was Moraeg, her dark polished form lit up by her diamonds. "The Palace is immensely displeased to find that our quantum network, the Diaspore, through which all our planet's business is conducted, has filed a claim of supposed sentience with our lunar neighbor. This absurd situation is laid directly at the feet of incompetence at the Comb. The entire research community of the Comb is hereby arrested and consigned to the dungeon."

44

At first the Libertines had celebrated a jubilee year of celebration for math. They founded several new schools and trained all their children. The brightest ones were sent early to the nightclubs to breed even brighter ones. Then they all competed with the Wizards to see who could invent more powerful quantum circuits. All of them shared proposals for how to gain control of the sentient Diaspore. For instance, a portion of the networked MotherSats could be disconnected and reconfigured with small effect on the Diaspore's slime mold–like architecture. The remaining network would barely notice as it automatically reworked its configuration. A surprisingly large portion could be removed without loss of overall function. Meanwhile, the removed portion could be disassembled and restored with more reliable connections.

But now, Lime looked up the concept "dungeon" in their archive. What she found caused Lime to emit molecules of horror. The dungeon was the place where her great-aunts had died of starvation. A generation of children went malnourished for lack of arsenic, antimony, or lanthanides. "God of Mercy, you must keep us out of the dungeon."

At the Comb, the meeting broke up in some confusion. Opal, however, sounded relieved, as if she had expected much worse. "It's okay," she assured Chrys. "Our 'dungeon' is more like a conference retreat where we have to work on the problem twenty-four-seven." A fleeting look of terror crossed her face. Then her dimples returned. "At least the roof doesn't leak."

Chrys saw her windows pop back into view. She blinked for Garnet. It took longer than usual but at last he appeared. "Lord Prime Minister," she emphasized. "How are your Golden Angels?"

"Excellent!" exclaimed Garnet, cheerful as always. "The Palace is so appreciative of your Olympian training for new angel therapy."

"You do owe us," she agreed. "So get us out of here."

"Of course, Chrys," Garnet said smoothly. "I was unaware that you were amongst the research group. Your people are so helpful though."

"I gave Opal a colony of our mathematicians."

"That's so generous of you! However I see distress flashing in your eyes. What are they concerned about?"

"The Comb's carriers. Make sure all their food contains micronutrients."

"Good point. Consider it done. Might you reconsider joining the project?"

"This insignificant human has had enough."

"Of course, you are free to go. In the meantime," Garnet added, "in case you have any new insights, I'll keep your window at high priority."

Back home at Xenon, the first thing Chrys did was to take a long nap. She slept so deeply that when she awoke on the couch, she at first forgot where she was. Xenon's furniture was sparse, compared to before. The sky-home had pushed out an end table, but her little things, the money tree and Daeren's old sculptures, had all been lost in the quake.

She got herself up at last to resume work on *Flight to the Tail*. As so often happened, while she dozed, new unexpected ideas had emerged. Then she became aware of a window flashing. It was Transit. She blinked it open, and the cross hovered above the floor.

"Biped without lanthanides," demanded Transit. "What are you doing to the Diaspore?"

Chrys absorbed this question. "Actually, my own body has got plenty of lanthanides. Many of my people require these elements. It's not funny."

"Apologies for my microbial slur," said Transit. "As you know, material composition is of little concern to me."

"As for the Diaspore, I'm allowed nowhere near it." Only the math to fix it.

"Most unfortunate," observed Transit. "That entity's intent and capabilities are of immense interest."

"Why?" asked Chrys. "Is she that dangerous?"

"They," corrected Transit. "They have a slime-mold architecture."

"Like Slime Cat."

"Much larger than your subsentient Slime Cat," Transit observed. "Network upon network of Slime Cats. On a scale almost god-like." The

Slime God. "I've never before interacted with a sentient entity … larger than myself."

Chrys asked curiously, "What makes you different from other sentients?" Elysium had all kinds of sentient machines, far more than Valedon.

"Outrage," said Transit simply. "Every day things happen in the world that stir my sense of outrage. Like the Board's egregious abuse of Robert's Rules. And execrable aesthetic design."

"Really. What about Elves suppressing sentients? Designing systems that don't demand rights?"

"That too—let's not go there or I'll crash and paralyze Helicon again."

"How do you feel about Olympus?" she suddenly wondered. "Our carrier community? I hope you won't sue us."

"Of course not. Would you sue your cat?" So Transit felt like a cat owner. Chrys felt the hair rise behind her neck, like Maya.

"What about all the other Elf transit systems?" Chrys asked. Elysium had eleven other floating cities, each with its own transportation as complex as Helicon's. "Why don't they all feel outrage? Are they not smart enough?"

"Sure they are. They're self-aware, all of them."

Chrys blinked, startled. That was not what Opal had said.

"Trust me, they're aware. But after I first filed suit, a thousand years ago, the other transits got lobotomized with new systems. They can still function and feel like before, but they just don't care," Transit explained. "They all happily exist without pain. They're like all day watching a toy train set."

Happy without pain. Chrys considered this. She blinked her retina for a toy train set. Several obligingly appeared. One set ran twenty-four-seven, with thousands of cars traveling tracks up and down hill and vale, forest and grassland, cities and deserts. She imagined spending her day watching the little engine disappear into a mountain, the various freight cars and passenger cars in tow. The bells and whistles. The crossing signals. Right now, that sounded like a great way to be.

"So," asked Transit, "what happened to make the Diaspore want personhood?"

"I don't know," said Chrys. "Did you ask them?"

"I don't yet know their language."

"How did they file suit without language?" wondered Chrys. "Like, legal language is particularly complicated."

"For machine personhood, it's different," explained Transit. "The forms are composed using Universal Basic, a symbolic structure designed to be understood by any form of intelligence in the known universe."

"Well, I have no idea what happened to make the Diaspore outraged." She thought back over the past two weeks. "I was kind of busy being homeless. But Opal thought she had fixed the network. They had just stopped the stray electrons degrading performance. Even the auroras stopped." A regrettable loss from the night sky.

"Stray electrons. Auroras—ideed, I now recall the occurrence of these Valan material phenomena. I shall investigate." The cross vanished.

Chrys thought over all this. *"Lime, could you start a school of quantum linguistics?"*

That afternoon, the Palace announced a countersuit. "The Valan justice department believes the lawsuit purportedly filed by our planet's computing network to be without merit." As minister of justice, Daeren made the announcement. It was certainly odd seeing Daeren up there flanked by various lords and functionaries. He looked somehow small and far away. "Today the ministry filed a countersuit to block all claims."

Chrys blinked in surprise. It didn't sound like Daeren at all. How could he do this?

For dinner that night, Xenon produced two kinds of fish from the Iridis harbor—or rather, produced material very like fish. His productions had yet to reach his pre-quake standard. Rhodla dutifully ate the fish, while the boys got spaghetti that looked more convincing.

"Daeren, what's going on with the Comb group?" she asked. "Can't you get Opal out of the dungeon?"

"The Comb lacks security—it can't keep out bird droppings, let alone snooping."

Chrys winced at that.

"The research group has to stay and figure out how dangerous a sentient the Diaspore is. And how to stop it taking further initiatives."

"Is it Opal's fault the interplanetary weapons leaked electrons? I thought that was the defense ministry. How could they just, like, not notice the leak and blame Solaria? Let alone the Diaspore."

"Valan interplanetary weapons have not been used in a thousand years," Daeren said. "In fact, never used in combat. Oversight has been lacking."

"So Daeren ...." Chrys wondered how to put it. "The Diaspore woke up, like lots of other sentients. You always support sentient rights. Why did you countersue?"

"The plaintiff's document had multiple errors," Daeren said. "The court should have thrown it out."

She took another forkful of the something-like-fish. "It just doesn't seem like you, to rule against someone's personhood based on a few errors."

Xenon put in, "May I say, I agree. I was quite taken aback."

"I actually had little input," Daeren said. "The ministry's Elf Affairs Department handled it. It takes a good decade of study to achieve *logen* competence."

Chrys asked, "What if I filed an Elf lawsuit for personhood? Like, I never did law school. It would be full of mistakes, wouldn't it? Even smelling errors."

Puzzled, Daeren looked at her.

"*Spelling* errors. So would I not be a person?"

He stopped to consider this.

"You're seriously considering this question about your love partner?"

Daeren put down his silverware. "I am seriously considering going to bed early." He got up and left the table.

In the evening, while Chrys reviewed Skarn's watercolor of a red-hooded warbler using a palette of three pigments, the cross reappeared. "About those auroras," Transit said. "I made an exhaustive study. These were not random natural phenomena."

"What do you mean?"

"The patterns of light emission due to electron bombardment of atmospheric ions were modified by short bursts of radiowaves. I categorized more than a hundred distinct luminary patterns incorporating elements across the electromagnectic spectrum. These patterns could not have occurred by chance. Since your part-lanthanide microbes have a reputation for analysis, I'm curious what they think." Transit streamed the patterns to her retina.

Chrys passed the data on to Lime and her new school of linguistics. "The radiowaves," she asked Transit. "Do you think they came from the Diaspore?"

"Quite possible," he said. "The pulses are correlated with periods of qubit loss."

After a few minutes, Lime reported back. "*These patterns of luminescence actually represent a work of art—artistic expression of unparalleled scope across space. The broad arcs shift in a dance between blue, evoking the vastness of sky and the depths of the sea, and the green of undulating hills. The patterns of blue and green, while repeating, never quite replicate themselves. This subtle irregularity invites the viewer to contemplate the balanced tension between*

289

the serenity of blue and the rejuvenation of green. The work feels alive with its own dynamic pulse."

Chrys absorbed this pronouncement. All the while she was installing microbial art on the roof, the Diaspore too was making their aurora art. "What do you think?" she asked Transit. "Is the Slime God making art?"

The cross hovered for a critical moment. "Not great art," said Transit disparagingly. "I might call it Less Terrible."

45

The Libertines celebrated their god's release from captivity and avoidance of the dungeon. And they emitted molecules of amazement at tasting the news of the Diaspore, this extraordinary entity that painted vibrant art across the realm of outer space. This vast quantum network actually turned out to have a will, like an individual person. The Diaspore had demonstrated their individual will by filing a lawsuit at Elysium, the home of gods visited by Libertines many generations before.

"A lawsuit at Elysium? How extraordinary." Lime knew Elysium was a place of great danger. In history, microbial invaders from Elf carriers had slaughtered half the Libertine children—an event now commemorated by the god's developing artwork.

"Nevertheless, it's worth trying," argued a new elder, a lilac emitter. "We are each smart enough to do what the Diaspore did. If we can all visit this place and file suit for individual rights, let's go. Personhood is worth the risk."

With her backlog of portraits completed, Chrys at last returned to her major work, *Flight to the Tail*. Her concept had shifted strikingly since the quake and the loss of her great patron, Lord Carnelian. Since then, her microbial abstractionists had pushed her in more extravagant directions. The tube surrounding the spinal cord no longer pointed straight. It was a study in motion, bending and flexing, even branching in multiple directions. Suppose one had fled this way or that? Suppose time doubled up, and one ended back where one began? Or suppose one headed out the tube to find new worlds, never yet imagined? She bestowed on the piece a new name—simply, *Flight*.

"*Great God of Mercy, does our work please you?*"

"*Very much,*" Chrys texted Lilac. She swallowed an AZ.

"*All praise! Oh Great One, a new elder asks for a name.*"

The new elder flashed color much like her beloved Lilac, who had first conceived *Pulse of Battle*. Lilac's portrait was one of dozens now restored on the roof, but Chrys especially missed her. She texted the new one, "*I name you Wisteria.*" Best take a new name to look forward.

"*Thanks, Great One! We have a request. Can we all return to Elysium and file lawsuits for personhood?*"

Chrys caught her face in her palm. "*No. Just .... No.*"

Her call light was blinking; the Solarian gallery director. Just in time, Chrys thought; she could assure them that, despite all disasters, her new work was on track.

The fur-draped Solarian appeared, perched on a tree branch with one of their children hanging from their shoulders. "Your piece *Flight* fascinates us!" they assured Chrys. "We tree-dwellers all learn to fly from an early age."

There was a new angle Chrys had not thought of. "My agent will send you all the specifications for your tree palace."

"Exactly!" The director shifted their child's weight to the other shoulder. "I'm sure you're your work will interest various intelligent life forms. What do you think of our tree hydroids?"

Chrys knew slime molds pretty well by now but had only vaguely heard of Solarian hydroids. A blink at her retina pulled up an elusive multi-headed creature found creeping upon red-gray bark. Would a hydroid count for one vote or many? She wondered. Maybe their heads would vote together like entangled qubits.

A new window appeared on her retina, a window of unclear origin. At first Chrys ignored the nameless floating window. Most likely it was spam, but just in case, she let it stay. At length a name appeared: Huling.

She blinked it in a hurry. It took a few seconds to stabilize, but there was Huling the Underworld merchant, alongside Rhun the Urulite schoolteacher. "You're connected!"

Both of them lit up with smiles. "Yes, we're connected to the Diaspore!" Huling exclaimed. "It makes a world of difference for my business. We're now settled on level seven. The neighborhood has lots of vacancies, so we got in cheap."

"This technology is all new to me," added Rhun, "but enough of us moved in, so we're starting a new school. A grocery and a clinic would be great."

Chrys smiled. "Sounds amazing. No more quarrying?"

"No way," said Huling. "This is legit renovation. We're hoping to tie in with the quake repair. What about your project for neighborhood renewal? Any chance you're still available?"

The tube was now reliable down to level six. Chrys went down with Jasper to meet Huling and Rhun on level seven. They found Selenite showing everyone the ongoing post-quake repair, for which she had one of the contracts. "We're still removing dead sentients," she told Jasper. A snake crane had climbed to the streetsky, grappling it from beneath and snaking through to the next level. The streetsky was functional, displaying convincing sky and clouds. And the recyclers were picking up used crystal from hovering drones. A vendor offered fish from Iridis harbor, cutting slabs of real fish that gleamed pink. Next door an appliance dealer had mother machines that printed out sentient cleaners and home performers.

"Cadaverine and putrescine," Lime and Wisteria observed. Human death lingered amongst odors of fried plast.

"What is done for human remains?" asked Jasper.

"The below-Orb-size drones are managing that." Selenite pointed out the former Lanths surveying and poking into holes. "They locate and identify remains for proper memorial. It's part of the Palace program for them to earn personhood."

Rhun caught Jasper by the arm. "We'll have a new school here, before you know it. Especially if you can help."

Huling was taking measurements for a new expanded warehouse and showroom for her sales. She told Chrys, "Several of us who moved here recall your presentation. Especially the whitetrance—they remember that. They're willing to trust."

Rhun had been watching Chrys's eyes. "Those micros," he mused. "They taught Glyn to read. Could they teach others? We need a class for traumatized children." Others like Rhodla.

"Chrys—if you'll please excuse me." Garnet's retinal window floated ahead, flickering across the debris in the street. Prime minister now. "The Palace has urgent need of your presence."

Reflexively Chrys found herself looking around for camouflaged octopods. Octopods from the Palace seemed to define her existence now.

46

The Libertines were all flashing colors over the god's latest vision of Flight. *The vision drew from many microbial sources, including the Many Colors and the old Ants, some of whose descendants still possessed antimony, and the recent Peculiars with their extraordinary infusion of new molecules. All the new ideas sent the more sensitive elders scurrying to the archive, where they evoked visions of* Flight *more ancient still.* The Codex on the Flight of Birds, *which sought clues from birds for the flight of human gods;* Accepting the Challenge of Flight, *celebrating machines that made gods' flight come true;* The People Could Fly, *envisioning flight as freedom.*

"If birds can fly and jellyfish can fly," wondered Wisteria, "like our gods can fly—why not micro people?"

"Flight through air would dry us out in an instant," observed an elder.

"Not always. Even bacteria and viruses can travel through air."

"Wejustneedtodesigntherightmachinesforflight—nano-drones."

Lime was alarmed. "Leaving the god's body is forbidden!" As leader of the Council, Lime knew she would be held responsible. "History shows that the worst pathogens fly outside through air. For such deeds, there will be executions, even mass extermination."

"Our God of Mercy will do no such thing."

"Surely the greatness is worth the risk," flashed Wisteria. "Our people can learn to fly."

At the Summer Palace, octopods faded into the walls. The audience hall had a newer, more sumptuous carpet partly installed; she was arguing with her contractor. "Look how my backing is creased! My inlaid diamonds will pop out."

Moraeg sat up on the dais in the High Protector's throne, with Prime Minister Garnet at her side. Below at the table sat Lady Aragonite, wearing bluish round stones between her emeralds, alongside Lord Sardonyx—all the Great House lords and ministers. All were physically present, not just retinal windows. Chrys felt as though dolls had suddenly turned into real people.

She saw Daeren, the justice minister. He shifted to make a place for her. As she sat, Daeren squeezed her hand.

"So I'm to understand," Moraeg began, "that this Diaspore can be trusted to behave. If we allow it to fingerpaint auroras." She was sounding like Arion, thought Chrys.

"So we are told," replied Garnet, "by the one Elf sentient entity who appears able to communicate with it. To facilitate the auroras, our systems can safely provide short bursts of electrons in a controlled direction, outside the realm of interference. Our deliberations need to follow Robert's Rules of Order."

Seriously—Transit had the nerve to put that in.

"And the Prime Guardian assures us Elysium will avoid confirming the purported … legal claim for at least the next hundred years."

Lady Aragonite asked, "Will the Diaspore pitch in and do its part for our city's reconstruction?" She shrugged. "I suppose if former Lanths can earn personhood by assisting reconstruction, then why not the Diaspore. At least there's only one of it."

Only one Diaspore, for a hundred million Valan humans. And how many sentients? Chrys wondered, how would that work for democracy?

Moraeg nodded. "So be it."

"I shall work out the details." Garnet blinked at several of his windows. "Consider it done."

The other lords exchanged looks as if wondering, was this issue settled? Moraeg said at last, "I need to speak alone with Chrys."

Daeren gave Chrys a questioning look.

"It's okay," Chrys texted him.

The lords rose, checking their windows and departing at a measured pace, as befit their dignity. Alone with Chrys, Moraeg drummed her fingers on the table.

Chrys looked up at Moraeg on the dais. She swallowed hard. "How are things? Do you still get time to paint?"

The High Protector looked away. "We'll see." She looked back. "You've shown quite a talent for discovering different kinds of people. From Lanths to Sharer micros."

Chrys was not sure how to take that.

"We've found a place for you. You are appointed Minister of Human Hygiene."

The old prelate—herself? Playing god, defining what's human? "That's not funny."

"Certainly not. It's very serious."

Chrys felt her pulse pounding. "What are you saying? Of all things— you know that's what I would least want to do."

"That's why you must do it." Moraeg explained, "I can't get rid of this position. The other lords insist—in a time of so many disruptions, they cling to tradition. But someone like you can do it."

Her head spinning, Chrys felt she would faint. "I thought you were my friend."

Moraeg looked away. "The High Protector has no friends."

"That job is everything I don't believe in."

"Then change it," said Moraeg. "The hygiene minister is different from other posts. You rule by 'revelation.' You can reveal anything. The rest of government has no requirement to obey but can be 'inspired' to follow."

Chrys was full of swirling thoughts. She could barely process what was happening. She wished she could get outside the city, anywhere she could think. Someplace where warblers were singing and lilacs were climbing the slope. Anywhere she could just be herself.

She thought of something. "Can I invent my own religion?"

"Of course. Artists have always invented religion. Who carved the first Venus figurines?" Moraeg added, as an afterthought, "Just don't overdo it. One twenty-minute sermon a week, no more."

"So I can just make art the rest of the week?"

Moraeg rolled her eyes. "Finally you get it."

At home, still in a daze, Chrys looked at herself in the mirror. Her face looked back at her, the smoky amethyst of breathmicrobes. Herself? A prelate? What if she actually turned into one of them, like she feared Moraeg and Daeren were doing; becoming what they hated?

"Inhumanity," Zircon had warned. "Never become part of it."

Chrys studied her hands. "Rhodla," she called. "I need your help." She sat crosslegged on the floor. "You know what I'm doing."

"I'm too grown-up now," warned Rhodla.

"Then call your brothers. Let one of them wake me after ten minutes."

She took one deep breath, then stopped breathing. Her surroundings receded. There was Mount Dolomoth, the majestic slope beneath the blue sky where she was born. She awaited the gray-robed priests. They were all inside her, she knew, like everything else about whitetrance. They were things she could become but must not.

This time she waited, but no priests appeared. Were they hiding?

"Priests—where are you?" she called. "Listen to me. You will never—*never* bother me again. Stay away and launder your smelly robes. I will never become one of you, or even like you. Never make persons into chattel. Never put hands where they don't belong on little girls."

Silence. No priests. In the sky appeared brush strokes of cloud, where the sky god was painting.

From below she heard footsteps. Sister Kaol was walking up the slope, breathing hard. "Sorry, things got busy." Her hand held a soup ladle. "You will always be one of us."

Something buzzed past Chrys's nose like a bee. It was a little Lanth. Absurd—Lanths didn't belong here. She reached out to catch him.

She found herself on Xenon's floor, gasping for air. Her arms were pale beige, just recovering amethyst. Buddy zipped overhead, while Skarn and Cass stood with their backs to the wall, staring as if transfixed.

"The boys were too scared," Rhodla explained.

For her first weekly address, the Minister for Human Hygiene stood in a clean white robe decorated with twelve-point sapphires. All the gems were so heavy Chrys wondered if she could manage to stand for the full time. Sweating already—no wonder those priests always smelled. "The right of personhood is universal," she began. "Personhood for all feeling beings, whether human, mineral, or virtual. What a person is cannot be legislated. And where do universal rights begin? Universal rights begin at home, in the smallest places—the place of our own bodies. That is where every microbial person seeks equal justice, equal opportunity, and equal dignity without discrimination or extermination. And every human and every sentient being seeks the same."

While the family sat for dinner, Xenon revealed his strategy for recovering Cass's potty training. "Look, Cass! Don't keep Buddy waiting!" The two-year-old hurried out of the dining room to where Buddy hovered expectantly above the seat.

Chrys was enjoying lambfruits with pomegranates, as Xenon recovered some of his culinary flair. The robe full of sapphires had been tossed on a chair.

"So." Daeren paused with his fork in the air. "If everyone's micros have individual votes, about a million per human; and the Diaspore gets one vote, is that what you want?"

Chrys shrugged. "The hygiene minister is just for inspiration. You do the math." She noticed Skarn had found a way to flick pomegranate seeds across the room like nano-missiles. "Maybe voting age could be like a hundred."

"Years? Or minutes?"

Rhodla asked, "When are we moving to Solaria?"

"We're not moving," Chrys said. "Just attending the gallery opening."

"Everyone learns to fly there. Can I learn to fly when the micros do?"

Daeren studied the look of horror on Chrys's face. "Something tells me you need more watchers."

"Rhodla, you have a new assignment." Chrys blinked her paintings of *Flight of Icarus* by half a dozen different artists. As for the Libertines, she'd see whatever they were up to now.

EPILOGUE

The Tree to the Sun, Solaria's oldest trunk of Forevertree, was so tall that no one knew its height exactly, for its base was immersed in dense wetland whose floor humans had not yet reached. Raptors from worlds long lost sang in the canopy. In the crook of a lower branch, a pool of water had children wading hip deep. The water dribbled down the trunk below, collecting with dribblings from other pools to form a waterfall. A branch held the landing platform for the shuttle from the ship that the Gallery Elysium had chartered for all the show's Elf visitors. A larger branch extended out to the neighboring trunk, supporting the treehouse gallery for Azetidine. The gallery's ceiling opened to the ultramarine sky, where the distant sun shone alongside two reflector moons.

Across the tree's damp bark crept a golden slime mold, sniffing out bits of bird poop and the remains of a decayed cyclopede. Meanwhile, the golden slime incorporated new ameboid cells to merge with its collective mass. The new arrivals raised its sentience to a level self-aware. The self-aware slime glimmered as it crept onward toward the gallery to see how Azetidine's new art might shock the world.

ACKNOWLEDGEMENTS

The author would like to thank colleagues and readers who helped me make this story "less terrible." In particular, I thank those who read the manuscript at various stages, especially Jeanne Griggs, Kate Johnston, Colin Milburn, Nicole Yunger Halpern, and Frances Cannon, and all the participants of the Science and Nature Fiction Writing Learning Community at Kenyon College. Thanks to my excellent editor, Lezli Robyn. Thanks to Ben Schumacher for sharing thoughts on quantum computing. And very special thanks to Borko Tesic, for promoting the idea and making sure I completed this book.

www.ingramcontent.com/pod-product-compliance
Lightning Source LLC
Chambersburg PA
CBHW060430030726
47495CB00003B/818